Also by Naomi Kritzer

*Fires of the Faithful*
*Turning the Storm*
*Freedom's Gate*
*Freedom's Apprentice*

# Praise for the Novels of Naomi Kritzer

## *FIRES OF THE FAITHFUL*

"This far-from-typical fantasy from first-time author Kritzer is like chocolate cake: instant addiction. . . . With habit-forming books like this, you can't read just one."—*Publishers Weekly*

"Entertaining."—*Booklist*

"Subtly brilliant from start to finish."—*Locus*

"Exceedingly well done. I couldn't put it down."
—Katherine Kurtz

"Thanks very much for the opportunity to read *Fires of the Faithful*, which I finished within 24 hours of starting—in my busy life a real trick. *Fires of the Faithful* is an engrossing book that tells a thoughtful and complex story of religious conflict and oppression. The protagonist, Eliana, is forging her own path through a famine-stricken, war-torn world that desperately needs a visionary leader. Yet Eliana is no Joan of Arc. A commonsense musician who loves people deeply and truly, she seeks above all to follow her own conscience and hopes not for power or victory but for the end of oppression and the healing of a desperate land. I was completely engrossed in this vividly depicted tale of ordinary people bravely and hopefully stepping forward to reclaim their country. I eagerly anticipate reading the next volume, *Turning the Storm*."
—Laurie J. Marks, author of *Fire Logic*

"Naomi Kritzer proves that music can indeed change the world, for those who have the ears to listen and the heart to follow."
—Susan Sizemore, author of
*The Laws of the Blood*

"Naomi Kritzer is a top-notch fantasy writer who combines the storytelling grace of Mercedes Lackey with political subversiveness to rival Ursula K. Le Guin. *Fires of the Faithful* is sure to be well received by critics and audiences alike. Brava!"
—Lyda Morehouse, author of *Fallen Host*

"A confident debut . . . Kritzer deftly captures a young woman's coming-of-age with heart and verve. A polished performance. I look forward to the next."—Peg Kerr

"One of those rare stories that grab you from the first page and compels you to keep turning the pages until you realize that you've finished the entire book in one sitting . . . If this first book is any indication, this woman is going to be hugely popular."—Barnes&Noble.com

"Kritzer has created a world that is deep, rich, and wonderfully imaginative, the closest thing to Tolkien for a long time."—bookshelfstores.com

"Complex and satisfying."—SFRevu

"One of the best novels by an unknown author I've been given to review in quite some time . . . The issues and plot devices used to speed the strong-willed and likeable music student heroine to her destiny have all been done before, but rarely with the freshness of voice that Ms. Kritzer brings to her work."—*Talebones*

"Kritzer's characters are well drawn and her plot is engaging and intriguing."—*Voya*

## TURNING THE STORM

"Mesmerizing . . . With panache and dexterity, Ms. Kritzer weaves complex plot threads and feisty characters into a tight story of political and social intrigue. Nebulous loyalties create fluid allegiances that contribute to the Machiavellian quality of the story."—*Romantic Times* (four stars)

"This series is a very promising debut, and I hope to see much more from this writer."
—*Philadelphia Press*

"Enthralling."—*Locus*

## FREEDOM'S GATE

"Good and Evil; Us and Them; humankind and demons; freedom and slavery; loyalty and treason—all these dichotomies begin to break down in the course of [the heroine's] ordeals and adventures, until the world becomes so maddeningly complex she loses any notion what her place in it should be. Since the myths, history and magics here don't all follow the patterns of our world (or its classic fantasies), *Freedom's Gate* should open the way to a

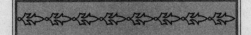

# Freedom's Sisters

## Naomi Kritzer

BANTAM BOOKS

FREEDOM'S SISTERS
A Bantam Spectra Book / August 2006

Published by Bantam Dell
A Division of Random House, Inc.
New York, New York

This is a work of fiction. Names, characters, places, and incidents
either are the product of the author's imagination or are used
fictitiously. Any resemblance to actual persons, living or dead, events,
or locales is entirely coincidental.

Bantam Books, the rooster colophon, Spectra, and the portrayal of a
boxed "s" are trademarks of Random House, Inc.

ISBN-13: 978-0-553-58675-6
ISBN-10: 0-553-58675-0

Printed in the United States of America
Published simultaneously in Canada

www.bantamdell.com

OPM    10   9   8   7   6   5   4   3   2   1

*To Ed*

# CHAPTER ONE

# TAMAR

When I rode into the camp of the Alashi spring gathering, I tried to sit tall and hide my fear. Lauria would tell me I was as good as they were—she'd tell me to look them in the eye. She'd say I had nothing to be ashamed of. And I wasn't ashamed. I was proud of what Lauria and I had accomplished. We had freed over a hundred slaves. The Alashi didn't free slaves because they thought those who deserved freedom would escape on their own. Well, the Alashi might not free slaves, but I did. Lauria and I did. I took a deep breath and raised my head.

What did the eldress want from me, anyway?

First, apparently, she wanted me to wait.

I had ridden back with Janiya, the leader of the sword sisterhood Lauria and I had spent last summer with. The rest of her sisterhood had stayed behind to escort the former mine slaves on foot. Janiya gave our horses to a girl to care for, then we sat down in the shade near the eldress's tent. I watched Janiya, and when she turned away from me, I looked around. Lauria and I had found the Alashi at the end of their big spring gathering, and we'd left right before their big fall gathering. I could smell lentils and rice cooking over fires made from dried animal dung. There were families nearby, with lots of children who weren't old enough to ride out with a sisterhood or brotherhood. Looking at them made my throat ache a little.

Janiya looked me over. She hadn't spoken much on our ride. Now she cleared her throat and said, "You look well."

I looked down at my muddy clothes and boots. Lauria and I had bought ourselves new clothes when we'd come into some money, but they were worn ragged now. My hands were filthy, and I thought my face and hair probably were, too.

"Oh, you could use a bath, but that's not what I meant," Janiya said. "You look very confident. You look like a woman who can stand on her own and defend herself. When I first met you ... well, you looked like you'd fight until the last drop of blood left your body, but you didn't look like you thought it would *matter*."

I let out my breath in a short laugh. "It's good to see you again," I said. Janiya looked pretty much as I remembered—well, maybe a little more gray in her hair.

"It's good to see you, too." Janiya clasped my hand. "I wish ..." She let the words fade. I thought she'd probably meant to say that she wished she could see Lauria, too.

"Why does the eldress want to see me?"

Janiya shrugged. I thought she probably knew but wasn't supposed to say. My guess was that this was about the slaves Lauria and I had freed and brought up. Well, the mine slaves really had freed themselves. I had nothing to apologize for. I chewed my lip, wondering if the eldress would like that argument. "How are the others from the sisterhood?" I asked. "Maydan, is she recovering?" Maydan had been badly injured in a fight with bandits, late last summer.

"Yes. Very slowly. She had to learn to walk again, as if she was a child, but she's still Maydan. She hasn't forgotten anything about healing, but her hands are very clumsy right now. She's frustrated, as I'm sure you can imagine. She's staying with the clan for the summer, not going out with our sisterhood. We'll have a different healer."

I felt a rush of longing at Janiya's words—*going out with our sisterhood*. I pushed the thought away. I belonged with Lauria.

Janiya glanced over at the eldress's tent, then stood. "It's time," she said.

The inside of the tent was dim and cool. For a few moments, I couldn't see. When Lauria and I had arrived a year ago, we had been brought to the eldress, who had listened to our story and accepted us as "blossoms," provisional members. This time, eight old ladies and five old men sat in a circle. The eldress I had met a year ago sat across from the door on a pile of cushions. Braided white hair wound around her head. She wore a long dress, a vest so covered in embroidery I could barely make out the black cloth underneath, and a necklace that looked like a spell-chain, though when I looked for a piece of karenite that would imprison a djinn, I didn't see one. These had to be the clan elders. Janiya and I bowed respectfully. The eldress pointed to a spot near the door and Janiya and I sat down.

"Good afternoon, child," the eldress said, her voice kinder than I expected. "You've come a long way since I met you a year ago."

I didn't know what to say to that, so I nodded, then said, "Yes, ma'am."

"I apologize for bringing you back against your will. Zhanna has told me the information that you and your blood sister have passed to her, but I wished to speak with you face-to-face." She fingered her necklace. "Zhanna said that when your blood sister was trying to bind djinni, you were able to stop her. Is this true?"

This was not the question I had expected. "For a little while," I said. "First I slapped her with a wet rag, so she hid from me. So then I went to the borderland and waited for her there. I was able to force her back out. Though later she tried again and was able to do it."

Murmurs, around the circle.

"I was a shaman's apprentice. Zhanna's, and before that, Jaran's."

"Yes. Jaran." The eldress raised an eyebrow, and *now* came the challenge I had expected. "The Alashi do not free slaves."

"I am not Alashi. I left when you exiled my blood sister."

Janiya, who was the one who actually had exiled Lauria, bit her lip and looked down.

"You *chose* to leave," the eldress said. "You could choose to come back."

"Why?"

"To teach." That was one of the other clan elders, a man I didn't know. His voice was a soft growl. "To teach the shamans how to guard the borderland and the djinni, so that we can lay siege to the source of the Sisterhood's power."

"I'm still not convinced that's a good idea." That was a clan eldress with only one eye, and a scar that stretched from forehead to chin. "That will just prove to them that we *are* a threat, and that they *must* move against us."

"They're coming whether we act or not."

"You don't *know* that."

"They're moving the army up! What else could it . . ."

". . . just guarding against our raids, and the bandits . . ."

". . . strike at the border, not the borderland, that's what I've . . ."

". . . could move all our herds north, find new grazing grounds, just get out of their way . . ."

The eldress sat back and let the others argue. I looked at Janiya. She gave me a quirk-lipped smile and a slight shrug.

"Let them come!" one of the eldresses said. "We'll back off and let the desert do our work. They'll never find our wells."

"They're not fools; they'll use their djinni to bring up water. *That's* why we need to barricade the borderland."

"So what if they can't make new slaves? That won't stop them from using the ones they've got.

They have thousands, tens of thousands! More than enough . . ."

"All right," the eldress said. "I've had enough of this. Back to your clans, all of you. I want to talk to Tamar alone. No, Janiya, you can stay. Sit down. The rest of you . . ." She gestured, and after a moment or two, they rose and went out, still arguing. The tent was very quiet with them gone.

"It's been like this for days," the eldress said. "I'm sure you can imagine. Now. Tell me. Do you think you can teach other shamans to do what you did?"

"I don't know. I wasn't trying to close off the whole borderland, I was just following Lauria. I could never keep *all* the sorceresses out."

"The djinni must have wanted you here for some other reason, then," the eldress said.

"The djinni told you to bring me here?"

"Yes. Evidently, they thought you'd be useful."

I raised my chin. "I don't want to stay here. I want to be with Lauria. Are you going to keep me here by force? Or . . ." My voice faded, and I swallowed hard. "Or are you going to let her come back?"

"You have great faith in your blood sister."

"Yes."

"Though you know she was a spy."

"Was. Once. Not anymore. And she tried to undo what she did."

"Alashi do not free slaves."

"I'm never going to stop trying to free slaves, eldress, even if you make me Alashi. What did the djinni tell you about me, anyway? And Lauria?"

"They just said to bring you here."

"Why not Lauria? She can free bound djinni by touching them. If they come close to her, she can send them back to the borderland. That's what *I* wish I could learn to do."

The eldress became very quiet for a moment, her eyes still fixed on me. Then she said, "Perhaps her path is separate from yours, because the djinni said nothing about bringing her here. They told me to bring you. They said that *you* would know something that would help us."

"I know something that will help you?" I shook my head. "I don't know what they're talking about."

"Then tell me what you've done this past year. Tell me what you've learned. Perhaps when I hear about your journeys, I will know what the djinni were talking about."

A barefoot girl brought in cups, a kettle of tea, and a tray of salty little fried cakes. She ran in and out several times to get all of it. She bowed to the eldress as she brought in a white sauce to dip the cakes in, and left for the last time. The eldress watched her without speaking, a faint smile on her face. Janiya poured tea.

As we ate, I told Janiya and the eldress where Lauria and I had gone, and what we saw and learned. I told them the Sisterhood of Weavers was running short of karenite. I told them about the rogue sorceresses who called themselves the Younger Sisters, and the Servant Sisterhood that wanted control of the Empire. I told them about freeing Nika and Melaina, Uljas and Burkut, Sophos's harem, Prax and the others from the mine. The eldress listened to my story without interrupting. Then she looked at Janiya. "Do you think the djinni were right? Did she bring us something we need?"

"Information," Janiya said. "Our enemies have enemies of their own."

"We can't trust the Younger Sisters," I said. "Any more than we can trust the Servant Sisterhood. We have karenite. They *all* need it."

"But perhaps we could persuade them to fight among themselves," the eldress said. "Perhaps we could offer an alliance to the Younger Sisters—a gift of karenite, provided they move now against their 'elders.' "

"The Younger Sisters would become their own problem, in time," Janiya said. "But in the short term . . ."

"Who would we go to?" I asked. "Do you know who the leader of the Younger Sisters is?" Janiya and the eldress both looked at me. "Oh, no. I don't know. I wouldn't even know where to start."

"With the corrupt steward of the Weavers' farm, Lycurgus," the eldress said. "Lauria tangled with the Younger Sisters when she went to rescue Burkut. Or perhaps the sorceress you approached in Daphnia."

"We almost got ourselves killed in Daphnia!"

"Last time. Surely you'd know how to be discreet if you went again."

It would have been disrespectful to shout "you're mad!" at an eldress, so I bit my tongue and lowered my eyes.

"We can give you karenite, enough to enslave an entire army of djinni if that's what the Younger Sisters choose to do," the eldress said. "Use it to sow discord among our enemies."

My stomach twisted at the thought of all those new spell-chains. "I don't want to help anyone enslave an army of djinni."

"Even if it saves the Alashi?"

I looked away again. I had tried my hardest to

keep Lauria from binding a single djinn, even though she was sure it was the only way to free Prax. I knew I should refuse now. But I also knew the Alashi really were in danger. So instead I said, "Alone? I'd be robbed by bandits."

"Of course not alone. Janiya can go with you."

Janiya's head snapped up. She hadn't expected this. "But my sisterhood . . ."

"I will arrange for another to lead it in your absence. You walked among the Penelopeians once, Janiya. You can do it again."

"We'll need a third," Janiya said. "Someone who could pass as Greek."

"I will consider it," the eldress said.

"You're forgetting something." I raised my chin. "Lauria."

The eldress narrowed her eyes. "I did not forget your blood sister." She rose and opened a wood chest. From deep inside, she drew out two black felt vests. Mine, and Lauria's. "I had Zhanna give these to me some weeks ago." She handed both to me. "Yours is yours again, if you want it. Lauria's can be hers again, if you give it to her. Her fate is yours to decide."

"She can come back?" I asked, just to be sure.

"Yes. She can come back. As eldress of all the clans, on my authority, I grant a pardon to Lauria. She came among us as an enemy, but I believe she had turned against her old master and was ready to become one of us in truth." She leaned back and looked at me appraisingly. "You will be initiated as one of the Alashi before you go. If you choose, Lauria can be initiated in absentia, just as Burkut was."

That night, I held Lauria's vest and tried to find her in my dream. I'd tried to find her while traveling with

Janiya and hadn't been able to. Tonight I saw her, but far away. She looked like she was made from smoke. I feared she'd blow away before she heard me.

"Come back," I said. She didn't hear me, so I shouted. "Come back! Come back to the Alashi, they will take you back!"

Lauria shook her head. I couldn't hear her words, but I thought I saw her lips move to say, *too late*.

"I'll help you free Thais, but come up to the steppe first," I shouted. "You can come back. The eldress has pardoned you."

The wind whipped across the steppe. I saw Lauria stop shouting and close her eyes in concentration. For a single heartbeat, the wind died, and I found myself in Sophos's courtyard. Lauria stood before me as I'd seen her the night Sophos raped her—shaking with cold, her torn clothes bloody. She looked into my face and her lips parted. "I love you," she said, and vanished from the borderland like the flame of a blown-out candle.

# CHAPTER TWO

# *L*AURIA

*T*amar," I whispered, though I had found myself in mist and shadow and had searched for Tamar in vain. Someone was nudging my ankle. Kyros.

"We're almost there," he said. "I thought you might like to see Penelopeia from the sky."

I blinked and looked around. I'd nodded off against the cushions of the palanquin sometime during the afternoon. I'd started out feigning drowsiness to avoid talking to Kyros, but I must have fallen asleep for real. I sat up and stretched. The cushions under me were damp from sweat. All the curtains were drawn; Kyros feared flying and hated looking out of the palanquin. *Well. He doesn't have to.* I drew the corner of the curtain aside and peered out.

We were still high up. Looking down, I could see golden fields. Farther away, something vast and dark caught the afternoon sunlight in rippling sparkles. I caught my breath and squinted, wondering what it could be. Blowing sand? Some sort of shiny rocks?

"It's the sea," Kyros said, though he hadn't looked out, only at my face. "Penelopeia is near the shores of a sea."

"That's all *water*?" I stared at the glittering expanse.

"Salt water," Kyros said. His voice was a little amused. "You can't drink it."

Still. I looked out again. *All that water.*

My thoughts drifted to Thais. After the Alashi had cast me out, I'd resolved to free the slaves I'd returned to slavery. I'd finally found the last of them, Thais, but instead of accepting my offer, she'd raised the alarm, and I'd been handed over to Kyros. Thais's master was one of Kyros's officers; she'd run away to be with him, and after I'd brought her back, Kyros had sold her to Casseia to punish both of them. It hadn't worked; he'd found a way to get down to Casseia and had bought her and brought her home. And I'd gone to free her anyway, not knowing, and now I was with Kyros. *Come back, all is forgiven,* Tamar had shouted when we'd touched in the borderland, but it was too late. We were going to Penelopeia, for me to plead my case before the magia, and probably be executed.

"How much farther to Penelopeia?" I asked.

"We'll be there soon," Kyros said. "Before sunset."

It was difficult to believe that in less than a day we had traveled a distance that should have taken weeks. Kyros had his feet kicked up on a bolster. I glanced at him again, wondering if he was going to ask me questions, but he appeared to be deep in thought. I looked out the window again.

I thought I could see farms now, below us. There were houses, surrounded by fields. The dark ribbon that ran alongside the farms was not, I realized, a river, but a wide, well-kept road; there were people traveling along it, with horses, wagons, camel trains. I had been studying the ground for so long, trying to pick out details, that I was startled to see movement out of the corner of my eye, in the air; I looked, expecting a bird, and saw something that looked like a flying barn, or a very large flying box. An aeriko caravan, I realized, shipping apples one direction and grapes the other. It was painted to look like a bright yellow bird, with eyes and feathers outlined in black.

"Your mother would be shocked by your hair," Kyros said.

I touched the cropped ends. "It's grown out a lot." I scratched an itch. "I think if my mother saw me now, she'd want me scrubbed raw and picked free of lice before she'd let me kiss her." *I'll certainly look the part of a bandit if I get taken before the magia like this.* I glanced covertly at Kyros. I'd found out near the end of my summer with the Alashi that Kyros was my father. Had he always spoken of my mother so casually? I couldn't remember.

Kyros chuckled a little and fell silent again. I sat back against the cushions and tried to practice, in my mind, what I would say to the magia, but my thoughts kept skipping ahead to when she didn't believe me. Would she have me executed? Or tortured like a captured spy? *Like the captured spy I am?*

What did I know? The camp locations of the Alashi camps, last year. But even a djinn could find that out; they didn't need me for that. How to infiltrate the Alashi—the tests I'd had to pass. The beads. I grimaced inwardly at the memory, but I was almost certain that the precise tests varied depending on what the leader of the sword sisterhood or brotherhood thought you needed to learn. Or the clan elder or eldress, if you joined the Alashi in the winter, or were too young or too old to go fight.

I knew that the Alashi had karenite, but the Sisterhood of Weavers knew that already. I knew something about the karenite trade in Daphnia—the names of the two sorceresses who bought, or tried to buy, my karenite. *I could turn them over, I suppose.* I knew about the Servant Sisterhood and the Younger Sisters, but little beyond the bare fact of their existence. There was Zivar, of course. Zivar, who'd been born a slave and then managed to pass herself off as a Weaver's apprentice. The green mouse, she had called herself, because there was no one else like her in the world—well, other than me. I flinched at the thought of having information about Zivar wrung from me, but I doubted that the Weavers particularly cared where Zivar came from. She made spell-chains for them on command, at least for now, so she was useful. Her origins were unimportant.

*I could tell them about Lycurgus.* Lycurgus, Kyros's cousin, was supposedly the steward of a farm owned by the Sisterhood. Tamar and I had taken Uljas there, looking for Burkut. Lycurgus had been drunk most of the time, and I'd realized while there that he'd been skimming farm profits to help the

Younger Sisters. *That's the sort of information I could give Kyros to convince him that I really was on his side all along.* I didn't really care whether I condemned Lycurgus or not; I had no fondness for the man. Solon had been kind, and far more competent. And loyal to the Sisterhood.

If I were talkative enough, could I convince them I really had stayed loyal to Kyros?

*They'll believe me. Of course they'll believe me.* I knew it was the cold fever whispering in my ear, but I embraced it because the alternative was despair. *They'll believe me because I am the one meant to free the rivers. I can only do that if I'm alive.*

"Can you see the towers yet?" Kyros asked.

"Towers?"

"Well, you've been to Casseia, you know the sort of thing I'm talking about. Casseia has one tower, built very tall by aerika. Penelopeia has over twenty towers like that. You should be able to see them soon."

I leaned a little farther out the window and squinted. I *could* see something, up ahead, barely visible against the blue sky. As we got closer, I could see the towers more clearly—first two, then six, then more. They spiked up toward the sky like glittering needles, and as we grew closer I realized that some were partially shod in polished copper and brass. *They must have aerika who do nothing but polish the metal.* It was an appalling display of power. Zivar had told me once that she never felt that she had enough aerika, though she lost a bit more of herself every time she did a binding. I was certain that the metal-polishing aerika had not been bound by women like the high magia, but by their apprentices and lesser sisters, acting on orders.

The sun was low in the sky. We were slowly descending now, and I thought I could see the Koryphe—the palace where the high magia and some of the other most highly placed Sisterhood members lived. White marble walls, partly clad, like the towers, in polished metal. A half dozen of the towers rose from within the outer walls; one had a glowing light inside like a beacon, and I wondered if the fire was tended by a human or a djinn. *An aeriko; I need to remember to use the Greek words.* My ears ached and felt as if they were filled with water; then I swallowed, and they cleared with a jolt of pain.

The aeriko set the palanquin down gently in the courtyard. Slaves were already waiting to help each of us out. I felt a little light-headed and accepted the arm offered to me. We were in an inner courtyard of the palace, large enough to accommodate several more palanquins. A fountain splashed lightly in the center, and the walls were decorated with mosaic pictures of olive trees.

Kyros was having a quiet conversation nearby; then he stepped over and said, "I've arranged for you to have a bath before you're presented to the magia."

*Presented to.* Like a gift. I followed a slave who led me to a room of warm water and herb-scented steam. If I had any hope for an opportunity to run later, I needed to restrain the impulse to run now. *There is nowhere to run to anyway. I am in Penelopeia, in the Koryphe.* I wondered what Tamar was doing. The realization of how far away she was made me slightly dizzy. *Weeks . . . months of travel.* I tried to tell myself that I would see her again, but for the moment, all I could do was submit to the ministrations of the slaves as I was immersed in water, scrubbed clean, and picked free of lice.

Once I was clean and dressed, I was escorted to one of the many interior gardens and left to wait . . . and wait . . . and wait. The night sky was dark; the courtyard was lit with torches. They'd dressed me in linen, with a light wool shawl for warmth, and sandals. I realized that my last material link to Tamar had been severed. The little talisman I'd made for myself—threads from her clothing knotted around my wrist—had disappeared in the bath. I rubbed my thumb against the palm of my right hand. *We are blood sisters. They can't ever truly separate us.*

My new clothes felt all wrong. Foreign. Everything was foreign. The night was warmer here than it had been back on the steppe, and the breeze had a strange misty softness, rather than the brisk edge I expected. There was a salty smell in the air, along with the perfume of the orange tree that grew beside the courtyard fountain and a warm, spicy smell that wafted from the doorway. Tea, I realized a moment later. The guard there was drinking tea.

I couldn't sit. I paced, instead, back and forth in the courtyard. In addition to the orange tree, there were copious flowers, even this early in the year, including some blood-red blooms shaped like a candle's flame. I forced myself to slow my step and study the flowers, as a way to calm my mind, but it did little good.

The guard in the doorway was female, I noticed.

Last summer, Janiya had confided in me that she had once been a guard employed by the Sisterhood of Weavers in Penelopeia; they had their own elite cadre of women guards. I wondered how many of the people in the Koryphe were women. There was at least one man—Kyros—but I'd seen no others. The sorceress I'd studied with during the winter, Zivar, had permitted no men in her house, not even slaves. Surely some of the sorceresses here were married, though . . .

The guard cleared her throat. I looked up, and she beckoned; it was time to go. She stood back to allow me to go first, then followed behind, as if she thought I might flee. *Maybe that means that there is somewhere to go? Or perhaps she always does this . . .* Despite her boots, her step was quiet on the marble floors. The corridor was lit with oil lamps. I wondered if they were tended by human servants, or aerika.

At the end of the corridor, we reached a closed door made from heavy wood. The guard rapped on the door and someone inside swung it open. The room was warm, and moist with the smell of breath and sweat, as if it hadn't been opened for days. There was a long table, with chairs clustered at the other end. Kyros sat in one, and a thin older woman sat in the other. Her hands were folded over each other on the table. Her fingernails had been allowed to grow extremely long, and had been painted; they made me think of bloodstained claws. Her face was deeply lined. She was dressed in red silk that matched her claws, and had a gold bracelet that looked like a serpent coiled around her upper arm.

Looking at her, I could see the cold fever lurking, but it did not master her—not today.

"So," she said. "You are the spy."

I swallowed hard. "Kyros sent me . . ."

". . . to spy, yes, of course, yet you didn't just say *yes, I am the spy.* That's very interesting. Why didn't you?"

"Because . . . because Kyros has lost his faith in me."

"Really? He seems to have a great deal of faith in you." She glanced at him dismissively. "More than I think is warranted. He brought you here, had you bathed and given fresh clothes, as if you were truly *his* spy, returning from the field, ready to report. Strange. We sent him orders to have you executed."

"But I—"

"Do you have anything *useful* to report? Anything that Kyros doesn't already know? You were out of contact for a while, but then he sent an aeriko to watch you, so I can't imagine you have all that much."

"Lycurgus," I squeaked out.

"We already know about Lycurgus. I'm done with you." She gestured, and the guard stepped forward, laying her hand on my shoulder.

"Wait—" This was happening so fast. "I tried—it's not my fault—" I wondered if they would use a sword, or a rope, or grant me some more gruesome death. *Let it be over with quickly, if they're going to kill me . . .*

The sorceress had started to turn away; now she turned back and looked me straight in the eye. "Kyros clearly wants you spared, so we'll leave your neck intact for now. Take her to the pit." She turned away again.

"Kyros," I said. "KYROS!" I caught a glimpse of his face, his eyes wide and worried, and then other guards came, and I was swept away with them like a twig in the tide.

# CHAPTER THREE

# TAMAR

Name your mother."

"My mother is the River that will return."

"Name your father."

"My father is the Steppe that gives us freedom."

Zhanna took my left hand. A priestess of Arachne whose name I didn't know took my right hand. Janiya stepped forward and looked into my eyes. "You took your freedom, and you proved yourself over and over again. You weren't born one of us, but you're one of us now. Walk through fire and come out Alashi."

Cheers rang out as shaman and priestess walked me to the fire. The Greeks told their slaves that the Alashi made initiates walk through fire, and for a moment I felt a breath of fear. But they had no intention of hurting me. Zhanna and the priestess dropped my hands, picked up torches and set them alight, then held them high over their heads so that the flames licked against each other. I walked under the flaming bridge, then they tossed the torches into the fire. The Alashi crowded around me, each person lacing their fingers with mine and then kissing me on the forehead in a gesture of welcome. I made my way around the huge circle, then back to where I'd started.

Now I would go through the ceremony again—this time, pretending to be Lauria. I slipped off my own vest and put on Lauria's, then stood before the shaman and priestess again.

"Name your mother," Zhanna said.

"My mother is the River that will return." Lauria's mother was alive, and I wondered fleetingly how she would feel about embracing the river as her adopted mother, even if she'd never much gotten along with her real mother. It was too late to ask. And the truth was, I was afraid that if I waited, the eldress would change her mind.

"Name your father," the priestess said.

"My father is the Steppe that gives us freedom." Lauria's father was Kyros. I had no doubt that she would willingly disown him.

Zhanna and the priestess clasped my hands again, and again Janiya stepped forward. Her eyes were bright and her voice very soft. "You took your freedom, and held it as tightly as any Alashi," she said. "You stayed true to us when we were not true to you. You were not born one of us, but you're one of us now. Walk through fire, Lauria, and come out Alashi."

I stepped under the torches again. The cheering this time was quieter. Meruert and Ruan and the other women from my sword sisterhood came to clasp my hands again, and kiss me. Beyond them, I saw a young man gazing at me. I couldn't remember whether he had clasped my hands the first time, but when I reached for him now, he recoiled like I'd offered him a cup of poison and turned his back on me. My stomach twisted. Swallowing hard, I turned back to those who were willing to accept Lauria as well as me.

There was kumiss and stewed lamb afterward, then drumming and dancing. The sword sisterhoods and brotherhoods would ride out tomorrow with the new recruits. Between Sophos's slaves and the mine slaves, there were too many to assign only one blossom to each sword brotherhood and sword sisterhood. They would have to go out in groups. The feast was wonderful. I'd gotten tired of Alashi food during my summer with the sword sisterhood, but now it tasted like home. Well, other than kumiss. I still hated the thick, sour drink that everyone tried to press on me during the evening celebration.

Ruan, who had been so nasty to me all summer, embraced me like a long-lost kinswoman and dragged me over to see the rest of the women from Janiya's sisterhood—Maydan, Gulim, Zhanna. Maydan's face lit with a warm smile. She leaned on a stick to help her walk. Erdene let me hold her new baby. Her daughter's downy hair was the color of a chick's feathers, clearly the gift of the trader who'd fathered the baby. Then Meruert spotted me and I went to see her and Jaran and the others who'd escaped from Sophos's household, lone blue beads hanging on cords around their necks. Jaran looked at me nervously—he'd fled north to the steppe after selling Lauria to the mine, certain I'd have his head if I caught up with him. I'd forgiven Lauria for going behind my back, though, so I couldn't really hold a grudge against Jaran. Much.

Zhanna had met us on the steppe and warned Lauria to flee. Now she poured me kumiss and told me to sit by her side. I had been Zhanna's apprentice during my summer with the sword sisterhood, but now she met my eyes like an equal. "I felt so proud when I heard what you'd done," she whispered.

"But you were the one who told me that the Alashi didn't free slaves," I said.

"I never said I agreed with that rule." Zhanna gazed for a long moment into my eyes, and I saw humor and the spark of something else. I looked down quickly. She sighed and stroked my back gently. "You are no longer my apprentice," she said. "You're a full-fledged shaman, though I think you know that."

I nodded.

"And you are fully Alashi now, as well. So there are rules that don't apply anymore."

What was she talking about? I lifted my head to look at her again. She gave me a level gaze and a hint of a smile. And I realized that she was inviting me to—I choked a little on my kumiss and put it down. I had no idea how to politely refuse. I had spent years not being allowed to refuse, but now—now—

"Excuse me," I said, and stood up. "I need to—" My mind went blank for a moment, and I almost bolted in panic. "I need to relieve myself. I'll be back soon."

Zhanna sought me out, later, on the other side of the encampment. "Don't worry," she said, and I could see sympathy in her face. "I'm sorry. I didn't mean to scare you away. I just—well, I'm sorry."

"There's nothing to apologize for," I said. I wanted to pretend nothing happened.

"Do you want to come sit with us again? Just for companionship. I promise."

"That would be nice," I said, and followed her back to the others.

In the late-night firelight, I could see that many others had paired off. Some reunited with summer friends. Others enjoyed a last night with their lover from the winter. Zhanna hadn't sought out anyone else, though I doubted she'd have had trouble finding company. I looked down at my kumiss and wondered what it would be like to spend an evening with someone I'd chosen. Someone I liked.

When I joined the Alashi, the eldress said they would teach me to live as a free person. But when it came to this, Sophos's hands still gripped me tightly. I shivered in the cold night wind, and wished Lauria were here.

I must have fallen asleep during the night because someone nudged me awake at dawn—Janiya. "The eldress wants us to leave today," she said. "Get your horse ready."

I'd drunk only the kumiss I couldn't refuse, but my head ached and my tongue stuck to my teeth. I washed my face and rinsed my mouth, but I still felt like something scraped off the bottom of a boot. Well, it couldn't be helped. I went to find my horse.

*J*aniya joined me as I saddled Kesh. "The eldress is sending us with remounts and packhorses. We'll be able to travel quickly."

"How much karenite did she give you?"

Janiya handed me a heavy pouch. I peered in. There were hundreds of pebbles of the stuff. I swallowed hard and closed the bag. "I don't want to bring this much."

"The Alashi don't lack for it."

"We don't need this much." I thought about the army of slaves the eldress had mentioned so casually. "There are hundreds of pieces in this bag."

Janiya studied me for a moment. Then she shrugged and said, "How much do you think we should bring?"

"Ten pieces each," I said. I was thinking that would be twenty pieces, but she took out three small bags and counted ten into each.

"Who else is coming?" I asked.

"Me," said a voice behind me.

I turned. It was the young man who'd snubbed me last night during the ritual. He was mixed Greek and Danibeki ancestry, and a little older than me. He had pretty eyes with long lashes, like a girl.

"Tamar," he said, and gave me a stiff nod.

Did I *know* him? Then I remembered: Alibek. The man who'd named Lauria a spy. I thought of him as her betrayer, although I had to admit I could understand why he'd done it. "Why are *you* coming?" I blurted.

"The eldress asked me. She seemed to think I'd have a better chance of passing myself off as a merchant than someone who was born Alashi."

"So, why you? Why not Ruan?"

"She's going to lead the sword sisterhood," Janiya said.

"Oh, you're joking. She'll be *terrible* at it!"

Janiya shrugged. "It's the eldress's decision, not mine. And it was her decision to send Alibek."

"The first thing we're doing is going to Elpisia to find Lauria and help her free Thais," I said. "Lauria may be coming with us."

Alibek's eyes narrowed, but he shrugged. "My lady Tamar," he said, "if you say Lauria is trustworthy now, I will hold no grudge."

"You will hold no grudge? You sought me out last night just to *snub* me when I was being Lauria!"

Janiya held up her hands, cutting us off. "Alibek, if Lauria joins us, will you treat her respectfully, as a sister?"

"Of course I will." He was breathing a little bit hard.

"Tamar, will you treat Alibek respectfully, as a brother?"

"Yes," I said, irritated that she'd even question that.

"Alibek, you have no feud with Tamar, do you?"

"No." Though the set of his jaw said otherwise.

"And Tamar. You have no feud with Alibek—right?"

No feud with the person who had betrayed Lauria? I ground my teeth and said, "Right."

"Then I think we can set out." Janiya mounted her horse. "Come on."

Alibek gave me another grim look and mounted his horse. I chewed on my lip as I settled onto mine. With Janiya, we turned south—toward Elpisia.

We approached Elpisia near twilight two days later. I had an idea of where Lauria might hide, so we picked our way along the dried-out riverbed, the horses following us. Alibek hummed a little tune to himself. It was a short tune, and he hummed it over and over. "Would you *stop*?" I muttered.

"Sorry," he said, but he started up again a moment later.

Lauria was not there. Kesh snorted, though, and a few minutes later I heard the whinny of another horse. I pulled myself up to the top of the bank and saw Kara, her saddle off and her halter loose. She trotted straight over when she saw me, and snuffled my hair and hands.

Janiya pulled herself up next to me. "That's an Alashi horse," she said.

"It's Kara," I said, my throat tightening. "Lauria's horse."

Janiya slipped something out of her pocket and Kara lipped it up. She stroked Kara's nose. "Nice to see you again," she murmured. Then she looked at me. "She hasn't been groomed in days."

My heart sank.

"Let's pull back from town for the night," Alibek said.

"But . . ."

"There's nothing we can do tonight," Janiya said.

We ended up moving as far away from Elpisia as we could and making camp in the growing darkness. Kara stayed close to us.

"What was Lauria's plan?" Janiya asked.

"We didn't really have one. I told her to wait here for me. She was traveling with just Kara. She should only have gotten here a few days ago . . ."

"Do you think she waited? She might have been seen hiding and detained."

"Honestly, I think she probably went into town after Thais."

"Thais," Alibek said. "She was one of the others that Lauria took back to slavery, wasn't she?"

"Yes," I said. "We were trying to free all of them. Nika and her daughter, Uljas and Burkut, Prax . . ."

"I see." Alibek looked grim, but also faintly pleased. "I know Thais. Kyros sold me to her master, and that's who I escaped from. She has no interest in freedom now. But she does hold a grudge."

I suddenly noticed how chilly the night was. "You're saying that if Lauria did try to free her, Thais would have turned Lauria in?"

Alibek thought this over. "Probably," he said.

"I want to go into town and look for her."

"Lauria, or Thais?"

"Both!" Even if Thais didn't want to be free, she might know what had happened to Lauria.

Janiya caught my hand. "Don't go into town tonight," she said. "You're a shaman—seek her out in your dreams. Ask her where she is, and what's going on."

I had to admit the sense in that, and after eating a quick meal, we went to sleep.

*I* found my way to the borderland quickly and looked for Lauria, but she was nowhere to be found. I hadn't been able to find her since that night when she shouted, *I love you*. Would I know if she were dead? I wouldn't be able to find her in the borderland if she were dead, but surely, I thought, I would know. She was my blood sister. I took a deep breath and tried again.

I didn't find Lauria, but as I concentrated, my hands reaching out to grasp her, I saw something else: a web of red silk threads that led from my hands to . . . elsewhere. They were my blood ties, I realized—the ties that linked me to other people. These were all people I could bring into the borderland with me if I tried. Well, maybe. Some of the threads, as I touched them, gave me a sense of resistance, like a full bucket of water at the bottom of a well. If I pulled, I could bring them in. Others were slack like a fishing line in still water. I could pull on those all I liked, but nothing useful would come of it.

As I held the threads up, I saw Lauria's. It glowed with a faint light but was slack. I saw no threads leading to anyone dead, so Lauria, surely, was just awake. I felt relief, then wondered what she was doing awake in the middle of the night. Were they waking her at night and letting her sleep in the day? Why?

Well, I might as well look for Zhanna. Did one of these threads lead to her?

The world turned to a blur around me, but when it settled, I was not in an Alashi tent, but in a Greek house. In front of me I saw a desk piled high with papers, a shuttered window, and a lamp. This was an officer's study. Sophos had something similar. I felt a stab of panic, but Sophos was dead. I took a deep breath, reminding myself I was a shaman. This was my territory, no matter what it looked like. No one could hurt me here.

"Tamar," a man's voice said.

It was Kyros.

———

*I* was sold to Sophos when I was ten years old. I'd been owned by a friend of his, and one day when he was visiting he saw me fetching water for the kitchen. Before I knew what was happening, my mother was kissing me good-bye and telling me to stay out of trouble. She died six months later. I found out from the Fair One, the djinn that visited Jaran.

Sophos brought me home with him. He had me scrubbed clean, dressed in white linen, given a glass of drugged wine, and taken to a guest's bedchamber. I wasn't told what to expect—not by Sophos and not by Boradai, who took me to the room and left without a word. It was evening. There was a lamp on the table, and the room was small but very comfortable. The large bed took up most of the space, piled high with quilts and pillows. It was winter, and the room was kept warm by a fire. In my innocence, I thought perhaps my job there was to keep the fire from going out, so I sat down on the rug by the hearth and tended it.

When the door opened, I had drifted off to sleep, and I snapped awake, afraid I'd be beaten for failing at my duty. The fire still glowed, to my relief, and the room was as warm as anyone could ask for. A man came in alone, wearing boots, and I kept my eyes on his boots as he sat down on the bed. He took them off and set them down on the floor, then chuckled—it was a kind-sounding laugh—and said, "What a pretty girl you are. You must have been very tired."

"Yes, sir," I said, keeping my eyes down.

"Come here," he said, so I stood up. "Lie down on the bed."

I lay down. I didn't understand why, but ten years

of slavery had taught me to obey without asking for explanations.

"Spread your legs apart," he said. "That's it, just like that. Now close your eyes."

The sudden pain was like a knife. I think I may have screamed, *What are you doing,* before I started begging him to stop, promising I'd never do it again, whatever it was I had done to deserve this. I didn't strike out at him, because to strike a Greek meant death. My hands knotted into fists, and I bit my knuckles until they bled.

When he was done with me, he called a servant to remove me from his bed. I had to be carried, as I was too hurt to walk. It was actually some months later that I learned the name of the friend that Sophos had "given" me to: Kyros.

*T*amar," he said again. He was seated behind his desk. "No, don't be afraid of me."

"I'm *not* afraid of you," I said. "This is my territory, not yours." And I wanted a tent. I pictured it, and the world tilted sharply. A moment later, we were sitting on cushions in an Alashi tent.

"Of course," Kyros said, and gave me a polite nod. "What do you want?"

"Just to talk."

"Where is Lauria?"

"Ah, yes. That's precisely what I wished to talk with you about."

"Where is she?"

"Safe, for now."

My stomach clenched. *"Where?"* I asked.

"Penelopeia," Kyros said. "We're the guests of the

magia. Or at least, I'm her guest. It would probably be more accurate to describe Lauria as her prisoner."

Penelopeia. Months of travel. *Months.* My mouth went dry. "Why are you telling me this?"

Kyros turned his palms up. "I need information. From someone. It can come from you, or from Lauria. Right now, Lauria isn't talking. The magia is willing to be a little patient, for now. She knows that Lauria is my daughter, but she has her limits—and so do I." He leaned forward. "Do I make myself clear?"

"You're saying you'll hurt Lauria."

"Yes. And kill her when we're done. Unless *you* give us the information we need. If you agree to help us against the Alashi, I'll even set her free. *You* are trusted."

"So is Lauria. Set her free now and she'll be accepted back."

"Really?" He raised an eyebrow. "Well, well, well. But no, I don't think I'm going to do that just now. I know my daughter pretty well, and I knew when she betrayed me. She's no longer of use to me as an ally among the Alashi. All that's left is the information she can give me. I'll give you a day or two to think it over, Tamar. I'm sure you can think of some scraps of information that might buy her some time."

I wanted to call him filthy names, but when I opened my mouth again, I was alone in the tent. "Lauria," I called. "Lauria!" Surely Kyros couldn't keep her from me here . . . but there was no answer.

*I* brooded over breakfast, and while loading up the horses. "Do we need to go back to Elpisia?" Janiya asked me.

"Kyros has Lauria," I said.

"Were you able to speak with her?"

"Briefly," I lied. I didn't want to tell anyone about my conversation with Kyros. "I think he took her to Penelopeia." He could be lying about that—she could be in Elpisia right now—but Kyros wasn't stupid. Lauria and I had broken slaves out from the heart of Helladia and organized a mine rebellion. If Lauria were in Elpisia, I might find a way to get her out, and Kyros knew it. No, he would have taken her somewhere far away. Penelopeia was the Imperial city, the seat of the Sisterhood of Weavers. I could believe that he would have taken her there.

Janiya furrowed her brow and nodded slowly. "Let's head to the farm, then, to see if we can find Lycurgus and make contact with the Younger Sisters." Her voice was firm, but I knew that she was giving me an opening to protest and insist we had to go to Penelopeia. But without a sorceress's palanquin, it would take months just to get there. Besides, the farm was sort of on the way. Janiya still looked at me, waiting, so I nodded.

Alibek didn't say much as we loaded the horses. I could hardly stand to look at him. It wasn't fair to blame him, but I still thought it was his fault.

"There was a story I heard when I was a boy," Alibek said. "About a man who sowed a field with blood and was surprised when an army grew there overnight, burned his house, and slew him."

"Are you saying that Lauria deserves whatever happens to her?"

"I'm saying that she planted things that will bear fruit for years, even if she's changed her ways. That's just the way the world is." Alibek undid the top of his shirt and slid it down slightly, exposing thick, ridged scars on his shoulders, and a shiny healed burn scar just below his throat. "There are reasons some of us hold grudges."

Shaken, I turned my back on him and mounted Kesh. Lauria sowed a lot more than blood, I thought. I knew the story that Alibek was talking about, but . . . Lauria had changed. She was not the person he knew.

There were fields beyond the field of blood. Orchards and gardens waiting to bloom. She deserved to reap from those fields, as well.

# CHAPTER FOUR

# LAURIA

The guards dragged me down a long spiral stair. After one last anguished scream for Kyros, I closed my mouth hard, clenching my teeth. *If I die, let me at least face it bravely. There's no hope of escape. Tamar—I wish I could return to you, if only for an hour . . .*

We were deep underground now. It was cool and lamps lit our way. A memory of the mine rose up unbidden and I tried to fight it back. When we reached the bottom of the stair, two of the guards opened a heavy trapdoor that was set like a lid into the floor. They loosed me, and when I didn't immediately try to run or attack them, one of them sized me up. All the guards were women, or I would have feared rape. As it was, it still took all the self-control I had not to shrink away from her. She kicked something down into the hole in the floor—a ladder.

"Get in," she said. When I hesitated, she said, "Climb down, or we'll throw you down. Your choice."

"I'll climb down," I said. My legs were shaking as I approached the ladder, and I crouched carefully beside it, fearing that I would fall if I weren't careful and that they would push me if I weren't fast enough. They waited until I had reached the bottom, then pulled up the ladder behind me. Then they heaved the trapdoor up and let it fall shut over me with a thud. I heard a latch fall into place, though how I would have opened the door from below with no ladder . . .

The darkness was absolute. I couldn't even see my hand in front of my face. I felt my way around the edge of the room. It was small. I could lie down, but if I put my hands over my head and stretched, my feet pressed against the opposite wall. The room was round, and lined entirely with seamless rock. It was rough, not smooth, but I couldn't feel the lines that would be present if it had been lined with brick. *How would you make something like this? Djinni, I suppose.*

I felt for handholds—was there any way to scramble up? No.

*Even if I learned how to fly, it's locked. There's no way out.*

*There's always a way out. There was a way out of the mine.*

*This place is darker than the mine.*

I'd heard stories about prisoners being thrown down into pits and left to die of thirst or starvation. I spent a long time, that first day of darkness, wondering if they would let me die here. I remembered the thirst of my trip across the desert, with Tamar, when we journeyed to the Alashi. *It would not be a pleasant death. At least it's not hot here, but I don't imagine that would make the thirst feel any more pleasant.* I swallowed hard, my throat clenching just thinking about it.

Or perhaps I wouldn't live long enough to die of thirst. Would the air go bad? The djinn at the bottom of the mine had been there to bring in fresh air; there was no djinn here. Perhaps my throat clenched because I was starting to suffocate . . . But when I sat still, I could feel a breeze waft across my knees, and when I felt through the dark I found some holes in the wall near the floor. I didn't know where the air was coming from, but there did seem to be air coming in.

After a time—it was hard to know how long—I heard a rattle above, and the trapdoor opened, just a bit. A bucket came down on a rope. It held a piece of bread and a waterskin. The water had a strange taste, and I was still hungry even after I ate the bread, but at least it looked like they planned on feeding me. They lowered another bucket and someone shouted down for me to use it for my wastes. So I wouldn't be left to lie in my filth, either.

I lay down a bit later on the stone floor. *Tamar,* I thought, but the blackness claimed me, and I dreamed of nothing. No borderland. No Tamar.

*I*t was very difficult to guess how much time was passing. I thought they were feeding me twice a day, but some days I thought they fed me three times and other days only once. I tried counting times I slept, but I knew that sometimes I napped in the middle of the day, and in any case I had no way to mark a count. This bothered me, and I spent a long time on my hands and knees, searching for tiny pebbles that I could pile up to mark the days. I gathered a small heap, and since I'd slept five times by then, I put five beside the bucket I squatted over to relieve myself. I added pebbles for several days, then reached for the pile one morning and found it scattered and lost—I had kicked it while not paying attention, or maybe in my sleep. I let out a stream of foul words. Would the guards above hear me and wonder what I was so angry about? *Were* there any guards up there when they weren't feeding me?

I tried again to count, then gave up. It had been about two weeks, I thought, but it might have been half that. Or twice that. I didn't know.

One time, instead of food, a ladder unrolled, and two guards descended with a lamp. As I shaded my eyes against the dazzling light, a blow to my stomach caught me by surprise. A lash cut across my back, tearing through the linen dress. They asked no questions, and by the time I wanted to offer information—*anything*—to stop the beating, I couldn't get the words out.

Then it was over, and they were gone, until the next time. My stomach lurched when the trapdoor opened again a few hours later, but it was just my dinner. I had little appetite today, but I was thirsty; I drank the water and curled up on the floor. Sleep came easily, despite the fear and the pain, but I couldn't find the borderland—nothing beyond thick darkness.

*E*ven in the darkness, the fever burned in my blood. I paced around and around the tiny circular shaft, pretending that somehow this was taking me closer to Tamar. *How many steps would take me back to where I belong?* Sometimes the fever told me that I was going to die here. Months might pass; years. I might go completely mad alone in the darkness, until I died an old woman, forgotten even by Tamar. Other days hope seized me with a violence that made me sob. I would escape; there was a way out of here. Prometheus had been bound to the side of a mountain, his immortal liver torn out daily, until Arachne had found him and they had freed each other. Spiders liked darkness. *Arachne is here; her messengers are close at hand.* I thought I could hear them, when the fever burned strongly enough. Or the djinni. *The djinni will help me. I am the gate.* Their *gate. A djinn could get me out of here. If I wait. If I hold on.*

Prometheus had been freed, but there was also Zeus. The story said that Alexander had imprisoned him under a mountain when he conquered Olympus. Though some believed that anyone who found Zeus and freed him would be granted immortality in gratitude, in nearly a thousand years he had not been found. *I am not going to live that long.*

Then I woke one morning and felt the darkness settling in around me like a blanket of snow, and knew that the hope I'd felt had only been the fever that was now leaving me. There was no reason to hope. No reason to continue. I left my food and water untouched. *There is a way out of here. One way. And with no Tamar here to force me to eat and drink, it shouldn't even take all that long.*

Perhaps a day after that, the ladder unrolled. I waited, curled in the corner, for the guards to descend, but no one did. "Lauria," someone called from overhead. "Come up the ladder."

*Stay here,* the melancholia whispered. *Let them drag you up if they want you that badly. You're tired, weak from hunger, you don't have the strength to climb the ladder.*

"Come up," the voice said again.

Curiosity won out. I stood up, steadied myself against the wall as my head spun momentarily, and climbed up the ladder.

*T*here was lamplight above; it dazzled my eyes, and I couldn't see much. The hands holding me were female, but I could hear a man's voice—Kyros. I heard him say *on my authority* and then *I'll make it worth your while.* Then his hand was on my arm and he was steering me out of the room, up the spiral stairs, and out into a courtyard.

It was day. If the lamplight had dazzled me, the sun blinded me completely. My knees buckled and I couldn't open my streaming eyes. "You need to come with me," Kyros said, pulling me back to my feet. "Your eyes will recover in a few hours. Just keep them shut for now."

It was galling to be so helpless. *At least I'm out of the pit.* I felt the sunlight leave my face as we passed inside into a cool hallway. Down a short flight of stairs, then out to another courtyard, under some sort of overhang that shaded me from the sun even as it let in a summer breeze. Inside again, up a spiral stair, and into a room. "Sit here." Kyros lowered me into a chair. I heard the rustle of curtains. "You can open your eyes now."

Kyros had closed the curtains, but even the thin lines of sunlight around the edges made my eyes water. I put my face down on my folded arms. "Let me get you some tea," he said.

I sat and waited; gradually my eyes adjusted, so that I could look around the room without tears pouring down my cheeks. It was small, but with a comfortable bed, a table with chairs, a wood door with a latch on the inside. Hangings with pictures of olive trees covered the walls. It was desperately ordinary. I nearly sobbed with relief. "Why did the magia change her mind?" I asked when Kyros returned. My voice was hoarse.

"I persuaded her to grant you a reprieve," Kyros said. His voice was gentle. He poured a cup of tea and set it down beside me at the table.

I picked it up; my hands were shaking so badly I had to use both of them to hold the cup. "After all this time?" *How long has it been?*

Kyros's fingers drummed on the tabletop. "The magia is actually four women. Or rather, it's a single office, occupied in turn by one of four women, so that decisions can be made by someone who isn't too despondent to rise from bed."

I wondered what happened when one magia didn't wish to give up her authority. This didn't seem like a good time to ask.

"The magia you met has given up the gold serpent—she has stepped aside. The new magia was more willing to listen to me. For now, at least, you have been reprieved from the pit. You're still under guard." He gestured briefly to the door. "I would appreciate it if you wouldn't do anything foolish," he added in a low voice. "I vouched for you. Please don't make me regret that."

"Why did you vouch for me?" It was a stupid thing to ask—*Do you want him to send you back there?*—but I asked anyway.

"Lauria. You're my daughter. I *know* that I can trust you." He stood up. "Let me get you something to eat."

Despite the darkness that still lapped at the edges of my thoughts, I was ravenous. Kyros brought a plate of sweet rice pudding, as if I were recovering from a long illness, and a cup of cider. I tucked in, relishing the sweet, creamy taste, the silky texture of the rice, the scents of the spices. Kyros watched quietly while I ate, and sent away for more when I finished what I had. I drank enough cider to make me tipsy before I thought to slow down.

"What were you going to say about Lycurgus, before the magia had you taken away?" Kyros asked.

"He's in league with the Younger Sisters," I said, my voice still hoarse. "Solon, the steward—he is loyal to the Sisterhood of Weavers."

"What do you know about the Younger Sisters?"

"Not much. Lycurgus was funneling them some of the goods from the farm. And he summoned a sorceress to help him at one point. I think she might have been one of them."

Kyros leaned forward, clearly interested. "What was her name?"

"I can't remember." I was telling the truth; I couldn't.

"Try." Kyros stood up. "For now, I'll arrange for

you to have a bath. Your meals will be brought to you. If you want to go anywhere, you can ask your guard to escort you." He turned back at the doorway. "If you can remember the sorceress's name, that would be very helpful."

*Cassandra,* I remembered a few hours later, as I soaked in a tub, a slave scrubbing the filth of the pit from my hair. I didn't really care what happened to Cassandra. *Should I give him the name?* I didn't have a great deal I felt willing to offer Kyros. *Not even to stay out of the pit.* I'd hold on to that for a while, in case I needed it.

*At least I'm out of the pit for now. Maybe now I'll be able to find Tamar in the borderland. . . .*

When I was clean and dry, the guard took me back to my room. More food, along with a glass of wine and a pot of tea, waited for me. I filled my stomach and took a hesitant glance out the window. Night had fallen. My eyes might be intolerant of light, but my night vision was no better than it had ever been; I could see little in the shadowed courtyard below. There was movement, however, and after a few minutes of watching I decided that it was not just my imagination: there was, in fact, a guard out there as well as at my door, despite the fact that it was too far to jump and the wall was too well kept to climb. I watched a few minutes longer, then let the curtain fall shut. *In time, they will be more likely to slip.*

I ignored the wine—I'd avoided wine for nearly a year, because it tended to remind me of the night when Sophos raped me. I took a cup of tea. Halfway through the cup, I felt sleepy and went and lay down in the bed. Despite my fear, despite everything, I fell asleep almost instantly. A dreamless sleep, again, where Tamar could not reach me. *Darkness.*

One of the slaves woke me the next morning. Steam rose from a cup of tea on the table by the door. There was also a tray with food—sliced cold meat, soft fresh bread, and yogurt. They had brought a basin and pitcher of cool water, and a cloth to let me wash my face. By the door, someone had set a basket with linen, needles, and colored thread. Again, I nearly wept over the homey comforts. I washed my face and had breakfast, then picked up the basket and tentatively opened the door. "Is there some courtyard . . . with shade? I'd like to get out under the sky," I said, my tongue awkward.

"This way," my guard said, and I trailed her outside to a garden.

Summer had come while I was in the pit. I was relieved that at least it hadn't passed. It was hot and sunny, though still reasonably pleasant in the shade. I took a seat in the shade of a tree and threaded a needle. I'd always hated embroidery, even among the Alashi. *If I ever get back there—when I get back there—I'll have another vest of sister cloth to embroider. Maybe I'll try to make a picture of a horse, so I'll be able to do it right next time.*

The garden was fully enclosed. The walls were high, but enough sun made its way in to sustain a couple of olive trees and some golden flowers. A fountain bubbled up in one corner; a slave dressed in white linen drew water out of the fountain in a blue pitcher to pour over the flowers and the roots of the trees. A white cat sat at the edge of the fountain, washing itself; after a while, I let my untouched linen drop to my lap and watched the cat as it licked its paw, then rubbed its paw behind its ears. It saw me watching, jumped lightly down from the fountain edge, and came over to say hello.

I scratched its bony little head with a fingertip; it lifted its nose and purred, then arched its back and settled itself into my lap, on top of the embroidery. I closed my eyes and stroked the cat.

My guard nudged me out of my half doze to bring me inside for lunch. Kyros had sent up a message: *let me know if you need anything.* I left the note on the table, reminding myself that he was my keeper, my prison guard. Nothing he did was for kindness, but because he wanted something. Still, somewhere in the dark cellars of my own soul lurked the Lauria who had once been Kyros's willing servant, and she whispered to me now. *You can trust Kyros. Kyros freed you from the pit. Kyros will never betray you.*

# CHAPTER FIVE

# TAMAR

"Zhanna wants to know what's wrong," Janiya said over breakfast.

I choked on my tea and said, "What do you mean?"

Janiya raised one eyebrow. "She hasn't been able to *find you,* what did you think I meant? So she came looking for me, instead. I hate having people meddle with my dreams—I'm no shaman. So. What's the problem?"

"I haven't been sleeping well," I said to my tea.

"Hmm. Well, do we need to go to an inn and get you a bed? Because I like having my nights for myself."

"A bed wouldn't help."

"What would help?"

"I don't know."

Janiya sighed. "Well, all right then. I'll let Zhanna

know that the next time she barges in. If she has some ideas, I'll pass them on to you."

Alibek was listening, his eyes flicking back and forth between us. "Couldn't someone talk to *you*?" I asked him.

"I'm no shaman," he said. "Janiya and Zhanna were probably once lovers, and that's why Zhanna could find her." He glanced at Janiya, whose ears had turned bright pink. "I have no blood brother, no old lover, no family other than my sister."

"You have a sister?" I asked. I remembered a moment later that Lauria had told me about her once.

Alibek narrowed his green eyes. "I told Lauria about my sister when she took me back to Kyros. She never told you?"

"She did," I said. "I remember, now."

He went on with his story anyway. "Gulsara and I were both born in Kyros's household. She was five years older than me. When we were young, we worked in the stable. Gulsara liked that job, because it was easy to stay very dirty and avoid being noticed by anyone. But eventually she was noticed anyway, and Kyros took her for his harem. She was there for, oh, perhaps a year. Then one night a door was left open and she slipped out and escaped."

"Good for her," I murmured.

"Yes. Good for her. Kyros sent out searchers, of course, but they returned empty-handed. When he gave up looking for her, he sent for me. I was eleven years old then and still working in the stable. I was terrified when his guards came for me. They took me before Kyros in his office, and he smiled at me and said that since my sister had run away, he would take me as her replacement. As I watched, he summoned one of his djinni, and told it to find Gulsara and tell her what he'd done. Gulsara was never particularly kind to me, but our parents were gone, and she'd been my protector for years. Had she stood before him bound and in his power, there was nothing he could have done to her that would have been worse than hurting me."

I shuddered, trying to shake the image of eleven-year-old Alibek—and of myself at ten—from my thoughts.

"Kyros's harem is hard to escape. I waited years, thinking I'd try for freedom when he tired of me and sent me back to the stable. Except he didn't, so finally I found a chance and ran. That's when Lauria brought me back. Kyros had me beaten nearly to death, then branded. He wanted to destroy me inside and out, to punish me and to punish my sister even though she didn't know what had happened. Then he gave me as a gift to a friend. I think I was supposed to be an example to the other slaves, in my broken, wounded state. And I probably was an example, but not the kind Kyros had in mind. As soon as my body was healed enough to travel, I ran away again—and this time I made it. I spent the rest of the summer with the sword brotherhood, then met you in the fall, and you know the rest." He tilted his head up at me and I realized for the first time that he was only a year or two older than I was.

"I was a harem slave, too," I said. Alibek raised an eyebrow, and he looked me over as if he were trying to decide whether I was pretty enough to be telling the truth. I flushed and stood up. "Can you talk to your sister in your dreams?"

Alibek shrugged. "I spent a full year trying, back

when I was eleven. I could never do it. Most people can't. I suggest you try to figure out what your problem is and fix it."

Janiya shook her head in disgust—with me, with Alibek, it wasn't clear. "When Zhanna came last night, I told her what we knew about Lauria. That's all we have right now, anyway. Let's get going."

I knew what was wrong, of course—Kyros. I feared that if I went to the borderland to find Zhanna, Kyros would find me first. I couldn't tell him anything. But if I refused outright, he would hurt Lauria.

At least it was morning. I had a whole day before I had to worry again about dodging Kyros.

We mounted up and rode.

*Was* there anything I could tell Kyros? Something harmless? Something that would make him feel like he was getting information but that he couldn't use against us? Part of me knew he could use anything at all, but . . . Was there anything he already knew that I could offer as if I thought he wouldn't know? What did I know that he'd want to know about, anyway?

Well, I knew about our mission to the Younger Sisters, and obviously I couldn't tell him about *that*. I knew about the Servant Sisterhood. Kyros might be interested, but that might matter. Besides, I'd liked the woman who'd told me about the Servant Sisterhood—Zivar's housekeeper, Nurzhan. I'd liked her a lot. If Kyros was willing to torture and kill his own *daughter*, he certainly wouldn't hesitate to do the same to Nurzhan.

I knew what Lauria had done with Kyros's djinni and he'd probably like to know that, but if he hadn't figured it out, I certainly wasn't going to tell him.

I could tell him how we freed Sophos's slaves. Kyros might want to know that simply because Sophos was his friend, but it was nothing he could use against us. We'd brought a trusted slave, Boradai, to our side. If Kyros was clever, he'd figure out on his own that we'd found her old lover and freed him, and that was how we'd turned her against Sophos. Boradai knew Sophos's household inside and out. She could have killed Sophos years ago if she'd wanted, but she saw nothing in it for her, so she'd stayed loyal until she had a better offer.

Kyros probably had a slave like Boradai—a trusted older slave who kept order, and secrets, and maybe even keys. He probably even trusted her. I smiled. Telling him about Boradai could be fun.

There were risks. He might learn something I didn't want him to know. But maybe it would be just enough to keep Lauria safe. I pushed away all thoughts of danger and spent the day thinking through precisely how I'd tell the story. Sophos had been his friend. It would be pleasant to gloat.

When I slept that night, I let myself slip past the darkness and into the place that shamans go—the borderland where I could speak with Zhanna, or with Lauria if I could find her, and where Kyros could speak with me. I looked for Lauria first. I held out my hands and thought of the red silk cords I'd seen before, binding me to Lauria . . . among others. The one that bound me to Lauria had given off a faint silvery light. I found the cord easily enough—Lauria was still alive—but again, it was slack. I couldn't draw her in. Didn't she ever sleep? She had slept very little when she was in the grip of the cold fever, I remembered. Perhaps that was all it was.

There were other cords, but some of them were to people like Kyros . . . I knew I should just find Zhanna, quickly. Maybe I could avoid running into Kyros tonight.

But no. Even as I spoke his name in my thoughts, I faced him. "You're a hard woman to find," Kyros said.

"I'm a shaman," I said. "You're not going to find me unless I'm willing to be found."

"Right." Kyros jerked his head. "Let's get to it. The magia grows impatient. What do you have for me?"

"I can tell you how we freed Sophos's slaves," I said.

"Not quite what I was looking for, but I'll take it."

"I conspired with Jaran. Together, we persuaded Boradai to our side. She had a lover once—Alisher. To punish Boradai for inattention after a slave escaped, Sophos sold Alisher to someone in Elpisia. I slipped into Elpisia and found him, and helped him escape. The rest was Boradai. She knew we had Alisher and he still wanted to be with her. She drugged Sophos and his guests and guards, then she and the concubines slaughtered them like sleeping sheep. Boradai took the spell-chain. Sophos trusted her. But she knew that she was a slave, and she had no loyalty to him. None."

"And Sophos's head?"

"Jaran was the one who killed Sophos. He brought his head. As a gift, for me."

"And for Lauria."

"Your *friend* raped her. He swore not to and broke his vow."

"And it just breaks your heart, doesn't it?" Kyros chuckled mildly, but when I looked into his dead black eyes, I started shaking. "That a woman loyal to the Greeks would be humiliated that way. That Lauria would have had a taste of what *you* lived with."

I opened my mouth but no words came out. Kyros gave me a kind smile that made my stomach twist like a wrung rag. I forced down my nausea, telling myself that he couldn't harm me here. Although I hadn't summoned it on purpose, I found a bow in my hands, the arrow nocked and ready. I loosed an arrow into Kyros's heart. He vanished from the borderland without so much as a curse at me, and I wished I'd held off. This would wake Kyros, but it wouldn't kill him any more than a violent dream would, and I hadn't had a chance to make him promise not to hurt Lauria. I knew it didn't really matter. Men like Kyros broke promises to slaves without a second thought.

I woke soaked in sweat, my stomach in knots, and lay awake until dawn.

Traveling with Janiya and Alibek was not like traveling with Lauria. Lauria had needed me for my knowledge of the steppe, since I knew where the wells were and she didn't. She was the better rider, but I was a much better shot. She left me with the horses when she rescued Nika, but as the months passed, she accepted that we were equals, partners. Then she'd gone and apprenticed herself to the sorceress for a while, but she'd come to her senses. More or less.

Janiya certainly didn't need me to help her navigate

the steppe. Instead, I was along on the trip for my knowledge of the Greeks.

We avoided Daphnia, but stopped in a village down the road to buy more grain for the horses and more food for ourselves. Janiya paid in foreign silver. That would stand out, but it was better than trying to trade karenite. The farmer squinted at the coin, round with a square cut out from the center, then bit it, and finally shrugged and took it for the sacks of rice, lentils, and oats.

As we set out, we heard the rattle of approaching wagons and moved aside to let them pass. I'd expected merchants. It was soldiers. When I saw the banner showing Alexander's helmet, I wished we'd moved on faster.

The first lines were on horseback. Foot soldiers followed. All were dusty from the road but well dressed and well equipped—not that I was an expert in judging such things. I was comparing them to Janiya's sword sisterhood.

I pictured Janiya's sword sisterhood facing these men. We had raided a Greek fort and defeated them soundly, but we'd taken them by surprise and fired their buildings. We had better horses and better archers, but . . .

*But djinni's mercies, there are so many of them.*

They passed us by. A few men glanced in our direction, but no one spoke to us or bothered us. Janiya watched them go, her face very still.

"Let's go," she said.

$\mathcal{D}$uring our fall journey, Lauria and I had watched people bringing in the last of the harvest. Now it was spring. Planting season. Janiya, Alibek, and I rode past farms of slaves planting crops in neat-furrowed rows, stooping to drop seeds into the wet ground. Men and women bent side by side. Watching them made my own back ache, and I rubbed the base of my neck, imagining the tickle of prickling sweat.

"Only the rivers' return can free them all," Alibek said.

It was an old saying, something I'd heard from my mother. I'd said it a few times myself, but now it irritated me. "How is that supposed to work, anyway?" I asked. "The rivers will come back, and . . . then what? The Sisterhood of Weavers will decide to free all Danibeki slaves?"

Alibek shrugged. "I've always figured that the point of the saying is that all our people will *never* be free. Only the rivers' return can free them all. The rivers will never return, so . . . some of our people will *never* be free. Surely you've known slaves who wouldn't take freedom even if it were handed to them."

"I've *freed* slaves who turned away from the gift."

"You freed others who should have. I met one who had nothing to say but 'The food was better when I was a slave' and 'My bed at Sophos's house was softer' and 'I'm tired, Sophos didn't make me work as hard as I have to work here.' "

I hunched my shoulders. "That's his problem."

"Ha. It's the Alashi's problem."

"Do *you* think that the only people who deserve to be free are the ones that free themselves?"

Alibek shrugged ruefully. "Well, I really like Uljas. But I also think some people are better off as slaves. It's what they want. Or it's what they deserve."

"Has Uljas ever told you about Burkut?"

"A little bit. I was there when we buried him."

"Well, no one but Lauria and Uljas would've freed Burkut. He didn't want to be free. Uljas had to talk him into escaping. But Uljas believed in him."

"And then he died on the trip, right? Sounds like Lauria and Uljas should have left him alone. Maybe he'd still be alive."

I wasn't sure how to explain what I was trying to say. I wanted to ask him who should decide who ought to be free, or why *he* ought to be the one to decide. I didn't know which question to ask, so instead I rolled my eyes and urged my horse ahead a little bit so I didn't have to talk to Alibek anymore.

Alibek caught up with me a few minutes later. "Burkut escaped once, anyway. It was Lauria who brought him back."

"He wouldn't have made it to the Alashi that time. He ran away without water. If Lauria hadn't gone after him, he would've been dead."

"And then he died after she freed him? Sounds like the gods wanted him dead. Free, but dead."

I shrugged.

"I sort of remember Burkut, from when he was owned by Kyros. He was always sick. I figured he was just trying to get out of work."

"I'd have figured the same thing."

"But he wasn't."

"Well, unless you think he wasted away and died just to get out of the trouble of serving in a sword brotherhood—no."

Alibek fell silent for a little while, to my relief. Then he said, "You know, you're not at all what I expected."

"What is *that* supposed to mean? You only met me once."

He shook his head dismissively. "I was in a clan with some of your sword sisters. I heard stories about you all winter."

I glanced at Janiya. "Who told stories about me?"

"Zhanna, mostly."

"So what did she have you expecting?"

Alibek shrugged, to my annoyance, and said nothing.

"What stories did she tell you?"

"She said you were really good with a bow."

I opened my mouth to say that I *was* really good with a bow, then snapped it shut. My bow was tied to my saddle. I untied it, bent it against my horse's withers to string it, placed an arrow against the string, and looked at Alibek challengingly.

He raised an eyebrow. "I see a rabbit over in the grass," he said, and pointed.

We had the rabbit grilled over the coals that night. It was tough but still a welcome change from the lentils and rice. Alibek chewed his thoughtfully, picking the bones clean. "Good shot," he said, as we laid out our blankets to sleep.

*H*ow do you think we should approach the farm?" Janiya asked the next morning. "Openly? Or should one of us sneak in and try to talk to Lycurgus?"

"I can show you where we camped, if you want to hide," I said. "Lauria went in and pretended that she needed a job. Solon hired her. We don't want to talk to Solon. We want Lycurgus, but that could be hard—Lycurgus was supposed to be in charge, but he was drunk all the time and Solon ran the place." I thought it over. "If we go in openly, we definitely won't be able to talk to Lycurgus without Solon knowing. If we sneak in, we can probably go talk to Lycurgus at night. One of us, anyway." Janiya looked at me. "Oh, all right," I said. "I could do it. At night. Though I didn't see the farm when I was here with Lauria. I stayed with the horses."

"Did Lauria describe the farm to you? Could you find your way around it?"

"She sort of described it. I could probably find my way around."

"If they catch you, could you talk your way out?"

"I convinced the mine guards that I was a sorceress from the Younger Sisters."

"That's not going to be a good story to tell Solon. Didn't you say he was loyal to the Weavers?"

"Last year he was. What are you going to do if I don't think I can handle it? Are we going to ride up together and say we're merchants who want to see the steward? Because if we do that, they'll take us to Solon."

"Hmm," Janiya said, and fell silent. As we were mounting up she said, "I think you should go."

After my months with Lauria, who left me behind whenever she could, it was nice to hear someone tell me she thought I should do something by myself. Until I started thinking about everything I could do wrong.

We made camp in the same clearing where I'd camped with Lauria and Uljas. No trace was left of that visit. We had hours to go before night. "How much of the karenite do you want to take with you?" Janiya asked.

"One stone of it should be enough to make my point," I said. "I can leave the rest here in case they catch me and, uh, kill me."

Janiya thought that over. "Take three," she said. "Just in case you need more." Her lip quirked a little. "But try to be a little less grim, Tamar, please. Didn't you free Alisher? Didn't you just tell me you convinced the mine guards you were a sorceress?"

"I always had to convince Lauria to let me do anything," I mumbled.

"So you're saying I need to act like I don't trust you to saddle your own horse properly, so you can convince me you can do it?" Janiya clouted me on the shoulder. "I don't think I can learn to lead that way, not this late in life. Go convince yourself. By sundown."

Fortunately, there was plenty to do. We needed to groom the horses, feed them, and put up our tent. I tried to imagine that Lauria was here. If Lauria were here, she'd tell Janiya that *she* should be the one to go. After all, she knew both Lycurgus and the farm. I imagined trying to talk her out of it. If she were caught, they'd know her, and besides, Lycurgus thought she was a spy. He'd hardly trust her now. I should be the one to go in. I'd heard Lauria's stories and knew the men I'd face as well as Lauria did, but they wouldn't know me. I'd have the advantage . . .

"I should be the one to go," I muttered out loud as I measured out grain for the horses. "I can do it."

I set down their dinner and looked up to find Alibek smirking at me. He'd heard me talking to myself. My face went hot. I met his eyes and pretended I had been talking to him all along. "I *can*," I said again.

"I believe you," he said mildly.

I turned on my heel and stomped away to fetch water.

At sunset, I walked back to the road with three pieces of karenite in my pocket. It was a dark night. By the time I drew close to the farm, I needed my lantern just to see the road. At the edge of the fields, I shielded the lantern and sat for a while in the grass, listening to frogs and crickets, waiting for the lights of the farm to go dark. When I was certain everyone had gone to bed, I took my lantern, unshielded it enough to let out a tiny ray of light, and picked my way through the deep wagon ruts to the farm.

The buildings loomed dark and still. The windowless barracks held the slaves, no doubt, locked in securely for the night. Another long building probably housed the guards. The brand-new brick house was probably the kitchen, rebuilt after the fire. But Lycurgus. Where would I find Lycurgus?

One of the houses had a little marble floor out front. That had to be the steward's house. The door was unlatched, so I shuttered my lantern and stepped inside.

I took a deep breath, first, sniffing for the smell of sour wine. Lycurgus was a drunk, and drunks smelled bad. But the air smelled fresh, like wood shavings and new-pressed cider. Upstairs, perhaps? I listened. Someone upstairs was snoring. Moving slowly, aware of every creak, I picked my way up the stairs.

There. The bedroom. Lauria said it was a mess, with dirty clothes scattered together with papers, dishes, dropped food, anything. I hesitated in the doorway and took a deep breath. Still no sour smell. I let out a tiny gleam of light from the lantern to take a quick look around.

The room was immaculate—the floor swept clean, the rugs free from dust, the table bare except for an open book and a lamp. I could still hear snoring from the bed. I swept the little ray of light closer. Was it Solon?

No. It was a woman, her black hair scattered across the pillow, a bare arm thrown out against the sheets.

"Good evening," a voice said quietly in my ear. "Let's go downstairs for a chat."

I froze.

"Slowly and quietly," the voice continued. "To the stairs, please. I'd rather not wake Selene." Something very narrow and sharp poked me in the back. My mouth was dry. I shuffled my feet toward the stairs and trudged down, one step at a time, my lantern still swinging from my hand.

Downstairs, the man behind me took my lantern and swung the shield all the way open. I blinked in the sudden light. "My office," he said, and pointed. Hopelessly, I went on in. He set the lantern on a shelf, checked me briefly and impersonally for weapons—I had a knife, which he took—and sat me down in a chair, studying me in the pool of light.

He was Greek, and young. Solon? If it was, how was I going to get out of this? Solon was a kind master and an honest man, but he wasn't stupid. And he was not in league with the Younger Sisters—at least he hadn't been last fall.

"Solon?" I asked. A flicker in his eyes told me that I knew who I faced, at least.

"Who sent you here?" he asked.

"No one." I swallowed hard.

"What were you *doing* here?"

"Looking for you," I said.

"In the dark? With a knife?"

"The knife was sheathed. I didn't come here to kill you." He nodded at that. "I wanted to talk to you. Privately. *Secretly.* I had to approach you at night. I don't know who the woman is—I didn't expect to find you with anyone."

"Go on," he said, when I paused.

When I was a slave, and new to Sophos's household, Jaran had warned me that if I got into trouble, Sophos would let me try to talk my way out of it, just to see how much worse I made it for myself. I bit my lip now and tried to smile. I needed to pick a lie, a simple lie, and tell it well. "Do you remember Lauria?" I asked.

"Who is Lauria?"

"She was here last fall. Xanthe. She called herself Xanthe."

"Ah. Yes. She lied her way into my confidence and stole a slave."

"It's because of her that you're the steward now, and not the assistant steward."

Another flicker, and a faint smile. Yes.

"Lauria is in trouble. Kyros has her."

"He does? Good."

"I came here to ask for your help," I said doggedly. "Actually, I came here to try to *buy* your help." I pulled the three pieces of karenite out of my pocket— he hadn't taken it out when he'd checked me for weapons—and scattered it across the desk. "It's karenite. Soul-stone. It's *valuable.*"

He knew its worth. I could tell from the way he

suddenly sat straighter in his chair, swallowed, and pulled his gaze away from the stones. "Help me," I said. "These are for you, if you do."

Solon laughed. "You're in no position to take them back."

"I have more."

"Where?"

"You'll never find it."

"How much?"

"How much do you want in exchange for Lauria? You return Lauria to me, I can bring you a great deal more."

"It can't be done," Solon said. "Or at least, *I* can't do it for you."

"Who can?"

"I don't even know where he has her."

"Penelopeia."

There was a pause. The Younger Sisters might be able to get her out, and for a moment I thought Solon would tell me that. Then he checked himself and shook his head. "I can't help you."

I stood up, trying hard to act as if I were a customer walking out of a shop, not a prisoner walking away from a guard. "What happened to Lycurgus?" I asked.

"The incidents last fall were quite a strain. He really wasn't in good health, and . . ." Solon turned his palms up. "Sad, but not surprising."

I wondered who had killed him—Solon? One of the sorceresses? He would have been an easy man to poison. Or maybe he really *had* just died.

I was almost at the door when Solon spoke. "I can't keep these," he said.

I turned back. Was he offering me the bribe *back*?

He really was as honest as Lauria said. If that karenite bought my way off this farm, it would be well
spent. I strode back to the desk, picked them up, then
set one down again. "For frightening you," I said.
Another. "For disturbing your rest." And then the
last piece: "If you have the chance to help Lauria, and
if it doesn't go against any other oaths you've
sworn—you liked her. I know you liked her. Help her
if you can."

A long moment, then Solon nodded.

I took my lantern and walked out. He didn't
stop me.

# CHAPTER SIX

# LAURIA

The days grew warmer. I spent my days in the garden, pretending to embroider. I wanted to make a horse, but it wound up looking like a badly done dog, and I picked out the stitches in disgust and started working on flowers, instead.

My nights were dark. I tried to dream of Tamar, but could never find the borderland; my dreams were a confused jumble of images and intentions. I dreamed of Tamar once, but knew as soon as I woke that it hadn't been a "true" dream. No djinni approached me.

The melancholia sapped my energy. This time I knew it for what it was, but that helped little. At least I didn't feel as bleak as I'd felt during the winter, when I had barely risen from bed for over a month. I got up every morning, ate breakfast, then went to sit outside through the day. I knew that I needed to watch for an opportunity to escape, but the melancholia pressed in on my vision like a veil. Besides, my guard was always at my heels.

One day, my guard had visitors—friends of hers, fellow guards, who stood with her a while to talk. I had the opportunity to study the three women without their noticing, distracted as they were by their conversation. All three were about my age, and looked like they probably had Greek, Danibeki, *and* Persian blood. Like every guard I'd seen in the Koryphe, all three were women. Even the guards that came down into the pit to beat me had been female, or so I assumed from their voices. The sorceress I had apprenticed with, Zivar, had disliked men; I wondered if this prejudice was common among the high-up Weavers, if that was why their corps of guards were all female. Out in the provinces, Kyros's soldiers had all been men. Of course, the Alashi separated their men and women warriors, too, during the summers. The Alashi did it to avoid the distractions, and the pregnancies. Perhaps the Weavers avoided using male guards for the same reason.

My guard was not happy about her current job; I bored her. I had been boring her for a while. She looked much happier talking with her friends. I studied the three women. All had long hair, bound in tight braids and pinned tightly to their heads; all wore gold hoops in their ears. My guard had three hoops in one ear and two in the other; one of her companions had a full half dozen hoops in one ear, and a single green glint in the other. The woman with the emerald in her ear also had a tattoo, I saw—a snake that wrapped around her left wrist.

My guard must have made a joke, because the

other two women laughed. And it was in the smile that I saw it—the quirk of her lip, the tilt of her head. Janiya. The woman with the green stone and the snake tattoo looked like a much-younger version of Janiya. Was this Xanthe? Janiya had been a member of the Sisterhood Guard once. She left a daughter behind in Penelopeia, to be raised by the Guard, when she was exiled and sold into slavery. It certainly *could* be her daughter.

The tattooed guard caught me looking at her, and her brow furrowed; I lowered my eyes to my embroidery. The stems had started winding together like a net. *I can't even stitch flowers anymore.* I started picking out stitches again, trying to take a covert look at the guards.

A fourth guard joined the three who were talking and said something to them, quietly. They all looked at me. My guard shook her head and her friends headed off as she trudged toward me. "Gather up your stuff," she said. "We need you in your room."

I picked up the embroidery and shuffled back upstairs. I sat down on my bed, once I arrived, wondering how long I would have to sit in there. Only a few minutes passed before I heard footsteps—Kyros. "Oh good," he said, with audible relief, as he swung the door open. "You're inside."

"What's going on?" I asked.

There was a veil of gauze that I could draw across my window to offer privacy while still allowing light; Kyros pulled it shut. "The magia who condemned you to the pit has retaken the serpent," he said. "You'll need to stay in your room for now and not go outside. She mustn't see you; I'm sure you understand why."

"Wait," I said, as he started for the door again. *This room is going to feel very small the next time the cold fever seizes me.* "Will you do something for me?"

"If I can," he said, pausing and turning to give me a sympathetic look. The look of a father with an errant daughter. "What is it you need, Lauria?"

"A different guard," I said.

"Why? Has this one mistreated you?"

I lifted my chin. "In the pit, I was beaten. I couldn't see faces—the light hurt my eyes—but I think *she* was one of them. It's the sound of her voice." I actually had no idea who those guards had been, but it was a passable enough reason. "It makes it hard for me to sleep, knowing she's the one guarding me. If she had the chance . . ."

"Of course," Kyros said. "I understand. I'll arrange a different guard."

"Her friend . . ." I said. Kyros had started for the door, and now he glanced back. "She had a friend I saw today—a woman with a snake tattooed around her wrist. I *know* she wasn't one of the guards who beat me, because I would have seen the snake, and remembered it."

Kyros nodded. "I'll see to it," he said.

The door closed. A little elated, I lay down on my bed to wait for my next meal. *This prison has daylight. I'm fed well. It won't be forever.* It was better, but it was still a cage. *Breathe. Patience. There will be a chance.*

*With Xanthe guarding me, I will find a way.*

**K**yros visited me again that afternoon, and every afternoon after. The days were long, and I found myself looking forward to the visits. They broke up the monotony and soothed my loneliness. He didn't push for information—we chatted about inconsequential things, or reminisced about old times, like my first trip to Daphnia. He described sights in Casseia that he wanted to show me—though he carefully avoided promising a trip anytime soon.

*I do not trust you,* I thought each time he came in. But I craved his company because it was the only company I had. Xanthe stood guard on the other side of the door, and the servants who brought my meals barely spoke to me. Kyros's voice was warm and kind. He laughed at my jokes, even the poorly made ones. He looked into my eyes and praised me, though he didn't call me his most trusted servant, since that would have been absurd.

I thought about Xanthe a great deal, during the long, boring days. If I could suborn her, she could help me escape. I knew her mother—surely that would prove an advantage. But I would actually have to speak to her, and she did not invite conversation. Also, she no doubt had been raised to believe that her mother was a criminal, unworthy of the Sisterhood Guard. It was possible she didn't even remember her mother. The fact that I *knew* her mother, and that her mother was now a leader among the bandits, seemed unlikely to be welcome news. Still, at the very least, the first step would be to talk to Xanthe, to get to know her. To befriend her, if I could. But she was a difficult person to know.

I had a nightmare one night—not one of the old dreams about Sophos but a starkly vivid dream of being lifted from my bed, bound in webs of some kind so tight that I couldn't move or scream, and could barely breathe; I was carried up and away as I struggled and gasped, *Xanthe*, knowing that I didn't speak loudly enough to be heard. Then I wrenched myself awake and was in bed, in the dark, soaking wet from my own sweat and shivering. I lay for a few moments, still terrified from the dream, even knowing that it had been a dream. *Just a dream. Not even a true dream, like my dreams of the borderland.* I sat up in bed to collect my wits and saw a shimmer in the air. A djinn.

"What do you want?" I asked.

It said nothing.

"Are you bound, or unbound?"

Still nothing.

"Once I could free your kind," I said. "I don't know if I still can. Once I could go to the borderland, and I can't do that anymore. Do you need my help?" I stretched out my hand. The djinn edged closer, and finally I touched it. I felt a coldness around my hand. "Return to the Silent Lands, lost one," I murmured, speaking the words of banishment that I'd learned from Zhanna. "Trouble us no more."

For a moment, I thought that it hadn't worked. Then I felt a blast of wind as if someone had opened a door into midwinter; I gasped from the shock of it. The djinn vanished from before my eyes, and I felt it whirl into my heart. As it crossed the threshold it paused for a moment, and I could sense that it was holding on against the current that pulled it away. "This was a trap," it whispered. "Do not trust the ones who keep you. They chain—" A gust of the unseen wind almost tore it away, and it fought back, staying long enough to say, "They chain your *mind*."

I got up and lit my lamp and sat down. *A trap*. I

thought that probably meant that Kyros or the magia had sent the djinn to me, to see if I freed it. I wondered why it thought I needed the warning not to trust Kyros and the magia, and what it meant by, *They chain your mind.* Kyros had used magic on me, to keep me loyal. Was he using magic on me again? Probably. *It doesn't matter. It's not working. I may look forward to his visits, but it's only because I'm lonely. I don't trust Kyros; I could never trust Kyros again.*

Still, I wondered what this would mean, if I had revealed myself. Would they have me killed? Were they coming now? I heard no footstep from beyond my door. The night guard must have noticed the light in my room, but she didn't come in. I put out my lamp, then drew back the veil from the window and looked out. I could see stars I recognized in the sliver of sky from my window—Alexander's throne, and if I craned my neck, part of Bucephalus, whose tail would lead you north if you followed him. No one wandered the gardens at this hour, and the air was crisp and chilly, even though the days now were hot. I let the curtain fall back after a moment or two and lay back down in bed. It was hours until morning. What else was I going to do?

Kyros said nothing about the djinn when he made his visit that afternoon. He seemed more tense than usual, though, and left early.

I glimpsed Xanthe as the door swung shut. "Xanthe," I said when I was certain Kyros was gone. "Hey, Xanthe."

The door opened again. "How did you know my name?" she said.

"Can you come in? I would really like to talk to you."

"Do you need something?" When I couldn't answer, she shrugged. "Let me know if you *need* something." She stepped back out and shut the door firmly behind her.

I knocked from the inside a few moments later. "Can I ask you something?"

She opened the door and glared in at me. "What?"

"Are there really four magias? What happens if one is seized by a dark fever and refuses to give up her authority?"

"You should ask Kyros your questions," she said, and shut the door again.

*This is impossible,* I thought, and sat back down. She was never going to talk to me. She had probably been ordered *not* to talk to me; Kyros wouldn't want me talking to anyone but him. Still. I held one set of weighted dice—weighted which way, who knew, but it was worth a throw. I knocked on the door one last time. Xanthe didn't say a word this time, just opened the door with a weary expression.

"I know your mother," I said. "Janiya. You look a lot like her."

Xanthe's face was briefly alive with something—rage, horror, amazement; she slammed herself shut too fast for me to tell. "You're crazy," she said flatly, and closed the door again.

Knowing that she could hear me through the door, I stood by the crack and kept speaking. "You've probably been told that she was a criminal and was punished. It was a lie—she never betrayed the Weavers or the Guard. She was sold into slavery and sent east . . . But think about it, Xanthe, if that happened to you, if *you* were sold as a slave, would you serve, then, contentedly, for the rest of your life? Or would you take your chances with the bandits and run? You'd run, wouldn't you? Your mother ran. She's with the Alashi now; that's where I met her. Did Kyros and the magia tell you that I was with the Alashi for a while? Kyros sent me there to spy. Anyway, Janiya leads one of the sword sisterhoods. She taught me to ride like an Alashi bandit, and to fight and use a bow. She taught me how to be *free*." I was treading on dangerous ground now, so I stopped for a moment, realizing that for all I knew, Xanthe was standing on the other side of the door with her hands clamped over her ears. I paused for a moment and listened to hear if she was saying anything. Silence.

"Janiya told me about you once," I said. "She said that she had a daughter back with the Greeks, named Xanthe. Leaving you was the only thing I think she regretted, even though it hadn't been her choice. I asked her why she had never gone to look for you, and she said that you had probably been told that she was a traitor and a thief; that you would have your own life, your own loyalties, and she had no right to intrude."

Silence, then a soft mutter, something I couldn't catch.

"I'll tell you anything you like about your mother," I said. "I wish you could meet her. She would be proud, even though you serve a different master than she does."

"She has no right to be proud," Xanthe said, just loud enough for me to hear. "I am not *her* daughter anymore."

"Maybe you're right," I said. "She'd probably agree that she had no right to claim you. But she'd be proud anyway."

"How did you know I was her daughter? There are other women named Xanthe."

"I knew before I asked your name. I knew from the way you smile. I saw you laugh, once, in the garden, and I knew then."

"Hush; someone's coming."

I fell silent. It was the servant with my meal. When she left, Xanthe stepped inside and said, in a voice cold enough to freeze molten metal, "Do not speak of my mother again. Not to me. Not to anyone. She is dead to me, and to the Guard. Dead." The door closed.

I stared at my meal for a moment. *It had been going so well.* Probably best to obey, at least for now. She couldn't really shut me up, not without doing me violence, but she could ask to have another guard put to guard me—someone I'd have no tie to. Perhaps her curiosity would get the better of her eventually. I knew my own curiosity would eat me alive, in her place.

And perhaps she would have had questions for me, in a day or a week. But that night, I got sick.

I woke up in a cold sweat with a feeling of impending doom. I bolted from my bed and just managed to pull out my chamber pot to vomit in; then I realized that my bowels were at least as urgent. I heard my door open—the night guard, whose name I didn't know, must have heard me. She lit the lamp, swore when she saw me, and sent for a servant.

I had been sick plenty of times, but never like this. My stomach hurt so badly it felt as if it would rend itself apart, and throwing up brought only slight relief. My head ached, my back ached, even my arms and legs ached. Lying down brought no relief, but sitting up made it worse. The slave they sent to sit with me and nurse me tried to give me sips of cooled tea to drink, but anything I drank came right back up. *What am I even vomiting?* I wondered at one point. *There can't be anything left in my body; will I vomit up my own blood next?*

After a day or so I realized that I was alone. There were voices in the hallway, arguing. I heard a woman say, *You can beat me bloody; I'm not going in there,* then a low voice—Kyros?—saying something I couldn't hear. The woman was speaking very quickly, or maybe it was the fever. "She made Euthalia sick—I'm not going in there." I had made someone sick?

"Euthalia ate some of the same bad meat."

"No, that was Eutropia. Euthalia was fine until *she* threw up on her. If you're so certain she won't make you sick, nurse her yourself. Has she no sister? No mother?"

*My sister is far away,* I thought, *far, far away, and so is my mother, and everyone else who cares enough to risk sickness to feed me sips of tea* . . . I remembered how Tamar had sat by me in my melancholia, last winter, urging me to drink broth, honey-sweetened tea, anything I would take the trouble to swallow. I was seized with a longing for Tamar's presence that was so intense I felt it in my bones—then I realized that what I felt was the urge to vomit, and there was no one in the room to bring me the basin so I stumbled out of bed and heaved as I knelt on the floor. Nothing came out of my mouth except a thin line of drool.

Back in bed, I could hear the argument increase in pitch and fury, and I closed my eyes and tried to let the fever take me *away*. Even in my sleep, though, I could still hear them. I dreamed that there were insects on my pillow, singing, screaming insects, shouting words I couldn't understand into my ears. "I can free you," I said to the giant singing cricket that loomed just outside of my sight. "I can send you home. Will you take me home if I help you get home?" I laid my hand on the cricket, marveling at the smooth, cold surface of its insect skin, and realized that it was far too solid to pass through my heart, at least without killing me. "Perhaps I will die to get you home," I said. "Well, maybe that's all right. Return to the Silent Lands, lost one. Trouble us no more." But it went nowhere. Perhaps it didn't want to go home. I wished it would be quiet, at least, if it were going to stay with me. After a while, its voice at least got a bit more melodic, like real singing, and I passed into true darkness.

The darkness was singing. Not the grating, high-pitched squeal of the crickets, not the singing of a human voice, but the singing of the beads of a spell-chain. It had been so long since I'd heard that sound that for a moment I couldn't remember what it meant. Then the knowledge swept me up in a rush: *I was in the borderland.*

*Tamar,* I thought. *I need to find Tamar.* I pictured her—her smile, her grumpy voice, her eyes, the smell of her hair. *You are my blood sister; my thoughts should bring you to me.* But I remained alone in the

darkness. "Tamar," I called tentatively. "TAMAR."
Silence.

*What does this mean? Is something wrong? Is she
hurt—dead? It probably just means that she's not
asleep, or not in the borderland.* I suppressed a shudder. I didn't know when I was going to be back.
*Zhanna. Can I find Zhanna?*

Instead, I felt myself seized by the hands and
dragged, as I had been before when the djinni had decided to show me something, in a whirl of light that
made my stomach lurch again with nausea until we
settled, finally, in a lamplit room. *"Listen,"* hissed a
voice in my ears.

There were three people in the room: two old
women, and Kyros. They were in a vast room of
shelves full of books; I had never in my life seen so
many books. Several volumes, one so old it was
nearly crumbling to pieces, had been spread out on a
table before them. One of the women was the magia,
I realized, though not the one I had encountered before. The gold serpent bracelet was coiled around her
arm; she slouched back in a cushioned chair. The
other woman, divested of her authority, was in fact
the woman I had met as the magia, the one who had
condemned me to the pit. She looked tired and worn,
her inner fire a flickering candle. Her hands were
folded in front of her; her long red nails rested against
the backs of her hands. Kyros sat at the end of the
table, withdrawn almost into the shadows. *He told
me she'd retaken the serpent,* I remembered. As if it
overheard my thoughts, the djinn hissed again,
*Listen.*

"I don't see what the problem is," the not-magia
said. "Cut her throat and be done with it. It's what

Kyros was supposed to do if he laid hands on her again."

"I got you out of bed because it's not that simple, Lydia," the magia said. "She's a *gate*. Right now the gate opens at her will, but when she dies . . ."

"When she dies, it will be flung open and will stay that way," Lydia said. "That's what always happens. So take her to some remote place and cut her throat *there*."

"I dislike that idea," the magia said. "It is untidy." She leaned forward and counted off on her fingers. "The first one was executed, and the gate closed. The second was executed, and the gate stayed open—and somehow, it was moved, but the books don't say how. The third was killed by an aeriko. The book goes into a great deal of detail about the act: how he had to be drugged senseless to keep him from freeing it; how they had the aeriko rip his heart from his chest; the copious quantities of blood that flowed out; the death of the magia who had bound that aeriko. The gate closed. But the fourth was killed the same way, and the gate stayed open. And again, the books are vague on what was done *then*. But there was a fifth."

"Yes." Lydia narrowed her eyes.

"You are the oldest. Surely you remember." Lydia's mouth opened, and the magia waved her to silence. "Think *hard*, Lydia. Don't just say you don't."

"Ask your aerika about it. Aren't you the one who swears you could get answers from a stone?"

"I want *your* answers."

"It happened years ago," Lydia said, her voice reluctant. "I was magia, but the most junior of the four. The girl was held prisoner for a time. Years." Lydia waved vaguely as if pointing toward the prison. "She was the daughter of one of the other magias."

"But she did die, in the end."

"She threw herself from the tower." Lydia grinned at the other woman. "The gate opened and stayed open. Here, in the heart of Penelopeia. You can imagine the problems *that* caused. One of the other four believed that blood magic could be used to bind a gate, if not close it. In the dark of night, we set the girl's mother over the gate and cut out her heart ourselves. We were right, that time. The gate was bound to the magia's corpse. We took her well away from the city and burned her body. The gate closed."

The magia sat back, her face showing clear relief. "Well, if it just takes a mother—*that's* not so bad. This one's mother is a former slave, Kyros's mistress. . . ." She glanced at Kyros; his face was grave, but he made no protest. Lydia chuckled nastily. "Why are you laughing?"

Lydia shook her head. "Nothing ever works twice. The aerika are clever that way—it is *their* magic that creates these difficulties. You would slay her mother for nothing. You could slay Kyros . . ." She gestured at him, and again his expression did not change. "But you'll anger our friends in the army—and again, probably for nothing. Perhaps you'd slay me, out of frustration. Her servants, a bandit dragged here from the steppe . . . All for nothing."

"There must be a way," the magia said. "You found lore in the books."

"The books will do you no good. *Cut her foolish throat.* Don't wait for her to take another fever and die of it. Or to take matters into her own hands as the last one did."

"If things get worse every time, how do we know that the gate will *stay* at the place where we cut her throat?" the magia asked.

"Well, if it doesn't, we'll hardly be any worse off."

The magia jerked her head toward Kyros. "We will consult the books. Keep her alive for now, if you can. As long as we hold her, and keep our own aerika away from her, she's harmless."

"She's mortal," Lydia said. "She'll die *eventually*, no matter *what* we do."

"Are you volunteering to have one of *your* aerika slay her?"

"How many times do I need to say that we should just kill her? I'll volunteer to hold the knife, how's that? Or we can use one of the cold chains, and I'll take the risk of the aeriko's wrath if you shrink from the danger."

"You're a fool," the magia said, and I saw her hand stray to the golden serpent.

They rose and began to prepare to leave. I thought the djinni would probably take me away—what was there still to see?—but then I gasped as the world tilted, and I wrapped my hands around my spinning head. When things steadied, I opened my eyes again and found myself looking down at one of the books on the table—the ancient one that threatened to crumble to pieces. There was a drawing on one page, beautifully rendered in rich detail, of a gate into a tunnel. It disappeared into darkness, despite the fact that from another angle it appeared to be simply a gateway through a wall, no thicker than the wall around Elpisia. *The Passage,* the book said. In different handwriting, below, someone had added, *Now Drowned.*

The darkness was fading to gray, and the singing had changed; it was a human voice now. I was waking, if it was reasonable to call it *waking* when you felt as sick and exhausted as I did. At least now I was no longer alone. Someone fed me sips of tea, then held the basin when I vomited them up again, waited a bit, and offered more. "Leave me alone," I muttered.

"Shhhhh," she said. "You need to try to drink."

"I'll make you sick. You should leave."

"I'll take my chances. Drink."

I recognized that voice. *What is she doing here?* "Mother?"

"Yes, darling. I'm right here. Now drink some tea."

I had never gotten along well with my mother. Even when I was a little girl, I had spent most of my time trying to get away from her. But right at that moment there was no one else I would have rather had at my side—not even Tamar. Even knowing that she might well have been brought here as a sacrificial goat, to bear my inner passage to some more convenient location. I closed my eyes, drank the tea as she bid me, let her wash my face and comb the flecks of vomit from my hair. "Mama's here," she murmured, unperturbed, when the tea came back up again. "You're going to be all right."

# CHAPTER SEVEN

# TAMAR

From the hills above it, Daphnia looked like a green gem cupped in a bird's nest. The grasslands around us were turning yellow and brown from heat and drought, but Daphnia was watered by canals. I'd seen those canals last fall, but Daphnia's gardens had been dead and brown from the cold. I remembered Lauria's disappointment that I hadn't seen it in its glory. Now I knew why.

Janiya, Alibek, and I went to Daphnia because of Zarina. Zarina was the bath slave at the inn I stayed at with Lauria. I had tipped her well, and in return she had warned us when we were about to be arrested. With Lycurgus dead, Zarina seemed like our best hope of finding the Younger Sisters. No one knows more secrets than a well-placed slave. And Daphnia wasn't far from the farm. Janiya agreed this step made sense. It would be up to me to talk to Zarina. I hoped she was still at the same inn.

I turned to Janiya. "We probably shouldn't bring all of the karenite into the city. If we get stopped . . . searched . . . well, you're supposed to be able to hand it over to the temple, but I think if they found our sacks of it, they'd just execute all three of us."

"We can't just leave it sitting out by the side of the road," Janiya said. "One of us will have to wait with it—either me or Alibek, since you're the one who knows Daphnia."

"I don't *know* Daphnia. I only went there once."

"I've never been there at all. Nor has Alibek. Which one of us do you think you want with you?"

I almost said I wanted Janiya just because Alibek was so irritating. But I made myself stop and think about it. "I don't expect I'll be recognized. But anyone who remembers me will probably remember that I was with a woman. If I'm with Alibek, there's less chance I'll be recognized. That's important, because Lauria and I got in some trouble."

Janiya nodded. "I'll wait for you outside the city. Do you want me to hold *all* the karenite?"

"Give me one piece," I said.

"Just one? Are you sure?"

"If we need more, we'll come to you."

Money we would need plenty of—money for the room at the inn, money for bribes, money to buy wine to bribe slaves, money for clothes that would let us move around the city without attracting attention. Janiya handed over most of the coin, and I divided it between myself and Alibek. We looked like bandits from the steppe, but there wasn't much we could do about that right now. Lauria and I hadn't attracted attention because we looked like bandits. Plenty of merchants arrived as dirty and ragged as us. We attracted attention because we came in with nothing, then visited a sorceress and suddenly had enough money for an excellent inn.

Alibek, though, looked doubtful. "What are we going to say we're here for?"

"We're traders. With money and no goods at the moment."

"Traders of *what*?"

"Exotic fragrances," I said. I raised an eyebrow at him. "Think you know enough about perfumes to pass?"

"Not if I'm talking to a real fragrance trader."

"Unlikely."

"Then yes."

I hid the piece of karenite inside one of my waterskins, in case we were searched. Only a very thorough searcher would find it there. "Let's go."

"Wait, one more thing," Alibek said. "Are we going to pretend we're married?"

Traders working together, a man and a woman—they'd likely have *some* sort of family relationship. "Cousins," I said. "If anyone asks."

The guards at the city gate waved us through. Alibek glanced at me. "Where to?"

"This way."

I found the inn easily. The outside was very plain, and for a moment I thought I might have the wrong place. But I remembered the old man who opened the door, and inside, there was a fountain that used a tortoise shell as a basin. Scarlet flowers spilled from boxes all around the courtyard, and a bench stood in the shade. The bathhouse was where I remembered it, the door opened a crack. I hoped Zarina was inside, because if not, I was going to be out of ideas.

As with my first visit, the innkeeper wanted to see our money before he showed us a room. My first time, he'd ignored me and spoken to Lauria. This time, he ignored me and spoke to Alibek. I wondered idly if he would take us to the room Lauria and I had stayed in, but no. Instead, he suggested a choice of two rooms. One overlooked the courtyard, he explained, and was shaded from the midday sun. The other had a view of the Temple of Athena, and got a bit of sun but also enjoyed a nice breeze in the evening. The courtyard room had a single, large bed. The room with the view of the temple had two beds, with curtains that could be drawn for privacy. "I'd like an evening breeze," I said, not giving Alibek the chance to make the choice. "Also, we've been on the road for weeks. I'd like to take a bath as quickly as possible." The innkeeper told us dinner would be up at sundown and said a bath would be readied as soon as I'd like to come down.

Alibek sat down on one of the beds, pulled off his boots, and drew his feet up to sit. "Mind if I take this one?"

"It's yours." I sat down to dig through my pack. I'd bought some spirits of wine just to tip Zarina. "I'm going to go down and see Zarina."

When we'd come in the fall, the bathhouse had been shut up tight, with a roaring fire, to keep it as warm as possible. Now, in the heat of the summer, the shutters had been replaced with loosely woven cloth that offered privacy without keeping out the breeze. The water was tepid to let bathers cool off. I was relieved to find Zarina, her blue-black hair gathered loosely mid back. She'd worn a light shift even in winter, but her clothing now was nearly transparent.

I set the wineskin on the shelf where she kept the soaps and oils. "Do you remember me?" I asked.

She looked me over and quirked an eyebrow. "Where is your companion?"

"I'm working with someone else now, a man. Alibek. He may be down later."

She gestured toward the bath, and I shed my clothes and stepped into the water. Zarina helped me scrub clean—I still found it uncomfortable to be bathed by someone else—then gave me a towel and a light robe and started combing out my hair. "You're as generous as always," she said. "Can I offer you assistance of some kind?"

"Yes," I said. "I need to find a sorceress who is one of the Younger Sisters."

"Still looking for trouble, too."

"It's what I need. Can you help me?"

"I can give you a name. What you do with it is up to you."

I nodded.

"Pelagia. Her house is near the Temple of Alexander. She has a statue of a leaping fish outside her house."

"All right."

"She's unpredictable."

"They all are."

"She's worse than most. I wish you good luck. Tread softly or you won't be back to share your generosity with me again."

There was a pause.

"Do you remember the question I asked you last

fall?" I had asked her if she would like to run away with us, to be free.

"I remember it well."

"Do you ever regret your answer?"

"Sometimes. But rarely."

"If you'd like to change your mind . . ."

"My answer hasn't changed." She'd said, *No thank you, I think you're likely to end up dead. And some things are worse than slavery.*

When she finished combing my hair, I left my clothes to be washed, slipped on borrowed sandals to go with the borrowed robe, and went back up to see Alibek.

"What next?" he asked. "Can we find Pelagia tomorrow?"

"I want clothes first. Something that will blend in. We'll have a tailor come tomorrow." I looked him over. "You should go bathe. New clothes on a filthy man—not good for blending in."

Alibek gave me a nasty look, which I didn't understand. "Look, you can tell her you want to bathe privately, if you don't like being 'assisted.' She knows you're with me. She likes me. I tip well."

"She will know me for a slave," Alibek said. He gestured toward his back. His scars.

"She knew me for a slave, too, when Lauria and I were here the first time. She will hold her tongue. Trust me, Alibek."

He stood up, finally, and went down. He returned a bit later, clean and wearing a robe, like me. He was silent for a while, then said, "I don't understand turning away from freedom. Especially . . ." He let his words trail off, but I knew what he meant. Alibek had been a harem slave, like me. Zarina was expected to offer certain other services, beyond a bath.

"Surely there were favored slaves in Kyros's harem—slaves who believed that their job wasn't so bad. There were slaves like that where I came from."

"Zarina has her wits about her, though. Not like some. She deserves better."

"I thought you said it was a bad idea to free slaves—that they were a burden on the Alashi."

"Some of them, yes."

"I don't think Zarina would really fit in, in a sword sisterhood." I caught his eye. "But I'd still take her with us if she'd come."

*S*laves brought our food up at sunset. It was even better than I remembered. The lamb was tangy, with a thick gravy I could soak up with the soft, chewy bread. There were also apricot tarts the size of my palm. I sighed happily over my food. "Did you get tired of the Alashi food?" I asked as I finished. "I got so tired of it during my summer with them I thought I was going to cry."

Alibek shook his head, absently. "I liked it. Why wouldn't I like it?" He looked up at me and narrowed his eyes. "The food was better when you were a slave, is that it?"

"No! Why do you take every word I say the wrong way?"

"Why would you complain about the Alashi? About their food, of all things?"

"I can't believe you never got tired of it."

"Did Lauria complain the way you do?"

I stood up, furious. "The Alashi were her life. She

loved the steppe, and so did I." I stomped off to my bed and threw myself down on it, turning my back on Alibek as if to dare him to say another word. He fell silent. I listened to him finish his own dinner, prepare for bed, and lie down. He took a breath, as if he was going to say something—then let it out, his words unspoken.

The tailor came in the morning, and we paid the rush fee. That meant we'd have new clothes by evening. In the meantime, our own clothes were dry, but I was reluctant to go out in them. Lauria and I had put on our coats and hoped no one would notice us—but we *had* been noticed, and in any case, it was no longer coat-wearing weather. I went down to the inner courtyard to sit in the shade and watch the other guests—and to avoid Alibek. Naturally, no sooner had I gotten settled on the bench in the shade than I saw Alibek coming out to the courtyard and looking around for me. "The room is getting very warm," he said, sitting down next to me. I thought it was probably more that he was bored, and irritating me amused him, but I moved over and made a space for him to sit down.

A new guest was arriving. He was a merchant, well dressed, with heavy gold rings on nearly every finger. He had an apprentice with him, and a couple of servants. I thought he would certainly have slaves at home, but traveling with slaves was a lot of trouble, and he had enough money to employ servants instead.

"Back in Kyros's harem," Alibek said softly, "I always liked to see guests like him. They have a tendency to be generous. All those rings—it makes it easy to slip a present to a slave who's pleased you."

"Ha," I said. I glanced quickly around the courtyard to see if anyone was listening, but no one was nearby. "I never got presents."

"You weren't very good at your job, then."

"I hated it," I said, trying to keep the edge out of my voice and failing. "Sophos gave me to men who wanted to hurt me, not who wanted to pretend I was their lover. Not the kind who gave gifts." I swallowed, then added, "Men like that always wanted Meruert. It would've been pointless for me to try to come on to them. If it was a busy night and I knew there was no escape, I'd sometimes look for a man who seemed very drunk. Sometimes I got lucky and he passed out right after he took me back to the room. I'd yank off his boots, untie his pants, mess up his clothes a little, and leave the bedclothes rumpled. I figured when he woke up in the morning he'd think he just didn't remember the good time he'd had."

Another guest was passing through the courtyard. This was a woman—wealthy and powerful, whoever she was. It was clear just from her bearing.

"Did Sophos offer the harem to female guests?" Alibek asked.

"He rarely had them."

"Kyros did, on occasion. I got picked to serve a female guest one time. She didn't really want much, once she had me back in her room. I think she was mostly showing off her importance. She had me rub her feet while she drank wine. I told her she was beautiful, and she gave me the rest of the wine. She was pockmarked, actually, but she liked the flattery."

Another man passed by—an officer. I felt myself

tense up as he passed, and once his back was to me, I pointed and said in a low voice, "That's the kind of man I tried to avoid."

"Why?" Alibek asked.

"He's the kind who hurts girls."

"How do you know?"

"I just know." My voice was flat. The conversation wasn't fun anymore.

"What tells you?"

"The set of his shoulders, the cold eyes—" I broke off. "The smirk, the way he walks, like he thinks he owns everything he sees. If they don't want to hurt you, they want to humiliate you."

"Yeah," Alibek said, and let out a breath. "I'd have said it was something about the boots. His boots were too well kept."

"I never noticed boots."

"The men with really grubby, filthy boots—they usually wanted something quick but were never generous, at all. The ones with well-kept boots were more likely to be generous. But the ones who were really meticulous, with the perfectly kept boots— watch out."

"All of them?"

"No, not all. Just some of them." He twitched his shoulders up, like he was trying to shrug away an unwanted touch. "I steered clear of all of them, though, if I could."

A sorceress's palanquin sat in the corner of the courtyard. As I talked with Alibek, the sorceress herself came down. She wore blue silk, a rope of pearls, and six spell-chains that I could see. She passed into the bathhouse, though she didn't look dirty, and closed the door.

"Did Sophos ever entertain sorceresses?" Alibek asked.

"No. Did Kyros?"

"No, but his wife had been a sorceress. She hated the harem—all of us." Alibek ran his finger along an old scar on the side of one arm.

"Have you ever met a sorceress before, aside from Kyros's wife?" I asked.

"No."

"They're a crazy bunch."

"That much I know. I've known people who were owned by them in the past . . ."

"Oh yes," I said. "Though you know . . . we met a sorceress last year who was really pretty much owned by her slaves. They knew her secrets and used them to control her. *That* was interesting."

"Surely they weren't open about that."

"We stayed there for the winter. The servants liked me. They told me the story."

"Hmm. Does she live in Daphnia?"

"No, she's in Casseia. It's a long way away."

"So what was the secret?" Alibek's eyes held only curiosity now. The mockery was gone.

"She had once been a slave herself—owned by a sorceress in Persia. She'd spied on her mistress, and then after her mistress died, she ran away, went to Casseia, and told someone in the Sisterhood of Weavers that she was her old mistress's apprentice. And it worked! They took her in, she learned sorcery—or finished learning, I'm not sure—and now she's a sorceress with a merchant company and a houseful of servants."

"A houseful of servants who own her."

"Well, yes." I checked around us for anyone listening, then added, "The servants approached me before I left. They have a conspiracy of their own—they believe women as crazy as the sorceresses shouldn't run an empire. Instead, it should be ruled by servants, and the sorceresses should serve them."

"They're right."

"They wanted me to help them."

"Why didn't you?"

"Because I think it's better for the Alashi for the Empire to be run poorly."

"An empire run by servants might not be invading the steppe."

"Not this year. But in a few years . . ." I'd had this same conversation with Lauria. "The sorceresses need karenite. They *have* to have it. They've used up the karenite down here, and the Alashi control what's on the steppe. You can't let your enemy control something you need that badly. You can't. Sooner or later . . ." I shrugged.

"We can't win against the Greeks," Alibek said. "We can hold them off—we can distract them with disorder. But unless the Empire *falls*, they can wait a year or two and try again."

"They'll never defeat the Alashi."

"They could kill most of us. And scatter the remnant."

"So you think we need to overthrow the Empire to be safe?"

"*We* need?" The mockery was back. "You *do* have ambitions for a former slave girl. Don't you?"

I had started to relax in his company at last—now my hands clenched. "I meant the Alashi. Not you and me."

"Oh." His lips twitched.

I wanted to scream at him to stop laughing at me, but that would only make him laugh harder. I stood, clenching my teeth. "I think our midday meal is coming," I said.

Alibek caught my arm. "I think that after we finish here we should go down to Casseia and talk with the servants again."

"We'd need to talk to Janiya," I said, hoping that Janiya would have more sense. "It's for her to decide. Not me."

Our new clothes arrived late in the day—too late for us to go out. I went to bed after dinner and pretended to go to sleep. I was tired of Alibek's mockery, and this way he would leave me alone. Again, I heard him rattling around for a while. He finally went to bed, and I heard his quiet breathing on the other side of the curtain.

I didn't mean to go to the borderland that night. I had nothing new to tell Zhanna, I'd given up hope of ever finding Lauria, and I did not want to see Kyros. But there Kyros was, almost as soon as I slipped into sleep. "Hello, Tamar," he said, with a friendly smile that made me want to punch him in the face. "It's good to see you again."

"What do you want?"

"It's been a while since we've had the chance to chat. Lauria still hasn't told us anything useful, but then again . . . you bought her some time. *Some* time. Would you like to tell me something that might buy her a little more?"

I felt sick. I had nothing prepared to tell him. "Go rot in Zeus's lost hell," I said.

"Oh, Tamar," he said, shaking his head sadly. "Don't you know Lauria is my daughter? We're on the same side here. Neither one of us wants to see her hurt—you don't, I don't. It's just a matter of giving enough information to the magia . . ."

"If you wanted to protect Lauria, why did you take her to Penelopeia?"

"My orders were to execute her immediately. I took her to Penelopeia hoping she'd be able to talk her way out if she were face-to-face with the magia. A mistake, clearly." He shook his head sadly. "What can you tell me?"

My breath was uneven. "I could tell you how we broke the slaves out of the mine." That seemed harmless enough.

"All right. That's something I'd like to know."

"Lauria slipped in by having one of the slaves from Sophos's harem sell her there as a slave. She was on the inside and I was on the outside. She took in poison and put it in the guards' food. Meanwhile, I went to the guards and told them I was a sorceress. One of the Younger Sisters. I tried bargaining with the officer in charge for some of whatever they were mining, with some success, until the uprising started and I cut the man's throat."

Kyros leaned forward. "Where did you hear about the Younger Sisters?"

"Lycurgus," I said. No reason not to offer up a dead man.

"Hmm. What do you know about them?"

"That you're in trouble. That they're after the Weavers and greatly outnumber them," I said. I was making this up—I had no idea if the Younger Sisters outnumbered the Weavers, but the whole purpose of our mission was to set them against each other as a distraction. Maybe this could be to my advantage after all. "You think the Alashi are the greatest threat to you, but you're wrong. Your enemies are in your own house. They're among you. You'll never know who they are—I couldn't tell you their names if I wanted to, I don't know any! But they're strong and growing stronger. If you had any sense, you'd change sides now."

That would be a good line to leave him with. I pulled back and felt the borderland slipping away. "Wait," I thought I heard Kyros say, and I shrugged and made some noise of false regret. I opened my eyes to the darkness of my own bed, and Alibek's breathing. "Arachne's web," I whispered out loud. "Let it turn out all right, telling him those things about the Younger Sisters." The fact that I'd made it up didn't make me feel better. It could be true, after all.

I closed my eyes again, because it was a long way to morning. As I slipped into sleep, I told myself firmly to stay away from the borderland. I didn't want to have any more talks with Kyros tonight.

*W*e dressed in our new clothes in the morning. I was struck by how very *Greek* Alibek looked, dressed in his white linen tunic. He visited the bathhouse for a shave and a trim. I went down so that Zarina could brush my hair and braid it. It had grown out over the winter, and I hadn't gotten around to cutting it short again. Back in Greek lands, I found it hard to shake off the thought that I was a runaway slave and not the merchant I pretended to be. But Zarina held up a mirror for me, and after looking for a moment, I felt calmer. I looked older than I remembered—a woman, not a girl. I saw certainty rather than fear. Besides, it hardly mattered what Pelagia saw when she looked at me. I would have karenite to offer her, and nothing else would matter.

Alibek and I walked together to the neighborhood of the Temple of Alexander. Soldiers filled the streets everywhere I looked. The crowd hummed with cheer, as if they were going to a festival. I could hear happy shouts as soldiers met old friends. I wiped my sweaty hands on my new clothes and I heard Alibek's breath quicken, but the soldiers were busy, and no one noticed us.

The Temple of Alexander made me think of a big tortoise, squatting over the city. Soldiers waited in a long line to make their offerings. For their own good fortune, most brought a male animal—I saw roosters, goats, sheep, and even a young bull. A few had fruit or flowers. Coming out, they looked eager—energetic. Sometimes, when Lauria was seized by the cold fever, it gave her strength, rather than merely driving her to distraction. The soldiers looked like that. One met my eyes and gave me a pleasant nod, and I felt a hint of pride until my knowledge—*enemy! Other side!*—caught up with me, and then I felt sick.

We didn't know exactly where to find Pelagia's house, and were too nervous to ask directions, so we wandered until we saw the statue of the leaping fish. The fish balanced lightly on the curve of its tail, mouth open. The doorstep had a mosaic made of white tiles, some shiny and others dull. I stepped close and knocked on the door.

No one answered.

I knocked again and waited. After a little while I

took a step back and looked at the house. No smoke rose from inside, but this time of year someone might keep only embers burning during the day to avoid heating up the house. Midday meals could be eaten cold.

I knocked again. This time the door opened a crack. "Go away," the servant hissed.

I offered him a small wineskin, but he pushed it back. "Not right now. It's a bad time."

"Your mistress . . ."

". . . will see *no one,* and your wine doesn't make it worth it."

"I could give you spirits of wine."

"She beat a doorman half to death once for letting someone in unbidden. *Not worth it.* She sees no one. Go away." He shoved the door shut. I snatched my hand clear just in time.

Alibek looked at me. "That's it, then? Do you have another name?"

I knocked again. The doorman said from the other side, "I will call for soldiers to come. I will have them search your pockets, don't think I won't!"

I stepped back, swallowing hard. How did he know? Oh, he was no fool. He could guess easily enough. I wondered how many others would know— was it time to lose our shiny pebble? But maybe Zarina would know another name. I held on to it for now.

"That's it?" Alibek asked again as we walked.

"I think the servant knew what he was about," I said. "Have you ever seen a sorceress in a dark fever? Have you heard stories?"

"But if you have something she wants . . ."

"They're not reasonable." I swallowed. "We'll ask

Zarina if she knows anyone else. Or maybe we can wait this one out."

"How long until she, you know, *changes*? And when she does, will she get more reasonable or less reasonable?"

"There's no way to know." Zarina had said this one was particularly bad. I shook my head in frustration. Surely other Younger Sisters lived in Daphnia.

But Zarina knew of no others. "How much of a hurry are you in?" she asked as she rinsed my hair. "Pelagia can't stay dark forever."

"Do you think anyone noticed me today?"

"Hmmm, maybe. You'll know if someone knocks on your door to buy your wares."

"Ugh," I said.

"Why are you so set on finding the Younger Sisters? I can give you a dozen names of discreet, halfway sensible Weavers who will pay you well."

"I don't need money."

"Then I can't help you. The Younger Sisters keep their names secret. I know about Pelagia because she's so shattered, she doesn't keep secrets well."

I shook my head in frustration and disgust. "No doubt some of your sensible ones are in the Younger Sisters, or at least sympathize."

"Yes, but I don't know which. Some are quite loyal to the Weavers, even if they feel that the Weavers are ungenerous with materials they need. It's as much to do with friendships as self-interest."

I caught Zarina's hand as she combed my hair. "Are you sure you wouldn't like to come with us?"

"My answer still stands. I think you're as mad as any sorceress." I turned to look at her, and she gave me a wry smile. "I know what you were. I have eyes and I know what to look for."

"Then you know why I don't understand."

"I am not abused here—in fact, I am well protected. I have enough to eat. I live comfortably."

"But you're a slave. Things could change. You could be sold."

She laughed. "You could be executed."

There wasn't much I could say to that, so I thanked her and went back up to my room.

"Did she know another name?" Alibek asked.

I shook my head.

"So now what?"

I lay down, thinking about what she'd said about friendships, rather than self-interest. "It's possible to send messages to sorceresses through the Temple of Athena," I said. "I'll go tomorrow."

"Who are you going to send a message to?"

I closed my eyes, reminding myself that she was a friend. "Zivar," I said. "The sorceress Lauria and I stayed with last winter."

# CHAPTER EIGHT

# *L*AURIA

*E*ven with my mother's care, I was sick for days.
Despite my fears, she didn't get sick as the servants had. I had fever dreams and black sleep, but no more trips to the borderland. When I was awake, my head and back ached terribly, and I threw up most of what I ate or drank, though at least a little must have stayed down because I stayed alive. *What would happen if I died of this—would the gate within me stay open, as the magia fears?* I wondered one day, lying in bed. *Perhaps I should try to let myself die; surely if the gate stayed open, that would be a miserable problem for the Weavers. But then I wouldn't be able to free the rivers . . .*

I had plenty of time to think about what I had seen in the Weavers' library that night, though my headache made thinking difficult. It was clear that they had been talking about me and wanted me kept alive, at least for now, because of the danger I posed. *So if I try to escape, the guards probably have orders to stop me, but not to kill me. Not that it would be difficult to stop me. Right now, I can barely rise from my bed.* But sorceresses on the other side of the borderland—a sorcerous djinn might be responsible for my ability to free djinni? *If I was chosen somehow, why me? Why now? And if they could turn me into a gate, why not everyone? Every Alashi shaman, every Danibeki slave? Surely that would make things even more inconvenient for the Weavers.*

I began to recover, finally. One day the headache and backache were mostly gone, and the next day I could drink without vomiting my tea back up. Then I could eat again, and my headache and backache were gone completely. I was terribly weak, and had lost a great deal of weight; I felt like a good stiff breeze would carry me right over the wall and away from the Koryphe. If the magia wanted me healthy enough to survive the winter, she needed to let me out of my room to walk around a bit. And someone would need to help me walk.

Kyros, it seemed, had the same thought. "The magia who sent you to the pit took to her bed again while you were ill," he said when he came to visit later that day. "You are at liberty to walk around again. Andromeda—your mother, I mean—can assist you." He beamed at my mother, who gave him an affectionate smile back.

"Thank you for bringing my mother here to nurse me," I said.

"You're welcome." He rose. "She'll help you walk down to the garden later today."

I could not remember ever having been quite so ill.

I was unsteady when I rose and tried to walk; I clung to my mother's arm as we made our way down the stairs. But the nausea was completely gone and the headache did not return. My mother settled me outside, in the shade. The day was hot. "Let me get you something to drink," she said, and went back inside.

No sooner was she gone than Xanthe stepped close to me. "If my mother ran away—if she's free—then why didn't she come back for me?" she hissed.

I'd asked Janiya that question, and remembered her response. "She'd been a slave for six years. *You* had not been accused of anything—you had your whole life ahead of you. She knew that you would have been told that she was a criminal, a traitor, disgraced."

"Or maybe she really *was* a criminal and feared to come back."

"Whether she committed her crime or not, the danger would have been the same," I said. "What did they say that she'd done? She never told me."

"None of your business," Xanthe said, and stepped away as my mother came back through the doorway.

"Here we are," my mother said, brightly. She had a silver tray with two cups and a pitcher; she sat down and poured a drink for me, then herself. The cup was earthenware and cool. The drink was sweet and a little tart, and it wasn't until I saw the deep ruby color that I identified the taste as pomegranate, sweetened with honey.

"Thank you," I said. When I finished my cup, my mother poured more.

"Do you think you'll be up for a bath today?" she asked, her fingers plucking at my hair. My hand followed hers; it was stringy and rank. I nodded, not speaking. "It's such a shame that you cut your hair."

"Cut it? It's almost grown out." The Alashi had cut it, when I'd joined the sword sisterhood. All the unmarried women cut their hair at the beginning of summer, then went off to train.

"It barely comes past your shoulders."

I shrugged. "Well, it will look better once it's clean, you're right about that."

She fell silent, satisfied with that for the moment, and I began to think about how pleasant it was to sit with my mother. Then she said, "This all could have been avoided if only you'd listened to me."

"*What* could have been avoided? If I'd listened to you about *what*?"

"There's no need to take that tone with me."

"What tone?"

"That 'don't you tell me what to do, you're only my mother' tone. If you'd settled down like I wanted you to, *all* this—unpleasantness—could have been avoided."

There were a million possible retorts to that, but the sheer absurdity of the statment left me speechless. Finally I said, "Yeah, and if you'd had a pet bird instead of a daughter, you could have kept it in a cage. *Much* less trouble."

"Are you saying that I kept you in a cage?" my mother said.

"No, I'm saying that you'd have been happier with a bird than a daughter."

"I never kept you in a cage."

"You couldn't have even if you'd tried. I'd have climbed out the window. Broken down the door." It occurred to me that someone might be listening to me, and I wanted to try to escape from *here* at some point—when I was stronger—so I shut my mouth and clenched my teeth.

"*You* could have chosen to stay where you belonged and behave yourself." I refused to rise to that. She sighed, and added, "Cybela's son Brasidas got married last year."

"How lovely for him," I said, sincerely, though I still found myself picturing Brasidas as the nose-picking little boy he'd been when we were six.

"Yes." She sighed again. "*All* the young men in our neighborhood are married now; Brasidas was the last."

"Mother. I don't want to get married!"

"Well, that's good," she said, her tone implying the opposite. "Because they're all gone. All taken. *All* the young men . . ."

"Mother, I'm not even a virgin anymore," I snapped. "That's the sort of thing that's important to the sort of men I grew up around. They want their wives to be pure and untouched. So look, just *drop* it. Stop thinking about it. I don't want to get married and even if I did, the men you have in mind *wouldn't want me*."

"Not a—" My mother was a step behind me, trying to wrap her thoughts around what I'd said.

"I was raped by Sophos." *It was Kyros's fault.* I bit back the words. I wanted to lull them, to convince them that I trusted him, that he could trust me.

"Oh." My mother was speechless, for once.

"So let's talk about something else."

There was a long silence. I sipped my pomegranate drink. My mother drained hers, then refilled the cup. I noticed that her hand was shaking slightly.

"Kyros sent you there," she said, her voice soft.

"Yes. Mother—"

"Did he *know*?"

I glanced around; Xanthe, of course, was nearby, and no doubt listening. "Maybe you should ask *him*." I swallowed hard and lowered my voice further. "Look. I think Sophos had orders from the Weavers to do whatever it took to make it work—to convince the Alashi that I really was an escaping slave. Kyros might have known that. Maybe."

"*Maybe*? Of *course* he knew. If they didn't tell him, he should have guessed." My mother's whisper was furious. I didn't dare meet her eyes.

"Well, I told him, afterward. I told him I wanted Sophos's head."

"And did you get it?" My mother's hand gripped my arm.

"What do you think? I did, actually, a few months ago, courtesy of Jaran, one of Sophos's former slaves. I had it delivered to Kyros's desk. Now you know why." *Shut up, Lauria, shut up! Just stop talking!* The novelty of having my mother *on my side* for once had overwhelmed my sense.

"That misbegotten, malformed bastard," she said, and let go of my arm. I wondered if she meant Sophos, or Kyros; then she added, "I hope he's rotting in Zeus's lost hell."

"Did you ever meet Sophos?" I asked.

"Did *I* ever . . ."

"I know you used to be Kyros's concubine."

She let out her breath in a long sigh. "You know what? It's not your business."

"Don't tell me, then."

"No, why not? You asked. Yes, I met Sophos, and

yes, he took me back to his room—that's what you were wondering. I was hardly a virgin by then. I was Kyros's favorite, and Sophos knew it. They were friends, but also rivals, in a way—and technically equals, though Kyros usually had the upper hand. Sophos had someone's favor, that week, and to rub Kyros's nose in it he took a privilege that would not normally have been granted to him. So I went with Sophos. I was very good at what I did—*all* of it. I told him I'd rub his shoulders, and then I poured him more wine, and still more wine—he drank so much he made himself impotent, which was what I'd hoped for. He was furious, and unfortunately realized I'd been pouring him generous cups of wine on purpose. He raised his hand—and checked it, just in time. He didn't dare beat me, knowing that I was Kyros's favorite—he knew that if he did, Kyros would have his revenge, somehow, sometime. Maybe not that week, but eventually. So he laughed it off, swore me to secrecy, and let me go."

"Did you keep his secret? Until now, I mean?"

"No. I told Kyros the next morning. He had a good laugh over it and gave me a bracelet as a reward. *Lovely work, Andromeda—I knew I could trust your cleverness.*"

She looked into the distance, remembering, a faint malicious smile on her lips.

"I would not have been a good concubine," I said. "I am not that clever."

"Clearly not."

*I got raped, after all.* That's what she meant.

"There was a moment," I said. "Sophos's knife was where I could reach it. I wanted to stab him through the heart . . . But he was Kyros's *friend*. I couldn't believe what was happening."

"If you'd done it, they'd have killed you," my mother said. "A slave who raises a hand to her master is food for the dogs. A slave who *kills* her master—you don't want to think about it. We wouldn't be having this conversation."

"I wasn't a slave, though."

"Did anyone other than Sophos know that? Would they have said anything? You could've claimed that you were freeborn, that Kyros had sent you, whatever, but they wouldn't have sent an aeriko down to Kyros to *ask*. They'd have cut your throat and sent their apologies, perhaps, if you seemed halfway credible."

"Huh." She was right, I supposed. I fell silent.

"But," she added, "*if* you had gotten married at a decent age—sixteen, perhaps—you'd have had your pick of the boys in our neighborhood. And *none* of this would have happened."

*A*fter my mother had finally taken herself off to bed that evening, Xanthe came in, furtively, and closed the door behind her. "Why are you so sure my mother was telling you the truth when she said she didn't commit the theft? For all you know she was justly punished, but escaped anyway. It's not as if a bunch of bandits would *care* if someone was a thief."

Xanthe's face was furious. She stared at the floor as I tried to meet her eyes. "I'm sure because I know her," I said. "She was a woman of integrity."

"People change."

"True enough." *I should know.* "Does it matter?"

Clearly the answer was yes. I cleared my throat. "Would you like me to tell you a little bit about her?"

"I don't care if she dropped dead while you were puking up your innards," Xanthe said, but made no move to leave.

"She's quiet. Nothing like *my* mother, who never shuts up." Xanthe suppressed a grimace at that. "The Alashi send out their young men and women in the summer as sword brotherhoods and sisterhoods. Janiya isn't young, but she's unmarried. She leads one of the sword sisterhoods. Tamar and I were sent out with her last summer; that's how I got to know her."

Xanthe was staring at the wall, not speaking. Listening, though. I kept talking.

"I was terrified of Janiya when we were first sent out with her. And those first weeks only made things worse. When a slave joins the Alashi they're tested, and taught how to live as a free person. I failed the first test and that made me *furious*. The tests are tricks—at least some of them are. As the summer went on, though, I grew to respect her. I learned what made her laugh. She's kind, even when she's angry." I glanced at Xanthe, swallowed hard, and added, "She spoke of you once. She thinks of you often."

Xanthe straightened and flashed me a furious look. "I hope she rots," she said, and stalked out, slamming the door behind her so hard a tapestry fell off the wall. A moment later the door swung open again; the servant had arrived with my nightly cup of tea. Giving Xanthe a look of terror, the servant tiptoed in, put down the tray and the tea, and fled.

I didn't really feel like tea—even the nights were warm now—but picked it up anyway and took a sip. I wished I could see Janiya again—I wished I could *speak* to her, at least, and tell her that I'd found her daughter. That Xanthe was alive and well, if not exactly friendly or eager to see her. If I could find the borderland . . . *I probably wouldn't be able to find her, any more than I could find Prax. But I could talk to Tamar, and Tamar could talk to Janiya.*

Why *couldn't* I find the borderland anymore? Except for that one night when I was sick. I wasn't a shaman, but I'd been a shaman's apprentice and a sorceress's apprentice. *I ought to be able to get there.* I had tried to meditate during the day; it didn't surprise me that this hadn't worked, as that was harder. But at night—*especially if Tamar is trying to find me, and I know she is . . .*

Why would being horribly *sick* have made me able to go?

And then, suddenly, I knew. *They're drugging my food.*

Last year, I'd seen my mother in a dream, and had said that I was afraid that Kyros would come. What had she said? *He has a remedy he takes for his headaches, and they make him sleep very soundly. Too soundly to dream.* Whatever the remedy was, they were putting it in my food. That's why they'd fed me every day when I was in the pit; that might have been why the water tasted funny; that was why I'd made it to the borderland once while I was sick. *But only once. Because even when I was almost dying, when my mother had to give me broth and water a sip at a time, that was in the food.*

Did *she* know?

*No. Surely not.*

But Kyros. *He* knew, without a doubt.

*They chain your mind,* the djinn had said. Now I knew what it meant.

I stared at the tea. *It's in the tea.* Was it in everything else, too? Had I drunk my tea every night? I could stop drinking my bedtime tea—that would be easy enough. I couldn't very well stop eating, though; I needed to regain my strength. Besides, a fast would attract attention. If they knew I'd figured it out . . . *They brought me out of the pit when I stopped eating and drinking,* I remembered now. *That was why.*

I had already started drinking the tea; I might as well finish my cup. My throat clenched, though, and I put my cup down. *To bed, and darkness.*

*M*y mother joined me in the morning with a tray of food—breakfast. Fresh bread and a pot of honey to share, some sheep's milk cheese, and tea. *Where is it? Do they bother putting it in my breakfast? Can I eat freely?* They couldn't have put it in the bread, surely, but the honey . . . the tea . . . I picked at my food. My mother looked at me, concerned. "Do you feel well?" she asked. She reached out and touched my forehead to feel for fever. "I thought you were better . . ."

It would be a good excuse not to eat, but they'd just have her spoon-feed me again, so I forced a smile and said, "No, I'm fine." I would eat breakfast and the midday meal, I decided, then claim illness at dinnertime if I needed an excuse to avoid eating. If I couldn't get to the borderland tonight, I would fast all day tomorrow.

It was another hot day. My mother brought pomegranate juice to the garden again to sip. I eyed it with distrust, but there was nothing else to drink; I held off as long as I could but by mid-morning I was too thirsty not to drink. I sipped, trying to identify the foul taste of medicine under the sweet taste of the juice. *Tamar and I walked for a whole day once without drinking, didn't we? And it was hot, too. I should be able to go without drinking for a day, if I have to.* But when we'd crossed the desert I hadn't been recovering from an illness. *Still. If I have to . . .*

Midday came, and slaves brought out a low table for us to eat at, in the shade, and our meal—bread, hummus, cold meat, and plums. I could easily imagine drugs in the hummus. The bread, meat, and fruit initially seemed safe, but as I reached for the meat, I started thinking of ways it could be concealed in each. Though perhaps it wasn't in any of the food. The sweet-tart drink would readily hide pretty much anything they slipped into it. *And doubtless they expect I'll drink it.*

And it was a hot day. I sipped a little more, spilled the rest of my cup so that my mother wouldn't realize how little I was taking, and poured more. I ate all the plums, as much for their juice as for their sweet taste.

My head ached in the afternoon heat. "I think I'm going to go lie down for a while," I said, and my mother helped me back up to my room. It was even hotter inside, though, and I lay on my bed, miserable, exhausted, and thirsty. I dozed, then jerked myself awake. Even if I somehow reached the borderland right now, I would never find Tamar; she was undoubtedly awake. As far west as I had traveled, it seemed likely that the sun rose over the steppe before it rose over Penelopeia, but the sun traveled more quickly than a palanquin; it might be later in the day where she was, but it would not be night. And if I napped in the afternoon I might find myself lying awake tonight. *I need to stay awake now.* I got up and sat in a chair, willing the afternoon to pass quickly, which of course was as useless as willing the moon not to wax and wane.

Finally, the sun was low in the sky and my mother appeared, servants in her wake with yet another tray. "Ugh," I said, turning up my nose at the curried lamb, yogurt, and rice, ignoring the tempting smell of the gravy even as it made my mouth water. "Do you know what really sounds good to me right now? More of those plums. I think I could make an entire dinner of plums." *It would be difficult to slip drugs into the plums.*

"I'll see what I can do," my mother said, and returned a short while later with a plate piled high. "There are orchards right outside the city."

"Lovely," I said, taking a bite and glorying in the sweet, untainted liquid. "Back home they're just not this sweet . . ."

I was still hungry when all the plums were gone, but I didn't quite dare send my mother looking for more. *One hungry evening won't kill me. The plums might try, though.* "Oh, no," I said, when my mother tried to persuade me to take some lamb. "I just wanted plums."

"Well, your appetite can do odd things when you've been ill," my mother said, still perplexed. I agreed, and pretended to drink some wine. It would be difficult to dispose of it without her noticing, but then she turned her back for a moment and I poured half my cup onto the rug under our table. It would stain, but hopefully no one would notice until it could be shrugged off as the result of some accidental spill while I was ill.

Finally, the meal was over and my mother took herself off, sending a servant with the tea, which joined the wine under the table since I didn't want Kyros to get suspicious.

It was night. *Finally.* I lay down, grateful for the cooler air that drifted in from the window now that the sun had set. Of course, now I couldn't fall asleep. I tossed and turned for hours, remembering that first night in the mine, when I had so desperately wanted to sleep in order to speak with Tamar, and couldn't. *Perhaps I could meditate, as I did when I was apprenticed to the sorceress, and reach the borderland that way . . .*

I had made myself a spell-chain, almost, and followed the singing of the beads to the borderland. I had no beads to sing to me today; I certainly didn't have any karenite. *There are plenty of spell-chains at close hand, though. Perhaps if I listen, I will hear them . . .*

I couldn't hear singing, but after a while I heard something else—a windy, thunderous sound that ebbed and flowed. I tried to follow the noise but kept stumbling back to consciousness, irked by an itch or by my own hunger. *I've forgotten how to do this.* I sat up, leaned against the wall by the window, and tried again. *Listen.*

There; a trickling sound, this time, like water melting from a roof in spring. *Follow it.* I focused, and this time the noise grew louder. I saw myself trudging down a muddy path, following a thin stream, and tried to contain my excitement that it was working and just focus on the stream, on the path to the borderland. Then I felt myself slip, and fall, and I jerked awake, bumping my head against the wall in my spasm.

I lay down on the bed again. *There's hours of night left. Hours. Just relax,* I told myself. *This is going to work. I'm going to find my way there.*

*Just let go . . .*

Y ou have a great deal to answer for."

"What?" I was in a tent; the light was dim, but that wasn't Tamar's voice. "Where is Tamar?"

The woman leaned forward, and I could see her face. It was Zhanna, the shaman from the Alashi sisterhood. She was dressed for battle, her bow at her side. My heart leapt: Zhanna was a good friend. "She's worried about you. *Terribly* worried." Zhanna was worried, too. I could hear it in her voice.

"Tell her I'm safe," I said. I wanted to sweep Zhanna into a hug and ask her to tell me everything that had been happening on the steppe, but this dream might be brief. I didn't trust that we'd have time.

"She's not going to believe that! She believes that you're in Penelopeia and Kyros has you. If you're safe, where are you?"

"Oh—well, I *am* in Penelopeia and Kyros does have me, and so does the magia. But—well, I'm safe for now. I was sick, and they brought my mother to nurse me back to health. They're afraid that if I die, something will happen with the djinni. It's hard to explain, but they need to keep me alive. And I'm guarded by Janiya's daughter."

"Who?"

"Janiya had a daughter, among the Greeks. Zhanna, can you tell me what the Greeks accused Janiya of, when they betrayed her?" *Does Zhanna even know what I am talking about?*

Zhanna nodded; she did know. "Theft of a spell-chain," she said. "An important spell-chain—the one that binds the Syr Darya."

"Are you serious?"

"I don't know if she really did it or not. When she told me about it, I rather thought she was falsely accused. But there was another time—well, I don't know."

I heard a shout outside the tent, and Zhanna started to her feet. Tears came to my eyes; I had *really* hoped to see Tamar, and seeing Zhanna was just not the same. "They're putting something in my food that keeps me from the borderland," I said. "I may not be able to come back anytime soon. Tell Tamar . . ." *That I love her* was too personal a message to give through Zhanna. ". . . that I wish I could see her," I said. "Tell her that I *will* be free again and will return to the steppe. And she should tell Janiya—her daughter has not forgotten her."

Beyond the walls, I heard the clash of metal. *Battle.* The tent vanished around me as Zhanna woke to face whatever was happening where she was. *Let me see,* I thought furiously. *Let me see her.*

The steppe formed around me again: whether it was a true vision or a picture painted out of my own fierce desire to know what was happening, I wasn't sure. It was gray dawn outside the tent, and I could hear the sounds of battle, though at first I could make no sense of what I was seeing. Men and women ran past me, on foot and on horseback, weapons in hand.

I followed on foot, searching for Zhanna in the confusion. I saw her, finally, on horseback, riding toward the crest of a hill, and followed.

When I had spent my summer with the sisterhood, we'd raided a Greek garrison. We'd had the advantages of surprise, speed, and arrow poison. The garrison had plenty of weapons and horses—we'd stolen some of them—but only one spell-chain, if that. The Sisterhood of Weavers, I knew from my service to Kyros, rarely entrusted more than one spell-chain at a time to their army.

That, apparently, had changed.

In the dim light of dawn, I could see flickers of light across the battlefield; djinni carried torches to provide light. At first I thought that the djinni were following the Greek soldiers, but that would have made them easy targets. The djinni were following the Alashi, offering targets to the Greeks.

Other djinni seemed to be circling the battlefield and snatching weapons away from Alashi. Another had been sent to wreak chaos in the Alashi encampment—scattering horses, emptying sacks of grain and rice, sabotaging pots. The one small mercy was that it was too risky to have the djinni do anything to the individual Alashi directly.

I had thought that Alashi women fought side by side only with other women, but today there were both brothers and sisters on the battlefield—quite a few of them. Even so, they were outnumbered by the Greeks. And they were losing.

I heard a horn give the signal to retreat. *But retreat to where?* I thought. This was no mere raid. The Greeks were making war on the Alashi. There was karenite on the steppe; the Greeks meant to take the steppe and wipe out the Alashi like lice.

Hearing the signal, Zhanna wheeled her horse; too late to dodge, I realized that she would ride it straight through me. The world went dark and silent around me; the battle, for me, was over.

I stood in darkness for a moment, then realized that I could still hear that sound I'd heard before—the sound of water. Holding my breath, I moved quietly toward it.

The darkness around me lightened to gray, and I found myself in an empty courtyard with a fountain at the center. The sound came from the fountain. It was a very simple fountain—more a pool, really, just a round thing with a wall, but when I looked down I saw endless deep water with no bottom. Something glowed near the bottom, and faintly, over the sound of water, I could hear singing—a thousand voices singing together in a vast powerful chord.

I took a deep breath, leaned forward, and let myself fall in.

The water around me was cold—shockingly cold, after the vague unreality of the borderland. I swam down, and farther down; I could see a blue glow, and through the water the voices sang loudly. There. THERE. It was the spell-chain. THE spell-chain—the chain that bound the Syr Darya, I knew with absolute certainty, lying at the bottom of this fountain, wherever it was. Miles of chain and blue beads and light; I started to try to gather it up, but my hands here had no more reality than they'd had in the vision of the library.

My lungs were beginning to scream for air, but I took a moment to look around. *Where is this? Is this*

*a real place? Could I go here and find the spell-chain?*
I was underwater, but around me I saw what looked like a ruined temple. There were walls, and a gate. A light flickered through the gate, then another light came back out again. It felt familiar, even though I had never seen it before.

*I need to breathe.*

I thrust my feet up against the rough stones, swimming back toward the surface. My head didn't break through; the water was endless, and I saw no light overhead. *Need to breathe to breathe to breathe . . .*

*Oh, shit . . .*

I sat up in bed, gasping for breath, choking the water I would have sworn was there out of my lungs. My heart beat frantically and after a moment I let myself slump back against the pillows, shivering in the warm night. My hair was damp, though from sweat, not swimming. The taste of the water was still on my tongue.

# CHAPTER NINE

# TAMAR

I could send a message to Zivar from the Temple of Athena. Of course, the message would not be private, so I would have to choose my words carefully. "Tamar wishes to speak with you" was definitely out. There weren't that many women named Tamar, and Kyros might have people watching for messages from anyone named Tamar or Lauria. Of course, he might also know where we spent the winter and read anything sent to Zivar. But we had to send a message, because we were running out of time. It would take weeks to ride down and speak to Zivar. If we sent the message through the temple, it would be carried by djinni.

Neither Alibek nor I could read or write, so I hired a scribe. I thought a bit longer, then said the message was from Photios, the man who ran her merchant company. Surely he sent her a lot of messages, so this wouldn't attract attention. But Zivar would know it wasn't his handwriting. I had the scribe write a simple message with the name of our inn, saying I had something to discuss and signing it with Photios's name. When the ink had dried, I rolled up the paper and tied it, then gave it to the acolyte who handled messages. "This is for Zivar, in Daphnia."

"Do you trust Zivar?" Alibek asked as we walked back to our room.

"Not really," I said. "She's still a sorceress. But I trust her more than the woman Zarina sent us to. Zivar is crazy and unpredictable, like all of them. But she's not a bad person, for all that."

"You have *exceptional* taste in your friends, Tamar," Alibek said.

My face flushed hot. "Go drown yourself in the Chirchik River, Alibek."

"What? Do you deny that you have unusual friends? You're friends with a sorceress. You're friends with—I don't even know what to call Lauria. A turncoat spy? And then there are the escaped slaves back with the Alashi. *Exceptional* friends. All of them."

"Lauria isn't just a *friend*. She's my blood sister. Take your mockery and go drown yourself, Alibek, really. I don't want to hear any more about how much you hate Lauria."

"Did I say *anything*?"

"You've said plenty!"

Alibek sneered. "I think you need to sit down in the shade and have some tea. You think you know what I'm thinking and you *don't*."

We'd reached the inn. "Fine," I said. "Fine! I'll sit down in the shade, but I want you to leave me alone."

"I'll go visit Janiya," Alibek said. "We need to let her know what's happened."

I nodded stiffly. It was a good idea. I wished I'd thought of it, because I'd have told *him* to sit down and *I* would have gone. Then I could have talked with someone who wasn't Alibek.

So it was a pleasant surprise, hours later, when the doorman for the inn fetched me. "There's a woman here to see you," he said. I jumped up—could Zivar really have come so quickly, or was it some strange sorceress here for my karenite? But it was Janiya. I led her through the garden and up to our room.

"Nice," she said, looking around. "Listen, I left Alibek with the horses. I had to come tell you something. Zhanna spoke with Lauria last night."

"She *what*?" My face burned. Why hadn't Lauria come to me? Because I was staying out of the borderland, of course. Avoiding Kyros.

"Zhanna had a conversation with Lauria, then sought me out to pass things along to you." She raised an eyebrow, as if she were going to ask me again why Zhanna couldn't seem to find me in the borderland—then shrugged and left it. "I didn't want to send her message with Alibek."

"Is she safe?"

"Well, sort of. She said to tell you she was safe— she wanted me to reassure you. But you were right— she's in Penelopeia, in the custody of Kyros and the magia. She says that for now, they don't want to hurt her. She was sick, and they brought her mother there to nurse her."

Her mother? I remembered Lauria complaining about her mother. But at least her mother's loyalty would be to her—mostly. Probably.

"Also—this didn't make a lot of sense to me, but she was quite certain that they want to keep her alive. There's something bad that might happen with the djinni if Lauria dies."

"Well, that's something, I suppose."

"They're putting something in her food that keeps her from the borderland. She wanted to tell you that she wishes she could see you, and that she *will* be free again and will return to the steppe."

Janiya fell silent.

"Was that it?" I croaked. My eyes were hot and my throat felt so thick, it was hard to swallow.

Janiya nodded, then sighed and said, "Also, she has seen my daughter. She told Zhanna something of that. But yes. That was all of her message to you."

I had to close my eyes and cover my face with my hands, because I *hated* having anyone see me cry. I heard Janiya rise and the clink of a cup on a tray. "Have some tea," Janiya said, and set a cup down beside me.

I wanted to curl up and tell her to *go away*—or else get my horse and start riding, even though I wouldn't reach Lauria for months.

At least Lauria was safe. Or safer than I'd feared, given what Kyros had said. Or else she'd lied to us—all too possible if she feared we'd get ourselves killed trying to help her. A drug to make her sleep heavily—that made sense. No wonder I had been sure she was alive but unable to find her in the night. They wanted her alive because of something with the djinni. That must have something to do with her ability to free bound djinni by touching them. But if they knew about that, why keep her alive? Even if they were keeping her alive for now, surely they would kill her as soon as their fear passed . . .

"She saw your daughter?" I asked when I was certain that my voice would be steady.

Janiya sighed deeply. "I have a daughter—Lauria told you of this?" I nodded. "She's nineteen years old now. I think of her every day, but I don't expect to see her again before I die. Lauria told me she hadn't forgotten me."

"How long has it been since you've seen her?"

"Thirteen years."

"She was six then? Of course she hasn't forgotten you. My mother died when I was ten, and I haven't forgotten *her*."

"But you're not angry at her, either. For leaving you."

"No." I took a sip of tea. "I was angry at her for a long time for not trying to protect me when I was sold. A *real* mother, I thought, would have fled with me in the night to the bandits. My mother . . . her spirit was gone, and she never thought of escape. She sent me away. And I never saw her again." My free hand knotted around the edge of my tunic. "Dying, though. She couldn't help dying."

"I was taken from my daughter. Sold. She's angry anyway."

"Well, of course. You could have run. Taken her and run."

"But I couldn't have! I was a prisoner. I was lucky not to be put to death. I think my—someone who liked me must have intervened on my behalf."

"Tell *her* that, not me."

Janiya poured another cup of tea and sat down. "I should have taken her and left right after she was born. Left Penelopeia, left the Greeks, left the Sisterhood Guard. I loved it there, but I should have known. Somehow. I should have run then, when I could have."

"To where?"

"The Alashi take all kinds of fugitives."

"Ha. So Lauria could have just left Kyros and run away, and the Alashi would have taken her in?"

"Yes."

"Funny."

"We would have been more suspicious. She would have been watched more closely. The tests would have been . . . different. Very, very different. But yes. We would have taken her in. For Kyros's purposes that would not have worked, though."

"For Kyros's purposes, the plan they tried didn't work either."

"True enough."

"So Lauria's seen your daughter?"

"Yes. My daughter is her *guard*. Isn't that strange?"

I caught my breath. Janiya's daughter, guarding Lauria? "You know how to go to the borderland," I said. "Go to your daughter."

"I can be *taken* to the borderland. I don't know that I can go there myself, let alone find someone else there."

"Try!"

"Do you think I haven't? I tried for years, when I was first taken."

"Try again. Persuade her to help Lauria."

"You think she would listen to me? Would you listen to your own mother if she appeared to you in a dream and told you to betray the Alashi?" I shook my head. "Do you think Lauria would have listened to *her* mother if her mother had shown up in her dream and told her to trust Kyros?" I laughed at that, out loud, just a little. "Well, I don't think my daughter is going to listen to me, either."

"You have to try."

"I could make things worse."

"Go to her," I said.

Janiya put down her tea and stood. "I need to get back to the horses. I told Alibek I'd send him back here before night."

"Can't you stay instead?"

"It would attract attention. It probably already has, don't you think? Do you get along with Alibek so poorly?"

"He hates Lauria."

"Well, he has a right to. Just as you have a right to love her." Janiya shrugged. "One of you can come visit me again in a few days."

I walked her to the door of the inn. She turned back, unsmiling, just before the door closed. "I will *try*," she said, and walked away.

The sun set very late that time of year. It was evening, but not yet sunset, when I saw a blue dot in the fading sky: a sorceress's palanquin. Its color made it difficult to see, but it was coming toward us. Down it came, until it came to rest in the courtyard, set down gently like a hand might set down a kitten. Was it Zivar? I stood up.

Zivar flung back the curtain and stepped out, her eyes alight. She didn't see me right away, but turned to the servant who'd come running. "I need a room," she declared loudly. "Your *best*. And a dozen wine-skins of excellent wine, a pot of grilled lamb, a half bushel of the best plums you can find this time of day, and a silk-covered pillow. And ready a bath for me; I hate travel." She tossed the servant a drawstring bag, but he didn't even look inside before rushing off to do her bidding. Then she saw me. "*Tamar*. My old friend, you are the most beautiful thing I have seen all day, and let me tell you, the view from a palanquin is excellent. Shall we go to your room to talk while they get mine ready?"

"That would probably be a good idea." I glanced around. I would give her that piece of karenite, just to have it off my hands before anyone came to search. Zivar was flying as high as her palanquin. I hoped that she didn't decide I was out to destroy her, like she had when I was her guest. If she tried to kill me, would anyone at the inn stop her? I found it hard to imagine that the Sisterhood of Weavers would worry much about my murder at the hands of a sorceress. Well, I'd brought her here, and there was no turning back now. "It's right this way."

Zivar glanced around as she came in. "I knew it had to be you, and not Photios, when I realized I could read the writing without getting a headache. Where is Lauria?"

"Penelopeia," I blurted out, then bit my lip and shook my head. "She's a prisoner of the Sisterhood. That's not exactly why I brought you here."

Zivar sat down, smoothed her robes, and daintily poured herself a cup of tea. The cold fever, for the moment, was leashed. "By all means, Tamar, begin at the beginning and tell me why you sent for me."

I took a deep breath, let it out, and began. "The

Greeks gather their strength to move against the Alashi. They want karenite, which can still be found on the steppe. To distract them, I want to offer a supply of karenite to the Younger Sisters, on the condition that they make trouble for the Sisterhood."

"Karenite. How much?"

"Lots. Here . . ." I dug in my pocket and took out the stone, pressing it into Zivar's hand. "A gift, from the Alashi."

She looked at it hungrily for a moment, then slipped it into a small pouch that rested under her robes, against her chest. "Do go on."

"Well, to do this, we need to find the Younger Sisters. Can you tell me how?"

"That's all you need from me?" She wet her lips. "*I* am not one of them. What's in this for me?"

"Do you still want to come to the steppe? Because you probably want to find the Alashi there, not the Sisterhood."

She shrugged. "I suppose."

"And I just gave you a lovely gift. Suppose you give me some names."

"Yes. I suppose I could do that." She stood up. "In Daphnia—well, there's Pelagia."

"We know about her, and she's melancholic right now, and not seeing anyone."

"Yes, her melancholias are dark. *Very* dark. She should probably have given up binding years ago, but she takes pleasure in the craft itself, unfortunately. Let me think. There's also Sophronia, Hypatia—though it might be difficult to get in to see her, she's kind of important—and Eudoxia. Can you remember all of those?"

"Sophronia, Hypatia, Eudoxia. Yes."

"Good. Surely *one* of those women will be in a good mood."

There was a knock at the door. It was Alibek, a servant at his heels with our meal, and another servant behind that one with Zivar's meal. Alibek sat down beside me and gave Zivar a quick look half-veiled by his eyelashes. We all fell silent as the nervous servants set down our food and fled. Just before the door swung shut, a young girl ran in with the basket of plums, set it down, and ran out again.

"Plums? Oh yes, I did ask for plums," Zivar said, and picked one up to eat it. She sniffed disdainfully. "Who are *you*?" she asked Alibek. "I didn't expect to find Tamar in the company of a male."

"My name is Alibek," he said, rising briefly and giving her a slight bow.

"Yes? And? Why are you traveling with Tamar? Even without the separate beds I'd know it's not for your long eyelashes and your pretty cheekbones."

Alibek shrugged. "We're working together." He shot me a cool glare, then looked down at his food.

"The Alashi sent us out together," I said, since I'd told Zivar we were working on behalf of the Alashi. "We've both spent time living among the Greeks."

"I see. Have a plum." Zivar held out the basket. I took one. "Getting back to Lauria. How was she captured?"

Alibek choked on his lamb and took a sip of wine, his eyes watering.

"She tried to free someone who didn't want to be free," I said.

"And how is your alliance with the Younger Sisters going to help her?"

"What makes you think she is our priority?" Alibek asked.

"She might not be *your* priority but I'm sure she's Tamar's," Zivar said.

I nodded, then shook my head, then shrugged. "Lauria is smart," I said. "If she sees a chance, she'll take it. I'm hoping that making trouble for the Sisterhood will give her the opening she needs. I can't . . ." I paused and put down my plate. "It would take me months just to reach Penelopeia. Riding. I have no other way to get there, unless someone with powers I don't have were to take me." I didn't dare *ask* for a ride. Zivar scared me. But that was the most obvious hint I could drop.

"Of course," Zivar said. The basket of plums was still on her lap. She set it on the floor and stood up. "Don't let those plums go to waste," she said, and left.

A few minutes later the innkeeper knocked on our door. "Can you tell the sorceress that her room is ready? Do you know where she's gone?"

I stood up and went down to the courtyard. Zivar was gone, along with her palanquin. I looked around wildly. "Zivar!" I shouted up at the dark sky. "Come back! Wait! Zivar!"

"I hate it when they do this," the innkeeper muttered, and went inside.

"ZIVAR!" I shouted, no longer caring who heard me. "COME BACK!"

Alibek appeared at my side a moment later. "Stop shouting at the sky, she's probably halfway to Penelopeia by now. Let's go inside."

"Why wouldn't she have taken me along?"

"Because she knew you had work to finish *here*?"

"You could have done it. I could have given you the names!"

"She clearly didn't think I was good for much. Maybe she didn't think *you* were good for much, either—maybe she thought you'd get in her way."

"Maybe," I muttered. I kicked the basket of plums out of my way. It tipped over, and plums rolled everywhere. I cursed and started gathering them up again. Alibek squatted beside me.

"Take heart," he said, putting the last few plums back in the basket. "Help is on its way to your sister. Even if it's not you. *Someone* is going after her."

"I wish that made me feel better," I said.

$S$ophronia's house was brick and sensible-looking. Unlike Zivar and most of the other sorceresses I had dealt with, she was married. Her husband stood idly in the corner of the sitting room. Sophronia sat, her hands folded, and waited for us to speak. I looked at Alibek. He looked at me.

I set a piece of karenite on the table between us— Alibek had visited Janiya again this morning. "We need help from the Younger Sisters," I said. I set another piece on the table. "We can pay very, very well." A third piece. "Can you help us?"

Sophronia struggled to control her face. She dragged her gaze up from the karenite on the table. "Who are you?" she whispered.

"I speak for the Alashi," I said. "The Sisterhood of Weavers threatens us. The Younger Sisters can stop them. We will give you karenite—as much as you need. More than you can use! If you will use it to overthrow the Sisterhood."

Reluctantly, Sophronia said, "I can't speak for the Younger Sisters."

"But you are one of them."

"Oh yes, I'm one of them." She looked longingly at the karenite on the table, then glanced over at her husband. "I can take you to one of our leaders."

"When? Now?"

"Tomorrow," she said. "I would need until tomorrow."

Sophronia wasn't really that well connected, then. She didn't know the leader, and could only pass a message up the line. Well, that was good enough. "Tomorrow, then," I said and stood up. I left the karenite on the table to say we had so much we could waste it on people who hadn't given us anything useful.

Alibek and I walked back to the inn. I hoped we could finish this tomorrow. Give our karenite to the Younger Sister and make our deal. Then Alibek and Janiya could go back to the Alashi and I could go to Penelopeia to help Lauria.

Kyros would come speak with me again. When should I tell him that the Younger Sisters were conspiring against him? Not yet, of course, but half the point of this alliance was to make the Greeks fight each other. If the Weavers realized that the Younger Sisters were a grave threat and turned their attention there . . . well, that would serve us, too. But not too soon.

I was thinking, and not paying attention to the streets around me. Alibek suddenly thrust me aside and drew his sword. We faced a dozen guards. Another six stood behind us.

"Drop your sword," one told Alibek, who measured the odds for perhaps a heartbeat before laying down his weapon.

"You need to come with us," the guard said, once he had us both in hand. "You're to be taken to the Temple of Athena to discuss your theft."

"Theft?" Alibek said, indignantly.

*Karenite,* I thought.

"Theft," the guard said. "Of the property of Athena."

# CHAPTER TEN

# LAURIA

*I* wasn't able to fall back to sleep after my trip to the borderland; I lay awake, hungry. I knew I would have to eat that day, both because I was ravenous and because it would attract attention if I tried to fast. I finally gave up on getting to the borderland again that night and rose to sit by the window. The sky was clear, and I could see the stars overhead, but only the bright ones—morning was near.

Was that battle I saw real? Were the Alashi fleeing from the Greek army even as Penelopeia slept? Or had I invented it out of my own worst fears? I stared out at the morning star, bright against the violet sky. *If it's not real now, I think it will be real soon enough.*

I felt sick—from the horror, not from a relapse of my illness. *I can't afford to think about this now. I am a prisoner and my own life is in danger.* But when I closed my eyes, I saw the battle again.

It was a relief when a servant brought in my morning tea.

My mother arrived soon after. "Since you liked those plums so much, I had some made into a drink," she said cheerfully, pouring me some from a silver pitcher. It was sweet and startlingly cold, flavored with mint.

"My appetite is back today anyway," I said with a shrug. "In fact, I feel like I could eat a horse. Rare."

"Lovely. I'll send for one for lunch."

Through the window, I heard a woman's voice, shouting; it was a long way away, far enough that I couldn't make out any words. My mother rose and drew the gauze over the window, which did nothing to shut out the sound. She sat down again and gave me an uncomfortable smile. She folded her hands; unfolded them. Then she stood up again. "Stay here," she said, and opened the door.

She nearly collided with Xanthe. "Stay in here today," Xanthe said, shortly. "Both of you. You're not to go outside."

The day passed slowly. I could feel the drug in me, slowing me down. Were they giving me more of it? Or was I just more aware of it because I knew it was there? My mother didn't seem to be affected. She paced back and forth in the tiny room. It made me dizzy to watch her. What was it she knew that had her wound so tight? It wasn't like her. *I should try to think, try to reason out what it is. It might be important.* Trying to reason out anything at all was difficult, though. *Is it the melancholia? Is that why I'm so slow, so stupid?* But somewhere deep under the surface I could feel the ice-flame agitation of the cold fever. It just didn't seem to bother me. It was like being kicked through a pile of pillows. There was an urgency somewhere, but distant, barely nudging me. *I ought to be bothered by the fact that this doesn't bother me. But nothing seems to be bothering me. So I guess . . . I guess I'm not.*

I dozed, in the afternoon. My dreams were disturbing, splashed with wet, red blood. *We cut her heart out,* I heard Lydia say. *We burned the body. The gate closed. The gate closed. The gate closed.*

When evening came, Xanthe brought in the meal. I had little appetite, and picked at my food. Xanthe hovered in the room, watching me; she *never* did that. "I'm just not hungry," I said.

"You have to drink your wine, at least," she said.

My mother's breath caught, and she gave Xanthe a look of open horror.

"What's going to happen if I don't," I said. It should have been a question, but my voice was utterly flat.

"Other guards will come, and we'll make you drink it, if we have to."

"That sounds unpleasant," I said. I picked up the wine; it felt as if my hand wasn't really *my* hand, but perhaps the hand of some intimate acquaintance. I took a sip. "How much?"

"All."

I drained the cup. My mother must have carried me to bed, and I was claimed by black, endless darkness.

C ome on. Wake up."

"It's no use. You should know it's no use."

"Wake *up*." I heard a loud clapping sound, and felt

my cheek go numb. It took a moment for me to realize that I'd been slapped. That whoever was slapping me had been slapping me, again and again, probably for a while. I struggled to open my eyes. A wave of water caught me in the face just as I got them open a crack, and left me sputtering but only marginally clearer-headed.

"Up." It was my mother's voice, in my ear. "*Up.*"

I was sitting up; then I was standing, dripping wet. My eyes were open, but the floor seemed to be tilted. Xanthe took my other hand and slung my arm over her shoulder. "You need to walk," she said. "Come on. There's no time to waste."

"I can walk," I said. My words ran together like syrup, and I tried again. "I. Can."

"No words. Just come."

I thought I glimpsed a guard as we emerged into the corridor, but she hastily turned away. Was it day or night? I wasn't sure. I expected to head down some stairs, but instead we seemed to be heading up—up a spiral stair, which made me dizzy, then through an enclosed bridge to another tower. Then out a door, and we were on a balcony built of pure marble—it was cool against my bare feet. The sky overhead was that in-between blue of dawn twilight, with the eastern sky streaked with yellow. *Day, but only barely.* "Hurry," Xanthe said, and I took a deep breath and tried to steady myself, to keep up with Xanthe and my mother. We ran across the courtyard—the two of them half-dragging me—and through another door, then down a narrow back staircase that was probably mostly used by servants. The stairs were rough and uneven, and I would have fallen without help. That stair led to a windowless room, stiflingly hot.

I tried to ask where we were going, but the words blurred together again. "Where," I said, and paused. "What—"

"Just shut up," Xanthe said. "Trust me."

"Does Kyros—" my mother started.

"You need to shut up, too. Come on."

My mother fell silent, a little daunted. I took a deep breath—my legs were a little steadier—and glanced around. I had no idea where we were; I'd seen little enough of the Koryphe anyway. I didn't know whether Xanthe was taking us toward the edge, or deeper toward the heart. Xanthe took my face in her hands and scrutinized me for a moment. I wasn't sure what she was looking for, but tried to look back at her; I saw two Xanthes, both of them too close. "Trust me," she said again. I nodded, once—I could manage that much. She pulled my arm over her shoulder again, to help me, and we went out the door and along a shaded walkway.

We reached a corner that was partly screened by a large pillar. "Wait here," Xanthe said, leaving us in the shadows. The sun was up, now, and it was already growing hot. I squinted at the courtyard. I was growing steadier; I thought I could probably walk on my own now, or at least with less help.

"Where is she taking us?" I asked my mother. My voice sounded thin and strained, but at least the words came out sounding like words.

"How should I know?"

"You seemed to have an understanding," I said. "She said *come,* and you grabbed my hand and followed."

My mother glanced after Xanthe, then toward the courtyard. "They were planning to kill you this morning. That's why you're so unsteady right now, they gave you enough drugs to keep you quiet."

". . . this morning?" My thoughts were still slowed by the drugs; I rubbed my forehead with the heel of my hand. "Why now? After all these weeks—the pit—bringing you here—"

"New magia," my mother said. "She gave the order as soon as she was in power."

"Which one?"

"I don't know. What, do you think I have tea with them daily?"

I swallowed hard. "Why is Xanthe helping us? Can we trust her?" It was tempting just to follow her, without question—I saw Janiya's face when I looked at her, and it made me feel as if we had a bond. But she was Janiya's *daughter,* not Janiya.

"I don't know why she's helping us, but I don't really see that we have much of a choice. Do you want to go back to your room and wait for them to come for you?"

"If you knew, why didn't you say something yesterday?"

"They'd have taken me *away* from you," she said. "There was no point in making you . . . worry."

"Making me *worry?* About them coming to *kill* me? I could have tried to escape. I could have at *least* drunk less of the tea—the wine—"

"Shh!"

Footsteps. We froze, silent and waiting, but it was Xanthe. "Come on," she said.

"I think I can walk, now," I said, but when she let go of my arm, I almost fell; my mother grabbed me again. "Where are we going?" I asked.

"Out of the Koryphe," Xanthe said. "I know a place we can hide."

But instead of passing out through a gate, we went back indoors and down a narrow staircase that led to a dim room full of musty-smelling wooden barrels. Xanthe led us around to the back of the room, where we crawled through a short, low tunnel that led into darkness. My head spun again as I knelt to crawl, but at least I was steadier on hands and knees than I'd been on my feet. Then my mother helped me up, and Xanthe unshielded a lantern; we were in a dark hallway built of bricks. Xanthe swung a door closed behind us and we followed her through the hallway. After a few minutes of walking, we had to duck and crawl again through a small opening. We emerged into a cellar, and Xanthe led us up and out into the streets of Penelopeia.

*There should have been a guard,* I thought, twisting against my mother's steadying arm to glance back at the unremarkable house we'd emerged from. Was my escape a conspiracy, or had Xanthe managed this some other way—bribery, calling in a favor? *Is Xanthe giving up her whole life, helping me like this, or is she following orders from someone?* I glanced back at the high walls around the palace, already half-lost in the bustle of the crooked streets. *This doesn't seem like a good time to ask.*

My feet were bare. This hadn't been much of a problem inside the Koryphe—the floors were mostly as smooth as polished metal, silky under my feet. Now, beyond the walls, I had to watch carefully where I stepped. From my distracted perspective, Penelopeia was a city of broken paving bricks and rutted dirt roads; animal shit of a hundred different

varieties, from horse to squirrel to dog; half-rotted refuse and broken shards of pottery. I smelled grilled
meat and garlic as we passed a street vendor, and my
mouth watered.

The gravelly voices of the men around us made the
hair on the back of my neck stand up. Kyros had been
the *only* man I'd seen since arriving at the Koryphe.
Every guard and servant I'd seen had been female. As
had happened during my months among the Alashi
with the sword sisterhood, I'd come to think of female voices as *normal,* female bodies as *the way
things are.* Suddenly seeing men again was disorient-
ing; I wanted to stop and gawk at the bearded men as
if they were some sort of exotic animal.

The street we walked on changed from brick to
broken stones, then to dried mud. We skidded down
a steep embankment to a muddy canal and picked
our way across on rocks. A stench rose off the water
and clung to me after we'd finished crossing. Rather
than scrambling up the bank on the other side, we
followed the canal, occasionally splashing through
the water, until we reached an overhanging rock. "In
there," Xanthe said, and I squeezed under and found
myself in a cave.

We could sit up, but not stand. There was a heap
of blankets along the back edge to serve as a bed.
Xanthe had also laid in some waterskins, a tiny stove
with a teakettle, and a basket of plums. Light filtered
in from under the rock—enough to see by, though the
cave was dim. Xanthe sat down on the blankets with
a sigh.

"This should be safe, at least for a little while," she
said. "Ensiyeh came to power yesterday morning. She
wanted you killed; the sooner the better." Xanthe

rubbed her forehead with her thumb and forefinger, the same way Janiya did when upset.

"Is she the one who sent me to the pit?"

"No, that was Lydia. She also wanted you killed, but . . . their plans differed somewhat. Lydia just wanted you dead. Ensiyeh had this idea that you had to be slain by an aeriko." She shook her head. "Phile, the magia who just slipped, usually longs for death during her melancholia. Ensiyeh knows that, so she was going to keep you drugged and quiet, then have Phile send an aeriko to kill you. The drugs were to keep you from speaking to the aeriko; they seemed to have some idea that you had power over them if you were conscious."

"How many magias are there?" I asked.

"Four. The fourth magia, Sophia, also wanted you alive."

"You're well-informed," my mother said, dryly.

Xanthe shrugged, and let slip a hint of a smile. "I have always preferred to know what was going on. Even if I wasn't supposed to. In a palace ruled by four separate women, nothing stays truly secret for long."

My mother pursed her lips and looked down at the ground. I wondered if Phile or Sophia had instructed Xanthe to protect me—if that was how she'd managed to slip me out so handily. I looked at her, trying to assess how nervous she was. From what I'd seen of her so far, I couldn't imagine her acting entirely on her own. But even in the dim cave, I could see that her hands were shaking. If she'd acted on Sophia's orders, or Phile's, why would she be so nervous?

I took one of the plums. I was *sick* of plums, after the day before yesterday, but I was also ravenous. I sat down beside Xanthe, leaned against the wall, and stretched out my legs. Then I ate the plum, sucking pulp and juice away from the pit. My mother sat down beside me and massaged her forehead with her fingertips. I stared at the wall, wondering when I'd shake loose the last of the drug. *I need to keep my eyes on the target. What is the target? Escape. No! My target is the rivers. I'm going to free the rivers. Escaping is just an important step toward that goal.* I couldn't very well escape with Xanthe right here with us. She'd said she'd go out in a few hours, but I couldn't imagine that she'd just leave me here.

Ideas for things I could do began to dart in and out of my thoughts like insects. *Create a distraction. Wait till night. She can't stay awake forever, she has no one to guard us. Don't escape at all—win Xanthe to our side. She's half joined us already—she kept me alive because I'm her only link to her mother. No, Xanthe is nothing but an obstacle; shed her as soon as possible. Kill her! She's the only thing holding me here. No, I can't kill her. She's Janiya's daughter. I could never face Janiya again . . .*

My mother checked the kettle; there was water, but no tea. Just the plums. She sighed deeply and took some of the plain water. The cave was warm and stuffy, and smelled like the canal.

"Why did you save me?" I asked Xanthe.

Xanthe had been staring at the shaft of light that slipped under the edge of the cave; at the sound of the question she jumped slightly, then folded her hands and put them in her lap. She looked me over—she was back to avoiding my eyes. "Tell me about Janiya," she said.

"What do you want to know?" I asked.

"You said . . . that she was mean to you," she said.

"Well, for a while. But it was for a purpose, not just out of malice."

"Tell me," Xanthe said.

I hesitated a moment; my mother was listening, and she was loyal to Kyros, and Xanthe was a member of the Sisterhood Guard, even if she'd disobeyed orders and done something that might cause her to be cast out. But there seemed little enough harm in this, and besides, if I couldn't walk—despite my hunger, despite the lingering sluggishness from the drugs, my body itched to *move*—I wanted to talk. My hesitation was brief, and then I started to tell her the whole story: how Kyros had sent me to infiltrate the Alashi, how Sophos had raped me and Tamar had escaped when I did, how the eldress had sent us out with a sword sisterhood, how we'd been tested to see if we'd learned yet how to be *free*, rather than slaves.

"For our first test, Janiya woke us early in the morning and told us that we needed to go out into the desert and hunt for a particular gemstone." Karenite, in fact, but I decided to leave that part out. "Tamar and I went straight out and spent the morning searching. And we found some, and brought it back. And do you know what Janiya said to us?"

"That you failed," my mother said.

"How did you know? Did you guess what we did wrong?"

"I have no idea what you did wrong," she said. "But this Janiya—" She glanced at Xanthe, sharp-eyed, then back at me. "You think you're smart. You think you're capable. Janiya would've wanted to slap you down. So of course you failed! You'd have failed no matter what you did."

"That's not fair," I said. "We failed because we

didn't take water with us, or food. We just headed out without thinking ahead to provide ourselves with what we'd need. If we'd asked for water, we would have passed the test."

My mother shook her head stubbornly. "If you'd asked for water, you'd have failed for some other reason."

"That wouldn't have been fair. Janiya was fair."

"Fair? She sent you out to find rocks and failed you for obeying orders. What's fair about that?"

"It wasn't a test of whether we could find rocks," I said. "It was a test of whether we could think like free people."

"You *were* a free person," my mother retorted. "You were free for your whole life."

"But I wasn't thinking like a free person."

"That's an absurd thing to say. Some free people think the way Janiya wants them to think. But some free people don't, *obviously,* since you were free and failed the test anyway."

I looked at Xanthe—she was the one I'd been telling the story to, after all. She was studying the floor. "That's not a fair test," Xanthe said. "She lied to you."

"Not exactly. I don't think she ever said that the *test* was to see whether we could find the rock."

"I would have assumed that the test was to see whether we would follow orders even when they didn't make much sense. Whether we trusted our commander enough to obey her without insisting that she hold our hand and find us water before we went out. What kind of commander abuses that trust?"

"Among the Alashi, you need to be more self-sufficient than that. You need to take care to provision yourself, to have food and water with you. Always. Or you could die."

Xanthe shook her head. "That still seems unfair." She crawled over to get a plum, looked at my mother sitting on the floor, and gestured for her to take her seat on the blankets. "Go on," she said to me, as my mother resettled herself.

I went on, telling more stories about the tests, about Janiya, about the night that Janiya had told me about her own past, working as a member of the Sisterhood Guard. I left out the details I didn't want Xanthe or my mother to hear, like that this was all part of a ritual to repudiate the vows I'd taken to Kyros, but nonetheless, when I paused, my mother said, "You *did* turn against Kyros. He's right; you *did* give your loyalty to the Alashi."

"That's not true," I said. "Everything I did, I did because I *had* to. I was a spy. I had to pretend to be loyal to them, or they'd have exiled me, or worse."

"You don't have to lie," my mother said. "Your secrets are safe with me." She glanced involuntarily at Xanthe, then shrugged. "Though I suppose you might need to lie to Xanthe. Carry on, then."

Xanthe pulled her bag open. "I need to go get some food; I'm hungry," she said. She took out a rope. "I can't leave you loose, and you can't come along. If you want me to bring you food, you need to let me tie you up."

"Can't I just promise not to go anywhere?"

"Do you think I'm stupid? Your choices are to co-operate and let me tie you, or to go hungry."

I grimly held out my hands. She made me put them behind my back and tied them; then she took another length of rope and tied my feet as well. She glanced at my mother. "I trust that *you* have the sense to stay put," she said. My mother nodded. Xanthe took her bag and the last of the plums, and left.

"Untie me," I said.

"Not a chance," my mother said. "You're safer in here."

"I'm not going anywhere, I just want to be able to stretch my arms."

"You're a bad liar. And I'm leaving you bound. Xanthe will be back soon." My mother settled beside me and stroked my hair; I flinched away from her. "So tell me, Lauria. When did you lose your loyalty to Kyros? When did you decide to truly join the bandits?"

"Never."

"Stop lying to me."

"I'm not lying to you."

"Was it when Sophos raped you?"

"I still trusted Kyros, even after that happened."

"Until he didn't send you Sophos's head in a bag."

I clenched my teeth and said nothing. I realized a moment later that this was as damning as if I'd said, *I trusted him for months—I told him over and over what had happened, and asked him to tell me what he'd done. When I knew that he'd sent me to Sophos knowing full well that Sophos might do this, when I realized that I was his tool and the tool of the Sisterhood of Weavers, to use and break and throw away, then I decided that he could rot in Zeus's lost hell.* I should have denied it, insisted that it wasn't Kyros's fault, but the cold fever was in my blood today, and when I was in its grasp, I tended to speak the truth.

"What does it matter," I said, finally. "I'm here now. I'll never be able to return to the Alashi."

"This Janiya you're talking about—is she Xanthe's mother?"

"Yes."

"I figured she had to be, or why would Xanthe care so much?"

"My nose itches. Can you untie my hands, please?"

"I'll scratch your nose for you."

"That's the wrong spot," I said. My nose really did itch.

"Well, tell me the right spot, then. I'm not untying your hands."

Xanthe was back a short time later—I thought that she probably didn't entirely trust my mother, either. She had grilled chicken and a little pot of cooked rice for us to share. She smiled a little grimly when she saw that I was still tied up and untied me. I sat up to eat dinner. I wondered if she was going to insist on tying me up to sleep. Probably. I wasn't going to get much sleep anyway; I didn't feel the least bit tired.

"The Sisterhood is looking for you," Xanthe said over the meal. "I think they've sent out all their aerika that weren't urgently needed elsewhere. Except they know they can't get too close to you, so . . . I think you'll be safe if you stay in here, but if you so much as poke your head out the opening, there will be guards here in minutes."

I nodded. Xanthe narrowed her eyes, glaring at her bowl of food. "Do you *really* understand that?" she asked. "Do you believe me? Or do I have to tie you up for the night just to make sure you don't try to creep off while I sleep?"

"I'll stay here," I said.

"You gave that promise very easily," Xanthe said. "I don't trust you." When we were done eating, she tied me again, though she let me have my hands in front of me this time. She let me lie down on the makeshift bed, tied my feet as well, and gestured for my mother to lie down beside me.

It was a hot night, and I was not sleepy. I listened to my mother fall asleep, then Xanthe. The drug they'd been giving me was surely out of my body by now; if I fell asleep tonight I could go to the borderland, but I didn't think I'd ever sleep. *Maybe if I meditate.* I closed my eyes and pictured beads dancing in the darkness—faceted gemstones, carved stone animals, polished wood, swirling colored glass. Karenite.

I found myself thinking of Zivar—of the beads in jars and bowls and vases in her workroom. *Count them,* I thought. *All the glittering thousands of them. Maybe I'll hear their singing, to lead me to the borderland.*

Instead, I heard trickling water again, and followed it down into the darkness.

$W$here are you?"

"On the steppe," I said, looking around me at the grasses spreading out around me. I could smell the sweet grass and gritty dust; I flung back my head to look up at the starry sky unrolled above me, stars gleaming all the way to the horizon. *I could walk for a hundred years if it would bring me back here. I could walk through fire. I could go without food or water for weeks.*

"No," Kyros said, and the steppe disappeared; we were in his office. I caught my breath. Kyros leaned across his desk, his dark eyes narrow and hard. "Where *are* you?" When I didn't answer immediately, his face softened, his voice became soothing. "Lauria. I know that you were taken—kidnapped?—by your guard. We found her missing, and *you* missing, and your mother missing. Is your mother all right?"

I wondered why he didn't just ask *her*. Did she know how to avoid the borderland? Surely *she* would tell him where we were, if he asked. Or maybe not.

"Whatever Xanthe told you that you needed to flee from, you've only made things worse for yourself. I had almost convinced the magia that you could be trusted again. Now—well, if you *tell me where you are,* I can convince her that you were taken against your will, tricked into running. Otherwise . . ."

"Otherwise, she'll have me killed the minute she gets her hands on me, won't she?"

"Probably your mother, too. And Xanthe."

"Well." I leaned back in my chair and smiled at Kyros. "I guess I don't have much to lose, then."

"You have nothing to lose by telling me where you are. You *will* be caught, and soon, even if you don't turn yourself in."

"Actually," I said, "that's not what I meant."

I'd changed the scenery around me a few times, back when I'd regularly found myself meeting Kyros in my dreams. One time I had summoned up a bouquet of roses to give to my mother. Now I pressed my hands together, imagined the hilt of my sword, and swung it at Kyros as it appeared in my hand. *I'll cut off your head, you bastard.*

He was faster than I expected; the office was gone,

and we stood on the steppe again, Kyros just out of reach and holding his own sword. "Well, I'm glad we have *that* little revelation out of the way," Kyros said. "It makes these conversations so much easier when I don't have to pretend that I don't know you're lying to me."

I lunged, and he fended me off easily. "If you knew I'd betrayed you, then why did you spare my life?" I asked.

"Because even when you do not serve me willingly, you are useful." He lunged toward *me,* and I leapt back. Getting run through with a sword in the borderland wouldn't do anything more than wake me up. But I hadn't found Tamar yet, and I wanted to.

"I have one question," I said, and he held back a moment, waiting. "Did you *know* that Sophos would rape me? When you sent me to him?"

"You're my daughter. Would I do that to you?"

"Yes," I said.

"I suspected that things would not go as perfectly as planned," Kyros said. "But I had a great deal of faith in you. More, apparently, than you deserved." He lunged toward me again; instead of leaping back, I changed his sword into a frantic cat, which clawed him and bit his hand in its desire to get away. Kyros let it go, then spread his hands wide and smiled at me. "Do as you will, Lauria. You know you can't hurt me here."

*Let the earth swallow him up.* There was shaking, under our feet, and the ground gaped open. "Go find Zeus's lost hell," I said, and pushed him into the hole. I'd hoped to hear him scream as he fell, but got no such satisfaction.

The night was quiet around me. "Tamar?" I called,

and then took a deep breath and shouted, as loudly as I could, *"Tamar!"*

The answer came as a breath of wind. Not Tamar—a djinn. I could see it tonight as a shimmer of light; it wrapped itself around me and lifted me up.

Back when I had worked for Kyros, long before he'd sent me to the Alashi, I'd once found myself in danger, with a spell-chain at my disposal. I'd ordered the djinn to pick me up and carry me bodily back to Kyros. It had been a terrifying ride, but it had set me down so gently that I hadn't even stumbled. This ride was rougher, but less terrifying. I felt a wind, but it only whistled past my ears, it didn't sting my eyes. When I closed my eyes, I could still see the djinn, but now I saw it like a man made of fire, his arms wrapped around me as we flew over the steppe.

Below us, the ground rippled, then thrust up into hills that became mountains. We slowed, and over the roar of wind, I could hear the trickle of water. We crested a mountain peak, and we looked down, and I saw it.

I saw a lake spreading out, vast and dark, below us. I knew it was *the* lake—the reservoir held in place by the djinni, the bound river. The Syr Darya. Looking around, I could see the djinni that held it. *I could free them,* I thought, *but I'd need to really come here.*

I fell, suddenly. I remembered to suck in a gasp of breath before I hit the water; I splashed silently into it and found myself going down, down, down. I realized a moment later that I was still in the grip of a djinn.

There was a light ahead; through the water, I could hear the singing of beads. *It's here,* I thought. *The spell-chain.* But the djinn didn't take me to see it, though I knew it was close. Instead, it drew me past the glow. *Look,* I heard it hiss, and I looked around, again, at what seemed like a ruined temple, walls and a gate. *Look.*

Stone on stone, the threshold buried under layers of sand and mud, the archway opened into a tunnel. It was dim, deep under the water, even with the glow from the spell-chain and the unnatural sight that I seemed to have when I traveled like this. But the gate opened into a richer darkness than the one that surrounded me. I could have sworn, peering in, that the water disappeared; you could step through that gate and be elsewhere . . .

*This looks familiar,* I thought, and then remembered: *The Passage. Now Drowned.*

Passage to *what?*

Could I step through it and see?

Very hesitantly, I slipped my hand through. The djinn did not stop me. I put the other hand through. Then I stepped into darkness, and darkness enveloped me. I turned back to see where I had come from, and it was gone. I was shrouded in darkness.

*I am still in the borderland,* I reminded myself, trying not to panic. *There is always a way out.*

Someone seized my hands, and pulled, and I was in the steppe again, facing Tamar.

"*Lauria,*" she said, joyfully. "I'd almost given up looking for you. And then Janiya said . . . Where are you? Are you safe?"

"I'm in Penelopeia. We got away from Kyros—well, I think we did. Are *you* safe?"

"Yes," she said, though somehow I was certain she was lying. "I've seen Zivar. She went to Penelopeia—

I think *she* wants to help you. But she didn't take me along. I want to see you again." Her hands gripped my arms. "I miss you. I've been traveling with Janiya and Alibek . . . I probably shouldn't tell you why."

"Don't."

"I want to see you again."

"You will." I could feel hands grasping me, pulling me away from Tamar.

"*Swear* to me!"

We'd each cut the palms of our right hands when we'd become blood sisters, and I pressed my right palm to hers now. "I swear by our blood. I *will* come back to you."

Someone was shaking me awake; my shoulders ached from my arms being tied all night. "The searchers are close," Xanthe said. "We need to move."

"*How?* As soon as we're out, they'll find us, won't they?"

"It doesn't matter. They'll find us here soon enough. Come on!"

I stretched my aching legs and looked down at my bare feet. Xanthe tossed me a pair of sandals and a light cloak. "You should stay here," she said to my mother. "Just tell them I made you come along and didn't let you go for help."

My mother turned and looked at me—then at Xanthe, then at me again. She wanted to protect me, I realized; she wanted to be there to throw her body between me and any threat, but she also knew that she would slow us down. My chances were better if my mother stayed here. Hers, of course, were *vastly* better—no one was looking for her. Except for Kyros.

"If you go back to Kyros, and I'm still alive, he'll take you as a hostage," I said.

I had expected her to deny it, but instead she lifted her chin and said, "Then I won't go back to him."

"You can come if you want," I said, hesitating a moment despite the urgent fear that prickled from Xanthe like sweat.

"No," my mother said. "Xanthe is right. You go." She reached out and took my head in her hands, and kissed my forehead; I felt her hands clench against my hair, and then unclench as she pulled herself away. "Hurry," she said. "Go now."

I followed Xanthe under the rock and out to the bank of the canal. Penelopeia was a huge, sprawling city, and within a few minutes I knew that I would never find my way back the way we'd come without help. *Of course, if we're caught, we'll have plenty of help . . .*

Tamar had said Zivar was coming to Penelopeia. She would help me—she could help all of us. *Where will she go? We are the green mice in a world of owls. Surely we will find each other somehow.*

Where would she go to look for me? Well, the Koryphe, to start with. She'd find out soon enough that I'd vanished, so then what? It sounded like every aerika under the power of the Sisterhood was looking for me. She could send her own out, and some of them actually *knew* me and would be more likely to succeed in finding me, but still. She knew me; where would she expect me to go? *Out of the city and east toward the steppe.* Except, that was where the Sisterhood of Weavers no doubt expected me to go as well. I'd said once that if I were a slave escaping from Kyros, I'd head *away* from the steppe, hide, and wait for Kyros to give up searching before heading to freedom. Zivar was smart; she might guess that this would be my strategy. Maybe. Then again, I'd outlined my strategy to Kyros, and he was helping the Sisterhood search.

What if Zivar guessed that I knew she was here? If Tamar knew, she might assume that I knew. *Then* where would she go? She would want me to be able to find her. But neither of us knew the city. Where would a mouse go? *The mouse who nibbles daily at the foundation of her mistress's house. Where would she go?*

I caught Xanthe's arm. "Where is the Temple of Athena? Is there a big one?"

"Of course there's a big one. It's back on the other side of the canal. You want to go there? Are you crazy?"

"A friend of mine is in the city. A sorceress. I think she might look for me there. If we can find each other, she'll help us get away."

"Why would she look for you *there*?" Xanthe asked.

"Can you think of a better place to look for a green mouse?"

"You *are* crazy!"

"Then can you think of a worse place to look?" I said.

"If you're wrong, we'll be right in the nest of the vipers that want to find you. Us."

"We could split up."

"I'd cut your damn throat before I let you go," Xanthe said.

"Which way to the temple?"

"Follow me."

Fortunately, this was one place that the Weavers were *not* expecting us to go. We ducked our heads as we passed guards, but no one stopped us. Xanthe led us through a maze of streets and alleys and out, finally, into a big open plaza of white marble. "We're here," Xanthe said. "I really hope you're right."

I took a furtive look around. The temple was huge. The façade arched up over the square, casting a shadow over most of it even in late morning. To get in, you had to pass a statue of Athena that was at least twenty times the height of a real woman, painted to be lifelike. *They must have to have djinni touch up the paint and keep it clean,* I thought, looking it over. Then I took a closer look and realized that two djinni were posted at its feet just to keep it from toppling over.

*I could topple the statue*—that *would certainly get Zivar's attention. Too bad it would get everyone else's, too.* I looked around for Zivar again. *Is she here? Did I guess right?* People streamed in and out of the big door, around the statue. Here and there, groups of women stood visiting with each other, some resting their offerings on their hips. Surely Zivar would not be in a group. Were any women waiting alone?

*There.*

She had seen me. I started toward her, Xanthe hurrying after me.

Then, from the doorway of the temple, I heard someone shout, "*There* she is! Lauria!"

"Pretend you don't know me," I hissed to Xanthe, but she was already falling back. I turned toward the voice; there was not much use running now. Who was it? I laughed bitterly. It was Myron, one of Kyros's loyal Greek retainers. I'd last seen him in Daphnia, where he'd recognized me at an inconvenient time. Kyros must have sent for him just to help look for me. Few enough of the others would know my face if he saw it.

Myron was waving at me, the idiot. I waved back; why not? People were starting toward me; I could see them out of the corners of my eyes. I broke into a run, heading toward the temple as if I were going to meet Myron. No one stopped me; why run after me when they could just wait for me to come to them? Myron stood right in the doorway, a big smile on his face. "I knew it was all just some weird misunderstanding," he said. "How have you been?"

"Great," I said. "Never better." Then I reached behind him to touch the two djinni at the base of the statue. "Return to the Silent Lands, lost ones of your kind, and trouble us no more."

I had never freed two djinni at once before. Freeing even one was overwhelming enough, but I had done it enough times now that I knew what to expect. Two— I felt as if I'd tried to open a door a crack, and found it blasted open by a gust of wind strong enough to lift me off my feet. I had planned to run in the confusion after I freed the djinni, but I was riveted to the spot, unable to run even as I saw the statue begin to tip. The world slowed as it fell. Sound stopped, and I still couldn't move. The djinn passing through the gate within me screamed something to me, begging permission of some kind, and I assented, though I wasn't really sure what I was agreeing to.

*My brothers,* the djinn's voice echoed back, and I realized a moment later that there were *more* djinni, all imprisoned within the same spell-chain, responsible for holding up the Temple of Athena. Since they were all so close, and imprisoned in a single spell-chain with the djinni that had been holding up the statue, they could *all* pass through me into the Silent Lands. *Hurry,* I whispered inwardly, thinking that the statue would crush me in a moment.

*Do not fear.*

There was warmth within me, then heat flaring outward, out to my fingers and down to my heels; my body rocked. Closing my eyes, I thought I could see through the gate. I'd always pictured the world of the djinni as dim and shadowy, like the borderland, but I saw a light as bright as the sun. *The secret of flight,* I thought, and wondered what would happen if *I* stepped through the gate.

*Not this one,* one of the djinni said. *Not here.*

*I'm going to die, you know.*

*Not today.*

I could hear thunder. No, not thunder. It was the temple falling. And then I felt a jerk, as someone—something?—grabbed me off my feet. "I am Zivar's aeriko. Don't fight me," a voice said in my ear.

The gate had closed; I was myself again. And I had been jerked inside a palanquin. Blue and white silk fluttered around us: Zivar and Xanthe were both inside.

"What did you *do*?" Zivar asked.

"You *are* the spider," Xanthe said. I was uncertain if her voice held respect or loathing.

I drew the silk to the side and peered out. The temple was collapsing, one section after another falling in a crash of marble and dust. Zivar had pulled me out in the midst of the confusion. I let the curtain fall shut again and sat back against the cushion.

"You're going to tell me what's going on," Zivar said. *"Everything."*

"Of course," I said. "But first, can we get away from here?"

"Far, far away," Zivar agreed.

I relaxed against the cushion for a moment, then asked, *"How* far?"

"The land with no night," Zivar said. "If I'm going to *have* to travel by palanquin, I'm going to take it somewhere I haven't seen a thousand times."

# CHAPTER ELEVEN

# TAMAR

They're treating us pretty well for a couple of thieves."

"Shh. I'm sure they're listening to us."

"All I said was . . ."

"Just shut up, Alibek. I know what you said."

We were alone. The room was windowless, but otherwise pleasant. There was a lamp for light, a tray of little cakes, and a pot of tea. The chairs had cushions. We'd been thrust inside and left to wait. And wait. And wait. I thought they probably wanted us to talk to each other—that's why they'd put us in the room together. They were listening to us.

Even knowing they were listening, it was hard to keep silent. I wanted to ask Alibek if he thought they'd found Janiya. If he thought they'd execute us for our karenite, or guess we were spies. If Zivar would get in trouble. I chewed my lip and stayed silent.

Alibek laced his fingers together, pulled them apart, and laced them together again. I saw mockery in his eyes, but if I let him bait me, we might let something slip. I turned away from him to pace.

The door opened. I expected a sorceress, but a priestess came in with two guards. She sat down, arranged her hands, and gave us a bland smile. "First, I'd like to make sure you understand the seriousness of your crime," she said. "Soul-stone is the property of the Goddess Athena. Her rightful custodians are her priestesses and the Sisterhood of Weavers. By trading soul-stone, you have committed theft from Athena herself. Your lives are forfeit. The method of execution is . . . most unpleasant."

I shuddered. But I knew that they must want something from us, or we'd already be dead.

"However, I have the power to grant you a reprieve," she said. "*Should* you hand over all your soul-stone, immediately, I will arrange for your punishment to be lightened significantly."

"Lightened to *what*?" I asked.

"It doesn't matter," Alibek said. "We have nothing. You can search us and search our room—in fact, I'm sure you already have. You won't find anything."

The priestess's smile never wavered. "We're not stupid," she said. "We've searched your room, of course, but we know you left your soul-stone somewhere outside the city. Hidden, or with a confederate. We want it."

"And?" I said. I still wanted to know—if we handed our karenite over, would she let us just go free? Because we could always go up to the steppe to get more.

"You're not in a position to bargain," she said. "If we find what you're hiding before you tell us where to look, the deal's off. And don't think we aren't searching."

If Janiya knew we'd been captured, she'd already be on the run, and I didn't think they'd find her. So I just waited.

"If you hand over your soul-stone, we will spare your lives."

"No deal unless you promise our freedom," Alibek said.

"We will free *one* of you. That one can go get another load of soul-stone and trade it for the freedom of the other."

"How on earth would we get soul-stone without money?" Alibek said. "You seem to think we'd just go dig for it. If you're not going to pay for what you're planning to take, we won't be able to *get* more."

"Maybe not this month, or this year. Eventually, I'm sure you will." The priestess's smile grew wider. She thought she had us.

I shrugged. "I don't trust you," I said. "What's to stop you from taking our soul-stone and cutting our throats?"

"Believe me, if you don't deliver it up to us, you'll wish for a death so quick and painless."

If it had been just the two of us, I might have taken the deal. But there was no way to hand over the karenite without handing over Janiya. Did I trust *any* of the Weavers? Zivar, but I wasn't bringing *her* into this. But thinking of Zivar reminded me of the names she'd given me. One of them had been someone important . . .

"There's only one person in this city I would trust the word of," I said. Alibek looked up, startled. "Hypatia," I went on. "The Weaver Hypatia. If *she* promises me that *both* of us will walk free, I will show *her* where to find the soul-stone."

The priestess's smile thinned. Then she rose, sniffed, shrugged, and said, "I will send word to her."

When we were alone again—alone, except for the listeners I was still sure were there—Alibek said, "Hypatia. I hope she's as trustworthy as you think."

"Yeah," I said. "Me too."

*F*rom inside our windowless room, it was hard to tell how much time passed, but I thought Hypatia arrived remarkably quickly. She was young and beautiful—smooth skin, straight white teeth—but what really impressed me was how much work she surely was for her slaves. Her dark brown hair was sculpted into elaborate curls around her face, and she wore a great deal of jewelry, all polished and glittering. Her fingernails shone wetly in the lamplight, each filed into a perfect oval, and I wondered if her toenails were perfectly kept, too. I even glanced down, but her robes brushed the ground and kept me from seeing her feet.

"The priestesses told me their side of the situation," Hypatia said, with a nod toward the door and a raised eyebrow that said, *They're listening—watch your tongue.* "Why don't you give me your version. Either of you."

"The priestesses believe we're soul-stone sellers," I

said. "They also believe we have a cache of it outside the city. They've promised to pardon us if we turn it over, but I don't trust them. I trust you, but only if you take us out of here, somewhere that we can talk to you *alone*."

"That's an interesting request." Hypatia tapped one of her painted fingernails against the table. "But easily arranged." She opened the door and gestured for us to follow.

There were priestesses in the hallway, of course. One of them rushed up, protesting, but Hypatia shrugged her off. "I am a Weaver," she said. "Surely you don't think they're going to simply walk away from *me*. Step aside." And after a moment or two, the priestesses did. We went down a corridor, through a room, and out to a balcony.

I'd half expected it to be midnight, but it was only late afternoon. The sun was low and cast shadows that offered no real relief from the heat. A palanquin hovered by the balcony railing. "That's mine," Hypatia said. "Climb in."

Did she expect me to clamber over the balcony railing? How high up were we, anyway? I scrambled up, then through the curtained door and into the palanquin. Alibek followed me. I turned to watch Hypatia. Carried by her djinn, she glided smoothly through the air, landed without a sound inside the palanquin, and reclined calmly against one of the pillows. I felt the djinni lift up the palanquin.

I had never traveled this way. I had watched the djinn-borne wagon arrive when we'd helped Sophos's slaves to break out, and I had imagined what it would be like to travel with a sorceress, but it was both more terrifying and less terrifying than I'd imagined. Less terrifying because it flew so smoothly that with the curtains shut, I could barely tell we were moving. More terrifying because when I drew back a curtain and looked out for a moment, I saw how very *far* we were above the ground.

I closed the curtain again and forced myself to lean back against a pillow, trying to calm myself. I felt like I was inside a jewelry box. Everything was silk or velvet or embroidered or cushioned. My bolster was dark pink silk with tiny glass beads sewn on it to make a picture of a tree. I wondered if the inside of Zivar's palanquin looked like this. It probably matched her housekeeper Nurzhan's taste more than her own—I couldn't imagine Zivar spending a lot of time decorating her palanquin. I looked over at Hypatia again. What if this was an imposter?

"Right," I said, my voice a little shaky. "Before we go anywhere, I need to know for sure that you are who you say you are."

Hypatia shrugged. "Sophronia sent me a message about you," she said. "It said you had a proposal for me. I assume you took advantage of the greed of the Order's priestesses to demand to speak to me?"

"I heard you were well placed. I thought they might believe me when I said you were the only one I'd trust."

"Clever," Hypatia said. "Yes. They believed you. We can talk freely here, so speak your piece."

"I am here on behalf of the Alashi," I said. "We want an alliance with the Younger Sisters." I watched Hypatia carefully. She raised her eyebrows, but otherwise her face gave nothing away. "We can offer you soul-stone—lots of soul-stone. In return, we'd like you to move against the Sisterhood of Weavers."

"An insurrection can't be launched overnight," Hypatia said.

"No."

"And the Weavers are already moving against you. I assume this is why you are so eager to see us move against *them*."

"Yes."

"How much soul-stone can you give us, and how soon?"

"We have a companion with a large supply. Unfortunately, the priestesses already know it's out there."

"Hmmm. And after that?"

"We can give you more. If you want an ongoing supply, you'll have to distract the Sisterhood of Weavers soon enough to draw off their invasion of the steppe." Her lips twitched slightly and I found myself suddenly defensive. "We're hardly going to be able to find karenite for you if we're fighting off the army.".

"Yes, yes, of course. In the meantime, you mentioned a companion . . ."

I hesitated, and Hypatia gave me a gracious smile that made my hair stand on end. "An alliance is based on trust," she said. "Right now you need to trust me. I will not take you, or your companion, back to the priestesses at the temple."

I glanced at Alibek, then nodded. It was a little late to worry whether we could trust the Younger Sisters. This was the point of the mission. This was why we'd come.

"Janiya is waiting for us outside the city," I said. "Alibek, you visited her last . . ."

Hypatia had the djinni take her palanquin over the

Daphnia wall, then followed the Chirchik River as Alibek directed her to Janiya's hiding place. The palanquin settled gently onto the ground, and Alibek climbed out. I followed, thinking they must have caught her—I could see our horses grazing, but I didn't see Janiya anywhere.

"It's all right," Alibek said. "We think you'll want to talk with this one."

There was a rustle, and Janiya's head popped up above the bank. She'd hidden in a small cave when she saw the palanquin approaching. She reached back in and took out the bag of karenite. "We'll be wanting this, I assume?" She whistled for the horses, then looked at Hypatia's palanquin. "The horses can't ride in that thing."

"My servants will be along to take the horses in hand. They'll be well cared for. All three of you need to come with me now. Once we deliver the soul-stone to the priestesses who covet it, I'm taking you to speak with some of my associates."

Janiya looked at me, and at Alibek, and must have felt satisfied with what she saw in our faces, because she climbed in. We all settled ourselves again. Janiya handed me the bag of karenite, and I gave it to Hypatia. Hypatia looked inside, and for the first time since I'd laid eyes on her, her carefully sculpted mask slipped off. I saw shock that we could offer so much, so casually, along with raw desire for the power the karenite offered. I felt a flush of pity for the twenty-three djinni that would be enslaved with the stones in that bag. Still, at least I'd refused to bring the pile Janiya had brought out at first.

"The priestesses will not expect this much," Hypatia said after a moment. She moved one of her cushions aside and took out a silver box set with black stones. She put six of the karenite pieces into her own box, then closed it with a snap and hid it again. "This will be enough to satisfy them," she said, and drew the bag shut again.

When we arrived at the temple, she handed over the bag as quickly as she could and told her djinni to take us away again. I was relieved to leave the temple, and it wasn't until I realized we'd passed over the wall of the city that I asked her where we were going. I'd thought we would go to her house, but surely we'd passed it by now.

"I need to discuss your proposal with some of my sisters," she said.

"Where?" I asked again.

"Another city. We'll be there by morning."

"By morning?" I swallowed hard. "It's going to be night soon, don't we . . . *stop* somewhere?"

"The aerika need no daylight," Hypatia said. "We'll sleep in the palanquin."

Hypatia's palanquin had not only the plush lining of a jewelry box, but also the endless tiny compartments. Out of one came a wicker basket with a hinged lid, and out of the basket came supper for all of us. She laid out sliced roast lamb, soft rounds of bread, a sauce of sour yogurt with mint and cumin, crisp slices of radish, and glistening plums. There was even a carafe with some sort of sweet wine, and a plate for each of us. I folded my bread around the lamb and yogurt sauce and tried not to fret about where she might be taking us. How far could a palanquin travel in one night?

The sky grew dark and Hypatia lit a lamp as we finished our dinner. Then she summoned a djinn and had it whisk the dishes away. It brought them back clean and dry a few minutes later and she stacked them neatly in the wicker basket. Then the curtains drew back and a gentle breeze began to waft through the palanquin. It was pleasant. Hypatia stretched out on the carpeted floor of the palanquin, arranged her curls on the silk pillow, blew out the lamp, and closed her eyes.

When her breathing was slow and even, Janiya whispered, "Alibek, Tamar. No—don't say anything, I know we need to assume we're still being heard. I wanted to tell you I think you've done an excellent job. I heard about your arrest and was afraid I'd never see you again. I don't know how you convinced them to let Hypatia take you away, but good work."

"We don't know we can trust Hypatia . . ." I said.

"We can't ever know how the mission will turn out until it's over. Sometimes not even then. You've been very resourceful. I have high hopes."

I closed my eyes, feeling a bit lighter. I fell asleep and dreamed.

Visiting the borderland felt like slipping on a pair of well-worn boots. Even with my fear of Kyros lurking, coming to the borderland made me feel expansive and in control. I could go anywhere, find anyone—well, probably not *anyone*, but nearly anyone. I really ought to start by visiting Zhanna.

First, though, I checked for Lauria. I looked for the thread that bound us, and saw it shining bright. She was here. She was in the borderland!

But finding her was not so simple. The thread didn't budge. I tried to follow it but it led on and on, wending its way across an endless dark steppe. I was getting nowhere, though the landscape obligingly shifted to a city, then to rolling hills. I still didn't reach Lauria.

Where was she? Why couldn't I get to her?

I closed my eyes and imagined her standing before me. "Draw near, sister," I whispered. I felt her closeness like the beating of my own heart, but when I opened my eyes—nothing.

She was close. I knew she was close, so why couldn't I find her?

I started to walk again, following the silver thread, then imagined myself a bird and flew, to travel faster, but again . . . on and on, and no Lauria.

I threw myself to the ground, becoming Tamar again, fighting my own frustration. Anger was my enemy. If I got too frustrated, I would find myself back in my own head. I unclenched my fists and took a deep breath. I would find her. I was a shaman. I would find Lauria.

I closed my eyes again and willed her close to me. This time, when I thought she was near, I didn't open my eyes. I reached out my hands, told myself firmly that I *would* find her, clasped her hands, and drew her to me.

It worked. I felt a surge of elation as I stared into Lauria's startled eyes. *"Lauria,"* I said. "I'd almost given up looking for you. And then Janiya said . . ." I broke off, not wanting to waste time on that. She knew she'd spoken with Janiya. "Where are you? Are you safe?"

Lauria told me she was in Penelopeia and had gotten away from Kyros. Then she wanted to know if *I* was safe, and I lied and said I was. I told her Zivar was on her way, but had left me behind. I said I had been traveling with Janiya and Alibek, then broke off when I realized I couldn't tell her why. My throat ached. I wanted to rip through the fabric of the borderland and fight my way to her in the flesh. "I want to see you again," I whispered.

"You will," she said. Someone was pulling her away from me—she was waking up.

"*Swear* to me!" I said. I knew it was an absurd demand, but Lauria pressed her palm to mine, and swore.

When I woke, for a moment I couldn't remember where I was. I could see silk draping over my head like a tent. The rug I lay on was softer than the ground but harder than a real bed. I couldn't actually feel movement until I remembered where I was. I sat up and looked around. The sun filtered in through the sheer curtains, and the air felt cooler than I expected. Janiya and Alibek still slept. Hypatia was awake. "Tea?" she said.

She had a kettle of hot tea, and poured me a cup. I saw no stove. "Where did the tea come from?" I asked.

"I sent one of the aerika for it."

"Back to your house?"

"No, that's far enough away that the tea would have gotten cold." She sipped from her cup. "I sent the aeriko down to the ground with instructions to build a fire and boil the water, then put out the fire and bring the water up here."

I wondered if anyone had seen the kettle sailing through the air. Where were we? I wanted to look out, but couldn't bring myself to pull the curtain back.

"Go ahead and look," Hypatia said. "You won't fall. If you *did* somehow fall out, or if you jumped out on purpose, I'd send an aeriko to catch you."

That was only a little bit reassuring, but—goaded—I pulled the curtain open and looked out.

For a moment, nothing I saw made sense. There was a wide green expanse that looked like cloth unrolled on a floor. Tiny houses were scattered here and there like bones from a dice game. There was a silver line where the green cloth had been cut with scissors. Then my eyes began to piece together what lay below: rolling green fields, houses and farms, a river. Something was moving, and with a lurch I realized it was a bird flying *below* us.

I pulled my head back and rested it against the pillow for a moment, closing my eyes. I heard Hypatia chuckle dryly. "Look forward instead of down, and you'll see where we're going," she said.

I took a deep breath and looked out again. With the light behind me, I could see a long way. A white-topped mountain rose in the distance. Closer than that, I could see a city spreading across the plain, arrow-thin towers glinting in the morning sun. Casseia had one tower like that—built impossibly high by the labor of the djinni. This city had thirty or more. I pulled my head back inside. "That's Penelopeia," I said.

"You've visited before?"

"No." I wished she'd told me where we were going when I asked her last night. I could have told Lauria I was on my way to her. But I was sort of a prisoner, and the last thing I wanted was for Lauria to try to rescue me. "I'm right, aren't I? Only the City of Weavers would build so many towers like that."

"Yes," Hypatia said. She handed me a cup of tea.

Hypatia was unusually steady in her nature, for a sorceress. I had seen her neither frantic nor melancholic. I sipped my tea and studied her over the rim of my cup. She sipped hers and studied me. I bristled under her level gaze. Sophos had looked at me that way. So had Boradai. I distrusted that look, even if the eldress of the Alashi had looked at me that way, too.

"How did you come to the Alashi, Tamar?" Hypatia asked.

I considered telling her I'd been born Alashi, but I wanted her to trust me and telling a lie just because I resented her seemed like a bad idea. Runaway slaves could be returned to their masters, but if Hypatia wanted to turn on me, she had many easier options than taking me back to a dead man. Besides, she had called them *Alashi,* not bandits. She was trying to be courteous.

"I was a slave until I was fourteen," I said. "Then I ran away. Crossed the desert, and joined the Alashi." I straightened a little and rested my teacup against my crossed ankles. "How did you become a Weaver?"

"Apprenticeship," she said. "I was fourteen. A long time ago."

I felt the palanquin shift slightly—we were slowing, then sinking. My ears ached, then felt clogged like I had a bad cold. I peeked out and quickly pulled my head back inside. It looked like we were going to skewer ourselves on one of the towers. I swallowed hard and let the curtain fall shut. I heard a popping noise, and my ears cleared.

"Almost there," Hypatia said.

We came to rest with a gentle bump that woke

both Alibek and Janiya. Hypatia stepped out and gestured for us to follow.

We were on an interior balcony. The floor was white marble. Another sorceress stood nearby, and I hung back and watched as she and Hypatia clasped hands and kissed cheeks. A slave waited in the shadows of the doorway, and I edged away from the palanquin, trying to see her face. At a gesture from her mistress, she fetched a small trunk from the back of the palanquin. Hypatia hesitated and looked back at me. "I'm going to discuss matters with Rhea alone, first," she said. "Her servants will make you comfortable. We'll send for you in a bit. Have some breakfast."

I nodded. The sun was already hot. "Where are we?" Janiya asked.

"Penelopeia," I said.

Janiya's jaw tightened, and I saw her glance around, but there wasn't anywhere to flee even if we wanted to. Alibek arched an eyebrow at me. No doubt he was thinking of Lauria. I shrugged and followed the slave.

"Is the sorceress's name Rhea?" I asked the slave. I wished I had wine to slip to her.

"Yes," the slave said.

"What's your name?"

She shot me a *what the hell is it to you* look and said, "Parvaneh."

"Does Rhea have any children?"

"No."

"Is she married?"

"No."

So it was possible her servants had the upper hand, like Zivar's. Parvaneh passed the trunk to a young man, then straightened her back and lowered her eyes, putting on a proper demeanor like a cloak. "Would you care to refresh yourselves before breakfast?"

"Yes, thank you," I said. She wasn't as skittish as most slaves of sorceresses . . . of course, we were on foreign ground here. Maybe she was a freeborn servant and not a slave at all. She showed us directly to a privy, then to a small bath house where we could wash our faces and hands with cool water and scented soap. Then we followed her through a garden to a room of polished wood and indigo linen. A large fan of woven rushes and huge feathers hung on the wall. Parvaneh took it down, held it up, and waited. The fan leapt lightly from her hand, hovered a moment, then began to fan us. A djinn, no doubt. The breeze gave only a little relief from the heat.

Parvaneh bowed. "I will return in a moment with some refreshment for you," she said.

As soon as the door closed, Alibek rose to glare at the fan. "That's a djinn," he said.

"Yes." Janiya, sitting on the couch, barely glanced up.

"Is it listening to us?"

"Probably," I said. "They aren't very good spies, but the Weaver could have it repeat our conversation word for word. At least it's fanning us while it's listening."

"What if we wanted it to stop?"

"Ask it to stop and see what happens," I said.

"What if it won't start again? It's hot." Alibek moved a little closer to the fan, to see what the djinn would do. It backed the fan up so it wouldn't brush against him. When he'd backed the djinn all the way to the wall, it flipped the fan up to the ceiling, sailed it across the room, and then set to work fanning us from the other side.

"Leave it alone, Alibek," Janiya said. "It's a slave. Would you harass a human slave?"

Alibek sat down. Janiya paced, then moved over and said quietly in my ear, "I did as you asked."

It took me a moment to think of what she might be talking about. *Xanthe.* "It worked?"

Janiya's eyes were shadowed. "She can't be trusted," she said.

"Why?"

"I can't explain right now. But—do not rely on her."

Parvaneh came back, trailed by a half dozen young girls carrying platters and pitchers. They had a pot of tea, a basket of fruit, a platter of cold meat, a platter of cheese, another basket of freshly cooked rounds of thin bread, a spread made from beans mashed with spices, and a silver pitcher. With a hint of a flourish, Parvaneh picked up the pitcher and filled three tall cups, handing them to each of us. I took a sip. It was some sort of juice, but *cold* like water from a stream. Colder. Parvaneh smiled at my shocked look. "One of the aerika fetches snow down from the mountain each morning, and we keep it in our cellar. Rhea finds chilled drinks refreshing in the summer."

A djinn to fan guests, another to fetch snow . . . There was a purpose to Rhea's fondness for luxury. It was a way to show her power. She had so many djinni at her disposal that she could use them for her whims. I wondered how many of these djinni were bound by Rhea, and how many were bound by her apprentices.

Probably most were bound by her apprentices, just like Hypatia's.

The basket of fruit held plums, grapes, and several fruits I didn't recognize, including one that looked like a stubby yellow finger. One of the young girls noticed me looking at it. She deftly stripped the peel off for me, then sliced it and put it on a plate. I had to at least try it after that. It was sweet, but had a strange, pasty texture—not juicy, like I'd expected. I washed it down with some of the cold juice and took some bread and cheese.

As we finished our breakfast, we heard a rumble somewhere far away. It grew louder, to a distant roar. Janiya leapt up. "Earthquake," she said. "Get outside—hurry!"

The djinn continued to wave the fan back and forth as we bolted out to the courtyard. Then we paused. I listened, but heard nothing more. The ground was still. I looked at Janiya. She shook her head. "I don't know what else it could have been . . ."

We waited a little longer. Beyond the wall, I could hear noise from the street—people coming out, talking excitedly. Looking up, I thought I saw the glimmer of djinni as every sorceress in the neighborhood sent one out to see what was going on. I looked around the courtyard. One of Rhea's slaves was scrubbing tile. "What was that noise?" I asked her. She gave me a mute shrug and went back to scrubbing.

"Excuse me." Parvaneh had come out looking for us. "If you are done with breakfast, Rhea would like you to come up to her receiving room."

We followed Parvaneh inside and upstairs. "What was that noise?" I asked.

"I have never heard a noise quite like that before," Parvaneh said. "I don't know what it was, but I trust we'll learn soon enough. Here we are . . ." We'd reached a closed door. She knocked twice, waited for a muffled answer from the other side, and swung it open.

I had expected to see just Rhea and Hypatia. Instead, a half dozen women sat around a table. Though I assumed they were all "Younger Sisters," not all were young. One had a deeply lined face, and another had white hair. Rhea held the box of karenite that Hypatia had set aside back in Daphnia. She opened it and laid out the six stones on the table. They caught the sunlight shining through the gauzy linen curtains.

"What is it you are offering, exactly, and what do you want in return?" Rhea asked.

I looked at Janiya—she was the leader, after all—but she gestured for me to go ahead. So I took a deep breath and stepped forward. "The Alashi are offering an alliance with the Younger Sisters. We'll supply you with karenite. In exchange—well, we know you're plotting against the Sisterhood of Weavers. We want you to move against them—now."

"Now?" Rhea raised an eyebrow. "Today? Tomorrow?"

"Soon. They're moving against *us*, you see. If we're to continue providing you with karenite, we need them distracted."

"And if we do move against them—if we overthrow them—then what? Will you continue to send us karenite?"

"We'll sell it to you directly."

"Exclusively to us?"

I glanced at Janiya, and she gave me a slight nod. "Yes," I said.

The women at the table exchanged glances. There was a pause.

"We would need karenite *before* we could move against the Sisterhood," Hypatia said. "A great deal of it, in order to make spell-chains. We could not move against them today, or even next week."

"We don't have a lot of time," I said.

Hypatia turned her palms up in a silent shrug.

"Can you get us more karenite?" one of the other sorceresses asked. "Say . . . five hundred pieces?"

Janiya stepped forward. "You ask for much, and promise nothing," she said. "We gave Hypatia what we had with us, and she handed most of it over to the Temple of Athena in Daphnia. We have no more *here*, far from the steppe."

I saw a flicker from the corner of my eye: a djinn. Rhea saw it, too, and I saw her look toward it, then back to me. She gestured to Parvaneh, starting to say something about talking more later, but was interrupted by the djinn.

"The noise you sent me to investigate was the sound of the Temple of Athena collapsing," it said.

There were gasps from around the table. *"How?"* Hypatia asked.

"The gate freed the bound ones that held up the temple roof."

"Where is she now?" Rhea whispered.

"I don't know."

"Go look," she said venomously. The shimmer in the air disappeared.

"It'll never find her . . ." Hypatia said.

"I don't care. I want it looking. Those *fools,*" she

muttered. "I thought Ensiyeh at least would have the sense . . ." Her voice trailed off, and her eyes focused on me. Her lips tightened. "We'll discuss your proposal more later," she said. "The servants will show you back downstairs."

I followed Parvaneh back to the room where we'd waited. The snap of her fingers brought a girl with a fresh basket of fruit and another chilled pitcher of juice. Parvaneh poured us drinks, though I thought she was almost as distracted by the news as I was.

The gate. That was Lauria, I thought.

And it sounded like she'd gotten away.

# CHAPTER TWELVE

# LAURIA

Zivar's palanquin smelled funny—she didn't use it much, and it had a musty odor. It was crowded full of all the strange things she'd thrown in for her trip. The basket of carefully packed food was no doubt her servants' doing; the uneven pile of notebooks no doubt Zivar's. The pillows were practical, but she'd put in so many you could barely see the rug on the floor. I had no idea why she had brought a silver pitcher, a freshly dug rosebush, or the huge seashell she normally used when she was working on a spell-chain. I arranged myself around the clutter. Xanthe, beside me, sat bolt upright, looking terrified.

"Are we being followed?" I asked.

Zivar pulled a spell-chain out from under her gown; she clasped it for a moment and murmured under her breath. "One approaches," she said a moment later.

*I'm only going to have one chance,* I thought. *Either they're sending it to kill me, or they're sending it to grab me and bring me back so that another one can kill me.* I looked around wildly—they could be hard to see in daylight. But in the curtained interior of the palanquin, I saw its light, and as it lunged for me I had the momentary impression of a face. *It's here to kill me,* I thought. I flung my hands out and hissed the words to banish it.

*It has begun,* it said before it vanished to the other side.

The palanquin was very quiet when I returned to myself. Xanthe and Zivar were both staring at me. "Lauria," Zivar said. "I'm going to just call you Lauria, and not Xanthe—I think it would be rather confusing to call you Xanthe, seeing as you brought along a Xanthe, don't you agree? *What did you just do?*"

"I freed it," I said.

"The aeriko?"

"Yes."

"*How?*"

"I don't know how," I said. "There is a gate. Inside me. That's what the djinni—aerika—all say. When I touch them, they can return to where they came from, even if they're bound." I glanced at Xanthe; her face was rigid and unreadable. "This is why the Sisterhood wanted me dead. This is why they thought they needed to kill me in some unusual way. Apparently there have been people who could do this before."

Zivar chewed on her lower lip, her eyes glinting. "They must be terrified of you," she said.

"They are," Xanthe said softly.

"I heard murmurs of this even last winter," Zivar said. "When your old master's aerika disappeared. Then more talk, after you left. There have been people with gates within them before. Their deaths caused *difficulties.*"

Xanthe raised her head. "They were going to have an aeriko kill her," she said.

"That wouldn't have worked," I said. "Nothing ever works twice."

"How do you know about this?" Xanthe asked.

I shrugged. "I . . . the djinni showed me one night."

"Can *you* close the gate?" Xanthe asked.

"It only opens when I will it," I said. "Zivar's aeriko isn't going to slip through and let the palanquin fall." Zivar cackled a little at that.

"More are going to be coming," Zivar said. "They can't just let you get away." She fished a half dozen more spell-chains out from under her gown; they glittered in her palm as she murmured something under her breath. "Might as well make it hard for them," she said. "I told my aerika to hurry it up, and to take a circuitous route. We'll try to lose them, or outrun them."

Xanthe looked pale and tense; her knees were drawn up against her chest. She didn't want to meet Zivar's eyes, or look at anyone else.

"Thank you," I said. "Without you, I'd be dead."

Xanthe let out a grim little chuckle and said nothing.

"Why did you help me?"

Her jaw worked and she lowered her eyes to stare at the rug under her feet. "My mother . . . Janiya appeared to me the other night, in my dream." She fell silent.

"Did she ask you to help me?"

"No, actually. She just said she was sorry she'd left me. She cried, and wanted to kiss me, but I didn't let her. I wanted to ask her more questions, but then the dream slipped away. I thought I'd ask *you* more questions instead, but then I found out they were planning to kill you *that day*. If I *ever* wanted a chance to question you more, I had to get you away, so that's what I did. It was an impulse." *A stupid impulse.* I swore I could hear the unsaid words echoing in her thoughts. "If I'd stopped to think, I'd have known the price was too high."

"You did the right thing," Zivar said. Xanthe turned her miserable eyes on Zivar, who was tucking her spell-chains back into her gown. "Their plan wouldn't have worked. Also, Lauria is a nice person. Saving her life was a good thing."

*I guess I'm glad to hear you say that,* I thought, and swallowed hard, thinking about how easily Zivar could let me be killed. I looked back at Xanthe, doubting her story. Could she really have gotten me out of the Koryphe entirely on her own? I thought I remembered a guard who'd turned away, and surely that secret door would ordinarily have been guarded? But perhaps the guards were so loyal to each other they'd do each other favors, without asking questions. When Janiya was a young guard, I thought she might have been willing to leave a door unguarded for a minute or two, "accidentally," if asked by a friend.

"If Janiya had asked me to save you, I'd have let you die," Xanthe muttered.

"Someone is coming," Zivar said.

I leaned out and looked. Another palanquin was approaching. "It's a sorceress," I said, pulling my head back in.

"You don't have to be a sorceress to ride in a palanquin," Zivar said. "I believe there are guards in that palanquin, with orders to seize you. Human guards, who can't be banished with a touch." She fingered her spell-chains again, and this time spoke aloud, so that I—not just the djinni—could hear her. "Keep us away from that palanquin. They're here for Lauria, for your *gate*. If you want her to stay safe, you'd better keep us away." She tucked the spell-chains back into her dress. "We'll see how much they want to protect you, now, won't we?"

There was no discernible change—though in the shuttered box of the palanquin, it was hard to tell how fast we were moving. I looked out. "They're getting closer," I said.

"We are outnumbered and cannot outrun," something hissed in my ear, and I nearly leapt to my feet before realizing it had the voice of a djinn. "We can outmaneuver."

Another voice spoke. "We will protect you. Trust us."

"And hold on tight."

I looked at Zivar, who arched one eyebrow and said nothing.

I looked out again. We were almost side by side. Someone was pulling back the curtains of the other palanquin; and Zivar had been right—I could see women, guards, crowded inside. Then one reached out for us, and our palanquin shot suddenly upward. I heard the guardwoman's scream as she plummeted, and I hoped her death didn't free one of Zivar's djinni. *Surely not. It just moved the palanquin, it never touched her* ... And Zivar didn't collapse screaming and dying to the floor of the palanquin, so apparently not.

They were approaching again, this time from below. One of them shot something like an arrow at us, a rope trailing behind. *An anchor.* It was deflected by one of the djinni—as were the next dozen that were shot at us.

Xanthe's hands were gripped into fists against the pillow she was sitting on. Her knuckles were white.

Another hail of arrows started—this time, they were fire arrows, and one of them found its way past the djinni and landed inside the palanquin. Xanthe jumped up and smothered the flame with one of the pillows. "Send a djinn to steal the arrows," I said to Zivar.

Zivar nodded, her hands already twisting the spell-chains. "Are you going to fire them back down?" she asked.

I hadn't really thought about it. "I could try ... I'm not very good with a bow. But if we take their arrows, they can't fire any more at us."

The djinn returned with a whirl of bits and pieces—arrows, bows, an extinguished torch, the grappling hooks—and set them in a tangle on the rug of our palanquin. "Steal the rest of their equipment, too," I suggested. "Whatever they've got that the djinn can take without hurting anyone ..."

This time, the djinn returned with a larger pile—swords, helmets, pillows and rugs, even—to my shocked amusement—a spell-chain, which Zivar snatched up and added to her own collection, sum-

moning the djinn a moment later to her side. I
watched for another djinn—surely, I thought, they'd
send one to try to get their stuff back. *Yes.* There it
was, and in a breath, I was able to lay hands on it and
send it *away.*

"It's slowing down," Xanthe said, looking out of
our palanquin. "Falling behind."

"Let's come around for one more pass," I said. "If
we pass underneath, I can free the djinni that are carrying the palanquin."

"No!" Xanthe sat bolt upright, horrified. "These
are *friends* of mine. People I *know*—you can't,
please . . ."

I bit my lip and didn't argue. "Zivar. Your new
spell-chain—have that djinn carry them safely to the
ground, so they aren't hurt. Is that all right?" I looked
at Xanthe. She nodded and wiped her eyes with the
heel of her hand. "They won't be hurt. Now take us
in under them . . ."

There were four djinni left. Zivar's djinn brought
us up under the other palanquin; looking out, I could
see them, but they were out of my reach. "We can't go
any closer," Zivar said. "Do you *need* to free them?"

"If I do, they can't follow us to see where we go," I
said. Holding my breath and keeping my eyes away
from the ground, I leaned out the door, grabbed the
roof of the palanquin, and hoisted myself onto it.
Then I crawled to the center. It was canvas, drawn
tight over the ribs of the frame; it easily held my
weight. But the djinni were still just out of my reach.
*I have to hurry and do this before the guards realize
I'm standing right under them.* My stomach lurched
as I let go. We were moving faster than the swiftest
horse, but the palanquin was at least the size of a

large wagon. *Even if I fall down, I'll just fall onto the canvas again. Not all the way to the ground.* I wanted to crawl to the edge and peer over the side before I committed myself, but that would have been stupid, and I knew it. *I have to do this, or coming out here was awfully stupid. I didn't fall when I let go, and I'm not going to fall when I stand up.*

I took a deep breath.

"I am the one who was sent to free the rivers," I said out loud. "I cannot fail."

I braced my feet against the ribs under the canvas and braced my body against the wind as I rose slowly to my feet. The slightest shift could knock me from my perch; I needed to do this quickly. I reached up, and realized as I tipped my head back that the djinni were reaching for me, straining to touch me from where they were held by their orders. I could touch all four. "Return," I said, and opened the gate in my heart.

I felt a rush of sudden heat like a blast of hot wind, and I threw myself down to the roof of the palanquin, grabbing the ribs under the canvas with both hands. Within, I could see the four djinni passing into a narrow tunnel, but it seemed to be closing on me even as I struggled to hold it open. I was being crushed, pressed, smothered. I thought I heard the djinni talking, then realized it was Xanthe's voice shouting. The tunnel was still there, a whirl of fire in the darkness around me, but everything else was going away; I couldn't breathe.

Then it was gone, and I could breathe again. "Lauria!" someone was shouting. Their voice was muffled. "Do we need to cut a hole in the roof or can you crawl back down here?"

I was sprawled on the roof of the palanquin. The voice was coming from inside.

"I'm all right," I said. My voice was a croak, but everyone inside fell silent, so I said it again. "I'm all right. I think I can get back inside."

"If you swear you won't *free* it, I'll send an aeriko to carry you in," Zivar said.

"I won't free your aeriko," I said. *Not right now, anyway.* It was a relief not to have to try to climb down and crawl back inside. My whole body felt bruised. I wasn't sure I'd have the strength in my hands to hold on.

The djinn was over me now. I had the sense of a woman looking solemnly into my face. I swallowed hard, and let go of the palanquin's roof. The djinn gathered me up as if I were a cat, supporting me gently as it lifted me off the roof. "Don't fear," it whispered. "You will not fall."

It slid me over the edge and for a moment, I hung in the air, nothing below me. I took a quick look down since I didn't have to worry about freezing up and falling. The ground was a *long* way down. Palanquins fly high, of course, but I could swear we were as high as a mountaintop with nothing—*nothing*—below us except possibly some birds. Then we went through the doorway, and the djinn laid me down on the cushions, and I could breathe again.

"Well," Zivar said, embarrassed. "*That* could have been planned better."

"What do you mean?" I asked.

Xanthe glared at me. "She means that she didn't give precise enough instructions to the aeriko that was supposed to pick up the other palanquin and take it safely to the ground. When you freed the aerika that were carrying it, they dropped it *onto you*. Zivar's aerika didn't pick it up because it was resting on our roof—its instruction was to *not let it fall* and, well, it wasn't falling, was it? She had to bring it back, give it a new instruction, and send it back up there to lift the palanquin off you. You could have died!"

Zivar gave me a mute, apologetic shrug.

"Well." I felt the tender spots on my face, my breasts, my arms and legs. "I don't think anything's broken."

Zivar still looked embarrassed. "I'm really sorry."

"This sort of thing happens when you're working with djinni," I said. "Aerika, I mean. I could tell you some stories from when I was still working for Kyros . . ." I shrugged again. "Did the other palanquin . . ."

"It's safely on the ground," Xanthe said.

"My aerika are watching to see if they have any other spies to send after us, but I don't think they do," Zivar said. "I think we've shaken pursuit. For now."

"Aerika aren't supposed to be very good at finding people," Xanthe said.

"No," I said. I had recovered enough to sit up, arrange myself on the pillows, cross my legs. "They're not. But if they're determined enough—if they send out enough—they'll find us. They'll find *me*. It's just a matter of time."

We traveled through the day and into the night without stopping. "Aerika don't get tired," Zivar said when Xanthe suggested that we put down for the night. She had a chamber pot for us to pee in, though no screen to hide behind. It was emptied by a djinn. When Xanthe hesitated to use the pot, Zivar offered to have a djinn carry her down to the ground, and then back up when she was done. She blanched, hesitated a bit longer, and finally used it. But she refused tea the next time Zivar offered it.

Zivar had a kettle and—terrifyingly—a tiny stove to heat water. Her servants, fortunately, had packed a generous hamper full of food before she left. I dug out some thin bread, slightly stale, and a covered bowl of hummus, along with a sack of plums. I was ravenously hungry; I tried to remember my last proper meal, and I was pretty sure it was lost in the mists of the drugs they'd given me. This wasn't exactly a proper meal, either, but we had a great deal of time and no shortage of food, so I ate bread and hummus until I was sick of both, then turned to plums, then to cheese.

"Where are we going?" Xanthe asked.

"North," Zivar said. "To the place where there's no night."

Xanthe bit her lip and looked at me. She wanted to talk to me privately. When I didn't say anything, she asked, "How far is that?"

"A couple of days . . . I don't really know. When we stop seeing night, we'll know we're there, won't we?"

I wanted to pace, as the day wore on, but within the palanquin I really couldn't. It was the size of a small room; there was room for all three of us to stretch out, side by side, but barely. The rest of the space was taken up by the hamper of food, all the gear we'd stolen from the guardswomen in the other palanquin, and the miscellaneous junk Zivar had brought along. Even just reaching for food from the hamper, I kept getting jabbed by the rosebush.

When I'd felt like this, traveling with Tamar, I'd gotten off my horse to run alongside for a while but that wasn't really an option here. I tried to stifle the itch that rose up inside me, without success. I fidgeted, instead—tapping my feet against the floor. *If my mother were here, she would tell me not to fidget.* That started me worrying about my mother. Was she alive or dead? Free or captured? Had Kyros spared searchers to find her, knowing her potential as a hostage? The worries circled through my thoughts like a noisy parade: *alive or dead? Free or captured? Alive or dead? Free or captured?*

It was a relief when Xanthe interrupted. "Tell me about my mother's crime. What do you know about what she did? Do you *know* that she was innocent, or were you just saying that to try to persuade me?"

*If even Zhanna isn't sure, I don't think I know either.* I evaded. "Janiya is no common thief."

"What did she steal?" Zivar asked. "Or what was she accused of stealing?"

Xanthe was waiting for my answer. "A spell-chain," I said. "An *important* spell-chain. The one that binds the Syr Darya."

"That was *your mother*?" Zivar said, turning to Xanthe.

"Did you know of this at the time?" I asked.

"When was this? A bit over ten years ago?"

"Thirteen years," Xanthe said.

"What do you know of it?" I asked.

"I was always a good listener—good at hearing things I wasn't supposed to hear. Mila—the Weaver I apprenticed with—was entangled, that spring, in some sort of conspiracy." Zivar gave me a brief nod, as if to acknowledge the truth she knew I knew: that Mila had been her owner, and she had been a slave who had learned sorcery by spying on her mistress. "I overheard rumors about a theft of something extraordinarily powerful."

"Was Mila involved?" I asked.

"I think so, yes. I think that's why she was killed."

"Killed?" I said. "I thought it was an accident. Someone misusing a spell-chain out of arrogance, or stupidity."

"Yes, that's what they wanted everyone to think," Zivar said. "That's what I assumed for years, but then we had that little chat, you and I, and you said that a certain Greek officer would only use a spell-chain that way *if he were ordered to do so by the Sisterhood,* and if they could give him certain guarantees of safety. I lay awake for weeks, thinking that over. And yes. I think that is what happened to Mila. They knew about the conspiracy and took care of it."

"If there was a conspiracy, why was my mother blamed?" Xanthe asked, softly.

Zivar looked over at her: at her earrings, her tattoo, the sword that rested by her feet while we traveled. "Tell me about your mother," she said.

"I don't remember her all that well," Xanthe said. "She raised me until I was six. Then one day she was arrested. Accused of theft of a spell-chain. An *important* spell-chain. For a few weeks, everyone thought she would be executed. Instead she was stripped of her rank and sold into slavery. I was raised by one of her friends, Photine, until she died from a sickness when I was twelve. After that, I joined the Sisterhood Guard myself." Xanthe cleared her throat. "You say some *conspiracy* was to blame. Surely they *knew* that. If this is true, then why—my mother—why?" Her voice went suddenly very thin.

Zivar gave her a long, level look. "There are several possibilities, of course. One is that the magias disagreed." She turned her palms up. "Surely there are loyalties, even now."

"My loyalty is always to the serpent," Xanthe said. "To whoever holds it."

*Yet you freed me when the magia wanted me dead.* I decided not to point that out.

"Anyway, it's awkward to admit a mistake," Zivar said. "It shakes the illusion that the magias operate as one. Another possibility is that they needed someone to blame publicly, having taken care of the erring sorceresses privately. Your mother was convenient. She might have angered the wrong person. Finally, there is the possibility that your mother *was* involved. I only know that Mila was involved, not who else might have been; I see no reason to assume it was *only* Weavers."

Watching Xanthe, I saw her relax slightly, at that possibility. *My mother really was a criminal. All is still right with the world.* Zivar saw it, too, and laughed, very faintly, under her breath.

"Make no mistake, Xanthe," she said. "These are not *nice* people. Whether your mother was guilty or innocent would have been irrelevant. She was not a Weaver; therefore, she was expendable. She had sworn her life to the service of the Weavers; therefore, if the Weavers needed for her to take blame for a crime she did not commit, in their eyes it was her duty and her privilege to submit to their punishment. They probably felt that they were being very kind and merciful, not having her executed."

Xanthe drew the curtain aside to stare outside. I studied her face; Zivar laughed softly to herself. Tension still coursed through Xanthe's body. Her face was rigid, impossible for me to read.

"One of the magias was removed shortly afterward," Zivar said. "Sometimes one will get unmanageable, and when that happens, the other three have her confined. There are loyalties among the guards—surely you do *know* of this, Xanthe. Perhaps your mother's loyalty was to the magia who was removed. Perhaps that's why she was punished so harshly."

Xanthe swallowed hard. "Yes," she said, very softly. "I believe you may be right."

*If Xanthe freed me on Sophia's orders, or Phile's, was Zivar part of the plan? Surely not.* Xanthe glanced back at me, her nervous eyes flickering quickly over my face. Her expression was still unreadable. *It took me a whole summer to turn against the Greeks. Surely Xanthe is hiding something.*

*I did turn against them in the end. And they took Xanthe's mother from her. But surely, right now, she's still hiding her real loyalties. She won't even meet my eyes, and that's not just shyness. Xanthe isn't shy.* I tried to remember whether she'd ever looked at me straight on before our escape, and couldn't. Before my illness, she'd spent as little time in my company as she could manage. I remembered her looking me full in the face when I was still too drugged to see straight. But other than that, it was hard to say whether she'd ever met my gaze.

Night fell. Zivar stretched out and went to sleep; I thought Xanthe lay awake for a while, then she fell

asleep, too. I lay awake, thinking about the djinni
that even now were no doubt searching for me, thinking about the battles that raged on the steppe. I could
hear my heart beating in my ears, racing like an out-
of-control horse. My whole body pulsed with energy,
but I had nowhere to go and nothing to do with it.

*Rivers,* part of my mind whispered. Or maybe
djinni? Was I hearing djinni, speaking beyond that
gate in my heart? *Rivers.*

I started listening for the sound of trickling water,
then pulled back. If I stayed away from the borderland, Kyros would not be able to find me; if Kyros
could not find me, he could not threaten my mother,
even if he had her. Of course, I wouldn't be able to
talk to Tamar, either. *Doesn't matter. I need to stay
away.*

I lay awake in the dark for hours, dropped into a
light doze for a bit, then woke again, still in darkness.
*Tamar said that I could return to the Alashi,* I remembered, *but surely they've sent watchers there. If I go
to the Alashi they'll find me. But is there anywhere I
can go where I can truly hide? Is there anything I can
do to help the Alashi, before the Greeks wipe them
out?*

The Greeks were using djinni against the Alashi. If
I joined the Alashi on the steppe, I could free the
djinni that were being used on the battlefield. Well,
some of them, anyway. I thought about what I'd seen
in the vision of the battle. *It wouldn't change anything. It would help, but it wouldn't make a real difference.*

*But if I freed the djinni that bind the river . . .*

Well, that might make a difference. The floodwaters would sweep away most of the outposts along

the frontier. That would be a potent distraction. Not to mention that everyone said that the rivers' return would free the Danibeki slaves. This would be only one of the two rivers, but still, it was hard to imagine that anyone, Greek or Danibeki, would look at the waters crashing down from the mountains and not see the beginning of the defeat of the Sisterhood of Weavers.

The palanquin was still headed north, and even with my hours of lying awake I thought the night seemed short. We ate the last of the food for breakfast, and to my relief, Zivar decided to stop somewhere to buy more. She selected a tiny cluster of houses from the air: "There." The descent made me feel a bit ill, and when we stopped with a gentle bump in the center of the village, it felt like we were still moving; I stood up to step out and immediately stumbled.

Everyone in the village had run out of their houses to stare at us, but we quickly realized they didn't speak Greek. Zivar tried some other languages— Persian, I thought, then something else—with no better luck. So she dragged out the empty hamper, gestured to it and pantomimed eating something. Then she opened her purse to show them the coins inside, then gestured again to the hamper.

That worked—mostly. They brought cheese and thick loaves of bread, but Zivar had to stop them from putting in a live chicken. "It has to be cooked. READY TO EAT," she said, shouting as if that would make her words easier to understand. "No chickens! No sheep, either!"

The villagers were odd looking. Their skin was much paler than normal. I'd seen someone that pale—who wasn't sick—once before, when the traders had come to the Alashi sisterhood during the summer. One had had pale skin, blue eyes, and yellow hair. I thought some of the villagers here had blue eyes; I saw no yellow hair, but some of them had hair the color of dry sand. They were polite and helpful, though, despite the fact that they couldn't speak our language.

Xanthe pulled me aside. "Where are we going?"

"Zivar said something about the land with no night," I said. "It's north of here . . . somewhere . . ."

Xanthe shook her head impatiently. "That's not where I want to go."

"Where do you want to go?"

Xanthe turned away from me, looking south, the way we'd come. "You can free djinni. So you could free the *river,* if you went to where the Sisterhood of Weavers dammed it."

"Yes," I said, and eyed Xanthe, who was still looking south.

"That would hurt the Weavers, wouldn't it?"

"Hurt them? I don't know. It would make them angry."

"Furiously angry." Xanthe was still looking south. Her eyes widened slightly at the thought.

"Do you want to hurt them?" I asked. "Make them angry?"

"Yes," Xanthe whispered. "They took my mother."

She was still staring south. *Why?* I wondered, but the curiosity about her motives was drowned out by my rising excitement—*this could be possible, really possible, I could do this . . .* "I'll try to persuade Zivar," I said.

The hamper full, the villagers counting their

money, one of the men gestured for us to follow him, making *eat, eat* gestures. Zivar glanced at us, then shrugged and followed. He led us into the largest of the houses, where we took seats around a table. Villagers crowded in to watch us eat and the man who'd invited us brought out a roast leg of mutton, with roast carrots and tiny fresh-shelled peas. The mutton was tough, but the vegetables were welcome; I thought I could have made a meal of carrots and peas. They filled our glasses with something I initially took for cider, but it was bitter instead of sour. After the shock of the first sip, I decided it was drinkable. Better than kumiss, at least.

When we returned to the palanquin, I waited until the djinn had lifted us high into the air, then said, "Do you think there's any chance they'll tell the Sisterhood where we are?"

"How?" Zivar asked. "They're months of travel from Penelopeia. They don't even speak a civilized language."

"Someone there might have a spell-chain," I said. "I bet the Weavers told everyone with a spell-chain to watch for us. And just because we didn't see anyone there who spoke Greek doesn't mean no one there does."

"A spell-chain? In that tiny little backwater? Don't worry about it." Zivar kicked her feet out and crossed her ankles.

"You don't *know* they didn't have one," I said. "Maybe they invited us to stay and eat because they were trying to delay us."

"They just wanted more money," Zivar said.

"They made us *think* they just wanted more money."

"You really think they might have had a spell-chain?" Zivar looked a little doubtful now. "Who would have had it?"

"There could have been a sorceress there," I said. "Or a trader. Or even an officer . . ." Unlikely, but I watched Zivar think it over, and I could see doubt creeping in. "If they know we've been here, they'll know where to look for us."

"That's true," she said.

"I think we should change direction."

"And go where?"

"The drowned valley, where they imprisoned the northern great river."

"The Jaxartes, you mean."

"The Syr Darya," I corrected her.

"Why do you want to go there? Oh, I know. You told me once you want to free the rivers! I told you the southern one belongs to Persia now—how are you going to get that one back?"

"Persia can keep it. I don't know how I would get it back."

"But you want to free the Jaxartes." Zivar's eyes searched mine. "Why?"

My answers spilled out, one after another: "Because it might save the Alashi. Because it will infuriate the Weavers. Because everyone says that the rivers' return will free the Danibeki slaves, and I think even one river returning will free more than I could free in a lifetime. Because I *can*." *Because I think I'm meant to.* I closed my mouth on that answer; I wasn't sure Zivar would understand it.

"What do you care about freeing the Danibeki slaves? If they had any gumption, they'd free themselves, wouldn't they? Isn't that what the Alashi say?"

"The Alashi are wrong," I said.

"Are they? I know a slave who lived thousands of miles from the steppe who managed to free herself. In an unusual way, mind you, but nonetheless. I know others who are 'slaves' in name only." Zivar leaned back against her pillows, then sat up as she got pricked by the rosebush. "But the Alashi—how would it help them?"

"The bandits—Alashi are threatened by the Greeks right now," Xanthe said. "The Weavers have sent the army to try to take the steppe."

The vision I'd seen rose up again in my mind, and I shuddered and leaned forward to press the point. "Zivar, you asked once about joining the Alashi. I can go back there now—the Alashi have said they'll take me back. But they won't be much of a refuge for you if they're being destroyed by the Greeks."

"If the Weavers realize that I helped you free the river," Zivar said, "they will have me killed. They don't need to know where I am. They have my spell-chains."

"Do you really want to see magic scattered through the world?" I asked. "Do you want to see green mice running through the grainery? Strike at the Penelopeian Empire this way, and you'll see it."

Zivar thought it over for a long time. Then she shifted her weight and drew her spell-chains out from under her dress. "South," she said. "And east. I want to go to where the great northern river is bound."

*I* grew up at the foot of a range of high, rough hills. But if you followed the track of the old Syr Darya to the east, you quickly reached the real mountains. The

Danibeki called them the djinni's mountains; the Greeks sometimes called them Zeus's mountains, since his lost hell was supposed to be hidden under one of the highest peaks. Their peaks were white even in the summer, and you could see them even when they were days of riding distant.

It was in one of those valleys that the Sisterhood of Weavers had imprisoned the river.

I craned my head out the window of the palanquin to look at the mountains as we drew close. I glimpsed them in the afternoon of our final day of travel, and thought that we were almost there, but when evening came, they were still distant, glowing white against the twilight sky.

It had become routine to sleep in the palanquin. We curled up around the chaos, stuffed pillows under our heads and tried to forget about how far we were from the ground. Zivar nudged me awake when it was still dark. "If you haven't ever seen the sun rise over the mountains," she said, "it's a sight worth seeing."

Zivar rose and stepped out of the palanquin; I lunged after her, then realized that we weren't moving and that I could hear her laughing. She'd had the djinni set the palanquin on the ground while I was still asleep. I took a moment to gather my wits and wrap my blanket around my shoulders, then stepped out after her. The night was still quite dark, but I thought we were at the summit of one of the foothills. The air was chilly and dry, like night on the steppe, and my breath hovered in the air.

Zivar didn't speak; just clasped her own blanket around herself and waited.

Xanthe climbed out a few minutes later, rubbing

her eyes. "You scared me half to death," she said to both of us. "What's going on?"

"We're watching the sunrise," I said.

"Oh." Xanthe ducked back into the palanquin, and I thought she'd gone back to bed, but she emerged again with her own blanket. "It's cold," she said. "Where *are* we?"

"The foothills of Zeus's mountains," Zivar said. "Hey! Maybe after we free the river we can go let Zeus out of his hell. They say he'll grant us all immortality if we can find a way to free him."

Sunrise over Zeus's mountains happened in pieces. The first rays of light broke through the teeth of the mountain peaks. Then the snow on the peaks turned pink, then gold. Streaks of cloud like ribbon wound through the peaks, and finally, the sun was truly up, the sky blue, and, warm in the summer sun, we'd dropped our blankets to the ground.

"When Alexander defeated Zeus, they say he dragged him from one end to the other of the empire he founded. Then he brought Zeus here, to the mountains of the djinni, ripped the tallest mountain from its roots, and imprisoned Zeus beneath it," Xanthe said, staring calmly at the peaks. "I never understood why they could say Zeus's hell was *lost,* when it was also supposed to be under the tallest mountain. I guess now I do, because I don't know how you'd know which one's the tallest."

"I've never seen Zeus *or* Alexander," Zivar said, echoing what the worshippers of the djinni said about the gods. "I'm not worried about either one."

"They say that Alexander took care not to make the mistake Zeus made when he imprisoned

Prometheus. His chains were forged, not from metal, but from Zeus's own immortal bones."

"I'd never heard that," I said, shivering a little. "That doesn't make a lot of sense. How would you get the bones out without killing someone?"

"Well, Zeus is immortal," Xanthe said. "Prometheus had his liver eaten every day until he got loose, didn't he? And he never died. It grew back. Same with Zeus's bones."

"You'd think a mountain would be enough," I said.

"Not for a god." Xanthe pushed a lock of hair out of her eyes.

"I don't know how you'd break chains made from a god's bones," I said. "I guess it makes sense that he'd be grateful if you could manage it, though. Prometheus granted Arachne immortality, why wouldn't Zeus grant you immortality if you freed him?"

Xanthe gave me a quick, half-lidded smile. "I've also heard that there are slaves who say that Zeus will make the river return."

"I've never heard that," I said. "Is this something slaves say in Penelopeia?"

"Maybe."

"We should get back into the palanquin," Zivar said. Xanthe looked at it with loathing, then climbed back in.

We found the track of the old river a few hours later and followed it up through the valleys and crevices where it had once flowed. In the height of summer, it was bone-dry. As I peered down, I caught a glimpse of something brightly purple, fluttering in the summer wind. "What is that?" I asked, and leaned out for a better look.

Zivar muttered something to her djinni, and the palanquin slowly descended to let me take a look. The purple was a torn piece of cloth—from a cape, or a large banner. But as we moved down, I could see the rest more clearly.

It was a battlefield.

Zivar shuddered, and would probably have taken us away again, but looked at my face and fell silent.

The bodies lay where they fell. Scavengers had been here, but this battle had happened recently; they hadn't had time to do much. There were no Greek bodies, only Alashi; the Greeks, having won the day, had no doubt removed their own dead for burial. They had taken no prisoners. Many of the dead had been struck on the forehead, as if someone had combed through the field after the battle, dispatching the wounded.

Men and women lay side by side. I felt an overpowering need to see if anyone I knew lay here, even as I wanted to run away. "We can use my djinni to bury them, if you'd like," Zivar said.

"Yes," I said, and swallowed hard. The Alashi normally buried their dead under a cairn of rocks. "Have them dig one big grave. We can't stay for long."

Zivar nodded and barked a short order to her djinni. I walked slowly through the battlefield, looking for faces I knew. I had almost concluded that I knew no one who'd died here when I saw a short male body that lay with its back to me. Not really wanting to grasp the dead man's shoulder, I moved slowly to the other side of the body and crouched to see the face.

It was Uljas.

Zivar saw me pause and came over. "You know him?"

"When I served Kyros, Uljas was a slave who tried to escape. I tracked him down and took him back. After I was banished from the Alashi, I went to the home of his new mistress and got him out again. He . . ." I cleared my throat. "He told me if he ever saw me again, he'd kill me."

Zivar looked at me, then at the body. "So he was your enemy."

"Yes, I guess he was."

"But you're not happy he's dead."

"No." I stood up and walked away to look at the rest of the bodies. *I guess I thought as long as he was alive, there was a chance he might forgive me.* I fought a wave of nausea that rose up with the battle-field smell around me. *It never would have happened. I hope he's found Burkut now, and they're happy.*

The bodies lay thick on the ground. I tried to remind myself that the Greeks had removed their own dead, and there might have been quite a few. Still, though the Alashi would make quick retreats if they thought it would be to their advantage, to leave behind their wounded spoke of desperation. They had lost this battle badly.

Zivar approached me again. "The grave is done. Shall we have the djinni take the bodies to the grave?"

I nodded. "I'll carry Uljas, though."

I retrieved the purple cloth that had first caught my eye and wrapped it around Uljas like a shroud. His body was heavy, and still stiff. I carried him over to the grave; it was too deep for me to lower him into gently, so I set him by the side so that one of the djinni could place his body in the grave.

The Alashi usually put things in with the bodies of their dead, but I had little I could offer Uljas, or any of the others. When all the bodies were in the mass grave, the djinni covered them with the dirt, then mounded rocks over it.

"Are we done here?" Zivar asked me.

I nodded silently.

Zivar strode back over to the palanquin, but didn't settle herself onto the cushions. Instead, she took out the live rosebush, which was looking a bit worse for wear. She scraped out a hole to plant it in at the edge of the cairn, and patted dirt around its roots. Then she poured water onto it from a jug.

We stood silently for a moment longer.

Then we climbed back into the palanquin, where Xanthe was waiting, and continued toward the lake in the mountains.

There were other lakes dotted here and there along the track of the river, and I wondered how we'd know when we reached the place where the river was bound. But when we reached it, there was no doubt.

Part of the river was dammed by rocks; it was not entirely magical. There were openings, though, and crevices, and instead of flowing through, the water was held in place, shimmering like a bowl of black glass. An *enormous* bowl of black glass. I thought I could see the djinni that held it. Hundreds of them, encircling the lake, holding back the waters. *All these years. All that effort. Are they tired? Do djinni get tired?* "Take me close," I said.

"Think it through first," Zivar said. "Remember what happened at the temple? You just about got crushed."

Once I'd freed one djinn, the water would come shooting out through the gap I'd left. I imagined the water, a thousand times more powerful than spring floodwaters . . . "Will we be able to get out of the way of the water?" I asked.

"I don't know," Zivar said. "My aerika seem to want to keep you alive. That might motivate them to get us clear." She thought it over. "The water might not come right away. Surely the aerika are supposed to patch holes, if anyone slips loose. Still . . ."

"Perhaps we should wait over the middle of the lake," Xanthe said. "One of Zivar's aerika can carry you to the edge and let you free the djinni one at a time. Surely it will be easier to pull you out of the way of the water than the whole palanquin."

The thought made me queasy, but I had to admit that it made sense. "Let's move out over the middle of the water." I want to see all of it.

The lake was blue from above, and unthinkably large—much larger than I'd imagined. I remembered my glimpse of the sea near Penelopeia and knew that was larger than this was, but I'd only caught a brief glimpse. This, I could lean out and gaze down and try to take it all in. Larger than Daphnia, I thought. No. Larger than Penelopeia. No. It would cover Daphnia, Penelopeia, and Casseia, were they placed end to end, and drown all the Alashi besides.

The thought gave me pause. I had known that loosing the river would bring a flood, but until I saw the water I didn't really understand just how big the flood would be. I had pictured something more like the spring flood after a particularly snowy winter, not the wrath of all the gods falling down from the heights like the end of the world.

*But I was chosen for this,* the cold fever whispered.

"Let's move down a little," Xanthe said. She was at my side, leaning out, looking down. Her hands were shaking.

Zivar brought us low and close to the water, and I leaned out to look, to see how close the nearest djinn was . . .

. . . and felt a sharp blow to my backside, and— *gods and djinni help me, I'm falling.*

# CHAPTER THIRTEEN

# TAMAR

H ave they forgotten about us?" Janiya asked. It
was late afternoon, and we were still alone.

"It's not every day that a temple collapses," Alibek
said.

I glanced at the djinn, still fanning us. The women
and men of the household might have forgotten us,
but we weren't *alone*—not alone enough to speak
freely. I picked up a piece of fruit. "They said *the gate*
made the temple collapse." I glanced at both Janiya
and Alibek. Janiya raised an eyebrow. Alibek was sitting on the couch, but when he saw my face, he pulled
his legs up and leaned forward, his eyes intent.

Back when I had been Sophos's slave, we'd had a
way of talking, in the harem, that let us speak a little
more freely even if we were overheard. We would say
the opposite of what we meant, and then touch our
lips as if to say, *don't believe my lying mouth*. Surely

Kyros's slaves did something similar. Surely Janiya had done something like this, when she was a slave.

"I don't have any idea what they're talking about," I said, and brushed my lips.

"That's too bad," Janiya said. "Right now, I feel like I'm standing blindfolded in a city I don't know." She turned away with a sigh.

I wanted to shout at her to pay attention. I bit my lip, frustrated. Alibek understood. He got up, caught Janiya's arm, and spun her around to face him. "Well, we may not be blindfolded, but we *are* in a city *you* don't know." He brushed his lips. "Aren't we?"

Her eyes went to him, then to me, then back to him. "Sure," she said, and tentatively mimicked the gesture. "*Yes.*"

Now that she was paying attention . . . "I think by 'gate' they meant a person. I'd like to meet her. *She doesn't sound like anyone I know.*"

"Certainly *not like anyone in your family,*" Janiya said, catching on.

"Nor our *sisterhood,* back with the Alashi," I said.

"If this person were to join the Alashi," Alibek said, "do you think the Alashi would want them?"

"Yes," I said. "They'd *never let a person like that go.*"

Nods.

So now we all knew that Lauria was in Penelopeia—or at least *had* been, a few hours ago. "From what the djinn said, it sounded like she got away. They don't know where she is."

"Do *you* know where she is?" Janiya asked.

"No." I shook my head and clasped my hands. "No."

"Your *own* sister, now," Janiya said. "Heard from her lately?"

We were still talking about Lauria. Janiya wanted to know if we'd met in the borderland. "Hmmm. Yes. Very recently."

"After all this time?"

"It has been a while, hasn't it? *Turns out there wasn't any particular reason. She just didn't think about trying to meet me.*"

"Some shaman *she* is," Alibek murmured.

"Ha! What can you do? Zhanna would be shocked."

"Did you tell her your own news?"

"*Yes, of course.*" No, of course not. "*She wanted to hear everything. We had a really long chat, got all caught up.*" I had told her about Zivar—how to bring that up? "An old friend of ours was going to visit her part of the steppe, so I told her about that."

"Old friend?" Janiya was lost again.

"We've known her—hmm. *All our lives.*" Alibek was nodding. He knew who I meant.

"Think they'll meet up?" Alibek asked.

"Oh yes," I said. "If they manage to find each other. It's a big steppe. Who knows, maybe they already have." I had a plum untasted in my hand, and I rested it lightly on the table. "Speaking of family . . ." I looked at Janiya. "That *most trustworthy* person . . ." Xanthe? Why shouldn't we trust Xanthe? Hearing that Lauria had gotten away should have made me feel better, but was Xanthe with her? Could I do anything about it if she was?

Janiya coughed, poured herself a drink, and sat down. "I'm not sure I can quite explain myself," she said. She glanced around the room, at the djinn that fanned us. "Perhaps I can just speak plainly. There are four magias; they take the office in turns, so that power can be held by someone who is not fully in the grip of either melancholia or the cold fever. Naturally, they do not always agree on the best course of action. There are alliances that form. This was true thirteen years ago. I believe it's still true now."

I didn't see what difference that made.

"I believe this person misleads many people about her loyalties. I believe that she was trying to mislead *me,* when we talked." Janiya swallowed hard, then drummed her fingers on her cup. "So. I think I do"— *not*—"trust Rhea."

"I feel the same way," I said. Alibek nodded.

"I'm glad we're agreed," Janiya said. She swirled her juice for a moment. "I'm not sure what we're going to do about it."

We heard footsteps and fell silent. Rhea came in. She looked us over, and I thought that if she'd been listening, she hadn't been fooled. "Let me speak plainly," Rhea said. "We are quite interested in your offer. We believe that this might indeed be mutually beneficial."

I tensed, fearful that some demand would follow, but she dismissed my concern with a wave of her hand. "It's late," she said. "I have always found it uncomfortable to sleep in a palanquin, and I'm sure you're less fond of it than I am. Why don't you spend the night here. Eat an excellent dinner and sleep in a comfortable bed. One of my associates will transport you back to the steppe in the morning; we want to come to an understanding as quickly as possible."

I nodded. My stomach still churned, and I would not feel safe again until I was back on the steppe, well out of the grasp of anyone with a spell-chain. But they would be fools to mess up this opportunity, and it sounded like they knew that.

"That's fine," Janiya said. "Thank you for the invitation."

We were shown to a single large room. Parvaneh arrived with an entire train of lesser servants with dinner: roast chicken, roast lamb, roast carrots and onions, two different kinds of bread, steaming rice that was a deep buttercup yellow, and another pitcher of chilled juice. My mouth watered. I wanted some of the crisp brown chicken skin. I'd seldom had roast chicken, and I could smell the nut-brown crispness from where I stood. But when the other servants had gone, Parvaneh still hesitated by the table.

"I need to talk to you," she said.

Janiya had started to reach for the food, but she turned and gave Parvaneh her full attention, so I reluctantly turned away from the chicken.

"I found out this afternoon that you've met an associate of mine," she said. "At least one of you has. In Casseia."

"The—" I clamped my mouth shut—someone might be listening. Was she speaking of the Servant Sisterhood? Zivar's servants?

Parvaneh nodded. "Servants," she said. "Yes."

I wanted to ask if she controlled Rhea, but the djinn was still right there. I asked instead, "Who exactly runs this household?"

"Ha. I'm here to observe, really, not to run things. Unfortunate, but true."

"And how far up . . . ?"

"You don't need to know that. What you *need* to

know is that it's not the Weavers who are behind the invasion of the steppe."

"What do you mean?" Janiya asked.

"Sorcery is an art that is not open to all," Parvaneh said. "Not to men, not to women without the right connections, not to anyone who hesitates at the price exacted. The army . . ." She glanced around and lowered her voice again. "There is a group, we don't know who, that came from one of the Temples of Alexander. They have risen to positions of leadership in the army—they're not the official leaders, but they're kind of like the Servant Sisterhood. They're controlling the army from the back rooms. When the conquest of the steppe is completed, they will control the karenite. They will measure it out and exact payment. The power is not in the sorcery; it's in the control over aerika. The conspiracy of Alexander understands this."

"Surely the Weavers must see that," I breathed. "Why are they allowing it to happen?"

Parvaneh shrugged. "They believe that they have enough power now to take the steppe from their allies once it is secured from the Alashi. I think they're wrong. But they are not behind the invasion of the steppe, and if they fall to squabbling with the Younger Sisters, it will only make it easier for Alexander's conspirators to take over, in the end."

"Gods." Janiya rubbed her forehead with her fingertips. "So who can we turn against the army? How do we distract *them,* if they're perfectly content to have the Weavers and Younger Sisters fighting among themselves?"

"I don't know," Parvaneh said. "I must say, this took us somewhat by surprise, as well. We had been preparing for years, working toward a certain goal—only to find that overnight, the ones we thought would someday be *our* servants were challenging us for control. It shouldn't have surprised us, but it did." She looked us over and said, "Let me tell you one thing. The Servant Sisterhood would be happy to come to an *understanding* with the Alashi. But what you need is to find a set of tongs that will allow you to grasp not the sorceresses, but the Greek army. And good luck to you, because we haven't found one." With that, she went out.

The chicken had cooled, and the skin was not as crisp as I'd hoped. We were silent.

"Well," Janiya said, and fell silent.

"Excellent news," Alibek said, finally. "I couldn't have asked for better news." Then he turned his head to the side and spat.

There was a great deal to discuss, but no privacy. When we were done with our food, and the lesser servants had cleared it away, I clasped my teacup and stared out the window into the darkness. My thoughts were jumbled. I wished I were back on the steppe. Or somewhere else—even Casseia or Daphnia sounded good right now. Anywhere but here.

But more than that—I wished I could talk to Lauria. And not the confused, rushed conversation that we could have if I found her in the borderland at night. I wanted to sit down with her face-to-face, tell her everything we'd done, and ask her advice.

On the one hand, we had the Sisterhood, with its generations of power and its four-headed leader. On the other hand, we had the Younger Sisters—restless for power of their own. On yet another hand, we had the Servants, like Zivar's servants and like Parvaneh, who hoped to find power through controlling the Weavers. And on still another hand, we had the conspiracy of Alexander—soldiers, not sorceresses, who hoped to control the sorceresses by controlling the karenite that they needed.

This could not hold for much longer.

The alliances—particularly the peace between the army and the Weavers—couldn't hold. It would shatter on the anvil of the conquered steppe, but that wasn't good enough. To save the Alashi, we needed it to break now.

A faint breath of breeze came in through the window, making me think of the djinn slave that still fanned us. I'd almost forgotten that it was there. I looked around and saw that it had followed Janiya to fan her as she laid down to sleep. "I wish I could free you," I said aloud. It occurred to me that I knew how Lauria did it, and I had never tried. For all I knew, I *could* free it. I got up, and went over to face it. I could see it in the air, when I concentrated. It hovered, a faint smudge of shimmer in the dark.

I saw djinni all the time in the borderland, but I rarely spoke with them here. Jaran had his friend the Fair One, but no djinn had adopted me the way the Fair One had Jaran. I touched it, and my hand tingled faintly as if it had gone to sleep. "Return to the Silent Lands, lost one of your kind," I whispered. I felt foolish, doing this where Alibek and Janiya could see me. "And trouble us no more."

Nothing. The fan continued moving. The djinn was silent.

"Are you forbidden to speak to us?" I asked. Not

that silence would be an answer. Maybe it was forbidden, or maybe it didn't feel like talking. I had just about decided it wasn't going to talk to me when it spoke.

"*You* are not the one I wait for," it said in a gravelly voice. "But your heart is kind." I felt something lightly brush my forehead.

I turned back to the window and saw that Alibek was awake and watching me. My face flushed. I waited for him to say something mocking.

"Is that how she does it?" he asked, instead.

I nodded.

He rose and came to stand beside me. Then he touched the djinn and murmured the words. Nothing. There was a faint rustle from the djinn. A laugh, I decided.

"Surely there are other gates," Alibek said. "Other people who *could* do what she can, if they ever tried."

"Yes," the djinn said.

"So you laugh, but should we wake Janiya, and have her try, too?"

"No," the djinn said. "*I* would know."

"Will they have you report on our conversation?" Alibek asked.

"Perhaps."

"Will you tell them anything useful?"

"Unlikely."

"Is anyone else listening? Can you tell?"

A pause. Then, "You must flee," the djinn said.

"What?" Alibek said.

"Run!" The djinn spoke urgently though the fan never broke its slow rhythm. "I tell you this because you tried to free me. Danger approaches. Take your friend and go now!"

I bowed to the djinn, then shook Janiya awake. "We need to go," I said. Janiya rose and followed without question.

The hallway was empty. "It didn't say what kind of danger," Alibek said. "Enemies? Earthquake?"

"Let's just get out," I said, and we went out to the courtyard. The outer door would be barred and guarded. "Should we climb the wall?" I asked. It was smooth marble, and didn't look good for climbing.

"Bribery will be faster," Alibek said, and held up a clay jug from our table. He'd snatched it up on the way out. "I doubt he's been ordered to keep us in."

Sure enough, we were out in the street moments later. We walked away, not running in case anyone saw us. "How far?" Janiya asked.

"I don't know," I said. "I—"

A bird's screech cut me off. I tipped my head back and looked. The moon was about three-quarters full, and it was too dark to see the bird, but I saw something else. Something large, black, and silent moved swiftly over our heads. I caught my breath and pointed.

Janiya and Alibek looked up. Another one was passing overhead now. The Sisterhood. Or the Sisterhood Guard.

Was this because I had told Kyros to fear the Younger Sisters?

"Follow me," Janiya whispered. "I know somewhere we can hide."

We hurried through the streets. Behind us, we could hear shouts, but they didn't grow closer. Rhea's house was in a fancy neighborhood. Each house was like its own tiny city surrounded by a wall, with a statue in front. The streets were almost as well kept as the houses, paved with bricks so that even in the rainy season they wouldn't be muddy, and even in the dark we could walk without falling. The walls loomed up beside us.

The air made my mouth dry. I smelled wood smoke and baking bread.

"Where are we going?" Alibek asked.

"A neighborhood where no one will look for us," Janiya said. "It's a long way from here."

We rounded the edge of a closed-down market square. I heard a sheep bleating and smelled rotting garbage. We crossed a bridge over a small canal, and I pinched my nose shut to block out the stench. From there we passed more houses and closed-up shops. I heard raucous voices, somewhere distant. They grew louder, and I saw lights and smelled roasting meat. The voices came from a large tavern—no, I realized as we passed, three taverns side by side. We kept walking.

The houses were getting nicer again, though they lacked the statues Weavers put out front. I could hear distant voices again, and the scrape of shovels. Janiya paused at that and listened for a moment, then led us on, only to stop short when we saw a bright light in the sky, like a small, low moon. "What *is* that?" I asked.

Janiya shaded her eyes and squinted. "I think—I'm not sure—I think they've got a bonfire on a platform, or something, to shed light below. We're very close to the temple. . . ."

"The one that collapsed?"

"Yes. I think we can hear them digging it out."

"That light makes me nervous," I said. "Do we have to get any closer?"

"A little, but we'll skirt the edge of the square. We're almost there."

We heard the voices clearly now, though we couldn't make out any words. They had djinni to help them, but human soldiers were the ones digging. I wondered why, and then realized that if a djinn accidentally let a rock fall on a survivor and killed them, that would free the djinn and kill the sorceress.

Beyond the edge of the temple square, we scrambled down a steep bank to another canal. There was no bridge here, just half-submerged rocks we could hop across. It was hard in the dark. Janiya made it first. The rocks were slippery, and I almost fell into the stinking, garbage-laden waters. "Bleah," I said, trying to wipe my feet on the dirt of the opposite bank.

"This is it," Janiya said.

The houses here were squat and run-down, built from mismatched bricks mixed with rocks, mud clay, and odd scraps. The narrow streets were bare dirt. Fires glowed inside a few houses, shedding the only light. Some of the shacks looked barely larger than the palanquin that had brought us here. There were larger houses, too—some built fairly well, with sturdy doors barred shut against the hungry crowds outside.

I thought we were simply going to hide here, in this part of town where the city guards didn't like to go, but Janiya seemed to know exactly where she was going. We followed her to a slouching, windowless house. The door was sturdy, and closed. Janiya raised her hand to knock, then hesitated. She looked back at me and Alibek, started to speak, then changed her mind and just knocked.

Silence inside the house. Then a voice called, "Who is it?"

"Janiya."

A long pause, then a bent, gray-haired woman flung the door open and glared out. "What are you doing here?"

"I need your help. I—"

She slammed the door shut.

Janiya pounded on it. "Look, just let us in. I'm not going to shout my story from the street, all right? I need to talk to you." She stepped back. I saw her shut her eyes for a moment, draw a deep breath, let it out. "You were right. I was wrong. I don't need you to do anything for me but let me in, with my friends, who don't deserve your scorn."

The door opened again. "What made you think you could come here and get *help*?" the old woman spat.

"All I know is, you're not going to hand us over to the Weavers."

"Who are these two?" the old woman asked.

"Alashi bandits. Now let us in, because even if you won't turn us in, your neighbors might."

The old woman stepped back to make way for us. It wasn't much of an invitation, but Janiya went in, and Alibek and I followed her. The old woman barred the door behind us. "It's good to see you again, Damira," Janiya said, her voice resigned. "You look well."

"Don't bother trying to lie. I don't look well. *You* look well, though. Which was it that agreed with you so well—serving the Weavers or being a slave?"

"Neither," Janiya said. "I escaped to the steppe and joined the Alashi. Quite some time ago."

Alibek sat down by the hearth. He hadn't forgotten how to fade into the furniture. I'd learned to do it as a slave, but it was a useful skill even for a free person. I sat down next to him. I did not want to get between these two women.

"You might have sent word," Damira said.

"How? The Weavers' messenger service? I'm no shaman. Besides, when I left to join the Sisterhood Guard, you said you never wanted to hear from me again. When did you change your mind?"

"Never," Damira said. "But I don't hate you enough to close the door on two *other* people who need help." She gestured toward me and Alibek, her eyes still on Janiya. "If you'd never come back, I'd have died a happier woman." She thrust her chin forward. "Go ahead and say it, Janiya. I saw the shock in your eyes when you saw me. I've gotten *old*. You were expecting to see the girl you used to know."

"I was just glad you opened the door," Janiya said, but she lowered her head as she spoke. "I suppose you're right, but it's not just you. When I come across a mirror, or a still pool, I'm always shocked by my gray hair. Who *is* that old woman staring back at me?" She raised her head, but turned away from Damira and looked at the light and shadows from the fire against the dark clay walls. "What happened to . . ."

"Anyone you're going to ask me about is probably dead."

"But you're not. I knew you'd still be alive."

"And still here."

"Where else would you be?"

For a moment, I thought that Damira would grab

Janiya in a fierce hug, but instead she turned away. "Who are your friends?"

"This is Tamar, and this is Alibek."

Damira looked us over. For a moment, I was reminded of the eldress of the Alashi, and the way she had looked at me before presenting me with my first bead strung on a thong. Then she hobbled over to a cushion in the corner and sat. "Why are you here?"

"We're on a mission for the Alashi," Janiya said. "How much do you think you ought to know?"

"Don't you trust me?"

"I do. That's why I asked you how much you want to know rather than just saying that I couldn't tell you more."

"Tell me what you think you can."

"The Greek army threatens the Alashi," Janiya said. "Even now they may be beginning their assault on the steppe. We left the steppe to sew dissent among the Weavers, hoping that this would distract their attack. There are cracks in the Sisterhood already—we hoped to widen them into schisms."

"And what went wrong?"

"The sorceress who had agreed to our bargain was found out, I think. We escaped just ahead of an attack on her house. And also—it's not the Sisterhood that's behind the invasion of the steppe, but a conspiracy from the Temple of Alexander. The Alashi control something the Weavers need. If the army controls it, they will control the Weavers."

"That is not an arrangement that can last," Damira said. "The Weavers will not tolerate it for long."

"You're probably right. But my concern is the Alashi."

"So now what?"

"We needed somewhere to go."

"No." Damira shook her head. "What are you going to do next? Walk back to the steppe? The war will be over before you arrive."

"I don't know what we're going to do," Janiya said. "Catch our breath, stay alive, and look for a way to turn the Weavers and the army against each other now, rather than later."

"Hmm," Damira said, her voice mocking. "Well. Despite your hard work, loyalty, and sacrifices, the Weavers turned on *you*, didn't they? Just as some of us warned you they would. Seems like you should have no trouble thinking of things that would piss them off."

Janiya turned away from Damira again, tense with anger. "You were always a troublemaker, Damira," she said, after a moment. "I knew that if we came here, you'd hide us, at least, and that's really all I'm asking."

"Did you have anything to do with what happened today?" Damira asked.

"You mean the temple's collapse?" Janiya laughed a little. "No. We heard the rumble, though. What happened?"

"I don't know. One rumor said that someone freed the djinni that supported some of the walls."

Janiya glanced at me, and Damira followed that glance. "You didn't do it, but *she* knows who did."

"We weren't involved," I said.

"But you *do* know who did it."

"Yes." I cleared my throat. Was there any reason at all not to tell her? After all, the Greeks knew who it was and were already trying to find her. "Lauria. It was a woman named Lauria. She's—she's a friend of mine."

Damira raised an eyebrow. "*That* sort of friend?" she asked.

My cheeks grew warm. "She's my sister," I said.

"Ah." Damira glanced at Janiya, and I saw, in that moment, that she and Janiya had once been *that* sort of friend. I felt a brief stab of envy, which I pushed aside. "Tell me about the woman who freed the djinni. How did she do it?"

"She touched them and spoke the words of banishment. She can free bound djinni. They call her a gate. It's her gift. I don't know how she does it."

"I see," Damira said softly. "And they let her slip through their fingers? Astonishing."

"I don't think they *meant* to."

"No." Damira rose and hobbled toward us again. "Stand," she said to Alibek. She put her hand on his chin, grasping his face like an apple, and gazed for a long moment into his eyes. Alibek shuddered a little and did his best to look back at her. He fell back a step when she finally let go of him, and I saw him tremble. "Now you," she said, and I stood up, clenching my hands into fists. I refused to show her fear. Her wrinkled hands were cool and smooth against my chin. Her eyes were dark brown, but when she stared into me, I saw not only *her* but something else as well. *Djinn.* She had a djinn within her, and it looked at me through her eyes.

"You are possessed," I whispered when she finally let me go. "But not unwillingly."

"We are companions," she said. "We have lived together, like this, for a very long time." She caught the quick look Janiya gave her and laughed a little. "Not quite *that* long."

"I have known a shaman with a djinn he spoke with regularly. But she only visited."

"Hmm." Damira said. "My djinn is a barley-eater, like me. Most of the rogue djinni are rice-eaters, like *her*." She glanced at Janiya, then smiled and brushed my hair back from my face. "You have been touched by the djinni—perhaps in time you'll understand what I mean. I will help you."

"Great," Janiya said, and sat heavily down on the floor. "All we really need is somewhere to stay."

"I expect you're hungry and thirsty." Damira dipped water from a jar in the corner to a kettle and a pot. "I'll go out and get water for breakfast." She lifted the jar onto her shoulder. Janiya started up to assist her, then fell back at Damira's glare. "Don't be ridiculous. Stay here and start tea. I'll make porridge after I get back."

I had thought it was still the middle of the night, but when Damira opened the door I saw that dawn had come. The sky was violet-blue, and people were out on the street. Damira closed the door quickly, leaving us in lantern light.

Janiya sighed and got up, lighting a fire on the hearth from the lantern, then putting out the lantern's flame. The house was already stuffy, and with the fire kindled it quickly grew warm. "Tea," she said, when it was ready, and handed Alibek and me each a cup. My stomach rumbled. Rhea's roast chicken had been a long time ago.

"Can we trust Damira?" Alibek asked.

"I don't see what choice we really have," I said.

"We can trust her, I think," Janiya said. "We were

good friends—a long time ago. When I volunteered to join the Sisterhood's Guard, Damira was opposed. She considered them enemies, even then . . . She said I'd regret it, and when I refused to change my mind, she cursed me and told me not to ever speak to her again."

"Ah. So that's why you came back here?" Alibek asked. "You had such fond memories of each other?"

"I had a hunch she'd still be here. And I thought she'd take us in, for your sake if not mine. And I was right."

"So what *are* we going to do?" I asked.

"I don't know yet. This way we have some time to sit and think about it, though."

Damira came back a short time later and started barley porridge cooking over the fire. "There are all sorts of interesting rumors flying about," she said. "Some about the temple's collapse, some about several sorceresses who were taken from their homes last night by the Sisterhood Guard. Soldiers dug among the temple ruins through the night, trying to rescue anyone who might still be alive under there. Today they're offering sacks of rice to anyone who can lift a shovel and comes to help."

Damira dished porridge into bowls. It was bland but filling. I washed it down with tepid tea.

"I'm thinking we should go dig," Janiya said, as we ate. "We can wear scarves to protect us from the dust, and that should hide our faces as well. The Guard won't be looking for us there. And we might hear something useful."

Damira raised an eyebrow, but didn't argue. "Bring back the rice," she said.

Alibek peered out the door and into the street. "If

we go out, all the neighbors are going to see us," he said.

"They've seen us already," Janiya said without looking up. "Everyone knows we're here. They'll likely assume we're fugitives, but probably no one will turn us in."

"*No one* will," Damira said sharply. "The people here are the ones who *didn't* join the Sisterhood Guard." She spat. Janiya shrugged.

"We're going to be conspicuous," Alibek said. "Our clothes, our boots . . ."

"Fall into the mud when you're crossing the canal," Damira suggested. "That should take care of your finery."

I looked down at my clothes. I'd had them made just a few days ago. At least they were dirty. I ripped off part of my tunic to make a scarf. Fortunately, the tailor had used cheap cloth, and the fabric gave way easily. We tromped through mud crossing the canal, and passed through clouds of dust going up the hill to the temple courtyard. When we got there we didn't stand out anymore, and the soldiers hardly looked at us anyway. If Lauria was still in Daphnia, she could probably hide in the temple courtyard.

The dust clogged my throat and made my eyes burn. Even at the canal, the breeze brought the stench of rot. At the fallen temple, the smell was overpowering.

The place where the temple had stood was now a shifting mountain of broken rocks. I'd expected to dig with a shovel, but instead we were sent to scramble up the heap and join a line passing buckets of loose rubble. "Do you know," said the man to my left, as he handed me the bucket, which I handed to

Alibek, "there was a soldier killed doing this yesterday. The stones shifted and he fell and died. *That's* why they were so eager to hire people today."

"Why don't they just use djinni?" asked the woman to his left.

"They might kill someone underneath," I said. "Someone who's still alive. And free the djinn."

"There *can't* be anyone alive under there," the man said.

"They found a priestess alive yesterday," said a man farther down the line.

"No!" the woman said, amazed. Another bucket swung from hand to hand, followed by a rough boulder the size of my head, followed by a piece of one of the big marble blocks. My arms ached. In the square below, people dumped out the buckets. Soldiers with shovels dug through the rubble there.

"They *are* using djinni," someone else said. "They're sending them hunting through the rubble to find the people who are still alive."

Weavers and soldiers mixed in the crowd. There were few people in Penelopeia who could recognize me—was Kyros here? He was nowhere in sight, of course. No doubt he was somewhere comfortable. Sweat trickled into my eyes. One of the Weavers scrambled up past me. I tensed, but it wasn't Rhea or anyone else I recognized. She climbed back down to argue with the military officer in charge. Soon after, a djinn lifted a wagon box to the top of the pile. The breathless sorceress climbed back up and reorganized us. She had us shovel debris into the wagon box instead of passing it down in buckets. The djinn carried full loads down and dumped them in the square. This went faster.

"How did this happen? Did you hear?" I asked the man who'd told me about the soldiers. "Was there an earthquake?"

"The official word was an earthquake—but I didn't feel any tremors until *after* the temple began to fall," he said. He lowered his voice. "I don't know what caused it, only that the Sisterhood of Weavers wants to hide the truth. They kidnapped one of their own last night—she had something to do with it."

"I know what caused it," said a woman nearby. "It was Zeus escaping his prison."

"Isn't his prison supposed to be thousands of miles away?"

"Sure, that's what they say. But who'd look for him here? Pretty good place to hide him!"

"It wasn't Zeus," said an older man who looked Danibeki. "It was the lost rivers returning."

"Those *are* thousands of miles away."

"It wasn't either one. There were aerika who held up the temple. Someone broke the spell-chain that bound them, and it collapsed."

I *knew* that voice. My hands and feet tingled as my blood turned cold. *Lauria. That's Lauria's voice.* I dropped my shovel and lurched sideways to grab her before she could slip away again, my certainty that I'd heard her voice overpowering all sense and the knowledge that she had to be far away by now.

I found myself staring into the face of an older woman, perhaps the same age as Janiya. *Definitely not Lauria.* "Excuse me," I said, trying to gather my wits, and let go of her. My face was already flushed from the heat, but my cheeks burned even hotter.

I heard a shout. Someone had been found in the rubble, alive or dead was not yet clear. We rushed over to help move rocks, though some rocks slid under my feet and I thought that anyone alive might be killed by the effort to get them out. The soldiers didn't want to risk climbing on the unsteady pile, though, and the sorceresses didn't want to risk having their djinni accidentally kill someone. So we did the best we could, and in the end uncovered the body of a woman who had clearly been dead for a while. I wondered if she were a priestess, a sorceress, or something else—it was hard to tell. One of the sorceresses sent up a small palanquin for the body, and we lifted the woman onto it to be carried down.

If she was a sorceress, she might have left behind a spell-chain. I went to work digging near where we'd found the body, trying to sift through without anyone noticing. I had, barely a half year earlier, convinced Lauria not to bind a djinn, but right now, a djinn seemed so very useful that I was more than willing to use a spell-chain if I could find one. I promised myself that I would free the djinn when I was done with it. Lauria, of course, had made that promise and I'd ignored her. Though now I'd helped put thirty pieces of karenite in the hands of the Sisterhood of Weavers.

If I was going to compromise my beliefs again, I hoped this time it did enough good to be worth the guilt.

The woman with Lauria's voice was digging near me. I wondered if she'd had the same idea about looking for spell-chains. She glanced at me warily, and I gave her a sheepish smile, still embarrassed by my mistake earlier. We dug side by side for about an hour, silently. No spell-chain turned up.

Just as well, really. Near sunset, we were all ordered off the pile and searched by the soldiers to make sure we weren't taking anything. If I found a spell-chain, I'd have to hide it well if I wanted to keep it.

I thought they might send us back up to dig through the night, but they handed out sacks of rice and sent us home.

"This is ridiculous," someone yelled. It was the sorceress who had thought of using wagon beds to move rubble. "Where are the cold chains? Let's use aerika bound by dead Weavers. I'll hold the chain and give the order, if you're afraid." One of the soldiers said something I couldn't hear, and the sorceress said, "Oh, I'll tell you where they are. They're off to war—the *army* has them. They'd rather slaughter bandits than save Weavers."

I nodded, wanting to shout, "Yes! Keep thinking that way!" Though thinking about her words made my stomach hurt. Cold chains. Dead sorceresses. You could use these spell-chains for murder without killing the sorceress who did the binding. I'd heard that if you used a spell-chain to kill someone, the djinn often killed you, too. But soldiers already risked death. They wouldn't hesitate to give the order to kill. At least each cold chain could be used that way just once. They'd run out eventually.

Though they'd get a lot more if they tracked down and executed all the Younger Sisters . . .

I found Janiya and Alibek at the edge of the square with sacks of rice under their arms. The sun was going down, and it was a little cooler. We slid down the bank, waited our turn to scramble across the canal on the rocks, and went back to Damira's house, putting the rice by her hearth. She scooped some into a pot and started it cooking.

"Did you learn anything interesting?" Janiya asked as we waited for the rice.

"One woman today knew why the temple collapsed," I said. "But no one believed her. Others thought it happened because Zeus escaped his prison, or because the rivers are returning. Or that Rhea did it somehow."

Janiya nodded, then looked at Alibek. He shrugged and said, "There was another woman working today named Tamar."

"That's funny," I said. "It's not a common name. Did you learn anything, Janiya?"

"I'd been thinking, maybe we could make trouble by organizing an uprising from within the barley district here in Penelopeia. I've decided that won't work. People may not trust the Weavers, but they have just enough comfort they're not going to risk losing it."

Damira snorted.

"Barley district?" Alibek asked.

"You know. This neighborhood. The poorest part of town. The people here eat barley because it's cheaper than rice. But they're not going to rise against the Weavers. They're poor but not desperate."

Damira had said something about barley-eating djinni and rice-eating djinni. I'd never seen djinni eat, though. Janiya rested her head on her hands and said, "I'm exhausted. I think we should sleep. Even if there's a simple way to snap the alliances like a dry twig, I won't see it right now."

Alibek and I nodded. We ate dinner, then lay down on the floor—Damira had only one bed, and she wasn't offering to share, even with Janiya—and tried to sleep.

I roused in the night and thought at first I was

dreaming of the borderland. But the voices I heard were Damira and Janiya, speaking quietly from beside the open door.

"I never should have let you go."

"How were you going to stop me?"

"I should have tied you down. Refused to cut you loose until you promised you'd change your mind."

"You tried something along those lines, as I recall. I beat you."

"Only because I let you."

"Hmmm."

"Think what you like." A low chuckle, and then the sound of a kiss. And then another. I closed my eyes again. I'd overheard this sort of thing before, but this was *Janiya*. My cheeks grew hot, but I also felt another stab of envy. Not because I wanted to be with Janiya or Damira. They were old. Well, older than me. But I could hear their ease with each other. They shared something I still shied away from.

Zhanna had flirted with me at the spring gathering. What would it have been like to say yes? Did I desire her the way Janiya and Damira desired each other? I didn't think so. Did I desire anyone at all?

I heard another kiss, and then a faint gasp. I rolled over onto my side, turning my back on the noises, and saw that Alibek was also awake. He met my eyes in the dim light. I expected him to laugh at me, but he didn't. Instead, I saw faint yearning in his eyes, then he turned his face away.

Before Kyros raped me, I was too young to desire anyone. In the harem, all I ever wanted was to be left alone. Now I was free. Free women could have desires of their own. They could choose, freely, to take others into their beds. I closed my eyes and tried to find that place in my own heart.

I didn't find anything, but eventually I drifted back to sleep.

*A* rooster crowed at dawn, over and over and over. I wished someone would wring the damn bird's neck, but the floor was too hard to sleep much longer anyway. Janiya was already up, pouring water into the pot for morning porridge. "Any ideas, now that you've slept?" I asked.

"Tea first," she said.

Damira was out. Janiya, Alibek, and I sat down to drink tea and stare out Damira's open front door to where chickens scratched in the dirt. "What did Damira mean yesterday?" I asked Janiya. "About the Weavers turning on you?"

Janiya didn't speak right away, and for a moment I thought she would refuse to answer. "You know I used to be in the Sisterhood Guard," she said finally. "I grew up here on the muddy side of the canal, but when I was a young woman they offered me a place with them, a sword . . . Damira was opposed, I think you probably guessed that, but I shrugged her off and signed up." She stared bleakly forward for a moment. A gust of wind stirred up a cloud of dust. "Is it horrible to admit that I loved it? In the same way that I love my summers with the sword sisterhood. I had a daughter, Xanthe. When she was a few years old . . ." Janiya sighed. "Ha. When I told Lauria about this, I said I was falsely accused, but I'll tell you the truth."

I waited.

"I stole a spell-chain. And not just any

spell-chain—I stole the one that binds the great northern river. The Jaxartes."

"You *what*?" I said. "*Why?*"

Alibek spoke at the same time, asking, "Why did they let you *live*?"

Janiya looked down into her teacup, a faint smile on her lips. "The magia who held the golden serpent—that means, the one who was in charge, who held the symbol of power—entered a dark fever. She meant to free the river—smash the binding stones, loose the djinni in a terrible flood. She told me what she intended. I could have killed her, but that would have gone against my vows to protect the Weavers, and especially the magias. I *did* tell someone, but they chose not to act as quickly as I thought they needed to. I was young, arrogant—so I acted. I stole the spell-chain, to hide it. To keep it safe."

"Surely they didn't want to let her break it," I said.

"No. In fact, after the incident, she was removed as magia. There are comfortable cages within their palace, the Koryphe, where they keep safe the sorceresses who are too disordered to be trusted, and she went to live in one of those cages."

"How did they catch you?" Alibek asked. "You had a spell-chain. Couldn't you have gotten away?"

"I had a spell-chain, but I feared to use it. Had I called on the djinni in the spell-chain to help me, they might have come—but that would have loosed the waters in precisely the cataclysmic flood I wanted to avoid. So I fled on horseback, and was found and brought back. And punished."

"Why?" I said. "You stole it to protect the Empire!"

"Oh, Tamar." Janiya eyed me. "Surely you don't

think that would excuse theft of a spell-chain. Of *this* spell-chain. This is the Sisterhood of Weavers we're talking about." She had a faint smile. *She* had believed they would excuse her theft. She had trusted them to trust her. "You recall that I mentioned allegiances to members of the four. It perhaps hurt my case that I had gone against my own secret allegiance, and there was no one in power to speak for me. Still, I think they did believe me. That's why they didn't execute me—only stripped me of my rank and freedom, took away my daughter, sent me to Casseia . . ."

"How long were you a slave?" I asked.

"Hmm. All my life, before I came to the Alashi. That's not what you asked—I know. But it's the true answer."

"Why did she want to free the river?" I asked. "I thought the river's return would be bad for the Greeks."

Janiya rested her cup on the ground. "There are some who believe that Zeus is imprisoned under the reservoir where the river is bound."

"That doesn't make a lot of sense. Alexander is supposed to have bound Zeus long before the reservoir was even there. And the stories all say he was imprisoned under a mountain."

"The reservoir is in the mountains."

"So the sorceress wanted to find Zeus?"

"Yes. They say—well, you know the story, that if you free him, he'll make you a god. The sorceress I knew believed that he would also restore her to *herself*. The sorceresses all know they're mad; this one could feel the last threads of control slipping away. She was desperate."

The porridge was ready. Janiya spooned it into

bowls, and we sat down in the shadow just inside the door where we could get a little bit of a breeze.

"What did they do with the spell-chain after they caught you?" Alibek asked as we ate.

"They certainly didn't tell me," Janiya said. "Before, it was guarded by the Sisterhood Guard, in a locked room deep under the Koryphe. After—I heard a rumor that they were going to use djinni to guard it. They can't hide it under a mountain with Zeus, because they need to keep it close at hand. The lake waters rise over time, and have to be drained off—some of the djinni carry it places that the sorceresses find useful. Also, when a sorceress dies, her bindings weaken. The bindings on this necklace sometimes have to be remade."

"I bet I know where it is," I said. "I bet it's at the top of one of the towers. You need a djinn to get into those, right? There aren't any stairs. You need a djinn to carry you to the top."

We could see some of the towers from where we sat, faint in the morning haze. Janiya stared off at them. "Maybe," she said. "But any sorceress can get into those towers. The four don't trust the other sorceresses any more than they trust their guards."

"Zivar had a locked box in the wall of her workroom," I said. "She had a djinn guard it. Lauria told me about it. If I were one of the magias, I think I would keep it at the top of one of the towers and guard it with djinni. That would keep it safe from everyone but Lauria."

"But Lauria was in the Koryphe just a few days ago."

"Surely she was closely guarded," I said.

"But she got away," Alibek said.

Janiya stared off at the towers again, resting her spoon on the edge of her bowl. "If they *do* have it in one of the towers, I bet I know which one," she said. "There's one that's plainer than the others. Most have carved marble blocks built into the base, but there's one that doesn't. It also has a larger base—plain gray rocks, cut large. It was used once to hold a prisoner."

"A prisoner?"

"Before my time," Janiya said.

"Surely you heard stories," Alibek said.

Janiya thinned her lips. The barley district was waking up beyond Damira's door. I smelled wood smoke and porridge, mixed in with dust and garbage and the faint reek of death blowing in from the collapsed temple. "Yes," she said.

"And . . . ?"

"Lauria isn't the first person able to free djinni. There have been others. One was, hmm. Over twenty years ago. The magias kept her imprisoned in that tower."

"Why did they lock her up, rather than kill her?"

"She was the daughter of one of the magias."

"What happened in the end?" I asked.

"She jumped out of the tower." Janiya set her empty bowl carefully down beside her. "And then . . . Well, the story said because she had opened her heart to the djinni, Hades refused to allow her into the kingdom of the dead. She stayed in the Koryphe as a ghost and wreaked all sorts of havoc. In the end, her mother had to die, as well, in order to plead her daughter's case before Hades, and Persephone took pity on them—thinking of her own mother—and they were both allowed in. That's the story I heard."

I shivered, despite the rising heat of the day.

"Well," Alibek said as we cleaned out our bowls, "I think we should do *exactly* as Damira suggested. We should climb to the top of the tower, steal that spell-chain, then make them think it was stolen by someone from the conspiracy of Alexander." His voice was mocking. Of Damira, I thought—not me, for once.

"Excellent idea," Janiya said. "All we need is to figure out who to fix blame on."

"Kyros," I said. "Surely he must be in on it. And he's here, in Penelopeia . . . or he was. We could steal it and kidnap him." I realized a moment later that my voice was far too earnest.

Alibek turned his mocking eyes on me, but instead of cutting me he said only, "I'd rather kill the bastard than kidnap him. Couldn't we kill him instead?"

"No," I said. Because if someone went looking for him in the borderland, they'd know he was dead . . . I shrugged back the words.

"Hmph. Kidnapping it is, then."

Janiya stroked her chin. "It would probably be easier to track down Zeus, break his chains, and re-cruit him for our side."

"I don't believe in Zeus," I said. "But Lauria and I freed a mine full of slaves once. If we somehow got a spell-chain . . ."

"Ah, yes. That would make many things easier." Janiya stacked our bowls by the hearth and stood up. "There are, no doubt, some spell-chains buried in that rubble heap. The soldiers are watching, but smuggling a spell-chain out should be easier than scaling a tower. Shall we go dig?"

The rubble pile looked nearly as big as it had yes-terday. I wondered how long this would take, and if eventually they'd conclude that anyone underneath *had* to be dead and switch over to using djinni. Maybe not. By now, they were probably more interested in finding spell-chains than survivors, and djinni were nearly useless for finding things. Also, I'd heard Zivar say something once about the risk of having djinni touch karenite. Sometimes they found a gate, like the one they'd found in Lauria, and slipped away.

We spent the morning shoveling rubble into floating wagon beds again. Then someone decided that the largest stones had to be taken out. They cleared all the people off the ruins, and two djinni were sent to pull out a couple really large blocks of marble. The sorceress watching from overhead shouted—there was a body down in the hole, where two blocks had leaned against each other. She sent her djinn down to bring the body up. The woman's body had not a mark on it, just dirt. Then someone shouted, "She breathes!" The sorceress elbowed everyone aside and knelt by the woman, tipping water into her mouth from a waterskin.

Alibek found me in the crowd. "Who is that?"

"I don't know," I said. "Some priestess." If a sorceress had found herself alive under the rubble, she'd have used her spell-chains to get out.

The sorceress who'd brought out the survivor now wanted to pull out the rest of the big rocks, to see if they found any more people alive. The officer overseeing the digging thought that was too dangerous. I sat down in the shade while they argued about what to do next. I saw the woman with Lauria's voice, looking at the injured woman with an anguished face. I edged over to her. "Do you know her?" I asked.

"Who? Oh, the priestess? No." She shook her

head. Her voice was still Lauria's, but it didn't rattle me now that I knew to expect it. "You're the girl who ran into me yesterday, aren't you?"

"Yes . . . sorry . . ."

"It's all right. Do you suppose they're going to send us back up?"

"Not right away. I think the sorceress is going to win the argument."

I was right. I stood in line by a well to get a drink of water as the sorceress's djinn lifted out huge blocks of stone and marble, stacking them neatly in a clear spot on the western edge of the square. "They could have the djinn rebuild the temple," I said.

My companion laughed darkly at that. "That's what got them into this mess."

I remembered from yesterday that she knew what had caused the collapse, but I gave her a surprised look anyway, to see if she'd tell me what else she knew. She raised an eyebrow. "They had aerika holding the temple *up*," she said. "Keeping the statues from toppling, the walls from tumbling, the roof from crashing down." She picked up a loose brick, holding it out with one hand, and piled pebbles on top. "Then something loosed the aerika, and . . ." She let go of the brick, and it fell in a rain of pebbles. "If they'd built it properly in the first place, they wouldn't be in this mess. Half of Penelopeia is built this way." She looked around thoughtfully, then fell silent.

No wonder they wanted Lauria dead.

We reached the front of the line. I drew up the bucket. The water was shockingly cold, and I drank deeply, then passed the bucket to my companion.

"What's your name?" I asked, as we stepped aside to let the next person drink.

"Tamar," she said.

"*You're* the other Tamar?" I said. "I mean—my name is Tamar, too."

"Really?" She had started to look away, but now she turned back to take a long, careful look at me. "I think—" She broke off. "I think they're ready to send us back up," she finished, and hurried away, leaving me to pick up my shovel again and scramble back up on to the heap.

We didn't find any more survivors that afternoon, though with the big blocks moved, we did start to find bodies. My shovel hit a leg in mid-afternoon. My first thought was fear that I had hurt someone. Then I realized my shovel had sunk into the flesh like a knife into ripe fruit, and I gagged. "Body," I said, and backed away. I remembered a moment later that I should have dug for a spell-chain, but it was too late. Others were arriving to dig out the body a rock at a time.

The stench of dead bodies was horrible everywhere in the square, but I *tasted* it when I found that body. As I tried to catch my breath and not throw up, Alibek appeared beside me. "Let's go get a drink," he said, and led me back down to the square.

There was still a line to drink at the well, of course, and we waited our turn. "I am weak," I said. There were soldiers nearby, so I said no more than that. Alibek knew what I meant.

He shrugged. "You know, it doesn't matter. I really don't think it does." He jerked his head toward the soldiers, very slightly. He meant that it didn't matter because we'd never manage to smuggle a spell-chain out.

"You don't know how resourceful I can be," I said.

"I've seen a fair sample."

"Anyway, even if it didn't matter—I was *weak*. And I've been around death before, so why?"

We reached the well, and took turns drinking. "Let's sit and rest a minute," Alibek said.

We sat down in the shade. "I've never seen anything quite like this," Alibek said. "Normally, if you leave a body sitting out, scavengers take care of it. The scavengers can't get to the bodies, with all the rocks here. So they rot, and overwhelm us with the smell. Don't mourn your weakness too much. Bodies aren't meant to sit like this. It's not natural."

I thought of the shovel sliding into the thigh and tried to shake the picture out of my head. "No," I said.

"Are you ready to keep digging?"

I nodded, and we went back up. I couldn't bring myself to use the shovel, though. Instead, I picked up rocks, one at a time, and moved them, until it occurred to me that I could put my *hand* onto—*into*—one of those bodies. Fortunately, when I had that thought, it was almost sunset. I slid down from the pile, got my rice, and headed for the canal.

"Hey," Alibek said, and fell into step beside me. "We should walk slowly tonight."

"Why?"

"Janiya left a little early, did you notice? I think she'd like some privacy."

"Oh," I said, and blushed. I hadn't noticed.

"I can't believe you're blushing. What kind of former concubine is embarrassed at the thought of someone having sex?"

"Don't *say* that," I hissed, and looked around to see if anyone had heard. No one was close enough. "We're not among *friends* here, remember."

"No one's listening. Let's cross the canal and go for a walk."

We scrambled across the canal, then walked along the bank. I still had my rice tucked under one arm. I wondered how long we needed to leave Janiya and Damira alone—I was hungry. In the warm evening, the canal stink hovered in the air, but it was nearly wholesome compared to the dead-body smell of the temple square.

"Did you ever take a lover?" Alibek asked as we walked. "Back, you know. Did you ever have a lover you chose?"

"One of the other concubines, you mean?"

"Or another slave. Or a Greek, even, if it was your choice, not theirs."

"No," I said. "When I had the choice—*any* choice—what I wanted was not to be touched. By anyone. Some of the others did, though. Why do you ask? Did you ever have one?"

"Yes, one time. One of the other young men."

"You wanted a man? I'd have thought—well, you know, just for the variety, if nothing else."

"I know, and there was actually a woman concubine . . . but I didn't trust her reasons, so I said no."

"I haven't had anyone touch me *that way* in a long time."

"Since the harem?"

I shook my head. "There was one time, after we escaped. We saw some bandits . . . Lauria told me they couldn't be Alashi, but I didn't believe her. Anyway, I decided to take a look on my own, and they saw me."

"Bandits."

"Yeah, the *real* kind." I forced out an awful-sounding laugh. I wondered why I could talk about the harem easily now, but not this. "When Lauria and I escaped, I kind of forced her to take me with her. So when the bandits caught me, I figured, that was *it*. I had defied Lauria and gotten myself captured—she wasn't going to help me. So I made the best of it. I pretended I was one of the girls who *liked*—you know the type. I figured they might not watch me as closely if they thought I wanted to be there. It didn't work."

"How did you get away?"

"Lauria came for me."

"Into the bandit camp?"

"Yes. I found out later—*much* later—that Kyros sent a djinn to make sure Lauria reached the Alashi alive. She made it help her get me out. They loosed the bandits' horses as a distraction." I rubbed the palm of my hand with my thumb. "I know you don't like her—I understand why you hate her, honestly. But I knew a different person."

Alibek nodded. He didn't really agree, I thought, but he didn't want to argue.

There was a bend in the canal. We found a spot that was clear of rubbish and not too muddy, and sat down. This time of day, the dogs and crows had returned to their dens or nests, but I could hear the scrabble of claws in the garbage behind us and knew that rats were nearby.

"So you didn't have a lover among the Alashi?" Alibek asked.

"Why do you care?" I shot him a glare, but he was looking at me so mildly that I lowered my eyes and turned it into a shrug. "It's not as if we had any privacy."

"Surely people managed. There were plenty of 'summer friends' in the brotherhood."

"People managed. Yes. But not me." Zhanna was none of his business, and nothing had happened anyway. "Why are you *asking* me about this?"

Alibek shrugged uncomfortably. "As a concubine, I was only ever—used. My body, another's pleasure. When *I* was with the Alashi, there was a man in the brotherhood who wanted to show affection to me, but I was terrified. So he left me alone. I have thought, of late, that I am tired of being terrified. You and I are a lot alike. I was wondering . . ." He stopped, suddenly awkward again. "Never mind."

I realized a moment later what he'd been thinking—*Me. He was*—and felt my ears, cheeks, and forehead begin to burn.

"I'm sorry," he said a moment later. "Don't worry, Tamar. I won't so much as touch your foot without your permission."

I thought about that night years ago with Kyros, and all the horrible nights that had followed. I thought about Zhanna, and Damira and Janiya. Alibek was right. I was tired of being terrified.

I stole a look at Alibek. He was a pretty enough boy. And he was here. And most importantly, he understood what it was like to be a former slave.

I stretched out my foot toward him. "Well, if you *want* to touch my foot, I suppose that wouldn't be too bad."

He pulled my boot off, gently. My feet were rank,

but he made no comment, just ran his thumb down the curve of my foot to my heel. I remembered he'd told me about the woman who'd wanted her feet rubbed. He pulled my other boot off, and rubbed that foot, as well. My feet hurt, I realized, and my legs ached—from weariness, from walking, from the cords inside me drawn tighter than a bowstring. He rubbed my feet for a while, patiently.

"If you want to touch the rest of me, I guess that would be all right," I said.

"Don't sound *too* eager," he said.

"Well, what do you expect? How eager do *you* feel? You want to try it, I want to try it, so let's try it."

Alibek nodded. "If you want me to stop," he said. "Just tell me. And—you understand—I'm not going to promise that *I* won't want to stop."

Our eyes met and locked. I saw the fear in his eyes, and I knew he saw the fear in mine.

"It always hurt," I said. "Every time."

"I won't hurt you," he said.

He began to rub my feet again, then began to work his way up. His hands traced the muscles of my calves, around my knees, up to my thighs. Then one hand brushed the inside of my thigh, and I felt a shiver run through my body even as I also felt a jolt of fear. I almost told him to stop, then took a deep breath. Maybe I would tell him to stop in a minute.

Still, his hand wandered up my side and touched my cheek. He cupped my chin with the heel of his hand and drew my face close to his. He kissed me lightly on the lips. I could feel his breath, warm against my face. His lips were very soft, though his chin and upper lip were scratchy. I had never been kissed before. The men who chose me as their concubine were not the *kissing* type.

Alibek's hand stroked my face, then down, tracing the side of my neck, my shoulder, the curve of my breast. I felt warmth flush through my body, and I reached out my own hand to Alibek's face, bringing his lips to mine for another kiss. Then he pulled my body against his. Even through the layers of our clothes, I could feel the warmth of him. Something hard pressed against me, rubbed between my legs, and for a moment I caught my breath; it felt *good*. Then old fear caught up with me. I didn't shove Alibek away, because of course when I was a concubine, resisting only ever made things worse. But I lay still out of terror, not anticipation, even though I told myself that this was Alibek, just Alibek.

After a moment Alibek realized something was wrong, even though I didn't say anything. He touched me again, tentatively, then pulled back.

"I'm sorry," I said.

"I'm the one who should apologize," he said.

"No—" I got to my feet, a little unsteady on the bank. "Do you think we can interrupt Janiya and Damira now? I'm *hungry*."

Alibek stood up beside me and really *did* lose his balance, skidding into the canal and soaking himself to his knees. He swore, then scrambled back up. We picked up our bags of rice and walked back to Damira's house in awkward silence.

The door was closed, so we knocked. "Oh, there you are," Damira said, as if they'd been waiting—but the inside of the house was stuffy, so I knew that the door had been closed for a while. We sat in silence while the rice cooked.

"I met the other Tamar today," I said, trying to fill the silence.

"Another Tamar?" Damira poked at the fire with her stick, then wiped sweat from her face. "Not someone I know. Perhaps she's also new in town." The rice was done. She set it on the table.

"More digging tomorrow?" I asked Janiya.

She sighed and rested her head against her hand. "I don't know. We aren't getting anywhere, but I keep hoping we'll get lucky. Or see some other chance. What do you think?"

I shrugged. Alibek shook his head.

"More digging tomorrow," Janiya said finally, and we lay down to sleep.

Alibek was close by, and I found myself thinking about our encounter that evening. Heat rose to my face, from cast-aside pleasure or pure embarrassment I wasn't sure. I rolled onto my side, away from him, then tried, unsuccessfully, to get comfortable. I wondered if Janiya and Damira were waiting impatiently for us to fall asleep, which of course made me even more awake. I rolled onto my back again and stared up at the ceiling, wishing I could go sleep outside.

Lauria once told me that during our summer with the Alashi, the djinni showed her a vision of herself in chains. She'd found that confusing, because she had not been born a slave, but she came to understand that as Kyros's servant, she wore a different kind of chains.

I was still in chains as well.

I thought about reaching out to take Alibek's hand. But the longer I thought about it, the more impossible it seemed. Finally, I decided to just do it, but in the darkness, instead of taking his hand, I put my cold fingers on his bare stomach. He jumped like a mouse had bitten him. I snatched my hand back and whispered, "Sorry."

Alibek rolled over. I couldn't see his face in the dark, but I heard a rustle. He'd held out his hand for me to take. I laced my fingers through his. His palm felt warm against mine. The skin was cracked from labor in the temple square. He squeezed my hand gently, and whispered, "Thank you."

After a time, I felt his hand relax into sleep.

I still lay awake, thinking about the steppe. I wished we were back there. We weren't accomplishing anything in Penelopeia.

I wondered how the slaves we'd freed were getting on. Prax, the mine slave. Jaran. Uljas. Nika and her daughter Melaina—Lauria had refused to let me come when she freed them. Nika had recognized Lauria, but had pretended not to, in a strange gesture of courtesy. That was why Lauria had called herself Xanthe for a while—she didn't want to reject that gesture, yet she wanted Janiya to know it was *she* who had freed Nika. I'd have to remember to ask Janiya tomorrow if it worked. It was a strange way to tell her, coming at it from a slant. Kind of like the way we talked when we knew the sorceresses might be listening to us.

If Lauria wanted to send *me* a message with a name, but had to hide from others who might be looking, what would she call herself? Xanthe again, perhaps. Or Zhanna, or Ruan. Or maybe Tamar. That would certainly get my attention.

That other Tamar. Was that a false name? Was that a message to me? No, surely not. When she heard my name was also Tamar, she never batted an eye.

But it *was* a false name, I realized suddenly, and I knew who the other Tamar was, and who the message was for. She wanted Lauria to find her—that's why she was using my name. She was hiding from someone else—that's why she wasn't using her own.

It was Lauria's mother. That was why she spoke with Lauria's voice.

I wanted to find Lauria, to tell her, to see what she said, if I was right . . . My excited discovery had pushed sleep even farther away, but I gently pulled my hand away from Alibek, closed my eyes and focused, and sank, finally, into the darkness I was looking for.

The web shone out for me like a dew-covered spiderweb. Lauria had gotten away, so surely I would be able to find her tonight . . . I looked for the thread that led to Lauria.

But it was gone.

I had to be mistaken. I looked again. Perhaps she was awake, but the thread should still be there.

It was gone.

Completely gone.

Where was she? Where could she have gone?

I kept looking, sure that I must just not be seeing it.

*She's dead,* my mind whispered. I shook my head, refusing to believe it, but I could think of no other explanation. *She didn't get away after all. She's dead.*

# CHAPTER FOURTEEN

# LAURIA

*I* learned to swim as a child, splashing in the river one spring as the floods ebbed. When I was fourteen, Kyros decided that he wanted me to become a better swimmer. So I practiced. One of his other servants taught me better form. I learned how to hold my breath and swim underwater, how to swim while carrying a burden, how to rescue someone in the water who didn't know how to swim. When I was ready, Kyros tested me by having me swim across a lake. It was tiring, and the water was very cold, but I made it. After all that, I thought perhaps Kyros would have some special task he wanted me to do that required me to swim. But no; he just wanted me to be able to swim, and swim well, if I needed to. In retrospect, it was probably one of his own crazy-like-a-sorceress cold fevers that told him to do it.

As I fell toward the mountain lake, I sucked in my

breath and tucked my knees against my chest. I hit the water butt first, and it stung like a blow. The water was shockingly cold, and I shuddered as I went down. Then I kicked my legs and swam back to the surface, breaking through to yell, "Hey!"

The palanquin looked very high from here. No one looked out at my call. Was Zivar in there, or had Xanthe managed to throw her out, too? Maybe they'd *both* fallen in while I was underwater.

"Hey," I yelled again. "I can swim, but I'm getting really cold." The water felt a little warmer as the shock wore off, but now my boots were weighing me down. I kicked them off.

There was still no response from the palanquin.

*Zeus's hell.* Now what? Could I swim to the shore? I splashed in place and looked around; I was nearly at the center of the lake, and the shore was a very long way away. We'd covered the distance quickly in the palanquin, but I thought that even trying to walk the distance would take hours.

I looked up again. The palanquin was moving *away.* "Stop," I shouted uselessly. "Come back! Zivar! *Xanthe.* Don't leave me here to die, come back!"

*Can they even hear me?*

I'd gotten a mouthful of water when I fell in, and the taste of it reminded me of the dream I'd had about the spell-chain. *Is that spell-chain hidden here in the very lake it binds? Well, if I find it, I'll have all the djinni I could ever ask for, at my fingertips.*

I looked up one last time, searching for the palanquin, then took a deep breath and dived down toward the bottom of the lake.

In my vision, the spell-chain had given off a glow,

which I had followed to its source. I'd hoped that when I dived underwater I'd see that glow and be able to follow it. Instead, there was water in my eyes, making it hard to see much of anything other than the greenish light of the sun through the water. I swam straight down, and the light dimmed. It wasn't a terribly deep lake, as it turned out: I bumped up against the rough gravel after a few moments of kicking. I wanted to kick myself back to the surface to gulp air, but I forced myself to wait for a moment, take a look around—*any glow? No?*—before I kicked off and shot back to the surface.

My head broke through the water; I gasped for breath. My clothes were weighing me down, soaked with water as they were. I had been reluctant to take them off because they offered at least a little bit of warmth, but if I was going to search for the spell-chain, I'd exhaust myself much faster with the clothes slowing me down. *Will I die from cold first, or exhaustion? Either way, I think I'm more likely to find the spell-chain with nothing to slow me down.* I kicked off the trousers and pulled off my tunic. Naked, I felt light as an eel. The exercise was warming me a bit.

My first impulse was to swim toward shore before diving down again, but surely, if someone were *hiding* the spell-chain, they'd have thrown it into the center. *Or the deepest part.* I wouldn't think about that now. I turned away from the shore, swam for a few minutes, then took a deep breath and dived down.

Again, I reached the bottom fairly quickly. This time I was able to pick up a good-sized rock off the bottom to weight me down as I took a look around. No glow, though a little bit of faint greenish light filtered down from the surface. If there was a spell-chain down here, I didn't see it. *This is hopeless.*

I set down the rock and thrust my legs back toward the surface. I wiped the water from my eyes as well as I could with my wet hand, once I was out, and took a big breath. The hot summer sun felt good on my head. *If I could just crawl up on top of the water and rest there for a while, I would be fine. If only the palanquin hadn't left me . . .*

*I don't have time to think about that now.* I swam for a minute or two toward what I thought was the center of the lake, and dived again. What would it be like to die from cold in a lake? I'd heard that dying from cold was normally not too bad—you fell asleep and never woke up. And I'd heard that drowning was awful. If you died from cold in the water, did you drown, or did you fall asleep? *I don't have time to think about this, either.*

The lake was deeper here. Down I went until my hands hit something hard. The ground? No—a wall, I realized, a stone wall. *This was a city once, before the water came.* I felt my way along it, and groping along the ground, my hand touched something smooth. My lungs were burning, so I closed my hand around and pushed off from the wall, shooting back toward the surface.

Out, and I gasped for air, then tried to float on my back to look at what I'd found: a glass teacup. I held it up for a moment, letting it shine in the sun. *My great-great-grandmother could have drunk from this. Could have been drinking from this when the water came.* I shook off the thought; probably *my* great-great-grandmother had been elsewhere, and that's why she had survived. I loosed the teacup and let it fall through the greenish water, to settle back on the ground below, and dived again.

There were buildings here, looming in the green-gray darkness; I had disturbed some fish, which darted through a hollow window and into the darkness. I still saw no spell-chain. I returned to the surface, swam a bit, took another deep breath, and dived again.

This time when I reached the bottom of the lake, I landed inside one of the buildings; the roof had long since fallen away. The walls were coated in a green mossy growth. Looking around, I thought I could identify a fireplace, and the remains of a table. In the corner, I saw a greenish lump; I prodded it tentatively with one finger and realized that it had once been a cask of wine.

I found more greenish walls on my next dive; there was a window to one side of me, and sand swirled around my feet. I found an overturned kettle and a cooking pot, or what was left of them. They were coated in slimy green weeds. If I'd had the palanquin close by, I'd have wanted to bring these bits and pieces up to the top simply as curiosities. Zivar would be fascinated, even if Xanthe wouldn't care. There was still no sign of the palanquin when I reached the surface, though, so I was glad I hadn't taken the trouble.

When I went down again, I saw a glimmer of *something* in the muck of the lake floor. *Could it be?* I pulled myself down and dug through the mud and weeds; my heart leapt as I saw the sparkle of a faceted gem. I closed my fist over it and pulled it free, already wondering if I could speak to the djinn right here underwater. But instead of a spell-chain, my fist held an ordinary—well, richly made, but worthless to me— necklace, set with gems. Diamonds, I thought—it was hard to be certain of colors underwater, and I didn't care enough to test to be certain. *Worthless*. I dropped it and pushed myself back to the surface.

I was growing tired. I floated on my back for a few minutes, trying to rest, and realized that I was also getting cold. I was starting to shiver; this wasn't good, it would only exhaust me sooner. I wondered how much of the day was left. Even if I managed to stay afloat through the day, night would surely finish me off. *Maybe Xanthe and Zivar will come back before then . . .*

I took another deep breath and swam down.

This time I found white marble steps—patches of white were still visible under the weeds and sand— and white columns. Beyond that, a carved statue like the ones the Weavers put in front of their houses. This one showed a bird in flight; I could recognize the shape even now. *Was this a temple? Or some other public building? Or merely the home of some very wealthy person?* I swam a little farther underwater and came to something that made me pause.

It was an archway built of stones—but unlike everything else down here at the bottom of the lake, it was *not* crusted over with weed growth. No—these stones were bare and weathered. Stranger still, when I stood before it, I couldn't see through the doorway. The light disappeared.

*The Passage,* I thought. *Now Drowned.*

*The spell-chain was near this, in my dream. It must be close by.*

I needed air. I shot back to the surface, caught my breath, and dived again.

In my dream, the spell-chain had been close by. It had also let off a glow, and a hum. I strained my ears and heard nothing but my own muffled heartbeat. If I could meditate, perhaps I would hear the singing that would lead me to the spell-chain, but it was difficult to relax and let go when I also had to hold my breath and struggle to keep from bobbing up back toward the surface. *A glow. Look for a glow.* I saw nothing.

*Air.* Up to the surface, then down again.

I found nothing. I found nothing. I still found nothing.

*I'm going to die here.*

*No. There's another option.*

I went back to the surface one final time and searched the sky for Zivar's palanquin. Then I took a deep breath, dived down to the temple, and swam into the darkness of the Passage.

*F*or the space of one heartbeat, I felt absolutely nothing: no water, no light, no cold, no heat. Then I felt a blast of cold air, and realized that I was lying on a smooth stone floor, in complete darkness. I gasped a deep breath—*air, there's air here,* I thought with some relief, and staggered to my feet. The chilly darkness reminded me of the bottom of the mine, but I heard no voices—in fact, I heard no sounds at all. I cleared my throat; that echoed very slightly, but there was no other sound.

There was no light. I could see nothing at all, in any direction.

I stretched out my hands and felt around the place where I stood. Each hand touched a wall. I'd expected rough stone, but it was smooth, almost slippery, like glass or polished metal. I felt hesitantly be-hind me. Could I return to the water? *Do I want to?* I took a step, another step, and found that the walls curved around and met in a dead end.

*Am I trapped? Is this a prison?* I turned and took a careful step forward, then another, and another. The hallway appeared to continue. *Well. Go forward, or stay here?*

*Go.*

I walked slowly, since I couldn't see anything. I kept one hand on the wall. In the darkness, I wasn't sure if I was walking straight or if the tunnel curved. I stopped a few times and listened, but heard only a faint breath of wind. No drips of water; no shrieks from bats. I called out and heard a faint echo, but no voices returned the call. After a while, I began to walk a little faster; I hadn't stepped on anything but smooth floor yet.

I had no idea how much time was passing, or how far I had walked. At some point, however, I realized that I was not getting tired, and not getting hungry.

*Perhaps I'm dead.*

*This could be the underworld. It's not exactly what I pictured, but it definitely* could *be the underworld.*

I stopped to sit for a few minutes, even though I wasn't tired. I thought back over my time in the wa-ter, trying to decide when I might have died. The Greeks believed that we crossed over a river after death. Perhaps I'd died when I hit the water, and the time I had thought I was diving and exploring, I was actually in that river, or something like it. I'd found the door, and gone through, and now I was journey-ing to the city of the dead.

There was that book where I saw the passage—

*The Passage, Now Drowned*—but for all I knew, that *was* a picture of the passage to the underworld.

*That would also explain why I've felt cold ever since I've arrived, but I'm not shivering . . .*

*That would explain why I couldn't go back, once I came through the door.*

After a while, I stood up and started walking again.

Dead or not, I didn't have anything *else* to do.

## CHAPTER FIFTEEN

# TAMAR

*L*ike yesterday, the rooster woke me up. I lay in a sleepy haze, listening. There was a weight on my chest, but I couldn't remember why. I thought back to the night before. Heat rose to my face when I remembered my awkward encounter with Alibek, but that wasn't it. Then I remembered: Lauria, gone. I rose heavily and moved out of Damira's way as she went to make porridge for breakfast.

Should I tell the others? In the morning light, I was no longer certain of what I'd known the night before. I might have been wrong. In fact, that seemed quite possible. I decided to say nothing.

"I think I know who the other Tamar is," I said instead. "She has Lauria's voice when she speaks. I think—perhaps—that she's Lauria's mother. She's in hiding, just as we are, and calling herself Tamar so that Lauria will find her if she comes back."

Janiya raised an eyebrow. "You said she was with Lauria. How do you suppose they got separated?"

"Maybe Lauria left her behind when she fled," I said.

"Should we make contact with her?"

"No," Alibek said. "I heard stories of Andromeda when I was still in Kyros's harem, though I never met her—she'd been freed years earlier. Kyros had slaves who were loyal, but Andromeda was more than loyal. She truly loved him."

"Lauria truly loved him once," I said. "And *she* turned against him."

"Andromeda is in hiding," Janiya said. "Would she hide from him if she were loyal?"

"Maybe she was sent out to look for Lauria," Alibek said.

"Lauria is long gone," Janiya said. "Or she would have found *us*."

Except that she was dead. My stomach lurched at the thought. But I couldn't be certain. There was a lot about the borderland I didn't know.

"Maybe she isn't fully loyal to Kyros now, but that doesn't mean we can trust her," Alibek said. "We've revealed ourselves to enough people in Penelopeia already. If she *is* in hiding, she's not going to be able to get us into the Koryphe, and if she's *not* in hiding, she's a threat to us."

Janiya looked at me. "Do *you* think we should seek her out?"

I still wanted to, but only because she had a link to Lauria. "No," I said. "Alibek is right. If we think of some way that she could help us—maybe."

We ate our morning porridge, then tied our scarves over our faces and stepped outside to go dig. I couldn't see well in the bright sun and almost ran into a woman outside Damira's door. Janiya and Alibek stepped away, like they might make a run for it. I squinted. It was my companion from yesterday, the other Tamar.

"Tamar," she said. "You're Lauria's Tamar, aren't you? *What are you doing here?*"

I glanced at Alibek. He shrugged. "Let's talk inside," I said, and we went back into Damira's house.

*D*amira glared as we came back in, then picked up the empty rice sacks and stalked out—to dig or do other work, I wasn't sure.

"I was right," Andromeda said as we sat down. "What are you doing here?"

"I could ask you the same question," I said. "I thought you lived in Elpisia."

"I did. I do. You know Lauria was here, though—Kyros and the Sisterhood of Weavers were holding her in the Koryphe. She became very ill for a while, and Kyros brought me here to nurse her back to health."

"So why aren't you still in the Koryphe?" Janiya asked.

Andromeda glanced at her, at her scarf-covered face, uncertainly. Janiya pulled off the scarf and said, "Tell her who I am, Tamar. I don't see much point in games now."

"This is Janiya," I said. "She was the leader of—"

"Janiya. Yes. I know who you are." Andromeda gave Janiya a wary look, and then sniffed, dismissing her. "And him?"

"Alibek," I said. "Another member of the Alashi."

"Alibek," Andromeda said. "Oh, yes." I realized that she knew him for Kyros's little bird, even if they'd never met. Alibek's face went pale, and he gave her a curt nod.

"How did you end up digging out the collapsed temple in exchange for sacks of rice?" I asked Andromeda. "Surely they didn't throw you out of the Koryphe."

"No." I saw a flash of humor cross her face, and then she grew sad. "Kyros held Lauria for quite some time, not really sure what to do with her. She has a power over aerika that makes her a threat—alive or dead. Finally, they decided they could kill her, but only if they had an aeriko perform the execution. They gave her a drug to make her sleep—a great deal of it—so she wouldn't be able to resist the aeriko. I knew what they were doing, but there was nothing I could do but stay with her." Her face became guarded. "Perhaps I should have tried then to resist, I—I don't know. I saw no way out, for either of us. I didn't want to upset her when there was no hope."

"What happened then?" Janiya asked.

"Our guard, Xanthe, decided to get us out," Andromeda said. I looked at Janiya. Her jaw was tight. "We had to half carry Lauria, but thanks to Xanthe's knowledge of the Koryphe—and her friends among the Sisterhood Guard—we made it out. We hid with Xanthe in a cave but then they started searching, and Xanthe realized they were near . . ."

"And then?"

Andromeda lifted her chin and swallowed hard. "Lauria and Xanthe had to flee. So I sent them on without me."

"You sent Lauria away?" I blurted out.

Andromeda narrowed her eyes. "More than *any-thing else in the world* I wanted my daughter to survive. Her best chance was *without* me. So yes. Yes, I sent her away. Because that was all I could give her." Her hands were shaking.

My own hands were shaking as well. "I'm sorry," I whispered. "I didn't . . . Well. What happened then?"

"Lauria warned me that if Kyros found me, he would use me as a hostage against her. I believed once that Kyros would *never* do that, but . . . I have come to believe otherwise. So I waited until they were gone, then slipped out and came here to hide. I think Kyros believes that I am with Lauria still, because no one has come looking for me. Oh, and Lauria caused the temple to collapse and escaped in the confusion. I can certainly understand why the Sisterhood wants her dead. If all my power in this world rested on the aerika, and someone came along who could free them with a touch—I'd want her dead, too, at least if she meant nothing to me otherwise." She looked up at the ceiling for a moment, swallowed hard again, and gave me a twisted little smile. "So. That's what *I* have been doing here in Penelopeia. What are *you* doing here?"

I looked at Janiya. She gave me a very small shrug. Apparently it was up to me to decide what to tell her.

"The Greeks are moving against the Alashi," I said. "We need to stop them."

"The three of you."

"Three can accomplish a great deal. Or two. Or one."

"Yes, but you've been digging rubble. Whatever your plan, I can't imagine *that* was part of it."

"No," I admitted. "But . . . The Empire rests on a

shaky foundation. If we can turn the army and the Weavers against each other, that will distract them."

"No doubt," Andromeda said. "But how are you going to do it?"

"Uh," I said. "We're open to suggestions."

Andromeda shook her head and laughed. "Good luck to you," she said.

"Let me ask you another question," I said. "Who is really in charge of Penelopeia? It's supposed to be the high magia, but there are four of them. And the army acts for them, but against them. Who rules here?"

Andromeda turned her palms up. "How would I know?" she asked. "Kyros brought me here, and I lived in Lauria's prison. I saw Lauria, Kyros, Xanthe, and a handful of servants."

"I was once a slave, too," I said. "If there was one thing I always knew, it was whose voice mattered. Always. There are some things you never forget to pay attention to."

Andromeda smiled slightly and met my eyes. "You were one of Sophos's concubines, weren't you? I heard bits and pieces of what happened, after Lauria first left on her mission."

"Yes. I was." Andromeda didn't look a great deal like Lauria, but I saw the same struggle in her face that I'd seen a few times in Lauria's. When Lauria had wrestled with her loyalty to Kyros, I hadn't known what I was seeing, but now I did. If I could take Andromeda to the steppe for the summer, I knew I could win her to our side. With an hour in a closed room . . . it was still worth a try.

I stood up, took Damira's teakettle, and made a cup of tea for Andromeda. There wasn't enough to make tea for everyone else. I hoped Damira wouldn't be mad.

"Andromeda," I said. "You used to love Kyros, didn't you? Before you realized that to him, your daughter was just a tool, that could be used and discarded."

"Not *just* a tool," she said quietly. "Or rather—not a tool that would be thrown away lightly. Because she was very, very useful to him. But I came to understand, finally, that he did not love her, even though she was his daughter."

"But you love her," I said.

"Of course." Andromeda stared down at her tea. "I am her *mother*."

"I love her, too," I said. "She is my sister." Or she was . . . I pushed that thought away.

Andromeda looked up again and half smiled. "Kyros has been making plans for a long time. When he sent Lauria on her mission, I believe that he was hoping to use her to take control of the steppe through treachery. That failed when Lauria was expelled, but he had made other plans, just in case. Lauria's turning up again—well, first I think he kept her alive simply because here was a tool, back again, and possibly useful. Then he *had* to keep her alive because the Weavers were afraid of what would happen if she died. If the magia gives an order, it is obeyed, no matter what Kyros says. But when Kyros speaks, all four listen. And when the army takes control of the steppe, Kyros plans to be there. And when everything is over, he wants to control the steppe. That's been his plan for decades—this is why he arranged to be posted to a backwater like Elpisia. He wants it very badly, for all that it's mostly desert . . ."

Desert, and karenite. I caught my breath.

"What?" Andromeda asked. She narrowed her eyes when I didn't answer right away. "I have been very honest with you," she said. "I expect the same courtesy."

"The steppe has a great deal of karenite. Soulstone. The rock that the sorceresses need to bind djinni."

Andromeda raised an eyebrow. This was not a complete surprise to her, but I could see her fitting the pieces together in her mind. "Ah," she said. "That explains quite a lot."

"What would happen if Kyros went missing?" I asked, thinking of the plan that Alibek had proposed yesterday. We'd joked about it, but with Andromeda's help, maybe we could try.

Andromeda turned her cup around and around in her hands. "I don't know. Surely there are others in the army who know about soul-stone and seek the power the steppe would give them. If the sword were knocked from Kyros's grasp, someone would pick it up. But if he were *missing,* rather than dead . . . I don't know. Do you aim to kill him?"

"No," I said.

"But you aim for him, at least. I'm right about that."

I tried to guess from her face if she'd help us. "I would love to aim for Kyros, but he's a distant target. Can you help us get closer? *Would* you help us get closer?"

"I would, but . . ." Andromeda's voice trailed off. "I don't know what I can do. I'm *hiding* from him, it's not as if I can just knock on the door and ask if I can bring a couple of friends up to chat. Or rather, I could, but I don't think any of us would like what would happen next."

I nodded.

"But into the Koryphe," she said, a few moments later. "Perhaps—it's possible I could think of a way to get all of us into the palace. Would that help?"

"Will you do that?" I asked.

Andromeda lowered her eyes to her own cup. "Yes," she said, finally. Her hands were shaking. "Yes."

*W*e followed Andromeda across the river, then around the square with the ruined temple. Down one narrow street, I glimpsed a white tower rising like an ivory needle from the Koryphe. Then we turned the corner and it was hidden from sight again. We passed through a narrow alley and came out onto a wide, busy street.

"People wait here to find day work," Andromeda said. "Some of it is delivering things to the Koryphe. If we wait here, we might get lucky."

We stood for a bit, then were hired by a man who seemed really pleased to see us. Apparently almost everyone was working in the temple square because the pay was so good. This man would pay in barley, not rice. He wanted us to carry furniture. He was a craftsman and had just finished a set of carved and cushioned chairs for a Weaver in the city. Not, unfortunately, inside the Koryphe, but we couldn't very well turn down the work, so we each strapped a pair of chairs to our backs and carried them across town. We lowered them carefully to the ground, then carried them in one at a time, arranging them in a line in the courtyard. The housekeeper inspected them for damage and paid the chairmaker, who in turn gave us each a small sack of barley. We returned to the craftsman's row to wait again.

The second person to hire us also had us make a delivery to the home of a Weaver—metal pots, this time. Then the third had us carry tanned hides to the workshop of another craftsman. At least we'd be able to feed ourselves at the end of the day. I wiped my sweaty face on my sleeve, frustrated.

"Sooner or later," Janiya said. "This is a good idea. If we're carrying in a delivery of pots and pans, or new chairs, no one will look at us twice. It will be easier to slip away once we're inside the walls."

"Are we really going to try this?" I whispered.

Janiya shrugged. "If we can get in . . . Well, if it seems suicidal, we'll go back out."

But no one hired us to carry anything to the Koryphe. At dusk we returned to Damira's house with the barley and Andromeda. Damira barely glanced at Andromeda, raised a pleased eyebrow at the barley, and cooked it up for dinner.

Andromeda sat quietly when we were done eating. Damira had bought more tea that day and gave each of us a cup of it. Andromeda turned the cup around in her hands again. "If you only want him dead, I could turn myself in," she said. "Kyros would not expect treachery from me. I could strike when he least expected it."

"He might not have expected treachery from you a week ago," I said. "But surely he would be wary of you now, unless you could persuade him that you've been a prisoner this whole time."

"I could tell him that I escaped from Lauria and

Xanthe far from Penelopeia. I've been traveling since then, walking back here to return to him. I'm ragged enough for that to be believable. He'd figure out I was lying—he has his ways—but not right away. At first, I think, he would believe me."

"It doesn't matter," I said. "For our plan to work, we need to kidnap him, not just kill him."

"Have you spoken with Lauria since she escaped?" Andromeda asked.

"Since she escaped? Yes."

"There's something you're hiding from me," Andromeda said.

I shook my head, even though I knew exactly what she was talking about. But I saw how she looked at me, and knew she knew I was lying. "I am a shaman," I said. "I tried last night to find Lauria in my dreams, and I couldn't find her. When she was a prisoner, and they were drugging her, I couldn't find her, but I could always see the thread between us. Last night, I looked, and I couldn't see it. Not at all. I . . . I don't know what that means."

Andromeda took a breath as if she were going to say something—then let it out, silently, squeezed my hand, and went to lie down to go to sleep. Maybe she was going to try to find Lauria herself. Well, and if she could—wonderful.

I lay down and saw Alibek hesitate, his blanket in his hands. He was looking at me, and I realized that he was trying to decide whether to lie down close to me or not. He was looking at me to try to see what I wanted. I turned my face away from him and closed my eyes. Alibek lay down, and I thought he might have stretched out his hand for me to take it, but I was too heartsick about Lauria to take it.

It was Alibek's fault, I thought. It was because of Alibek that Lauria was cast out.

I had a hard time going to sleep that night. I thought I'd try to find Lauria again, too, but I was afraid of what I would find—or what I *wouldn't* find—and that fear kept me wide-eyed, trying to get comfortable on the hard dirt floor. I hated this house, Penelopeia, the barley district, everything. I wanted to be home. That got me thinking about how I wouldn't have a home anymore if we couldn't stop the Greek army.

Lauria had thought she was going to free the rivers. My mother had always said that when the northern river returned, it would sweep away the Greeks and their empire—Weavers, army, and all. We'd lived right in its path—if it had returned in a huge flood, it would have swept us away, too. There were times I would have welcome it anyway, as a child.

*Only the rivers' return can free us all.*

In the darkness, I could hear Andromeda breathing. I knew which breath was hers—after all the weeks of travel, I knew the sounds Janiya and Alibek made at night, and Damira had a raspy wheeze. I thought Andromeda was still awake. I knew from things she'd said that Lauria didn't get along with her mother, but I could see the inner strength that Lauria shrugged off. Andromeda got her freedom by manipulating a master of manipulation. She'd raised her daughter as a freewoman—and despite her own loyalty to Kyros, she'd escaped and hidden quite well since slipping out of the Koryphe with Lauria and Xanthe. Lauria didn't give her enough credit. But then, I'd never had to listen to her nag.

My mother . . . had been the one who told me that the river would free us someday. I couldn't remember her face anymore, but I could remember her voice saying, "The djinni promised us." The first time she said it, it was right after one of the other slaves had run away. I wanted to run, too, and she'd stroked my hair and said, "No, no, we can't do that. We'll all be free someday, when our river returns. The rivers' return will free us all." I'd imagined our river returning for days after that. Of course, in my fantasies, it came in a gentle rush, rolling down from the mountains but never so much as splashing beyond the banks. "Look," I'd imagined shouting to my mother—of course, in my fantasies I'd somehow been on the riverbank to see it coming, not closeted up in the household of our owner. "Look! The river! It's coming! The river has returned!"

Alibek thought the saying meant some people would never be free because the rivers would never return. Except, if it was bound up by djinni, Lauria *could* free the northern river. She could go to the valley where the water was bound, and free the djinni. The water would come crashing down like the temple had. And then what? Then we'd see death that would make the fall of the temple look harmless. Janiya had sacrificed her life to protect the spell-chain that kept that river bound. But that was when she was loyal to the Greeks.

The river would kill anyone in its path—Greek, Danibeki, Persian, foreigner. But the Danibeki slaves believed that the rivers' return would free them—and many slaves, like my mother, were really only thinking about the northern great river when they said that. If it came back, would their belief make it true?

Slaves often outnumbered their masters—maybe not here in the heart of the Penelopeian Empire, but in Elpisia, Daphnia, Casseia . . . If the slaves believed that they were *destined* to be free and rose up, the Greeks around them wouldn't stand a chance. And neither would the army. With no one to watch its back . . . nowhere close by to get food and supplies . . .

Besides, if the river returned, the Greeks would also believe that their empire was doomed. They'd heard the same stories. Just because they mocked the slave stories didn't mean they wouldn't believe them if they looked up to see the flood coming. Even if only the northern one returned.

The flood wouldn't touch the steppe.

That made it much easier for me to feel that the destruction would be worth it.

But Lauria was dead. Lauria was dead, and the river would never be free. Not in my generation.

I gave up on sleeping, and opened my eyes, staring into the darkness. Andromeda was asleep now, I thought. Janiya and Alibek were asleep. Damira had gone to sleep ages ago. I was the only one awake. I sat up and leaned against the wall, feeling a restlessness stirring inside me. I wished I could go for a walk. I wondered if this was how Lauria felt when the cold fever had her. Probably not exactly.

It was during one of her cold fevers that she decided that she was supposed to free the rivers. That it was her destiny. I was no crazy sorceress, and I could think things through sensibly, even on a restless, sleepless night, even fearing the worst about Lauria. And so it wasn't until some dark, dark hour that I decided that even if Lauria was dead, I refused to give

up hope. If she could not free the river, then I would.
Janiya had stolen that spell-chain once. It was still in
Penelopeia, and stealing it again had to be possible.

   *Maybe*, I thought.

   I would try.

# CHAPTER SIXTEEN

# *L*AURIA

*W*hen I first heard a sound, I thought I was imagining things—that I had been walking in the dark, in silence, for *so* long, my mind was beginning to make things up to amuse itself. I stopped walking and listened, and heard nothing until I held my breath. Then, there it was, very faint: the sound of trickling water.

I walked for a while after that without the sound growing any louder. Then I realized that I could hear it even when I was not holding my breath, and sometime after *that* I realized that the darkness around me was no longer complete. I could see the outline of my hand when I held it up before me—barely, faintly, in the dark.

Then I walked for another long while before I realized I could see light, somewhere up ahead.

First, I saw a faint gleam, like one of the stars that

disappears when you look straight at it. That grew brighter, then larger. The speck became a glint, then a crevice of light. I kept walking. And came, at least, to the doorway, where I could look out of the tunnel. I saw hills—green hills, and mountains beyond them— and bright sunshine. I stepped out onto the grass, still damp with dew, and stumbled almost immediately. The world felt wrong around me—or perhaps *I* felt wrong. In that first moment of confusion I wasn't sure. But I put out my hands to catch myself, and realized that I couldn't see them. *Surely I am dead,* I thought. *A ghost in the world.* I turned to look back. The tunnel was gone. Instead, I saw the city.

The city was set into a valley. From the hill I stood on, I could see it all like a box of jewelry spilled onto a table. The buildings glistened in the sun like pearls, but pearls of a hundred different vivid colors. A path led down from where I was, and I started down it.

Last winter, during my melancholia, Zivar had become convinced that if only we ran fast enough, we would be able to fly—this, she was certain, would cure me. She'd dragged me outside and made me run around in the snow before letting me go back to bed. As I walked along the path, my recollection of that day came back to me with a vivid force, and I started to run again, even though I was barefoot. After a moment or two of running, I kicked off with a foot as if I were pushing up from the bottom of a lake, and the air lifted me as water would have. *I can fly. Truly. Just as Zivar said . . .*

Flying took no particular effort, as it turned out— merely intention. I probably hadn't needed a running start. I set myself toward the shimmering flower garden of a city, and a short while later I soared over it, then down into it, alighting like a bird on the roof of one of the tall buildings.

The buildings here were tall and narrow, as if they'd been stretched out, and the colors shimmered within the rocks themselves. The building I had lit upon was blue, with an orange roof. I slid down to the edge and peered at the street below. There were people here, and they looked like people. Tall, but otherwise fairly ordinary, at least from above: black and dark brown hair, tanned skin. No one looked up at me. I hesitated for a moment, then slid off the edge and floated gently to the ground, landing in the street itself. No one looked at me. They passed quickly, busy with their own errands. They all had a faint shimmer, I decided, just like their buildings. Perhaps the shimmer was in my eyes and not my surroundings. And I saw the eyes of a woman as she passed. They weren't brown, like normal eyes, or even blue. They were *red*, and with slitted pupils like a cat's. I recoiled, and for a moment her eyes flicked toward me and I thought she would see me. But they looked right through me, and she kept on.

I raised myself to my toes, then up into the air again, gliding over people's heads. They couldn't see me, and that made me wonder if they also couldn't touch me—but I flinched at the thought of trying to stand still and let someone walk into me, or through me. I skimmed along the edges of the buildings; I could smell the velvety scent of the red flowers that cascaded from window boxes. When I hovered just outside a window, I could smell a delicately earthy scent like rice cooking. I wondered if I could *eat* here. At least I could smell.

I could hear their voices, too, but no words. Each

voice I heard was singing—humming, really. Some of them seemed to be humming in harmony. Just a few of the people in the streets seemed to be doing it; most were silent.

*If this is the underworld, why is everyone else* different *from me?*

*If I am a ghost, why am I a ghost somewhere so strange?*

The city was *very* strange: the brightly colored buildings and the oddly colored eyes were the least of the strangeness. There were no horses here—none at all. There were large animals that looked a bit like oxen who pulled wagons, and there were people who rode in the wagons, but no one rode astride the oxen. The clothing was all as bright as the buildings: red, blue, green, yellow. Dyes like that would cost a small fortune, but even the simplest clothing seemed to be colored that way. Finally, when the sun went down, the city didn't become as dark as it should have. In nearly every window, I could see the soft glow of a steady white light, as if every person in this city owned bottled moonlight and took it out as needed. I peered in windows, and each household seemed to have a stone the size of my cupped hands that glowed brightly, giving them light as they went about their business. The white stones never stopped glowing; if someone wanted to go to sleep, they simply tossed a black cloth over it to dampen the glow.

I stretched out on the roof of one of the buildings and stared up at the sky. I felt no urge to sleep, no tiredness. *Well, that could just be the cold fever . . .* Or it could be this strange place. The moon was in the same phase as it was at home; the stars were laid out in the same patterns. I saw Alexander on his throne, and Bucephalus with his tail that pointed north. Somehow the stars being right, with everything else that was *wrong*, almost made things worse.

*I miss Tamar.*

*If this is the underworld, then surely I will see her again—someday. Surely we'll be able to find each other when she dies.* But I didn't feel convinced. I wished I could sleep, but I couldn't, so I lay awake and waited for the sun to rise again.

*A*s the sky began to lighten with the edge of dawn, I heard the rattle of a wagon in the streets and the scrape of a bucket as someone drew water up from a well; the city was beginning to wake. I heard the squawk of a bird—it was as noisy as a rooster, but its call sounded like it was saying *rrk-awk, rrk-awk,* rather than the *erk-a-rrk-a-roo* of a rooster. As the sky grew lighter I could see a wagon below, drawn by a pair of the oxen. I glided down for a closer look and saw that there were people riding in the back of the wagon, looking haggard and exhausted as they clung to the hard wooden benches.

*The other dead?* I wondered.

I followed along behind the wagon, which rattled to a stop in front of a small house. Three people—a man, a woman, and a little girl—climbed out. They were each presented with an armful of clean, brightly dyed clothing and a box of fresh fruit. The door to the house was open, and the family went inside. The wagon moved on.

*Surely they're the other dead, and this is the underworld. But why did they arrive here so differently from me?* I felt suddenly chilled. *Is it because I lacked for funeral rites? I had no burial, but drowned in that lake?* I slid into the wagon anyway.

We stopped at five more cottages. Each was small but clean, freshly painted the same bright colors as everything else, and with a pot of bright red flowers next to the front door. Each person was presented with clothing and fruit, then left at their house. At last, I was alone in the wagon. I looked into the face of the driver, but like everyone else, he did not appear to see me. Instead, the oxen began to pull us up the hill, toward what seemed to be the center of the city.

We passed through a market square. Like everything else, this was both familiar and foreign. I could see all sorts of goods available. The uncut cloth was the same vivid colors as all the clothes; the fruits, vegetables, and other foods were utterly unfamiliar, though they looked rather tasty. The people shopping at the market used glass beads rather than metal coins; they carried them on thongs around their necks, tied with complicated knots, and when someone wanted to make a purchase they untied their necklace and counted out the sum. This seemed reasonable enough until we passed a stall near the edge of the market square, where people were being handed the necklaces of beads in exchange for nothing at all.

I had seen no books, I realized as we pulled away from the market. No paper or ink. No scribe for hire to read and write letters.

Beyond the market was a large building of green and blue stones—grander than the other buildings I'd seen. It had pillars, and a huge staircase leading up that looked like it was mostly there to impress people. Most of the people going in seemed to be carrying baskets of fruit, artfully arranged; a few carried flowers. *A temple.* I left the wagon and followed the faithful up the stairs and inside.

Beyond the pillars I hesitated for a moment to let my eyes adjust to the dimmer light. I was in an entryway. White-robed acolytes accepted the baskets of fruit and offered blessings, but the faithful seemed to penetrate no farther. There was a hum coming from within the building, and I realized it was the sound of many voices singing in unison.

The laypeople did not seem to go beyond the entryway, but the door to the interior stood open. Not only was it open, on looking a little closer I realized that the edge was decorated with a mosaic that looked exactly like one of the designs Saken had done on her vest last summer. My heart leapt a little. *Is Saken here? Maybe she can explain to me what's going on . . .* I went through the door.

The interior of the temple was a huge, shadowy room with a high ceiling. It was filled with white-robed singers. They weren't singing words, merely holding a note together, endlessly; it echoed in my head and in my bones. *The note has a color,* I thought, but I couldn't place it. *Or a taste. Zivar would love this.*

The people faced inward, their eyes closed as they sang; there were men and women. I took a hesitant step forward out of the doorway. There was a path of green stones set into the floor, leading into the circle. White flowers—real ones, not mosaic ones—were scattered along the edges of the path, and the scent rose up to embrace me. I could glimpse the inner mosaic that the singers surrounded, and I realized that one of the pictures looked just like something I'd embroidered on *my* vest last summer. A wineglass, except that the one I'd embroidered was broken, and this one was whole. And a horse.

I took another step forward. No one looked at me. Did they know I was here? Certainty rose up that if I stepped into the circle, they would. *This is for me. They are here for me.*

I took another step forward. The singers were smiling, their arms linked. An image nudged at the edge of my thoughts, and at the edge of the circle, I suddenly realized what this reminded me of: a spell chain. The way a spell-chain looked when you held it in the borderland, hunting a djinn.

I hesitated and backed away a step. I thought I'd go around the circle, or maybe fly up over it. As I leapt up, I brushed against one of the singers, and her thoughts echoed loudly into my own, as if she had just shouted into my ear. "Welcome home, chosen one. Welcome home, chosen one. Welcome home, chosen one."

Shaken, I backed off a step. Then I touched another one, and again heard the words in my ear. "Welcome home, chosen one, welcome home, chosen one, welcome home, chosen . . ."

Did they know I had touched them? I saw no rising tension.

*They want me to step into the circle. That's what I'm supposed to do.*

*Well, maybe I should. It's not like I have some better idea of what to do next.*

I touched one more singer, a young man.

"RUN AWAY, LAURIA. RUN AWAY, THEY'RE GOING TO KILL YOU. RUN AWAY, LAURIA. RUN AWAY, THEY'RE GOING TO KILL YOU."

I stumbled back. If hearing the thoughts of the others had been like having someone shout in my ear, this was an anguished scream. I suddenly noticed that every white-robed acolyte in the circle had a silver knife on their belt, gleaming in the dim light.

I touched the man again.

"IT'S A TRAP. IT'S A TRAP. IT'S A TRAP. IT'S A TRAP."

*He* knew I was here, so surely the others had an inkling of it. But if I left—how would I find him again, to ask him what was going on, where I was? *If they're going to kill me, does that mean I'm not already dead?* There were others coming into the room now, and I saw the man's eyes open just a fraction. I touched him again, and this time, instead of words, an image washed over me: a hill outside of town, a particular rock. And then a word, so forceful that I felt my head would break from the impact: *GO.*

A new circle was forming along the edge of the room—more white-robed singers, the sharp knives at their belts. Rather than passing through the door again, I lifted up, past dust and cobwebs and muttering birds, out an upper window and over the town. No force held me back, and I didn't wait around to hear whether the hum turned into a shriek of frustration.

As I glided back down the hill, I realized that I could see the white-robed acolytes everywhere, their silver knives at their sides. How had I not noticed them before? The brightness seemed to have gone out of the day. My own fear seemed to be reflected in the faces of the ordinary people in the streets now; how had I ever thought this was a peaceful place? They didn't shrink from the people with knives, as I did, but their eyes darted around, and their bodies were tense.

As the echoes of the man's shout faded, I realized that there was something oddly familiar about his voice. Where had I heard it before? If this was the underworld, could he be someone I'd known, who died? It wasn't my long-ago friend Nikon, nor was it Thales, the soldier who'd probably died with his garrison because he recognized me when I raided with the Alashi. *Not that he'd be inclined to help me out even if he could,* I thought. It couldn't be anyone from the Alashi because I'd spent my time there with women, and this had been a man.

*No. Wait a minute.*

I remembered a man's voice speaking within the camp of the Sisterhood. *You ask me to make a choice? I would stay with you.*

The djinn from the bandits' spell-chain—the spell-chain I'd used during that final fight. The djinn I'd freed by smashing the binding stone. The first djinn I'd ever freed. *How could that man have been him? How could he be here?*

And then I knew. *I am in the borderland—the Silent Lands. When I passed through that gate, I came here with my body rather than just my spirit.*

*When the people here go through that gate to my side, they become djinni.*

*And now I have passed through to their side and am a djinn myself.* A rogue djinn, with none of the substance or power lent by binding. Was that what they'd hoped to do with the spell-chain in the temple? But we didn't kill djinni when we bound them, and the man—djinn—had told me that they meant to kill me. Why?

I decided to forget about finding the man who'd warned me—I needed to get home. I flew back to the hills, to the place where I'd come out of the tunnel. Surely there was a way back. Somehow. *Even if I drown in the lake, better that than whatever they're planning for me here.*

I found the place in the hills where I'd come through, but no tunnel, gate, or secret door—just rocks, grass, and scrubby bushes. Then—*There.* I saw a flickering light appear in the air. It was almost like seeing a djinn, but I knew that's not what I was seeing. *It's one of ours. A shaman or a sorceress.* I eagerly looked for a doorway behind it and tried to slip through. I could see a glittering thread that fastened it back to its own side, but I couldn't follow.

The spirit hesitated for a moment, then approached me. I tried to grab its arms, to shout, "Help me get home!" but it was already moving on, as if it could tell that I was not what it was hunting.

Then it began to fly, much as I had, but skimming along the ground like a low-flying bird. I followed it to a creek near the edge of the city, fed by water running down from the mountains. A group of women squatted at the edge, scrubbing clothes and spreading them out to dry. The women all wore crimson, with crimson scarves to keep their hair out of their faces; they hummed as they worked, and as I came near, following behind the spirit, I could hear that they hummed in harmony.

Then one of them saw the spirit and let out a piercing trill. She flung the clothes she was scrubbing at it, and the women scattered.

For a moment I couldn't see the spirit. Then I spotted it, pursuing one of the running women.

Something glittered, and a moment later I saw the woman surrounded with a burning light. My eyes watered and I had to look away. *This is what a spell-chain looks like to the djinni, when Weavers come for them.*

The woman let out a high, horrified wail. Then they winked out together like a snuffed candle, and the sound was gone.

The other women drifted back to the bank of the creek. They gathered up their work and left, their voices silent, their shoulders slumped.

I felt sick. *Could I have intervened? I don't see how. I couldn't even touch the sorceress.* I drifted slowly back to the hill where I'd come through. Near it, I saw the acolyte who'd warned me, hiking toward a spot higher up. I followed behind him silently. He'd shed his white robe and was wearing vivid blue clothes instead. He glanced behind him, but didn't see me—he was looking to make sure no one had followed him. Surely they hadn't wanted him to warn me. Had they known who sent me away?

He reached a flat rock—the one he'd shown me—and lay down on it with a sigh, looking up at the sky.

I brushed his shoulder, not sure how else to get his attention, and he jerked upright; his cat's eyes focused on me, and I saw him smile faintly. He stretched out his hand and thrust it into my chest.

*You are bound either way,* the woman said. *Would you rather that we continue to hold your chain, or would you like us to return you to the bandits?* And then—*How do I free you?* The woman was me; I was seeing what the djinn remembered.

"Yes," I said. "I remembered your voice." I gestured toward where I had come out of the tunnel. "You warned me to run—thank you."

The man bowed, and pantomimed taking a hand and kissing it.

"What is your name?"

This was a harder question than I had expected. Finally, he said, "Kasim."

"Kasim—why did they want to kill me?"

Kasim held up his hand, flat, for me to touch. I gently pressed my hand to his, and again the pictures washed over me. Again, I saw myself—and I saw the gate the djinni saw, within my body like a whirling flame. Then, the drowned gate, the gate I'd found under the lake.

Then another set of pictures—these were rough, sketchy, and I realized he was trying to show me what *could* happen, not what *had* happened. I saw a woman in white robes stabbing through my chest, pinning my body to the floor with a long, thin knife. And then a dark slit in the air—my gate, fixed to the spot where I had died. And then stones laid on stones, building a doorway like the one under the reservoir. *Gate.*

"Why?"

Kasim dropped his hand and thought a moment, his face showing impatience and frustration. Then he held up his hand again. This time his pictures showed me first one gate, with glints of light passing through it, then two. When I still shook my head, baffled, he took a deep breath and spoke aloud. The words came out thick, and difficult to understand. "*You* have a gate. Now"—he stabbed a finger at my chest—"now *we* have a gate."

"Are you saying there isn't a gate on this side? Or

wasn't until I came through? But I've seen djinni—
your people—on our side, who weren't bound!"

Kasim held up his hand, and I touched it. This time
he told me a story in pictures. First, I saw a ghostly
sorceress: a silver thread led back to her own side, to
her body, and I watched as she dragged a reluctant
djinn with her. Then I saw a shaman, also with a silver thread; a djinn grasped his hand as the shaman
followed his own thread back through the gate, van-
ishing in a brief flare of light.

What would it mean for the djinni to have a gate of
their own?

"Would a gate on this side help your people—the
bound djinni—to return?"

"No," Kasim said aloud.

"Then what—"

He raised his hand, and when I touched it, he
showed me another picture: a woman with cat-slitted
eyes, twisting wire into a necklace. *She's making a
spell-chain.*

"You could enslave us," I said. "The way we enslave you—you could do that to us."

"Yes," Kasim said.

A wave of panic and horror crashed through me,
rocking me like Kasim's voice had, back at the temple. Kasim was holding out his hand—he had more to
tell me. Grimly, I took his hand to see the pictures. It
was sketched pictures again—a trail of nuts leading
to a crude trap, only the animal walking into the trap
was me.

"You're saying I was lured here? How?"

This time the images Kasim showed me were a
jumble of my own memories. Dreams, messages,
hints from the djinni. "This was all to lead me here?

The idea that I was supposed to free the river—the message about where Thais was—all of it?"

Kasim said, "Most." He held out his hand to pass me another picture: Xanthe's face, avoiding my eyes.

"How was Xanthe ever mixed in with this?"

A picture of the magia, the one I hadn't seen. Lurking in her eyes, there was a djinn. She was not possessed, exactly, but . . . inhabited. And then Xanthe, kissing her hand.

"Xanthe never met my eyes," I whispered. *She didn't want me to see* . . . "I need to get home. How do I get home?"

Kasim shook his head. "I don't know," he said aloud, and his face reflected the horror I knew was in mine.

"Maybe the gate will work for me, since I don't belong here."

Kasim offered his hand and gave me a picture of sorceresses and shamans flickering in and out from a hundred different points, like a tapestry sewn with a hundred different needles.

"You're saying they come through randomly? All over?"

He shrugged and gestured toward the valley.

"They come through randomly, but only in this valley?" He nodded. "Why live here, then? When the sorceresses come here to kidnap you?"

Kasim chuckled a little, an unnatural laugh. The images he sent made no sense: a gang of children wandering through the streets, an acolyte at the temple, a woman who looked like she was starving to death. I must have looked baffled, because he tried another: meat, flung to savage animals, to keep them satisfied.

"You're saying that you live here because *someone* has to?"

Another image: a family climbing out of a wagon, receiving gifts of clothing and food. The marketplace stall where all comers were given the strands of glass beads that could be used to buy all they needed.

And then I understood. "They *pay* you to live here. You came here because you were starving, and here they feed you. And they pay people to live here because that way, the Weavers won't stray beyond this valley to look for prey."

Apparently I'd gotten close enough. He folded his hands.

"I'll try going back with a shaman," I said.

I thought about walking around to try to find one, but I wasn't sure that would accomplish much; I lit on the rock beside Kasim and waited, instead. Shamans were more likely to come through at night in any case. "Why aren't there more gates?" I asked. "I mean, gates like me. I know there have been others, but if it's the djinni who made me into a gate, why not make every shaman into a gate, or every slave?"

Kasim showed me someone cooking, making a complicated recipe with a rare ingredient. It wasn't quite that easy, in other words.

"How many others are out there?"

Kasim shrugged.

"Do you think we can wait here safely? Or are the people from the temple looking for us?"

Kasim shrugged again, pointed at me, and gestured upward. *Oh—he wants me to go look. Yeah, I could do that.* I lifted and circled for a bit, looking to see if anyone was coming. No one was.

"What are they going to do now? If I'd stepped

into the circle, they were going to kill me, but I didn't, so now what?"

Kasim held out his hand. The picture he showed me was a sketch of me in the pit.

"You're saying they think there's no escape, so they've got time to figure it out?"

"Yes," he said aloud.

The afternoon passed slowly. Several times, I saw sorceresses come through; Kasim tensed, but all moved in another direction. I wondered if there were always this many hunters in a day—if they came through all over the valley, there were doubtless many we weren't seeing. Kasim knew at a glance that these were sorceresses, not shamans; apparently the sorceresses burned more brightly because of the weapon—the spell-chain—each held. I had met a couple of sorceresses, back at home. I wondered whether I might recognize one of the sorceresses here if I stood face-to-face with her—wouldn't it be strange to meet Zivar here?—but I feared drawing their attention to Kasim.

In late afternoon, I saw a shaman come through. Kasim pointed him out to me as someone we had no need to fear. I tried to grab him, but I lacked the substance to seize his robe. It wasn't Jaran, or Tamar, or anyone else I knew; he didn't seem to even know I was there, though he made a respectful bow toward Kasim. When he left, he was gone, and I was left behind.

Night was falling around us. This was when most of the shamans would be coming. *Perhaps it will work yet,* I thought. *Perhaps I just need a shaman that I know—someone I have a connection to.*

Kasim had come without food or a blanket; he

curled up in a hollow place under the rock to sleep. *I will keep watch over you,* I thought, though I doubted I could protect him from much of anything. I rested on top of the rock, staring up at the sky and the all-too-familiar stars. I thought about the river—the distant river I had thought I was meant to free. *It was all a lie. They didn't mean for me to free the river, or the djinni that bound it—they just wanted me to come here, die, and become their gate.*

I tried to tell myself that it didn't matter what *they* had meant for me. I reached for the certainty that had once filled me with strength like a flooding river. I found only a still, placid pool within. *The madness is gone,* I realized with a sudden clarity. *The sorceress's madness, it's left me. Or I've left it.*

I thought back over the last months—the dizzying energy I'd felt when the cold fever raged, the stark despair of the melancholia. *It was the cold fever that told me to free the rivers. It was the cold fever that told me I could do it, and it was the djinni that told me I was chosen for the task—but they were lying, trying to lure me to the northern river's source so that I would come here. Come here to die.*

*I wasn't chosen. This was not my appointed task—it was a lie.*

*I need to go home. And when I get there, to hell with freeing the river. I'm going to find Tamar and go with her back to the Alashi.*

*If the river's going to return, it's going to have to find its way out without me.*

# CHAPTER SEVENTEEN

# TAMAR

*I* woke to the sound of wood splintering, and a woman's voice shouting, "Open, in the name of Athena!" The house was full of women with swords in their hands. I realized with sick despair that it was the Sisterhood Guard. Who sent them here? Had one of us been seen? Or was Andromeda reporting on us? It couldn't be Andromeda, I decided, because they'd have come sooner.

They jerked me to my feet and took me outside to stand against the wall of the house. "Stay calm," Alibek whispered as they shoved him beside me. "Fighting right now would be suicide."

Where was Janiya? Damira? Had they slipped out earlier? They must have. The guards brought Andromeda out, bound her hands, and stood her beside me and Alibek. One woman who seemed to be in charge touched Andromeda's cheek and smiled at her. "Remember me?"

"Xanthe," Andromeda said. Her voice shook. "I thought you were on our side."

"Your daughter is dead," Xanthe said. "Drowned. No longer a problem to the Sisterhood. But Kyros would like to see *you*." She turned to the other guards. "Bring the other two as well."

At least Janiya hadn't been here. Surely Xanthe would have recognized her. I felt sick as I stumbled along through the dark streets. The sun was rising when we reached the Koryphe. As soon as we were inside, Xanthe took Andromeda in one direction, and the rest of the guards took me and Alibek in another. Andromeda glanced over her shoulder as she was being led away. Her lips moved. "Xanthe lies," I thought she said.

Alibek and I were marched down a long spiral stair and into a dim hallway lined with barred doors. It was cold. The guards opened one door, shoved Alibek inside, and then touched a spell-chain nailed to the wall and muttered something. On to the next cell, where they pushed me in. The door shut, and as the guards touched the spell-chain, I felt a heaviness seize my limbs. I stumbled, then lay down on the floor as there was nowhere else to go. I had thought that Alibek and I would be able to talk to each other, but it felt like my mouth was full of cotton. I could breathe and groan, but not speak. The spell-chain, I thought. They must be using djinni to help guard prisoners. I was bound up like a fly in a spider's web. I couldn't even shift my weight to ease the ache in my bones where they pressed against the stone floor.

My stomach lurched and I fought down nausea. If

I threw up, I wouldn't be able to spit it out. I would choke to death. Finally, my stomach settled, but fear still hummed in my ears. I forced myself to breathe deeply, to tense and relax my body. Fear was useless to me now, but I was a shaman. I had one door still open to me—I could go to the borderland. Perhaps I would find Zhanna there. It was only just dawn, and she might still be sleeping. I could tell her what had happened, and what we knew. And not to expect us to come back.

I closed my eyes and took another deep breath. I focused my thoughts on my breath, and on the drip-drip-drip of water I could hear somewhere far away. After a time, I felt my mind float free.

*Zhanna,* I called in the grayness. *Jaran.*

Silence.

It was day. They were probably awake.

I could come back tonight. Well, unless I was dead.

I decided I might as well stay in the borderland as long as I could. It wasn't as if I had anything useful to do back in my body.

I had spent a long time in the borderland once before, when I had tried to keep Lauria from binding a djinn. Day or night, I saw the borderland as a misty twilight unless I wanted it to look like something else. Djinni were flickers in the mist. I bowed when I saw them.

Zhanna and Jaran were both awake, but could I find anyone else? When Andromeda said, "Xanthe lies," maybe she meant that Lauria wasn't dead. Suddenly hopeful, I looked for my tie to her, but it was still gone. I closed my eyes and rested my face against my hands. I would see her again. For now, I needed to look elsewhere.

I focused on the web of threads that tied me to people. Kyros found me because we were bound together by the rape, and I could see the thread to Kyros, though it was slack—he was awake.

Unfortunately, a depressing number of threads bound me to people like Kyros. There were ties to the Alashi sisterhood, as well—the women I had served with last summer. But I saw no threads I could use to let me pull someone into the borderland with me. Either they were awake, like Zhanna and Jaran, or they weren't bound to me strongly enough.

Then I realized that one thread was much stronger than the others—it pulsed with light. It was Alibek, I realized, and I smiled a little to myself as I thought about the kiss we'd shared. Well. Why not?

*Alibek? Can you hear me?*

And he was there—with me, in the borderland. He looked confused, and I quickly made it look like an Alashi yurt. "Am I dreaming?" he asked. "Or did they come and kill me, and we're dead?"

"You're dreaming," I said. "This is the borderland. I brought you here. Since they're probably going to kill us in a few hours, I thought we might as well keep each other company here. So we can talk."

Alibek looked out. "I see the steppe," he said.

"I can make it into something else, if you'd like. Any place I've seen."

"I can't think of anywhere I'd rather be," Alibek said.

"Me either." I stepped outside and stretched. The wind rippled across the grass. The sky was cloudless blue. A perfect day.

"Can you talk to Zhanna? Tell her what happened?"

I shook my head. "I tried. It's too late in the morning. Everyone's awake."

"Surely there's something we can do."

"Something useful, you mean?" I shook my head. "Bringing you here was the best I could come up with."

He let out his breath in a silent laugh and opened his mouth to say something mocking. But then he fell silent for a moment, and said, "I am honored." He brushed my hand with his, then let it fall to his side. "I assume it's my company you wanted, and not . . ."

I laughed a little, nervously.

"You would be happier with *someone else*, wouldn't you?" he said.

"What do you mean?"

"Lauria. For, you know." He clasped my hand again. "*That* kind of companionship." His grip went a little tighter. I jerked my hand away.

"Look, Alibek. I know you hated her, so just leave it, please. She was my blood sister, and I wasn't even there by her side when she died." And she'd sworn that she'd come back to me. "She was never *that kind of friend*, she was my sister. And I can't take defending her from you. Not right now."

"Tell me something," Alibek said. "Why did you follow her? You could have stayed with the Alashi. Was it because she saved you from the bandits? Because you were blood sisters?"

"No." I rubbed my palm. "I followed her because I loved her, and she loved me." I stared at the ground for a moment. It had started to drift to grayness, but I narrowed my eyes and it re-formed itself into cracked earth and dry grass. "Do you at least believe now that she spoke the truth when she said that she had turned away from Kyros?"

"I never doubted it," Alibek said. "The Lauria I knew—Kyros's perfect servant—never would have come back to defend you. But she is still the one who took *me* back to slavery. Surely there are people that *you* will never forgive."

"Kyros," I said. "Though, you know, that gives him power over me. We're bound together. He can find me in the borderland." Alibek glanced around. "I don't think he's coming right now," I said.

"Kyros was never *your* owner, was he?"

"No. Kyros was . . ." I tipped back my head to look up at the sky for a moment. "Kyros was my *first.*"

"Ah," Alibek said, and nodded. "Yes. He was my 'first' too, of course."

"I was ten," I said.

"That's very young," Alibek said. "I was eleven."

"If the djinni could give me a knife that would sever the tie between Kyros and me, I would use it in a heartbeat," I said.

"But if they said that to break that tie, you had to forgive him—what then?"

I shook my head. "I don't know."

"But you would have me forgive Lauria?"

I turned away. "Kyros, to me, is *only* a rapist. Lauria is far more than that."

Alibek held out a fistful of grass. After a moment, it turned into a wreath of flowers, like the wreaths Prax and the other mine slaves made after their escape. "Tamar," he said. "Show me Lauria through *your* eyes. Help me to see the person you love."

Well, this was the borderland. I could make that

happen. I closed my eyes for a moment and made the tents and the steppe fade away.

The first time I saw her was in Sophos's harem. The room pieced itself together—the carpets, the scent of perfume, the low strum of the dombra. The door opened, and Boradai brought Lauria in. She was the oldest pretty virgin I'd ever seen. Her eyes flicked around the room, and her smile was nervous.

"You didn't love her then," Alibek said. He sat beside me on the carpet, barefoot, his ankles crossed. I saw him as *he* had been in Kyros's harem: pretty, smooth-skinned. Kyros's little bird.

"No." I resented her. She was so much older than me. All those years working in the stables. And she wasn't afraid. I envied her fearlessness even though it made no sense.

I cupped my hands and closed my eyes, trying to gather together *everything* I saw. When I opened my eyes, Lauria looked like a giant. Enormously tall, with a booming laugh, she walked like a Greek even though she was one of us. Below, I was no longer Tamar, but a snake, coiling at her feet, tasting bitterness.

"What changed?" Alibek asked.

A flicker, and we stood outside in the courtyard— Lauria clutching her torn shift, covered in her own blood. She crept into the bathhouse and scrubbed herself raw in the cold water.

Lauria was small now, like me. And I was no longer a snake: I was a woman, but covered in blood as well. Lauria's blood, because I knew that this was at least partly my fault.

"*Your* fault?" Alibek asked.

I took a deep breath. I had never admitted this to

Lauria. "When Sophos sent for her, he called me in first, briefly, and asked me how nervous Lauria was." The courtyard vanished, and Alibek saw me speaking to Sophos. This time, I saw myself as a mouse, shrinking back from a cat. "Not nervous," I said. "Hardly nervous at all." I hadn't wanted to give Sophos the pleasure of her fear. But I'd also known that Sophos was always more brutal when he thought a slave needed to be taught a lesson.

"And he did teach her a lesson," Alibek murmured. "Do you really think it would have made a difference if you'd told him she was terrified? He had eyes. She was only able to infiltrate the Alashi because he raped her."

"That's also why she turned against them," I said.

"Yeah, that was the risk they took. But Sophos must have known the first Lauria you saw could never pass as anything but a spy. But later . . ."

The night she escaped, she covered me with her shawl before she slipped out. That's what woke me. I followed her, and saw she had the means to escape. She had somehow arranged for food and water, even a pair of boots. The hunger to escape had risen in me like a flood.

What was Lauria, in my eyes, at that moment? She was a horse. An ox. A palanquin. A means to an end—I would have said anything at all to make her take me along.

"I told her if she didn't take me along, I'd raise the alarm," I said. "I didn't know that Sophos had planned the escape. He *had* to find a way to get her out. If I'd raised the alarm, it wouldn't have mattered. But the next time . . ."

The bandit's tent formed around us, rank and

dark. I had ached from the way he had used me. I wished for death, and when it didn't come, I tried to take my mind somewhere else, and half succeeded. Then I heard a horse screaming, and then the rough sound of tearing fabric, then Lauria's voice. "We have to hurry. Can you run?" She cut the ropes that bound my hands.

I gathered in the truth of what I saw, to show Alibek. To me at that moment, Lauria was Arachne freeing Prometheus from his chains on the mountainside. I had despaired, but she had restored me. So I offered her the only thing I had—my blood, my loyalty, myself as her sister. We cut our hands on the bandit's sword and swore.

My hands had clenched. I let go, and Lauria faded into mist. "We walked," I said. "We reached the Alashi. Joined the sisterhood."

"And passed the tests, of course," Alibek said.

"Yeah. We should compare sometime. I'd love to know how different yours were."

Alibek snickered at that, and we fell silent, neither of us wanting to say that we'd probably be executed side by side for banditry the minute Kyros figured out who we were. If Lauria were still alive, he'd have used us as hostages, but with her dead . . . well, it was possible he'd have us tortured first, then executed.

I took a deep breath and made the steppe again. I wanted to show him one more thing.

The night after Lauria was exiled, we made camp alone on the steppe. "I'm not going back to Kyros," Lauria said quietly, looking at the campfire. "I'd rather die. But there were five other slaves I took back. They're all still slaves. I want to find them, and free them. And take them to the steppe."

I studied her face in the dancing flames, trying to let Alibek see her as I did. She was no goddess now. I knew her secrets and her hidden darkness. But in her face, I also saw my own, and when she looked at me, I knew she saw herself reflected in my eyes. We hadn't grown up together but she really was my sister. She was my family.

If I had to choose between Lauria and the Alashi, I would choose Lauria.

My sight blurred. I let her image fade away.

Alibek was silent for a moment, then sighed, and stretched, and lay back in the grass to look up at the sky. "She spent years serving Kyros. *Years*. It wasn't until she met *you* that she realized that was wrong."

"It was the only life she knew," I said. "When she met me—well, I opened a door. But Lauria stepped through. She opened her heart. Changed. And tried to atone."

"Do you remember when you went through the initiation as Lauria," Alibek said. "When I turned my back on you?"

"Of course I remember that," I said.

"If you can summon up that night, the way you summoned up your other memories—I'd like to do that bit again."

The steppe darkened. Excited sisters crowded around the bonfire. I blinked back more tears when I saw Janiya and Zhanna. Zhanna and the priestess held torches high and I passed under the archway. They tossed the torches into the fire, then clasped my hands and kissed me.

I made my way through the crowd until I came to Alibek. He faced me as he had that night. A flare from the fire lit his face. I could see him hesitate, and for a moment I thought he would turn away from me *again*. But then he smiled into my eyes, laced his fingers through mine, and kissed my forehead. His lips felt warm and real against my skin—a true touch, not an echo.

I felt a ripple of wind that I realized, a moment later, had not come from my own thoughts.

Alibek looked behind me, and his grip on my hands went tight. "I can see her," he said. "She's standing right behind you. Did you put her there?"

I shook my head and turned, letting the steppe dissolve to grayness around us. In the twilight of the borderland, a djinn wavered in the air before us. I bowed. "It's a djinn," I said.

"It's not a djinn. It's Lauria," Alibek said.

I squinted my eyes. I didn't see Lauria's face, but Alibek was right. It was her. There was something about the djinn that made me certain it was her.

"If we're seeing Lauria, they killed us in our sleep and we're in the underworld," I said.

The djinn bobbed in the air. "She's shaking her head," Alibek said. "She's reaching out her hands to you."

Hesitantly, I stretched out my own hands. "Why can you see what she's doing so clearly?" I asked.

"Maybe it's because of the ritual," Alibek said. "I welcomed you, standing in Lauria's place. Maybe the power of the ritual is letting me see her clearly."

"What's she doing?"

"She's clasping your hands," Alibek said.

I could feel nothing.

"She looks frustrated."

"Maybe she should try grabbing your hands, since you're the one who can see her . . ."

Alibek held out his hands. "She tried, then shook her head. It's yours she wants. Keep holding them out."

I remembered the time I had brought her to me after hunting through the darkness, and I closed my eyes. "By our bond as sisters," I said. "You swore to come back to me. Let your oath bind us now."

I felt hands clasp mine. "Go," Lauria's voice whispered in my mind.

Go where? There wasn't anywhere *to* go except back to my bound, helpless body. Was that really what she meant? I hesitated and her grip tightened. "Hurry," she said.

I tried to return to my body, only my grip on Lauria held me here now like a weighted chain. It was like trying to drag a boulder with me. *I can't,* I thought, but refused to speak the words aloud—she might let go.

Surely there was a way I could get back with Lauria. If not the way I came, then another way.

There. I felt a breath on my face, as if through a crack in a door, and when I yanked this time, I felt Lauria follow. Usually returning to my body felt like nothing more than waking up, but this time I fell into my body from a great height, and jerked like a fish even in the grip of the djinn. I struggled to open my eyes. Something warm and heavy lay on top of me.

It was Lauria.

# CHAPTER EIGHTEEN

# LAURIA

Night in the Silent Lands passed as slowly as the day had. I spent much of the time thinking up ways that the djinni might yet manage to kill me, as insubstantial as I was. If they could find a way to speak with me, they could threaten people I cared about—Tamar, Janiya, my mother, Zhanna. Rogue djinni could possess the unwilling. They could seize control over someone like my mother at a critical moment and leave her defenseless.

But even if they threatened people I loved—*no way*, I thought. I couldn't hand myself over, not knowing what they planned.

But they'd find some other way. After all they'd done to bring me here, they'd find another way.

And what a great deal of trouble they had taken. They had seen my potential, even before I had the gate within; I remembered the djinn speaking to me through Jaran, back in Sophos's harem. They sent me dreams and visions, and visitors with warnings. They had encouraged me to free the people I'd taken back to slavery, then gave me directions to Thais, which had put me in Kyros's hands. *What if he had just killed me? Perhaps they sent messages to him, too.* Kyros had taken me to Penelopeia, where I had seen the picture of the drowned gate, and been shown a spell-chain lost under the water. *Was it ever really there? I bet it was not.* Then they'd whispered in Xanthe's ear to free me, and whispered to her again when it was time for her to push me out of the palanquin into the reservoir, right over the drowned gate.

*They could not force me to walk through. But they could lead me to that door and give me no other choice.*

Kasim roused after a few hours and got up, looking around to see me.

"Who built the gate?" I asked. "Your people, or my people?"

"Yours," he said, stretching, then held up his hand to show me something. The images I saw this time looked different. The details were missing, I realized after a moment. They were blurry or shadowed, impossible to see. Still, I could see the woman at the center, her long hair gathered loosely where it swept against her waist, her cat's eyes shining red. Her anger rang in my ears like jangling brass bells. Then I saw a vast boulder of shifting iridescent colors—*karenite*—shattered into dust in a sudden hot white light. Then another light, this one growing brighter, and not fading.

"The angry woman," I said. "She was one of you? And she opened the rift?"

"Yes."

"And—the boulder of karenite. What was that?"

Kasim gave me a picture of a well. I didn't understand, so he changed the picture of the well so that it held heat instead of water, then something else. Finally, he spoke aloud. "Like a well of . . . power."

"How did she destroy it? The vision didn't show that part."

"It's . . . not supposed to. That was forgotten so that it could not be done again."

"And the gate. Who built it? Ancient shamans? It couldn't have been the sorceresses . . . they drowned it."

Kasim offered a new image. I saw a Danibeki man laying bricks made of karenite. Complete, the gate opened into darkness. I wondered what he had thought he was building. Of course, djinni had been around for centuries before the Sisterhood of Weavers had had the idea of binding them, making them slaves . . .

The image faded like mist as I pulled my hand away. *The sorceresses drowned the gate,* I realized. *They can use the gate whether it's drowned or not— everyone from our side who comes to the borderland sends their spirit through that gate.*

They had always told us that the Sisterhood of Weavers flooded our ancestral lands because our ancestors fought them. It was a lie. They were hiding the gate.

"If someone destroyed the gate," I asked, my voice shaking a little bit, "could the rift be closed?"

Kasim shrugged, but his face was intrigued. "Maybe," he said.

I remembered Zhanna telling me there were many

gates, but sorcery, at least, depended on the gate at the bottom of the reservoir. Without that gate, there would be no more spell-chains. There would probably be no more shamans.

Unless the djinni killed me here and built their own gate. Then there would be spell-chains, with *us* as unwilling servants.

*I have to get back.*

Near me, I saw a shimmer in the air. *One of us.* Kasim looked at it. "Shaman," he said. I was certain he was right—it didn't pursue Kasim and, anyway, it lacked the brilliant power lent by a spell-chain. I squinted, and thought I could see the outline of a man. He bowed toward Kasim.

I approached him; he gave no sign of recognition. After a few minutes another shimmer broke into the air. He had brought someone into the borderland with him. I didn't recognize either of them. They conferred silently for a while, then one vanished abruptly. I seized the other, or tried to, knotting my hands around his wrists in an attempt to follow him back to my own side. But it was like trying to lay hands on smoke. He was there, and then he wasn't; I was on my knees on the dark hillside. Or I would have been on my knees if I'd had a proper body here. *Smoke, indeed.*

I drifted back to Kasim. "It didn't work," I said. "Show me how your people do it." I held out my hands.

Kasim touched his palm to mine. I saw a dark hillside, and the sparkle of the visitor; the djinn and the visitor clasped hands, and vanished together. *The shaman saw the djinn. They don't see me. Perhaps that's the problem?* But then he showed me a djinn clasping the ankle of a visitor, following him back like a burr caught on his clothing. *That's what I tried to do . . .*

Another sparkle, in the distance. I flew toward it: it was a woman, again a shaman, but again no one I knew. When I thought she was about to leave, I threw myself toward her, wrapping arms and legs around her. I might as well have flung myself against moonlight or mist.

"How would they even have killed me?" I asked Kasim, settling down next to him again. "I'm not solid here. I don't know how someone would kill a djinn, in my own world . . ."

Kasim raised his hand for a moment, and I started to reach to touch him, but he pulled away; he just wanted my silence. "The singing," he said.

"It would have made me solid? For long enough to be killed?"

"Yes."

The sky was growing lighter; soon I could see the sun break over the edge of the eastern mountains, like the morning when I'd watched with Zivar and Xanthe. The sky was clear today—a perfect blue. *I should be able to feel the sun's warmth,* I thought; I felt neither warm nor cold, just as I felt neither hungry nor tired. *I want to go home.*

Kasim rose, suddenly. "Come," he said, and began to walk deeper into the mountains, away from the city. His face was alive with sudden fear.

"What is it?" I asked, and he gestured for silence. Very faintly, beyond the sounds of birdsong and wind, I heard humming.

Were we already surrounded? I touched Kasim's hand, trying to find out what he thought, but he was too afraid to be coherent. He seemed to want me to stay with him, but I wasn't sure if this was because he thought he could protect me, or because he thought I could protect him.

*Fly, or stay?* I looked at Kasim's terrified face, and knew that abandoning him, after he had saved me, was wrong. It might be *better,* but it would still be wrong. I had never yet regretted saving Tamar from the bandits . . . I stayed by his side.

*Tamar,* I thought. Tamar was home; Tamar was who I wanted to return to. I rubbed the scar on my palm.

Perhaps it was my thoughts of Tamar that drew her to me when she came through. I didn't see her come through, and when I saw her and Alibek, I didn't recognize them right away. I saw two spirits, and knew they must not be sorceresses, since the sorceresses never came through in pairs, ever. Even distracted by the humming—still faint, but growing louder—I paused for a moment to look. If the humming made me solid enough to kill, it seemed unlikely that I'd be able to slip through to the other side like a djinn.

Then one of the spirits took form: the outline of a man, flickering every now and then into the outline of a songbird. *Alibek.*

*I need to make him see me.*

*He is not here alone. Could the other person be Tamar?* I studied the other spirit: after a moment or two she also took form. *Yes. It's Tamar.* "It's people I know," I hissed to Kasim. "Tamar." I tried to grab her, and couldn't. "*Tamar.* Alibek!"

They didn't notice Kasim, either. They were no doubt talking with each other.

I tried again to grab Tamar. I tried to touch her hand, where she'd cut herself when we became blood sisters; I tried to touch her hair, which I'd helped her cut when we joined the Alashi. My hand passed through her, or she passed through me. I tried to grab Alibek. I nearly screamed in frustration.

We still couldn't see the singers, but the humming was growing louder.

Alibek turned out, away from Tamar, and our eyes met. *He could see me.* I tried again to grasp his hand, to speak to him. "Listen, you need to help me. I know you hate me, but please believe, if you want to cut my throat once I'm back where I belong, it would be better than leaving me here . . ." *He can't hear a word I'm saying.* But a moment later, Tamar turned. She saw me, and I saw her recognize me, but I was as intangible to her as to the djinni. ". . . *in the underworld,*" I heard her voice say. I shook my head frantically and held out my hands.

"Take my hands, Tamar," I said. "Please. If there is a way back, it will be with you."

Tamar held her hands out, and I tried *again* to grasp them, but I still felt nothing more tangible than air. "This has to work. This *has* to work, or there's no way back . . ." *And the humming . . .* They were coming, I knew. *They'll build a new temple here—a shrine, to guard the gate . . .* The humming was making me more solid, but Tamar was intangible here, so we still couldn't touch.

*Let our oath bind us,* I heard Tamar's voice whisper in my mind, and suddenly I could feel her hands clasp mine.

*Go,* I whispered back, and when nothing happened, I tightened my grip. *Hurry.*

There was a jerk, and I felt a moment of intense cold. *I can't breathe*—and then I was through. With Tamar, in body—in fact, I was lying on top of her. I rolled off her and scrambled to my feet, and realized that she was being held on her back, helpless, by a djinn. I touched it, and opened my gate. *At last,* I heard, and it was gone.

I helped Tamar to her feet.

"We're in a prison cell in the Koryphe," Tamar said. "Alibek is here, too. Your mother—they took her somewhere else. Everyone thinks you're *dead. I thought you were dead . . . oh, Lauria.*" She gave me a tight hug.

"I wasn't dead," I said. "But you got me out just in time." Tamar was taller, and her hair had grown longer. I stepped back a half step to look into her face. No one would take her for a slave now. "A prison cell? Is there a way out?" *If they used djinni to hold the prisoners, did they still lock them in, or did the djinni make them careless?* The cell door was barred.

"There's a spell-chain over there," Tamar said, and pointed to the far wall. "That's where they get the djinni to hold us."

No one had come to investigate our voices, and when I peered out, I saw no human guards. The spell-chain was out of reach, and cemented in somehow, not hanging loose from a chain. "Djinn," I whispered, knowing they could hear me. "If any of you can open this door, and let me out, I will free *all* of you. I am the gate. You know what I can do."

There was silence for a moment. Then the bar of our cell slammed back with such force it almost broke the door. I touched the djinn and set it free, then unbarred the next cell. Alibek lay on the floor inside; I could see the djinn embracing him, like a haze of light. I freed the djinn; I could see Alibek relax, but it took a moment before he took the hand I offered him and scrambled to his feet.

I picked up a piece of brick to smash the karenite, then hesitated. I was naked; we were in a prison. "I will help you, but I want you to help me. I need clothes. Tell me if there's a guard at the door . . ."

"Weapons," Tamar said.

"If you can bring us weapons without being noticed, do it." I had been stumbling over my words, and now I backed up, to make the instructions more explicit, then shrugged. "If the Sisterhood Guard realizes that something's wrong and comes down here to check on us, I'll free you if I can, but I can't promise I'll have the chance. So don't do anything to get us caught."

The djinn flickered away. A few minutes later, a shower of loose clothing fell at my feet, including a pair of sandals. There were no weapons. "The guardswomen would notice the theft of their swords," it said. "The armory is locked, and the sound of the lock breaking would attract attention."

"Thank you," I said.

"No one waits by the doorway at the top of the stairs."

I glanced at Tamar and Alibek, trying to think if there was anything else I needed from the djinni before I freed them and we got out of here. "How did you end up here?" I asked Tamar.

"Xanthe came for your mother. Alibek and I were brought along because we were with her. Janiya escaped."

*Xanthe returned here. So what happened to Zivar?*

*If they took my mother away, where is my mother?* I felt something like heat rising inside of me, sending my thoughts scattering in a thousand directions at once, and tried to rein them in.

"We need to get out of here," I said. "But first, I need to keep my promise." I picked up a piece of rock that had crumbled out of the wall, and turned to the spell-chain.

"Wait—" Tamar said. "What if we need its help again?"

"We can't bring this spell-chain along," I said. "And I don't want to stay here." I smashed the six soul-stones with the rock. When I was done, Tamar raised her hand to point silently at one more djinn hovering before us.

"Do you need to free that one?" she asked.

I knew, looking at it, that this was not a bound djinn—it was one of the others. I shook my head.

"Maybe it can help us," Tamar said.

"We can't trust them," I said. It approached me, and I flinched away.

*Trust,* I heard it whisper. *Let me within.*

A rogue djinn, here and now—was it Kasim? Had Kasim followed me back? Or was this a trick—one of the ones who had lured me through the gate, trying even now to seize control, to drag me back to the other side to meet the death they'd so carefully planned for me? *Surely it is Kasim. If this djinn wished me ill, he could possess me and I couldn't stop him. Or could I? I've never heard of a shaman or a sorceress being unwillingly possessed by a djinn; perhaps they can't be, and I can't either.*

I closed my eyes, trying to listen to my own heart, and finally held out my hand. "Kasim?" I whispered.

I felt a burst of heat; the djinn had passed within me. When they passed through me, through the gate in my heart, I had felt that heat, but only momentarily. For a moment now I felt as if I were being consumed. *Is this how it feels to be possessed? Surely not.* Then the heat eased, and I could hear Kasim's voice within my head. The mingling of our thoughts here was not like it had been in the Silent Lands. There, I'd felt a chaotic rush of pictures and feelings when we touched, as if his memories were being poured into me like water out of a bucket. Here, I heard a voice in my head that was not my own. He spoke words, cool and measured; here, he could borrow them from me like a set of boots. His words were slow and careful, unlike the rest of my whirl of thoughts. It was tempting to push away my own madness and cling to whatever he said as if his words were my own rational thoughts. *I still can't trust him,* I thought.

*Where is my mother?* I asked Kasim. *Where is Zivar?*

Kasim stirred. *I can go look,* he said, and I felt him slipping away. It felt rather like peeling away the dead skin from a healed burn—not painful, just odd.

"He's gone to look, hasn't he?" Tamar asked. "Your eyes are different." I nodded, remembering how Xanthe had always refused to meet my eyes.

"What happened to you?" Alibek asked. "Tamar thought you were dead."

I told Alibek and Tamar about my escape with Xanthe and Zivar, our journey, the drowned passage and what I found on the other side. "They lured me there," I said, finally. "I was their tool, to be used and discarded. By enticing me through, and killing me, they could use the gate in my heart as their own, anchored on their side of the borderland. We can't trust them—we never could. They seek to make us *their* slaves, as we have made them ours."

Tamar listened, her eyes steady. "How did you find all that out?"

"Someone told me—a djinn. Kasim. The one I freed from the spell-chain when we were with the sisterhood."

"Yet you trust him."

"Well—" I thought it over. "Yes," I said. "I had helped him; he wanted to help me. He seemed to risk quite a lot, doing so. Judging by his fear."

Alibek said, "So what you're saying is, the djinni have an empire of their own; they have the elite, powerful few and they have the many ordinary people who get by as they can, just like here."

I remembered the image Kasim had given me, of the free bread given to those who became prey to the sorceresses. "Yes," I said.

"And we can't trust the djinni in charge."

"Definitely not."

"But 'the djinni' don't all agree. Any more than we agree with the Sisterhood."

"Exactly."

"Sounds like what we heard Damira say," Tamar said. "Except she called them the barley-eaters and the rice-eaters."

Kasim was back. *I could not find your mother. But Zivar is not far—underground, like you, but with a human guard.*

"I don't know if we can help her without weapons," I said.

"Does she have a guard?" Tamar said, anxiously.

Kasim was speaking at the same time. *I will seize the guard.*

"We can do this, then," I said, and started to follow the directions Kasim was whispering.

Tamar ran after me, catching my elbow. "What? Do what, and where are we going?"

"We're going to get Zivar," I said. Tamar fell into step beside me, Alibek following behind, even as part of my mind—not Kasim's part—said, *she's following me, and she doesn't even know what I'm doing or why I think I'll succeed, and I'm the crazy one?* "This will work," I assured her. It was too difficult to give her the whole explanation.

We passed a stairway and went down another corridor. There was a light ahead, spilling out of an open doorway. *It's time,* Kasim said, and I felt him leave again. When we reached the doorway, we saw that the guard had slumped to the floor, her eyes half-closed. The room was brightly lit with lamps. Inside, Zivar sat at a bare wooden table. There were jars of beads spilled out across it, and silver wire. She worked feverishly, twisting wire; the necklace was close to done, I realized.

"Zivar," I said.

She looked up: her eyes were wide and hungry, and she scanned first my face, then Tamar's, then Alibek's. "You can't be here unless I'm dead," she said, her voice shaky.

"I'm not dead, and neither are you." She was still sitting on her stool, and when I looked closer, I realized that she'd been chained to the wall, feet and wrists.

"They took my spell-chains. All of them," Zivar said.

"And forced you to bind for them," I said.

"They said—ten, and they'd set me free. Ten." She pushed her damp hair back from her face. "I considered refusing, but then thought that perhaps, *perhaps,* I'd have a chance to use one of the chains before they took it away, and escape."

"Is that the first?" I said.

She shook her head. "Third," she said.

Alibek edged in to take a look. "That looks almost done," he said. "Why don't you finish it? The djinn will make it easier to get out of here."

"Isn't there some other way?" Tamar asked. "Lauria, what about your friend who followed you back? Could he help us?"

"Help us do what?" I asked, glancing at the guard. She had slid to the floor, and was slumped over, her eyes rolling back and a thread of drool coming from her mouth.

"We had this idea to help the Alashi," Tamar said. "It was a joke, but now, well, if we could actually do it . . ." She took a deep breath and went on. "If we kidnap Kyros and steal the spell-chain that binds the great river, we think the Sisterhood will think that Kyros stole it. I think I know where the spell-chain is. Janiya had a guess—we think it's at the top of one of the really high towers, the ones you can only get into with a palanquin."

I shook my head. "A rogue djinn can't carry a palanquin. The binding gives them their strength. Unbound, they have eyes and ears but not much more. They can't *do* anything—well, other than possessing people."

"But when you freed him from the spell-chain, he moved the bandits . . ."

"He still had the strength from the spell-chain, even though the binding had been broken."

Zivar had stopped listening; she had gone back to twisting wire as quickly as she could. She clearly intended to finish the spell-chain whether Tamar liked the idea or not.

Tamar touched my hand. "Once we steal the spell-chain, we can free the river," she whispered.

*All that water.* I remembered how it had looked, shimmering in its vast bowl. With the spell-chain, I wouldn't have to hope my helper snatched me away from the water in time to avoid being swept away— we could just smash the stones, free the djinni who'd stood there for centuries. *And expose the gate,* I thought.

*Without the gate, there will be no more sorceresses, no more Sisterhood of Weavers. No more enslavement of Kasim and the others who are desperate enough to live in that valley.*

I wondered what Tamar would say about that idea. Or Zivar. Or Alibek, for that matter. *Well, we can't free the river and have the gate stay open. It would make it far too easy for another person with an inner gate to stumble through.*

Zivar had almost finished the necklace now; Tamar bit her lip and averted her eyes. One link undone, Zivar closed her eyes for what seemed like mere heartbeats, then closed the final link.

She opened her eyes: the djinn hovered beside her. "Break my chains," Zivar said sharply. There were four sharp snaps and the chains fell away. Her eyes alight, she looped the spell-chain over her head and leapt to her feet. "Stealing a spell-chain, you said? Kidnapping Kyros? Let's do it. Come on."

I took a moment to rob the guard of her sword and boots, and tie her with her own belt. Kasim left her and joined me in my mind again. *Up*, he said, and we ran for the stairs.

*W*e came up the stairs into the heat of the day. I could almost see Zivar's fever rising off her like steam; I wondered if my own was as visible to her. There was no one at the top of the stairs. *Up*, Kasim urged again, and I saw another staircase across the hall and followed it. *Up*. He was scouting ahead; I could feel him leaving, returning, and leaving again. It made me feel dizzy and a little sick—or maybe that was the sudden heat, and the ache of hunger in my stomach.

We emerged onto a small balcony, a fair way up. *Now what?* I asked Kasim.

*Send the slave for a palanquin,* he said. *Take it and get out of here.*

"Send the slave—the *djinn*—for a palanquin," I said to Zivar. I turned to Tamar. "Where's the spell-chain you want to steal?"

"I think it's there," she said, and pointed.

It was one of the needle-like towers that rose up, built by djinni and inaccessible except by palanquin. She was still speaking—saying something about gates and the magias—but I found my own thoughts seized by a flood of memories that weren't my own. *Yes*, I thought, and I wasn't sure if my certainty came from myself, or from Kasim. *There. It's there.* "Let's go," I said.

"We need to wait," Tamar said, eyeing me nervously. "We still need the palanquin."

I tried to nod crisply. "Well, of course," I said. Tamar exchanged a glance with Alibek; I ignored it.

It seemed to take hours for the palanquin to arrive. The one that arrived, finally, was scarlet and gold silk, and very small. It was as luxurious inside as any larger palanquin—the interior walls were lined with blue and green silk, embroidered with golden pictures of fish. We piled inside and the djinn took us up. It took us up *fast*—my stomach lurched and my ears felt as if they were underwater, then suddenly out again. Tamar pressed her hand to her head. Then we stopped. "There's a djinn out there, just outside the window," Zivar said. "Lauria?"

I drew aside the curtain and looked out. There *was* a djinn; it hovered in the air just outside the window. We were just out of reach.

"Can we move in a little closer?" I asked.

Zivar looked out and mulled it over. "There are djinni who were bound by sorceresses who are now dead. It's still risky to tell them to kill someone, because sometimes they kill the holder of the chain, but there are times that the dead chains are used that way. If you're right about what's up here, this *will be* one of those times. If we come too close, it will kill us."

"I have to touch it in order to set it free."

"Yes." Zivar sighed. "We could just get out of here, you know."

I met her eyes for a moment. She was nervous, but I could see excitement lurking. "You don't really want to do that," I said.

Zivar looked out at the djinn again, then at me. "Lean out," she said. "We'll hold you."

Tamar and Zivar pinned my legs. Alibek took my left hand, bracing himself against the edge of the palanquin. I inched forward, leaning out toward the djinn. I found myself looking straight down at the ground. *That is a long way down,* I thought, and was momentarily almost overwhelmed with nausea. *A long, long way down.* The people below me were so small I could barely make them out; the flying birds below me looked the size of insects. *Just pretend that's what they are—bugs, crawling things. A tiny world, not the distant real one. Don't imagine falling . . . hitting . . .*

I reached for the djinn. It was still beyond my hand. "We need to be a little closer," I said. "*Carefully,* so I don't fall." I heard Zivar's voice murmuring to her djinn. Despite her instructions, we moved with a lurch, and I felt Alibek's hand tighten on mine.

*I've trusted my life to my worst enemy,* I thought. I didn't dare look up at Alibek; I wasn't really positioned right to look at him, anyway. *All he has to do is let go. The weight of my fall would pull my legs away from Zivar and Tamar.*

"Trust me, Lauria," Alibek said softly. "I've got you."

I wriggled forward a little more. *Almost there.*

The djinn turned on me; with the part of my mind that was Kasim, I could see its face, wild with anger, mad from its years of solitude and slavery. *Die,* I heard it scream, as it came at me like a thornbush caught in a whirlwind.

I flung open the door in my heart. *Go,* I screamed back. *Find your home.*

The djinn tore through me like a barbed arrow; it had aimed to tear me to pieces, and even thrown through into its own land it came close to succeeding.

My body jerked, trying to escape the agony and nearly wrenching away from the hands that held me. I screamed. There was a sharp pain in my shoulder, and then I found myself lying on the silk rug of the palanquin.

*Kasim?*

Silence.

Had he been forced through the door when I opened it? Had he dragged the other djinn through in order to save me? I had no idea.

"Lauria? Can you hear me?" Tamar asked.

My mind was quieter now, at least. "Yes," I said. "I'm all right." My chest ached, and I rubbed my breastbone with my clenched fist. "Are there any others?"

"I don't think so," Zivar said.

"Then take us in."

Here at the top of the tower, there was a tiny balcony to land palanquins on; there was also a stout door, locked. "Break it," Zivar said to her djinn, and it smashed the door open.

"I'll go first," I said. "In case there are any more . . ."

The room was empty. Built into the wall was a strongbox: the djinn smashed it open. One final djinn emerged. "I am the guardian and the messenger," it said in toneless, perfect Greek. "I was bound first by Nikephoros, apprentice to Sostrate, apprentice to one of the First Twelve; I was re-bound most recently by Lydia. What say you of Athena and Alexander?"

I looked at Zivar. She shook her head, her eyes wide with alarm. "Free it," she hissed. "If we give the wrong answer, something bad is going to happen."

That was clearly already the wrong answer; I could

see it pulling back from us, whether to give the alarm or take us all prisoner or both, I wasn't sure. I stepped forward, grasping with my fists, feeling the djinn solid under my hands for an instant, like carved rock—and threw open the door. This djinn passed through like melting smoke. *We say of Athena, praise her, and praise her name, and praise her Weaving. We say of Alexander, that he is a fit servant for our mistress. Now you know the answer, if you are asked again* ... and it was gone.

I stepped forward and took the necklace out of the strongbox.

The necklace that bound the Syr Darya was not quite as big as I had imagined. It weighed less than a good cooking pot. Still, where most spell-chains looped twice or even three times around the neck this chain would loop at least twenty. The strands glittered with cut glass and gemstones, but also glinted with the shadows of karenite—this spell-chain held scores of karenite beads, each binding a different djinn. They were in one chain, so they worked together. The guardian-messenger I'd freed had probably carried instructions to the rest. *Surely there's another way to speak to them* ... *Well, I could summon them all here, that would be* one *way to free the waters* ... I picked up the necklace.

"Wait," Zivar said, her voice tense. "You are a sorceress. As am I. Why should *you* have this?"

"I'm not going to keep it," I said.

"So you say."

I handed it to Tamar. "Tamar is no sorceress," I said.

Zivar shrugged and acquiesced.

"Now let's get going before anyone notices we're

up here." Tamar started toward the palanquin, then paused. "Do you know where we'll find Kyros?"

"No. Kasim—" I bit my lip. "Let me see if I can find Kasim and ask if he'll come back, and scout for us again." *He could find Kyros unseen, and lead us there . . .*

I took a deep breath, let it out slowly, and closed my eyes. *Surely the gate in my heart opens both ways. Can I pass this way to the borderland? Or at least look-through?* Behind my closed eyes, I imagined a door, wood and iron with a latch. *Hello?* I nudged it open a crack, and peered through into the shadowy darkness. *Anyone here?*

I felt a jerk as if someone had grabbed the front of my shirt with both hands and yanked with all their strength. And then I stood, facing a furiously angry white-robed woman, in that central hall of the temple in the djinn city.

"You fled us," the woman said.

"You were going to kill me!"

"We *need* a gate. Need one! It is your duty to return—you *must*. Swear it."

"I'm never coming back. I'm doing this *my* way." I felt dizzy and strangely weak, standing there—like I had felt those times that I had spent too much time at the bottom of the lake. *I need to get back—get back—*

And there I was, hunched on the floor, Tamar's arm shaking my shoulders as she tried to rouse me. I sucked in a deep gasp of air and realized that I had not been breathing in my absence. *No wonder I felt odd. . . .*

"Did you find him?" Tamar asked. "Is that Kasim?"

There was a flicker of light in the room with us—a djinn. "That's not Kasim," I said. My voice was hoarse. "This isn't one we can trust. Why did you come back with me?" I addressed the djinn. "What do you want?"

"Will help," the djinn hissed.

"Sure you will," I muttered.

"Give it a chance," Tamar said. "Would it serve their purpose for you to die here?"

"I don't think so."

"Then it's to their advantage to help you get away."

"They set me up to get caught by Kyros," I said.

"But if you were caught *now* . . ."

"The Sisterhood would cut my throat and figure out what to do about the gate later, I think," I said. I tried to laugh to cover my own nervousness, but it sounded ghastly. "Maybe the djinni want a gate here."

"No," the djinn said.

"If you want to be helpful, find Kyros for us," I said. "Tell us where he is, then possess him so that we can take him with us easily."

"Show me Kyros." The djinn approached. Nervously, I put out my hand and summoned a memory of Kyros to my mind. The djinn touched me; I felt a feather-light brush against my thoughts. "Stay. I will return in a moment."

It was gone.

"Stay?" Zivar said. "Let's get out of here. Forget Kyros. You have the necklace to free the river—what do you need Kyros for?"

"She's right," Alibek said. "It would be nice if we could make it look like Kyros stole it, but the

Weavers aren't idiots—they'd probably figure out what happened. Just freeing the river would be enough of a disruption."

*There's something they're forgetting,* I thought. *Something they told me back when I first returned.* It came to me a moment later. "My mother," I said. "She's with Kyros, isn't she? I'm not leaving without my mother."

"I thought you didn't even *like* your mother," Zivar said.

"That doesn't mean I'm going to abandon her here!"

"No," Tamar said. "You're right. We'll stay, and look for Andromeda."

The djinn was back. "I'm not letting you in my mind, so don't even ask," I said. "You'll have to tell us where to go as we fly down. Can you possess Kyros?"

"No. He has a strong will." The djinn's glimmer brightened for a moment. "Like you."

We climbed back in to the palanquin and descended from the height. I felt pressure build in my ears as it had when I'd been diving to the bottom of the mountain reservoir. The djinn guided us to a tower; I recognized the enclosed garden where I'd passed time as a prisoner, below. "Within," the djinn said when I pointed at a window.

"The rogue djinn may not be able to possess Kyros, but Zivar's bound djinn could hold him," I said. "Keep him from speaking—which is important, because he has a spell-chain."

"It's not going to be able to do that and hold up the palanquin at the same time," Zivar said. "Let's land this on the roof and go down the stairs."

It was high noon. The sun was scorching hot on our heads as we climbed out of the cramped palanquin. I shaded my eyes with my hand as we went down the stairs from the roof. There was a single door at the bottom. "Is Kyros behind this door?" I whispered to the rogue djinn.

"Yes."

I glanced at Zivar. She gripped her spell-chain; I could see her lips moving, instructing the djinn. She waited a moment, her eyes intent. Then she nodded.

I swung the door open.

And found myself face-to-face with Xanthe.

# CHAPTER NINETEEN

# TAMAR

*A*n angry woman drew her sword as we came through the door. "You're dead!" she shouted. "How can you be standing here? You're dead!"

"Yeah, I'm dead, Xanthe," Lauria said, grinning fiercely. She snatched up a heavy clay pitcher to swing like a club and threw herself toward the other woman.

Xanthe—I remembered her now, from the raid—fell back a step and her eyes went wide. Her free hand moved to her collar. "Stop her," Xanthe shouted. "Grab her!"

Xanthe had a spell-chain, I realized. Lauria whirled to face it. She thrust out her open hand and for a moment I saw a hand clasp hers. Then the djinn spun in the air, shrinking to a pinprick of light, and plunged into Lauria's chest like the point of an arrow. Lauria shuddered as it happened, and her eyes closed.

Xanthe raised her sword. "No!" I said, knowing what was happening too late to stop it. Someone brushed past me, and Alibek threw himself between Xanthe and Lauria, holding the sword we'd taken from Zivar's guard. He caught the edge of Xanthe's blade with his own sword and threw her back. Lauria opened her eyes, then leapt onto the bed, out of the way. Kyros stood frozen by the bed, held by Zivar's djinn, and Lauria snatched a spell-chain from around his neck. "Take Xanthe's sword," she shouted, and I saw the sword fly through the air as the djinn snatched it out of her hand. A moment later Xanthe knelt on the floor panting for breath. With Alibek guarding Xanthe, Lauria jumped down off the bed and faced Kyros. "Where is my mother?"

"He can't talk," Zivar said. "Should I release him?"

"Yes—No. Wait." Lauria searched Kyros. She found a dagger and a small knife, but kept looking. "I need to get at his feet," she said to the djinn. It lifted Kyros up, and she yanked off his boots. Looped around one of his ankles was a second spell-chain, made from gleaming black stones. Lauria held it up and looked it over, a faint smile on her face. She nodded and gave Kyros a knowing look.

"The one he had around his neck was rightfully Zivar's, I think," Lauria said, and tossed it to her. She handed Alibek the black one. Kyros's eyes were open, and I saw fury and despair pass through them as he watched. She searched his other boot, then said, "All right, Zivar. Let him talk. Where's my mother?"

"Why should I tell you anything?" Kyros asked.

"I don't know. Do you want us to keep you alive? Or do you want to die? We don't have a lot of time."

"Then kill me and get it over with."

"Not with a sword. We'll take you up in the palanquin and shove you out."

Kyros blanched. He opened his mouth silently, then began to stammer. "You have to understand, Lauria, I trusted your mother. I trusted her. I trusted you, too, and *both* of you betrayed me."

"What did you do to her?" Lauria whispered.

"As soon as she was brought to me, I—" His voice faded. Then he straightened his shoulders, as much as the djinn would allow, and said, "I took her down to the courtyard, and had it cleared. We sat in the shade. I told her to close her eyes. Then I cut her throat. She died in seconds."

"I betrayed you," Lauria whispered. "And you didn't kill me."

"I promised myself not to make that mistake again."

Zivar stepped forward and caught Lauria's arm, gently. "We need to hurry," she said. "I think someone's coming."

"Have the djinn carry him," Lauria said. "Stop his mouth again."

Kyros's eyes bulged with protest, but no sound emerged. Zivar went out, Kyros carried behind her like a big sack of rice. Xanthe had pressed herself into her corner, as if she hoped we'd forget about her, but Lauria turned. "Stand up," she said. Xanthe stood. "Alibek, have your djinn hold her still, if you would."

He twitched the spell-chain between his fingers, and I saw Xanthe go rigid, held by the djinn as Kyros had been.

"She's Janiya's daughter," I whispered.

"She took your mother to Kyros," Alibek said.

Lauria raised the knife to Xanthe's throat, and I caught my breath. But Lauria only used the blade to force Xanthe's head up and make her meet Lauria's eyes. "You have a master, I see," Lauria said softly.

"Not a master," Xanthe said defiantly. "A guest."

"No wonder you never met my eyes. How many are like you?"

"Few."

"To whom are your loyalties, really?"

"To the Sisterhood of Weavers!"

"Truly?" Lauria pressed her palm to Xanthe's forehead. "Return to the Silent Lands, lost one, and tell them this: *I will never be your tool again.*"

There was a moment of silence, then Xanthe swayed, even in the grip of the djinn, as if her legs had suddenly lost their strength.

Lauria put away her knife, took Xanthe's shoulders, and looked into her eyes. "Do you know why the djinn told you to throw me into the reservoir? Because under the water is a gate to the Silent Lands, and they wanted to force me to the other side. Because if they killed me there, *they* would have a gate. And *they* could make spell-chains, and enslave humans to serve them—and not just the other way around."

Xanthe shuddered, but didn't answer.

"I live because they failed. But you served *them*, Xanthe—you served the aerika against our kind. You were their tool. Don't let that happen again." Lauria turned away. "Alibek, have your djinn hold her here for a quarter of an hour, without letting her call out. Then have it let her go. Her weight would slow us down, and I don't have the stomach to kill Janiya's daughter."

We went back up to the palanquin. It was even more crowded now with Kyros, but at least we had more djinni to carry us. I wondered what happened to the rogue djinn who showed us where Kyros was—it had disappeared. We pressed inside, and the djinni lifted us up. "Hurry," I murmured.

"Don't worry," Lauria said. "If they follow us and we need some extra speed, we can just unload Kyros." There was an edge to her voice that made my hair stand up.

"Why do you keep talking about throwing him down, Lauria?" I asked.

"Kyros is afraid of heights. He doesn't like flying."

I leaned close and whispered into Lauria's ear, "I want the Weavers to think that Kyros stole the river chain. If he's dead, they'll know he didn't. It's possible Xanthe will run away without telling anyone what happened . . ."

Lauria nodded slowly. "We'll need to keep him out of the borderland, then. He knows how to go there. They gave me a drug . . ."

"We'll put the palanquin down somewhere and see if we can buy some."

Kyros's eyes were wide with terror or cold fever. "Unstop his mouth," I said.

Kyros licked his lips and swallowed. He couldn't move his head but his eyes traveled from me, to Lauria, to Alibek, to Zivar. Zivar caressed the beads of her spell-chain. She had a faint smile. Alibek's face was strangely serene. He held the unsheathed sword across his lap. Lauria's eyes burned with rage, cold fever, and grief.

"May I have some water?" Kyros asked. His voice was scratchy and weak.

"Do we have any in here?" I asked Zivar. "Where did this palanquin come from, anyway? Whose is it?"

Zivar shrugged and dug through a lidded wicker basket. She found a clay jug of water, a clay jug of wine, and a whole roast chicken. Lauria reached for the water jug, but I didn't want her drowning Kyros with it, so I took it and let him have a swallow, then passed it around. "Anyone hungry?" I asked. I was. The chicken smelled of herbs and crisp skin. Alibek and I each tore off a leg and sat back to eat it. If Kyros was hungry, he didn't say so.

His thirst only slightly satisfied, Kyros looked from one person to the next. His face grew desperate. He couldn't hope for help from me, or from Alibek, or from Lauria. I wasn't sure if he knew who Zivar was, but he wasn't likely to get help from her, either.

We couldn't really talk in front of him, though. The weight of the river chain rested against my chest. I had looped it around my neck, and the strands kept bunching up, sliding so that one or two wrapped tightly around my neck. I tugged at it to loosen it. Could I simply summon all of the djinni at once? Let the river just—go? I wasn't actually sure how to summon djinni with a spell-chain. Did I have to take it out and look at it, or could I put my hand on it to use it? Would I say "djinni—come," or just think it?

Zivar gave me a secretive smile. "The spell-chains I've made have just one aeriko each. It can be sent on any errand and used to do whatever I want. Not all spell-chains are like that. Some aerika are bound to a particular task: to hold up the stones of a temple, for instance. Those aerika can't be easily summoned away from their task even if you have the spell-chain. You can break the spell by breaking the binding stones. Or, if you're Lauria, you can touch the aerika and free them that way. That's what she was about to do when Xanthe pushed her into the water."

"I see." I let my hand fall to my side.

Zivar looked at Lauria. "I heard you cry for help after Xanthe pushed you," she said. "I wanted to kill her. She had hidden spell-chains and used her aerika to hold me still and silent. If she hadn't, I swear I'd have told my own to rip her heart out, I was so angry." Zivar shuddered. Her voice had started shaking. "I thought you'd surely drowned."

Lauria looked up and met Zivar's eyes. I could see a glint of humor despite her sadness. "Dying to kill Xanthe wouldn't have done me much good."

"I was too angry to care," Zivar said.

"Is anyone following us?" Alibek asked.

"I don't think so," Zivar said. "My aerika are supposed to be watching. You could have yours keep watch, too."

"They might not tell us in time," Alibek said. "Is there a hammer in here? Can we free the djinni in the river chain *now*?"

Lauria raised her head again. "I don't know if we should," she said.

"You what?" Alibek said.

"Why?" I asked. Janiya had risked her life to keep the river bound, but Lauria?

"I don't think this is a good time to talk about it," Lauria said, and jerked her chin at Kyros.

We fell silent. "We'll find the drug soon," Zivar said. "In the meantime, if we see anyone coming . . ." She held out a pair of pincers like she'd used to twist wire. "You could probably break the stones with this, if you had to." She gave them to me. Lauria watched but didn't say anything.

We put down a few hours later, in a good-sized town. "I'll go buy the drug," Zivar said.

"Do we have any money?" I asked.

"Kyros has jewelry," Lauria said, speaking for the first time in several hours. "Two rings. One has a ruby in it."

"That would be too noticeable. Besides, we won't need money. I'm a sorceress; I'll trade a bit of work for what I need. The rest of you—no, I take it back. Lauria and Alibek, you stay here with Kyros. Tamar, come with me." She slid out and I followed.

"Wait," Alibek said. "Are you just going to take the river chain with you?"

"Do you think anyone in this backwater is going to take it from her with *me* standing right there?" Zivar snapped. "I certainly think I can protect it better than you. Come along, Tamar."

"Why do you need me?" I asked, falling into step beside her.

"I don't. But this way we can talk privately." She waited until we were beyond earshot. "Why do you want to free the river?"

"Because when the rivers return, that's supposed to free the slaves. *All* the slaves."

"Rivers. Not river. And do you really believe that?"

"I think that enough people believe it that if even one river returns . . . it will happen."

"Or it won't, and they will despair because even the prophesied return didn't help them."

"You may be right." The necklace had wrapped itself tight around my neck again. I tugged at it. "But it's the best I can do."

"I have seen the northern great river where it's bound," Zivar said. "Lauria has, too. It's bigger than you realize. If we free it, thousands will die. Didn't you live near the old course of the river? People you know will be among them." She lowered her voice. "How many Greeks are you willing to kill to save the Alashi? How many Danibeki?"

"I don't know," I said.

"Well, think about it."

We were at the edge of the town. A curious crowd was gathering. "I wish to see an apothecary," Zivar called. There was a nervous shuffle, and then an older man stepped forward.

"I'm the apothecary," he said. "What do you need?"

"A remedy for sleeplessness. I have trouble sleeping—*great* trouble. I've had a remedy in the past that would put an ox to sleep. Can you prepare it for me, quickly?"

"At once," he said. "My shop is this way."

We followed to a cottage. Herbs hung in bundles, and the shelves along the walls held jars stopped with corks. The apothecary brought down a large jug, opened it, then used a funnel to pour thick syrup into a smaller bottle. He corked it and gave it to Zivar with a tin spoon. "One spoonful should do it. Don't take more than three. If you've drunk a lot of wine, take less than you would otherwise."

"How shall I pay you?"

"My roof leaks near the chimney. If you could have your aeriko patch it, I'd consider it an excellent trade."

While one djinn did that repair, Zivar had another split firewood in exchange for a pot of stew he'd made for his own dinner, and a cask of wine. We were soon on our way.

"They tricked Lauria into drinking this," I said, holding up the syrup. "I don't think we'll be able to trick Kyros."

"I think that if he's given the choice between drinking the syrup and being thrown down from the height, he'll choose the syrup," Zivar said with some satisfaction.

"Why do *you* hate Kyros?" I asked. "Because he held one of your spell-chains?"

Zivar's eyes flickered. "The spell-chain that Lauria found in his boot," she said. "*He* made that. I'm certain of it. Men are not supposed to learn sorcery, but he married a sorceress who failed in her apprenticeship, and I would wager he persuaded her to teach him. Magic . . ." She shook her head in disgust. "Magic is for *women.*"

"What about shamans?"

"Eh. They're nothing to do with me."

"Why do you dislike men so much?" Even among her servants, there were no men. "I spent years as a concubine, and I don't dislike *all* men."

Zivar sighed. "Do you really insist on a reason? They smell bad. They shed. Some of them have *hair on their backs.*" She threw up her hands. "They're men. What more of a reason do you need?"

I would never understand her. I resolved not ever to trust Alibek's safety to Zivar, and followed her back to the palanquin.

———

*I* poured syrup into the spoon and held it up where Kyros could see it. "This will make you sleep," I said. "Nothing more. Open your mouth."

Kyros hesitated. I wondered if he feared it was poison. I saw no advantage to poisoning him over killing him some other way, and neither did he, apparently, because he opened his mouth and swallowed it. I dosed him with two spoonfuls, then thought it over and gave him another half spoon. He was bigger than Zivar. His eyes soon took on a glazed look and he fell asleep, drool running from the corner of his mouth onto the cushions.

"It smells like rank feet in here," Zivar said as the djinni lifted us up.

I sniffed. "I've smelled worse," I said.

"Oh, I've smelled *worse*," Zivar said. "It still smells rank. Ugh. I wish I'd had the aeriko steal a larger palanquin."

"Wouldn't that be heavier?" Alibek asked. "Slower?"

"I don't think anyone's following us."

"Sure they are," Alibek said. "Even if Xanthe lied or ran and they believe Kyros stole the spell-chain, he'd head in this direction."

"Maybe."

"It's the most likely possibility."

"Have your aerika seen anyone coming? Mine haven't," Zivar said.

"And of course, no aeriko has ever chosen not to see something it was supposed to be watching for," Alibek said.

"What would you have me do? We could abandon the palanquin and go on foot . . ."

"I think we need to take care of the spell-chain *now*," Alibek said. "We have it. We can break the rocks and free the river, and no one will be able to put it back together."

"That's not true," Zivar said. "We can free the river, but the Sisterhood can just bind it back up again."

Lauria stirred, but said nothing. "Kyros is asleep now," I said. "Lauria? You used to say that you wanted to free the river." I thought about all the people in the path of the water. "Did you change your mind?"

Lauria straightened up and looked around at all of us. "The real reason the Sisterhood bound the northern great river was to hide the gate that leads to the Silent Lands."

This was not what I had expected her to say.

"You're going to have to explain that a little more," Alibek said.

Lauria sighed. "There's a gate that leads to the Silent Lands—the borderland—the place where the djinni live. It's a real gate, built out of stones. I found it after Xanthe threw me out of the palanquin. Tamar, you send your spirit through that gate every time you visit the borderland. Zivar, you go through that gate to find djinni when you make a spell-chain. It opens into their world. They have no gate into ours.

"They lured me through because I have a gate in my heart. If they'd killed me on their side, *they* would have a gate. They could use it to bind *us,* to make spell-chains that enslave *our* kind.

"If we free the northern great river, that gate will be exposed. If we leave it, they'll lure another person like me through to their side. If we destroy it, there will be no more sorcery. Maybe even no more shamans." Lauria tipped her head back against her cushion and sighed.

"There was a Weaver who believed that Zeus was under the reservoir," I said. "She was going to break the spell-chain to find him. Janiya stole it to stop her." I swallowed, thinking about what Janiya had sacrificed to keep the river bound.

"Yes. I heard that story from Xanthe, shortly before she dumped me in. I think the story might have been invented by the djinni, as bait for someone before me. They failed, but the story lives on."

"If we destroy the gate, what will happen to existing spell-chains?" Zivar asked.

"Bound djinni will stay bound unless they're freed. If they're freed, well, there *are* other gates. I think they'll find their way back eventually."

"If the aerika can go back, why wouldn't I be able to get to the borderland?" Zivar asked.

Lauria shrugged. "Well, I could be wrong. But it's not easy to get there now. This gate is big and it stays in the same place. If you go there once, you can usually find your way back. And it will be gone."

No more Sisterhood of Weavers. But no more shamans, either.

"And a lot of people will die," Lauria said. "The reservoir is huge. All that water, coming down from the mountains . . . It will go far past its banks. I don't know how far or fast it will go, but it will be a bad flood."

"But it wouldn't just save the Alashi," I said. "It would save the djinni. The Sisterhood couldn't enslave them anymore."

"And it would save us," Alibek said. "Or—maybe

not us, but our children or grandchildren. The djinni came really close to getting Lauria's gate. There are other people like her out there. They failed with Lauria, but surely they'll succeed eventually."

"But *thousands* of people will die," Lauria said. Her eyes were shadowed.

"Is there a way to drain it slowly?" I asked.

"If we drain it slowly enough to avoid a flood, that will give the Sisterhood time to stop us. When they realize what we're after, they'll guard the gate. Even if they *don't* realize what we're after, I expect they'll guard the reservoir as soon as they can."

"Can you try telling the djinni to start letting the water out tonight, and maybe we can break the spell-chain in the morning?" I said. "At least there'd be *less* water to unleash. Right?"

Lauria still hesitated.

"Why not?" I said. "Even if we decide tomorrow not to break the spell-chain, just the water coming down will make a lot of people think the river has returned."

"For a time, I thought I was *meant* to free the rivers," Lauria said. "I thought I'd been chosen. But that was a lie. That was just the djinni trying to lure me through the gate." Lauria closed her eyes for a moment, then went on, her voice shaking. "I am afraid that by freeing the northern river I might somehow be making myself their tool *again*."

"The rice-eaters wanted you to come through the gate," Alibek said. "The barley-eaters—surely they want you to destroy it."

Lauria raised her head slightly and looked at Alibek.

"I always thought the old line about the rivers' return just meant that we would never be free," he said. "But now we *can* make one of them return."

Lauria looked at Zivar. "You agreed once to let me free the river, but that was before we saw it. And before you knew what it concealed."

Zivar touched the two spell-chains around her neck. "You would infuriate the Sisterhood," she said. "And my servants, as well. But—I think I would enjoy that."

Lauria nodded. "I'll need to hold the necklace to summon the djinni in it," she said to me. I untangled the strands and tugged it off. My shoulders felt suddenly much lighter. Lauria held it in her hands and closed her eyes. Usually it was easy to summon a djinn, but this necklace was supposed to keep them where they were. Still, after a bit, I saw the sparkle of a djinn in the darkness of the palanquin.

"Your freedom is at hand," Lauria said. "But first, I want you to let the water out gradually. Start with a stream. Then let more and more come, faster and faster. Let those who no longer need to hold back water carry it in enormous raindrops to places where it will do no harm, and leave it there. Let two others come here to watch for sorceresses coming toward us—if they catch us, they will take the spell-chain, and you will stay slaves. Can you carry my bidding to the others?"

"Yes," the djinn said.

"Will they obey the commands given through you?"

"Yes."

"Then go, and carry out my orders."

When it was gone, I asked Lauria, "What will happen if someone dies from the water they let out?"

Lauria shrugged. "I don't know. If they kill me, I guess you'll get to decide without me whether to break the binding stones. And it will be up to the three of you to break the gate."

There was nothing to do until morning. Zivar made herself a nest and lay down to sleep. Alibek wrapped one of the silk cushions around his sword and tied it with a ribbon, so that it wouldn't cut anyone who rolled over in the night. He set it where he could reach it, arranged some more pillows under his head, and closed his eyes. I checked Kyros, who was still breathing, but not moving otherwise, then lay back against some of the pillows. Lauria lay beside me. I heard Alibek fall asleep, and I thought Zivar slept as well, but Lauria was still awake.

"Do you want to kill Kyros?" I asked softly.

"There's no harm in keeping him alive a bit longer," she said. "Just in case the plan worked."

"I suppose," I said.

"It won't bring my mother back."

I had expected to hear rage but Lauria's voice was worn and quiet.

"Did I ever tell you what my mother did the first time I got into a fight?" she asked.

"No."

"I was, oh, probably five years old. Maybe six. I fought with a boy down the street, a year or two older than me. He was mixed blood, like me, but everyone considered him Greek because he had a Greek father who actually lived with him. Anyway, I think technically he won the fight but I bloodied his lip and gave him a black eye, and later his mother showed up at our door to demand that my mother punish me for hurting her son. What she wanted was for my mother to summon me downstairs and then beat me in front of her. What *I* wanted—I was listening, of course, from the upstairs window—was for my mother to stand up for me. I hadn't started the fight. The boy was *older* than me, bigger than me! Instead, my mother wept about the difficulty of being a woman alone—she always implied that my father had died in a skirmish with bandits before he could settle down with her—and how she just didn't know how to handle me, a girl who didn't act like a proper girl. After a bit the other mother left in disgust. I was relieved, but disappointed."

Lauria let the spell-chain rest on her stomach. I could see the glitter of the stones, but it was too dark to see her face.

"That was always the way it was. My whole childhood. She always found some way to get me out of trouble, but it was always a *spineless* way. Always the way with the least risk to her. I guess I assumed . . ." She broke off and took a harsh breath. "I guess I assumed this meant she'd always find a way to get herself out of trouble. Out of the trouble *I* got her in."

"You can't blame yourself," I said.

"Of course I can blame myself. She wouldn't have even *been* in Penelopeia if it weren't for me."

"I met your mother in Penelopeia," I said. "She sought me out when she heard my name. She was not what I pictured."

"Other people's mothers never are."

"True." I thought that over, wondering what Lauria would have thought of *my* mother. "Your mother would willingly have traded her life to save yours. But . . . she'd have gone to her grave more happily if she'd had one more chance to tweak you for never getting married like a proper daughter."

Lauria let out a short laugh at that.

"Could you ever have been the daughter your mother wanted?"

"No," Lauria said. A long pause, then she added, "She didn't raise me to be that daughter. Even though she always said she tried."

"Maybe that's not really what she wanted. Maybe she really wanted *you*, even if she couldn't admit it."

"Maybe."

"Is there anything *you* could have done differently to protect your mother?"

"Not gone after Thais. That put me in Kyros's hands."

"We wouldn't have the river chain."

"My mother's life, for the river's?"

"Would she make that trade?" I asked.

"No. Remember, she always looked for the weak way out."

"But she raised you to choose otherwise."

"Yes. My mother never would have made the trade, but . . . it's not impossible that she would choose for *me* to make it. So long as I felt properly guilt-stricken afterward." She fell silent, and after a while, I fell asleep.

*I* looked for the borderland that night. I wanted to talk to Zhanna or Jaran, to tell them what we had done. Instead, I found myself face-to-face with a djinn. "See," the djinn whispered, and I felt myself caught in a whirlwind and blown distant. *See.*

I saw a stone room, and four women shouting at

each other in Greek. A bracelet like a coiled serpent lay on its side on the table in front of them. They were all talking at once. I could barely make out what they were saying, but they were talking about Kyros, Lauria, and the river chain.

"Of *course* the army aims to betray us," one of them said. "I never doubted this. But they hadn't the means, until—"

"—surely he won't dare," someone else cut in.

"Surely! Surely you won't assume *anything* this time!"

"Why go to all the trouble of seizing the karenite if they were going to render it worthless?"

They all started talking again.

"Are they the high magias?" I asked my guide.

*Yes.*

"Where is Xanthe? Didn't she report what happened?"

Silence.

Piecing together the conversation, I thought that they did think Kyros had stolen it. They thought that Xanthe had lied about Lauria's death, and Kyros and Lauria had been working together. "She's his daughter, after all," one of them said.

I wanted to find Zhanna or Jaran, but someone was shaking me, dragging me back. It was still mostly dark. "Someone's coming," Alibek said.

I sat up. "Are we going to break the spell-chain?"

"How much water remains?" Alibek asked Lauria.

"I don't think we have time to ask," Lauria said.

"Put down the palanquin," Zivar said to her own djinni. "I know you're going to do it."

Lauria looked at me. "I'm not going to decide this on my own. But yes. I've thought about it, and I think we should do it. It might not be worth the destruction if it were just to save the Alashi or just to free the Danibeki. But it's also to free the djinni. And to prevent the djinni from ever enslaving *us*."

I nodded. So did Alibek and Zivar. Kyros was still sleeping.

"Let's do it," I said. "Let's do it now."

We put down somewhere on the steppe. The eastern sky was faintly gray. I smelled dry grass and cool air, and felt a rush of longing to be back with the Alashi. *Soon*.

"Everyone find two rocks," Lauria said. We were near a rockfall, and I dug out a flat stone, and another I could hold comfortably in my fist. Lauria dropped the spell-chain on the ground and spread it out into a big circle.

"I think it's best if we space ourselves out and all smash the first stones together," Lauria said. "On the count of three. Then move on around the circle, breaking the binding stones as fast as we can."

We took our places.

"Do you want to count?" Lauria asked me.

My mouth went dry and I almost couldn't speak. "The world will be made new," I said. Then I raised my stone. "One," I said. "Two." In the lantern light, I saw Zivar, Alibek, and Lauria raise their stones, as well. "Three."

I brought my stone down. I had seen djinni freed this way before, but this time, I thought I heard a clap of thunder as we brought our rocks down. The binding stone shattered to dust under my own rock. I moved quickly to the side, searching for the next karenite bead.

In the twilight, the karenite beads were hard to see.

If I wasn't sure whether a bead was karenite or something else, I smashed it. I had hoped to hear the voices of the djinni—Lauria could hear them speaking when she freed them—but I didn't. Maybe they were too far away. I could hear my own heart beating, and I could hear the clatter of the rocks against each other.

The sun was rising when we finished. I scanned the sky to our west but couldn't see our pursuers yet. Lauria took the pincers and snapped one of the links, then started passing the chain through her hand to look for any last pieces of karenite. "Now what?" Alibek asked

"I dreamed last night about the Sisterhood," I said. "I saw them arguing over what to do. It seemed like a djinn-sent dream. They believe Kyros did it. I think they think he wants to destroy the gate."

"We need to keep them uncertain," Lauria said.

"They won't be looking for travelers on the ground," Alibek said. "We could bait them by sending the empty palanquin away—they'd probably never catch up."

"We have no horses . . ."

"So? We have feet."

"We'd have to carry Kyros, unless you think we can wake him up," Lauria said. "He'd have no reason to try to walk quickly."

"Sure he would," Alibek said. "He knows we'll settle for leaving him dead."

"The palanquin will only work as bait if they're looking for a palanquin, rather than the five of *us*," Zivar said. "Or the spell-chain."

My head came up. "They're probably looking for the spell-chain," I said. "We could leave it on the palanquin."

Zivar shook Kyros awake and dragged him out of the palanquin.

"Let's lighten the load as much as possible," Alibek said. We took out the wicker basket, the jugs of water and wine, the remaining food, and of course the bottle of syrup and Alibek's sword. There were cushions and blankets inside, so we pulled all those out, too, leaving silk-covered walls and the rug on the floor.

"All done?" Lauria asked, walking up with the spell-chain bundled in her hands. We nodded. She had coiled the chain, and she set it neatly inside the palanquin.

"Where should I send it?" Zivar asked.

Lauria thought it over. "Casseia, perhaps? It's where the other great river turns south—perhaps we'd make the Weavers think we meant to free *both* rivers." Zivar shot her a narrow-eyed look, and Lauria gave her a shrug. "I still haven't thought of a way to free *that* one. But the Weavers won't know that."

"We kidnapped Kyros to persuade the Weavers that the army had turned against them," I said. "Is there some way to send the other half of the message to the army? Let them know that the Weavers are turning on *them,* and persuade them to break off their own attack and turn on the Weavers?"

"Yes," Lauria said, and her eyes were suddenly fierce and intent again. "We can send *them* the old river-chain. And a note."

We found paper and ink among the goods from the palanquin. Lauria spread out a piece of paper, dipped the pen, thought for a moment, then wrote. She gave her note to Zivar to read. "What do you think?"

Zivar read it aloud. " 'The Weavers have turned on us prematurely, but never fear; plans have changed. Their power will shortly be at an end. Move south and ready yourselves. The bandits and the steppe are no longer a concern.' Why should they believe this?"

"Other than the fact that it's accompanied by the broken river chain?" Lauria looked Kyros over. "It would help if it were clearly from Kyros, wouldn't it? Kyros, take off your ring." She pointed at a ring on his finger—a ruby nearly the size of my thumbnail, set in gold. "We'll send this along."

Kyros had been rubbing his eyes, still foggy from the drug. Now he straightened up slightly. "Let me sign the note," he said.

Lauria narrowed her eyes. "Why?"

"Because you're right that the Weavers will likely turn on the army now. I'd like them warned."

Lauria thought that over, then handed him the pen. He dipped it in the ink and carefully signed his name. Lauria blew on the ink gently to dry it, studied the note, then shrugged and tucked the note, the ring, and the broken chain into a silk-lined compartment built into the palanquin.

Zivar murmured to one of her djinn, and the palanquin rose and flew away. Kyros watched it go, then said, "I'm thirsty. May I have something to drink?"

Alibek sent his djinn to fetch water for us, and we had it fill our jug to pass around. We let Kyros drink his fill and eat some of the food. There wasn't much point in taking him with us if we were going to let him fall dead from thirst on the walk. We gathered up the useful things from the palanquin, bundling them together in knotted blankets and ripped-open silk pillows. I loaded Kyros down with a share of the heavier stuff, then bound his hands. "If you try to run," I said, "or if you try to hurt us, I will think up a very painful and unpleasant way to kill you."

"I believe you," Kyros said, and gave me a grim smile. "I won't try to run. Or try to hurt you."

He wouldn't run or try to hurt us today, anyway, I thought. Tomorrow might be different.

"Why *did* the Sisterhood of Weavers bind the southern great river?" I asked Zivar. "Do you know? Is it covering anything?"

"I don't believe so," Zivar said. "There's no reservoir, as there is with the northern river. They just diverted it, through a tunnel under the mountains. Perhaps they just wanted water in Persia."

"Alibek," Lauria said, "I think you should let me carry the black spell-chain."

"Why?"

"Because if anyone comes after us, we can use the black chain to kill with. If you gave the order, the djinn might kill you. I think I could avoid being killed. If not, well, I'll take my chances."

Alibek pulled the chain over his head and gave it to her. "Who's the sorceress who made it?"

"Kyros," Lauria said.

There was a shocked pause. I glanced at Kyros. He did not deny it. So Zivar was right.

"Better start walking," Zivar said, and we set out.

# CHAPTER TWENTY

## LAURIA

When I closed my eyes for a moment to rest them from the glare of the sun, I could see the river. First, the vast black pitcher, shimmering under the moon; then the pitcher splitting open and water spraying out like white foam. A tall, rangy pine tree was caught by the spray and ripped out by the roots as the water boiled down the mountainside, and the torrential rush swept away everything in its path. Trees, houses, boulders, animals trying to swim, mountainsides washed away, mud . . . When I closed my eyes and meditated for a moment I saw it all, and then a single bright red flower bobbing to the top of the foam.

*The river unbound.* Even in my grief for my mother, and despite the horror of knowing what kind of destruction I'd brought, I felt a dizzying sense of triumph. We had done it—we had freed the river.

Whether the Sisterhood turned against the army or not, I thought the renewed river would likely prove to be a serious distraction. The ordinary Greek soldiers would be as shocked as the Danibeki slaves.

But we'd exposed the gate. What if we couldn't destroy it? That gate had been open for a long time before the Penelopeians ever came along, but before Penelope figured out how to bind djinni with spell-chains, that gate was used only by shamans, and I thought it was unlikely that the ancient djinni had been trying so desperately to get a gate of their own. Now it would be open and unguarded. They wouldn't need a helper to push someone into the lake at precisely the right spot—with the right misleading messages, they could probably persuade someone to go to the valley and walk right on through.

There were other people with gates inside them—at least, there had been in the past, and there could be again. It was easy enough to think of things that could have convinced me to find the gate last year and walk through it, if it hadn't been underwater.

I pushed the thought away. If we were unable to destroy the gate, the Sisterhood would still be able to do sorcery and would undoubtedly bind up the river to flood the valley again. If they had to send the entire Sisterhood Guard to shoot anyone who came near it, they would.

*Though one of the magias is on the djinni's side,* I remembered. *Or she's been deceived into serving them.*

There were four in all. They knew what was at stake, didn't they?

*They don't know that the djinni want to build their own gate.*

Well, we'd just need to find a way to destroy it, then.

Kyros fell into step beside me at one point during the long afternoon. "So you really did it? You broke the bindings on the river?"

I didn't answer. *Why would I tell you?*

"So now what?"

"What do you mean?"

"You know what was under the water, don't you?" When I didn't answer, he went on. "The source of the Weavers' power is in that valley. If you destroy it . . ." He paused, and I thought that if his hands hadn't been bound, he would have flung an arm out in a grand gesture. "No more sorcery."

"What's that to you?" I said. "I thought you served the Weavers. You certainly always sounded loyal."

"An Empire should not be run by a quartet of madwomen," Kyros said. "Don't you agree?"

I didn't answer.

"My wife is steadier than any of the high magias, and she's bad enough. The purpose of seizing the steppe was to ease control away from the high magias and pass it to someone who could be served by sorceress and soldier alike. I'm sure you realized that; you're quite intelligent. That's why I valued you so much."

I turned on him, suddenly hearing my heart pounding in my ears; my head throbbed in the heat. He lowered his head in the face of my fury. "You killed my *mother*. Shut up, you lying bastard, or I'll cut your intestines out and feed them to you."

Kyros fell silent.

———

*A*n hour or two later, Alibek shouted wordlessly and pointed to the sky. In the distance, I saw a speck of something dark. It moved too steadily to be a bird—it could only be a palanquin. As I watched, squinting my eyes against the glare, I realized that I could see more than one—it was a cavalcade of palanquins. "They're coming closer," Tamar said.

I gripped the spell-chain Kyros had made. One newly freed djinn had transported an entire pack of bandits for me, once. If I didn't care whether they lived or died, I could be a match for whatever we faced. Maybe. Of course, the bandits hadn't had any djinni of their own.

"They're closer, but they're not heading for us," Alibek said a few minutes later. "They're following the palanquin."

"You hope," Tamar said.

"No, I'm sure of it." Alibek shaded his eyes with his hand. "If they were coming for us, they'd be closer by now."

Zivar was watching, too. "He's right," she said. "They're not stopping here. They're going to keep going."

"Do you think they'll catch up with it before it reaches the army?"

"Hard to say," Zivar said. "The empty palanquin was moving awfully quickly."

We watched a bit longer; the distant palanquins faded into the sky.

"They'll come back looking once they catch up with it," Zivar said. "Looking for people on foot."

"Maybe," Tamar said. "Or maybe they'll be distracted by the rebellious army if our message arrives."

"That's not the biggest problem," I said. "We need to get to the gate before they do, or they'll set guards over it. We won't be able to destroy it."

"Well, they're ahead of us now," Alibek said. "How are we going to manage that?"

"They're not going to go straight there. If we send our djinni out to find something we can ride in—it doesn't have to be a palanquin, an old wagon or something will do—we can probably get there first."

"You'd have us ride in a *wagon*?" Zivar said.

I took out my spell-chain. "Listen, I need you to go get something and bring it back here," I said to the djinn. "We need something that all of us can sit in and be carried by you. It can be a palanquin, or a wagon, or a sky boat, or a giant stew pot. Anything with sides and a bottom, sturdy enough that it won't fall apart while we're riding in it, and light enough for you to carry. Go and find something and bring it back as quickly as you can."

Zivar shook her head in disgust. To her own djinni she said, "Go find a palanquin and bring it to me."

"We might as well keep walking," Tamar said.

My djinn, to no one's surprise, was back before either of Zivar's. It carried an ancient, desiccated fishing boat. The hull was intact enough to ride in, but there were gaps between the shrunken boards big enough to slip my hand through. I climbed in and checked it over: it was sturdy enough to serve. As everyone else watched dubiously, I spread out the silk cloths we'd raided from the palanquin, using one to line the bottom and one to stretch over the top to keep grit out of our eyes. "This will do," I said.

Tamar shrugged and climbed in, making herself as comfortable as she could. Alibek half lifted, half shoved Kyros in, then climbed in himself. I looked at Zivar.

"Not a chance," Zivar said. "I'm waiting for a palanquin."

"If we wait for a palanquin, we'll be too late," I said.

"I'm not saying *you* have to wait. I'm saying that *I'm* going to wait."

There wasn't time to argue. "We'll see you later, then," I said.

"Good luck," she called as the djinn lifted up our boat.

*I* had traveled once in a djinn-borne wagon. It was not a comfortable way to travel. Traveling by palanquin was much easier—the sturdy sides protected riders from falling out, while the silk cushions and other padding made it comfortable to sit still for the hours (or days) of travel. The wagon had no padding, and neither did the boat. The boat's sides sloped up sharply, and the four of us sat along the bottom edge, leaning against the sides.

We'd thrown away most of the silk cushions from the palanquin, and I regretted that as I tried to get comfortable. There was a missing board near my head; it let me see out, which was a pleasant surprise, if disconcerting when I first looked down at the ground far below us.

Through the afternoon, I watched the textures of the ground change. The steppe was a muted brown-green carpet; we passed over more arid places where the green gave way to the gray-brown linen of dust and sand. Then the ground became more rugged; first I could see ripples in the earth, then rocks like breaking waves, and finally the climbing crags of mountain foothills. Near the end of the afternoon, I saw what looked like a blue silk ribbon caught in the rocks. I looked closer, and caught my breath. *The river. I'm seeing the river.*

Here, far from its source, the frantic flood had slowed to a more manageable flow—rapid, and swollen like you'd see after a very heavy spring rain, but still, not too bad. It had fallen into the old track like a foot into its boot. I wished I had told the djinn to follow the course of the river so that I could have met the returning waters as they came toward us.

I thought about the djinn, bearing us steadily toward the drowned city. "Thank you for your help," I said softly. It didn't answer. "I want you to know that I will free you when this is done."

That brought a response. "Why?"

"I don't keep slaves. When we get to the drowned gate, I mean to destroy it, so that it will be impossible—or at least much harder—for my people to enslave yours. I can't do that without your help—not quickly enough, not with the Weavers trying to stop me. There's no way. But once that's done—I will free you."

Silence.

I shrugged, and rolled over a little, trying to get comfortable. I lost my view, but my shoulder felt bruised; it was time to bruise the other shoulder, or my back. I stared up at our makeshift silk roof for a while, closed my eyes to rest them from the glare, and dozed off.

I had expected to see the waters again, but instead, I saw a battle.

There was no warning; I was thrust into the heart of it. I heard the screams of the dying, and smelled acrid smoke; I saw the blur of a horse passing me and flinched away even as I realized that this was a vision and I was not truly there.

I was lifted up, giving me a vulture's view of the battlefield. Sword sisters and sword brothers fought together against the Greeks. As I looked over the battlefield, I saw a familiar face—Ruan. She had a breastplate strapped on over her black vest, and a helmet salvaged from some previous raid. Her bow was in her hand, and she stood up in her saddle, her horse at full gallop, to fire on the Greeks. There was a bottle of arrow-poison on her belt but she was firing so quickly she wasn't using it—or maybe she'd run out. She was laughing, or snarling—then someone else surged forward, hiding her from my view.

*Is this happening now?* I wondered. *Or did this already happen?* Had our message reached the Greeks, and had they believed it?

Somewhere beyond the Greeks I heard a rumble, then a roar. I knew what it was, even if no one on the battlefield did. *The river. It's coming.*

The floodwaters descended like the hands of the gods, sweeping away everything in their path. The heart of the water reminded me of the collapsing temple. It might be a wall of water, rather than rock, but it would strike with the weight of a thousand boulders. Shallower streams spilled out from the edges, tearing away bushes in their wake.

The wall of water struck the camp of the Greek army.

One moment, I could see the tents, the horses, the wagons of supplies, the livestock—the next, nothing but churning water. Here and there I saw a horse struggling to swim in the deluge, or a person desperately clinging to floating debris. Everything else was underwater or swept away.

The battlefield was at the edge of the flood; the waters rose up around the ankles of the horses, but not high enough to drown them or knock them off their feet. Ruan clung to her horse, looking down at the water, then over at the river; everyone else was similarly transfixed. "The river returns," I heard someone shout. *"The river returns."*

*I* woke, my stomach churning. *The river returns* echoed in my ears even as I thought, *death, so much death.* How many people had been in the path of the river? How many cities had been swept away—was Elpisia even still standing? I thought of all the people I'd known growing up, from nose-picking Brasidas to the stablegirl in Kyros's stable. If Elpisia had been swept away like that Greek camp, none of them would even still be alive.

Elpisia made me think of my mother: *her death is my fault, too.* When I closed my eyes a moment later, instead of the flood, I saw my mother, weeping as Kyros cut her throat with his knife. *I could kill him. Neither Alibek nor Tamar would care.* I glanced at Kyros; he lay beside me, his eyes closed, his hands bound in front of him. We'd forgotten to give him the syrup, but it was broad day and he was unlikely to find anyone he needed in the borderland. If I killed him in his sleep when he'd been a quiet, obedient prisoner, would that make me as bad as him? *It hardly matters, with all the blood on my head for freeing the river . . .*

*I could do it. Alibek's sword is within reach. I could probably hack his head off with a single blow. I didn't get to kill Sophos, but I could kill Kyros.*

I had killed before—not often, but I'd done it. But it had always been in battle, when fear was surging through my body and giving strength to my arm. To slaughter a man like an animal—even Kyros—I didn't want to do it. I thought about waking Tamar or Alibek and offering to let them do it, but somehow that seemed even worse.

*We'll take him with us to the Alashi and let them deal with him, when we're done here.*

I looked out the gap and saw that we had reached the edge of the valley. "Slow down," I said to the djinn. "I want to take a look outside." I pushed the blanket aside and crawled up the edge of the boat to take a look.

The sun was low in the western sky; we were deep within the mountains, and the sun had fallen behind the edge of the mountain, putting most of the valley into shadow.

When I had seen the reservoir before, it had looked to me like a vast black bowl from the side; from above, the water had been blue. It had been smooth, barely rippling in the breeze, and it had been vast. Sea gulls had circled overhead, scolding us as we'd approached in the palanquin, and when Xanthe had pushed me in, I'd realized that I would drown if I tried to swim for the shore.

Now, I saw an endless mudflat. The valley was black with mud and silt. I could see the ruins of the city rising from the bottom of what had been the lake. The buildings jutted upward, coated in waterborne weeds, slick black mud, settled dirt, dead fish. Nothing had dried yet—the valley was a vast swamp. I wondered how long it would take before people could live here again. Years? Generations? Or perhaps it looked worse than it was and would dry out in a month of summer sun . . .

I had explored only a tiny portion of the underwater city; it was vast. *The djinn must have had Xanthe push me out at precisely the right spot.* With the water gone, had I looked for the gate with just my eyes, it might have taken me weeks of searching to find it again. But I could feel its tug within me, its gate calling to my own. "That way," I murmured.

Tamar and Alibek climbed up next to me and looked out as well. "It looks so desolate," Tamar whispered. "Our people really *lived* there? Do you think the Alashi will want to live there again?"

"Not anytime soon," I said.

"It will dry out, eventually," Alibek said. "The soil here will be fertile—excellent for farming."

"It looks burned," Tamar said. "Though it doesn't smell burned." She inhaled. "It smells pretty bad, though."

Alibek took a whiff. "It could be worse. The ruined temple was worse."

"*Nothing's* worse than that . . ."

The gate was ahead. It stood at the top of a hill that rose high above the rest of the city. Steps led up to it, and a marble floor lay at its base. The crumbled remnants of walls surrounded it. "There," I said, and pointed. "That's it."

"That archway?" Tamar asked.

"Yes."

The stones were as blackened from dirt as the other buildings, but had fewer weeds growing on them. In the sun, I saw a glint, and realized that the entire gate was built from karenite. Tamar studied it for a long moment, then said, her voice hesitant, "I can't see through the gate. Is that a trick of the light? I should be able to see the mountains on the other side, but there's just . . ."

"Darkness, yes," I said. "That's not a trick of the light. Don't go sticking your hand into it to see what happens or anything. I only sort of know how *I* got back from the other side." I leaned against the edge of the boat. "Take us close," I said to the djinn. "But don't you go touching it. I swear I will free you when I'm done here. To free your people from mine forever, we have to destroy this, and we need firm ground to stand on."

The djinn brought the boat so that the base rested on the floor in front of the gate, then held it there, balanced for us. I could feel the pull of the gate; I felt that if I tripped, I would be swept through like a gnat in a wind. *Surely the djinn feels it.* But it either chose to stay and help us, or was powerless to let the gate sweep it away.

"We need a hammer," Alibek said. "I don't suppose you have one at hand . . ."

"Lay the boat down gently," I said to the djinn. It let the boat settle onto its side. The upper side of the hull curved up behind us, while the lower side made a squishing sound as it settled into the mud. We stood on the inner curve of the hull, looking at the gate. "Bring us some rocks we can swing to destroy the gate. A hammer, if you can find something like that. Hurry."

"Can we use something as a rope and maybe try to pull it over?" Tamar asked.

"You'll have to do it," I said. "I'm afraid that if I get too close, I'm going to be pulled through whether I mean to go through or not."

We took the silk we'd used as a roof, twisted it, and Alibek and Tamar passed it around the back of the gate; it was just long enough to work. They grabbed the ends and we pulled as hard as we could, but the gate didn't budge.

The djinn returned with a shower of useful things: three large rocks, a hammer, a sledgehammer, an axe, a sword, and a perfectly new bow and quiver of arrows. I blinked at the bow and arrows for a moment, puzzled. Xanthe must have cleaned out Zivar's palanquin on the way back to Penelopeia, after she threw me into the water.

Tamar strung the bow while Alibek picked up the sledgehammer and took a swing at the gate. It rebounded; the gate didn't break. "Let me try," I said.

"Don't be an idiot," Alibek said. "If I fall through the gate by accident, I'll be of no use to them. You'll never get away from them again." He took another swing, with no discernible effect.

In the distance, I heard a voice shout, "Stop!" And then, "Stop them!"

"Protect us," I said to the djinn, and we dived behind the shelter of the boat's hull. I heard a deafening rattle like hail against a metal roof and risked a quick peek up; the djinn had formed a rigid shield against a rain of arrows. Some way off, still, I could see a palanquin.

"It's the Sisterhood Guard," I said. "The djinn is protecting us from their arrows." I straightened up, feeling my face flush with defiant delight. The arrows rained down again, but they bounced off the djinn like a brick wall. "Thank you," I whispered. "You won't regret this."

Tamar fired an arrow, wounding one of the people leaning out of the palanquin. Alibek picked up the small hammer and tried swinging that at the gate instead; no use. Kyros stayed hunched in the hull of the boat, clasping his bound hands, which was just fine with me. Alibek tried the sledgehammer again, and must have swung it harder. It rebounded with a sharp crack, but still didn't so much as chip the stones of the gate. Another hail of arrows came down. Tamar flinched as she saw them coming, but gripped her own bow and fired an arrow back.

"Let's try having the djinn pull on the rope," Alibek suggested.

"I don't think it can do that and shield us at the same time . . ."

"We can shelter in the boat while it tries."

He and Tamar each picked up an end, then held them together. "Djinn—pull," I said, and we ducked behind the hull as the rope stretched taut. I heard the fibers creak. The gate looked undisturbed. "Pull harder," Alibek said under his breath. "Come on."

The djinn gave a sharp yank, and the rope snapped, the ends flying out to the sides; Alibek threw himself backward to avoid being hit, and almost fell. "Shield us again!" I shouted as the arrows rattled against the hull.

Alibek gave me a grim look. "*Now* what?" he said. The palanquin was much closer. Alibek struggled back to his feet, his sword in hand. "I'll do what I can if they get in here," he said, his tone saying, *and that won't be much, not against that many people.*

"We can use Kyros's djinn to do something with them—all of them—"

"That'll only work once. And there *must* be more coming."

Weavers or no Weavers, this was starting to feel futile. *Do we need a bigger hammer? An anvil to swing? How did they destroy gates in the past?* I remembered that they used human deaths to bind the gates and destroy them—but this gate had received the opposite treatment. Someone had built a physical doorway out of karenite to *keep* it from collapsing. To bind it to the spot and force it to stay open, so that it never slipped quietly shut like the gates left by people like me.

The Weavers' palanquin stopped with its djinn just beyond my reach. They took out planks, and I realized they aimed to climb onto our boat without ever coming close enough to let me free their djinn. Tamar nocked an arrow; Alibek's hand tightened on his sword.

"Protect us if you can," I whispered to our djinn.

The planks stopped in the air, and then spun away, dropping into the mud some distance below. I turned back to the gate, desperately trying to think of a way to destroy it.

Karenite was not normally all that sturdy. I'd smashed dozens of pieces of it just the day before, between a pair of rocks. *Why is this holding so firm?* I tried to still my own churning thoughts for a moment to really *look* at the gate, and suddenly I saw them;

the faint gleam of djinni. *The gate itself is a binding spell.*

*But the Sisterhood of Weavers didn't make this.*

The Weavers hadn't made it—it was a different sort of magic—but the center remained the same. *Djinni.* I fixed my eyes on the keystone of the arch, and with the same sight that let me see the djinni, I saw the burning light within that stone. *The heart of the spell.*

"Get behind the boat," I said. "I think the djinn is going to have to shield me while I do this."

I stepped up to the very edge of the gate and laid my hands flat against the sides of it. I could feel the pull, but I could fight against it; I would not be forced through. Arrows rattled against the djinn, and I knew the Sisterhood Guard would close in on me in moments. I closed my eyes, trying to still myself. "Return to the Silent Lands," I said, my voice sounding rough and hoarse in my ears. "Lost ones of your kind. Return."

I could hear a rumble under my ear like distant thunder. Behind my eyelids, the world went suddenly white. I could feel the djinni passing through me like a river through a broken dam. *There are more here than I realized. A lot more.* I had freed multiple djinni at once before, but not like this. This was a flood, a torrent, and as it went on, and on, and on, I feared that it would overwhelm me.

Then I heard Tamar scream. I looked over my shoulder.

Kyros was coming toward me. He had freed his hands somehow, and I realized as I stood with my hands against the keystone that he meant to shove me through. *No,* I thought, but no sound came out. I couldn't move any more than I could flee from the falling temple. Alibek and Tamar had tried to grab him as he left the boat but he had evaded Alibek and kicked Tamar aside. "Lauria, *look out,*" Tamar shouted, scrambling back to her feet. I could see the wildness in Kyros's eyes and feel the heat of his breath; *he is their tool,* I knew.

Then something yanked me up and out of the way. Kyros, unable to stop, plunged through the gate and disappeared. Around my neck, the binding stone of the black spell-chain exploded, burning my chest.

*And now home,* a voice whispered, and dropped me to the ground.

The djinni were still coming. *The dam was breaking; the water was coming. I looked up to see the water breaking forth over me like spit from a world-eating dragon, like the end of the world . . .*

The river of spirits was going to carry me away like a stick in the flood—I would be lost, taken to the other side of the gate never to return. Then I felt hands clasp mine. *Tamar. Our bond holds me here.* I tightened my grip and felt the pounding ease as the last of the djinni passed through and away. *It's done.*

I opened my eyes. Above me, the archstone cracked, and the stone doorway began to collapse. Tamar knelt beside me, clutching my hand. Alibek stood over both of us, his sword drawn. Facing us was what looked like an entire phalanx of women from the Sisterhood Guard. Beyond them were palanquins of sorceresses.

Shielding us still was the djinn from Kyros's spell-chain, even though the binding stone had broken when Kyros passed through the gate. It wavered in the air as I watched; it was fighting the pull of the gate to continue to protect us, but I knew looking at it that it had fought that pull as long as it could. It was slipping away before my eyes.

*Good-bye*, it whispered, and was gone. In another moment, the Sisterhood Guard would realize we no longer had our shield.

But with the finality of embers finally quenched with water, I felt the gate close behind me. *It's gone. It's gone. We've done it, we've remade the world, even if we die here, we've remade the world . . .*

A guard bent back her bow.

But I felt something snatch me up off the ground—me, Tamar, and Alibek together. We were held side by side like three pebbles in an enormous fist. A djinn—a djinn had us. *The Weavers must want us for questioning,* I thought, but we were leaving—flying absurdly fast into the growing darkness, leaving behind the wagon, the palanquin, the ruined gate, and whatever remained of Kyros.

*And whatever the djinni took with them when they passed into their own world.*

Something felt as if it were missing, but I realized as I prodded it that it was the borderland. Of late it had been so close to me that I could touch it almost as easily as breathing. Now . . . when I reached, there was only darkness.

*The world is made anew.*

I closed my eyes and surrendered to the dark.


The djinn set us down carefully next to a palanquin at the edge of the steppe. Zivar was waiting, a faint smile on her face. "Did my aerika serve you well? One doesn't seem to have returned."

*Of course,* I realized. The one that pulled me away from Kyros had been sent by Zivar. She'd sent both her djinni to help us.

"Your djinni saved our lives," I said. "What did you tell them to do? Surely you didn't know Kyros would try to push me through the gate before it closed?"

"I told them to go, and serve you as well as they could. I'm pleased to hear that was sufficient. Kyros tried to push you through? *Why?*"

"Someone must have been whispering in his ear. That djinn that helped us find Kyros, back in the Koryphe—it was probably her."

I had been burned by Kyros's spell-chain, and Zivar gave me cold water to soothe it. She'd bought food somewhere, and so we had dinner, then lay in the grass.

"Where now?" Tamar asked.

"Home," I said.

"That doesn't really answer my question," she said.

"Home is where my sister is," I said. "And the Alashi are her people."

Alibek was silent. Tamar sat up and looked at him. "Alibek?" she asked.

He gave her a very faint smile. "Home is where your feet are," he said. I wasn't sure why, but this made her blush, and also seemed to please her.

"Zivar?" I asked. "Do you still want to join the Alashi?"

"Do you think they'll have me?" she said.

"Yes," I said, though in all honesty I wasn't sure.

"I might as well go back with you," she said. "The Sisterhood of Weavers would be delighted to see me, but not for any reasons that would be good for my health."

Zivar used the palanquin to take us very close to where the Alashi were camped, though not all the way, for obvious reasons. We were a few hours' walk from the camp of an Alashi clan when she had the djinn put us down; I saw her glance at me when she tucked the spell-chain under her clothes.

When we reached the clan, the elder present remembered Tamar and Alibek from the spring. He heard Zivar's story, and the rest of ours, and ceremonially presented Zivar with a blue bead. This clan had heard stories of the river's return, but they hadn't seen the river yet themselves. The elder sent riders to escort us to the eldress of all the clans, since she needed to hear our story and Tamar and Alibek's report.

Zivar was uncomfortable on horseback, and I walked beside her to keep her company. "Lauria," she said. "The elder saw my spell-chain—I know he did. So the Alashi are willing to take me with my spell-chain?"

"Yes," I said.

"Are you?"

"What do you mean?"

She took my hand, and spun me to face her. "I think you know what I mean."

"Zivar . . . I guess I'd have to think about it. It's a slave. I don't like to keep slaves—though I have to admit that I kept Kyros's for a bit because I knew I would need it. I'm not going to tell you what to do. It's not as if you can make another spell-chain if you destroy this one."

"All I wanted, once, was to be free," she said. "But I lived a long way from the steppe. I couldn't imagine getting that far on my own . . ."

"You're free now," I said.

"Yes," she said. But I wasn't sure she believed it.

# CHAPTER TWENTY-ONE

# TAMAR

The world was made new, but it wasn't exactly the world I had imagined.

When Lauria, Alibek, Zivar, and I arrived on the steppe, we were the first of a flood of refugees—former slaves who'd heard of the river's return and had simply walked away and headed for the Alashi. The river did *not* free all the slaves. The slaves who made it to the steppe brought stories of slaves brought back and beaten or killed. Other slaves were too sick, old, or beaten down to run away.

But the Greeks had more urgent problems than the loss of their slaves. The army and the Weavers turned on each other, scrambling for control of the remaining spell-chains. Rumors traveled slowly now that hardly anyone could get to the borderland, but the refugees brought plenty: riots over food, assassinations of sorceresses to get their spell-chains, an uprising of slaves in one city that left every soldier dead.

With a great deal of effort, I could still find my way to the borderland at night. Lauria could not, and neither could Zhanna or Jaran. I did meet another shaman who could—one of the old men. We seemed to have found other gates to reach it. I wondered sometimes if I used the one in Lauria's heart.

Zivar was sent out to a sword sisterhood for the rest of the summer. The world shook around us, but the eldress was bent on doing things the way she always had. Lauria was still weak from her time as a prisoner of the Greeks, so she stayed with one of the clans. I wanted to stay with Lauria, and Alibek wanted to stay with me.

They set up a yurt for the three of us.

It was less awkward than I'd feared. Alibek and Lauria got along very well when they didn't think too much about the past. Lauria was sad and distracted, grieving for her mother and thinking about the destruction she'd brought. Alibek treated both of us like sisters.

The clan was busy getting ready for winter and dealing with all the new arrivals. Our yurt had space for more people, but the elder of the clan didn't trust us not to give the blossoms tips on passing the tests, so he didn't put anyone in with us. The elder knew that we had freed the river, but he didn't tell anyone else, so neither did we.

Despite the war and the flood, it was a very peaceful couple of weeks.

Having Alibek treat me like a sister was a relief at

first. Thinking about the kiss we'd shared still made me blush. But as the days passed, I began to think again about how nice it would be not to feel terrified. Late at night, in the dark of the yurt, I ran my palms over my skin and imagined someone else's hands touching me. Back in the harem, Meruert and Aislan sometimes felt pleasure. I had wondered if part of me was broken and that was why I always hated it. I decided in those nights that I was not broken. At least not anymore.

But did I want to share Alibek's company? That evening in Penelopeia, it had seemed so reasonable. We were both former concubines. We were comfortable together because of all we'd been through. But now that I was back with a clan, surrounded by families, I remembered that Alashi couples were supposed to marry if they were going to have a child together. They were supposed to stay together at least until the child was old enough to go off and join a sisterhood or brotherhood. I knew ways to avoid pregnancy, but they weren't foolproof. Did I like Alibek enough to have a family with him? Of course, right now I was living with him, and it wasn't too bad. He was even courteous to Lauria. That was a good sign.

A week before we were to ride out for the fall gathering, Lauria invited me to go riding with her. We borrowed horses, packed food and water, and headed out in the early morning. We rode for an hour or two, then stopped to rest. I saw a rockslide and Lauria picked up a piece of karenite. "They say merchants still buy it," she said.

"For how much longer?"

"Who knows?"

"What do you think the Alashi will do once everyone realizes it's not valuable anymore?"

Lauria looked up at the sky. "I think we'll see a lot more overland merchant caravans, like the one the sisterhood met last summer. Even if no one wants karenite, people will still want silk and the other stuff you can buy beyond the edge of the Empire."

"Are you thinking the Alashi will turn to banditry?"

"No, I'm thinking they could offer to guard the caravans from bandits, for a fee, and sell them water and other supplies that they'll need as they pass."

"I suppose."

"Anyway, that's not why I dragged you out here. I wanted to talk." She swatted a bug. "Do you and Alibek need me to move out?"

"What?"

"I've seen the way you look at each other. But you never touch. I was just wondering if maybe you needed some privacy."

I blinked. "I—uh—you don't have to move out."

"Are you sure? Because if that's not it, what's the problem?"

"It just seems so complicated," I said, finally.

"Life is short," Lauria said. "Don't waste too much time thinking about how complicated things are."

I looked up at Lauria. Alibek had thought I might desire Lauria, and I wondered suddenly if she desired me. But I saw no hint of that in her face. "You're a good sister," I said. "Did you ever want to be, you know—" My voice failed me.

Lauria took my hand and looked into my eyes. "Where I came from, blood sisterhood didn't mean that you were *sisters* in a way that would make it wrong to desire each other. But when we first met, you seemed very young to me. While I was in Penelopeia, I longed to be with you, but what I wanted was your company. If we had taken a different path together, maybe . . . but I can tell that you love Alibek. And you know, between us, we could really use a larger family, don't you agree? Some kin-by-marriage for each of us."

I felt a sudden relief, though I hadn't thought I was worried.

"You love Alibek. I don't know what's holding you back, but—try not to let it chain you any longer."

When we returned to the camp, I sought Alibek out. He was whittling a whistle for one of the children, and I waited until he had finished before I spoke.

"I'm ready," I said.

# CHAPTER TWENTY-TWO

## LAURIA

When fall gathering came, Ruan invited Tamar and me to stay with the sisterhood, for old times' sake. Alibek had been invited to stay with his old brotherhood, and wanted to see the men from the brotherhood again, so the two agreed to separate at least for a few nights. They had a whole winter ahead to spend together.

Ruan was tanned and confident; leadership was good for her, and she hadn't made nearly as much of a mess of things as I would have predicted. They'd had three blossoms spend the summer with them—a woman from the mine, and two from Sophos's household. Zhanna seemed to be keeping company with the former mine slave; they had the casual, affectionate air of summer friends who'd greatly enjoyed their summer. There were many others I recognized from last summer, including Maydan, the healer who'd been badly wounded in the final bandit attack. Maydan had spent the summer with one of the clans, but came to spend fall gathering with the sisterhood. She was looking good; she carried a walking stick but rarely used it.

On the second night of fall gathering, we were sitting around the fire when we heard the rustle of someone approaching; I looked up to see a lantern growing nearer. "Who's coming?" Ruan called.

"A former sister. May I approach?"

"Former sisters are always welcome," Ruan said, a little cautiously.

I shaded my eyes against the lantern glare, and saw three figures. Then Janiya strode into the circle of firelight. She grabbed Tamar in a hug, then clasped hands with Ruan and with me. The other two women followed behind—Xanthe, and then an old woman I didn't know. Xanthe had gotten rid of her guard uniform, though she still had her sword.

"I heard from Xanthe that you escaped after your arrest," Janiya said to Tamar.

Tamar nodded, then glanced at me with a faint smile; she was wondering how much more Xanthe had told her. I craned my neck a bit to look at Xanthe. She was staring at the ground, but raised her head after a moment to meet my eyes squarely. No djinn looked back at me; only Xanthe, nervous and a bit shy. I nodded, since I knew Tamar was looking at me. Xanthe shrugged slightly and dropped her head again, letting her mother speak for her.

Janiya introduced Xanthe as her daughter. The old lady was named Damira, and she seemed to be a long-ago friend of Janiya's. Everyone made them welcome, even Ruan, who seemed to have learned how to be kind to newcomers during her months as the leader.

Late that night, when most of the sisterhood had gone to sleep, I asked Janiya what was happening in Penelopeia.

"Well, we left quite some time ago," Janiya said. "The news about the river reached the city right away. Within a couple of days, we heard rumors that the sorceresses couldn't bind djinni anymore. The Sisterhood mostly withdrew to the Koryphe with their families—they're using djinni to bring in supplies, and shutting out the army."

"What about the rest of the city?"

"There were riots. The homes of the Weavers had been left empty, and some people broke in to steal what was left behind. The city guard started out trying to stop them, but then joined in."

"Did you run into the army on your travels?"

"We tried not to. You'd think they'd realize their opportunity to seize power, with the Sisterhood's power so sharply limited, but right now most of the soldiers are frightened and just trying to get home, wherever home is." Janiya cocked her head and looked at me. "The Empire is on its knees, Lauria. If a great leader steps in who can bring together what's left of the Sisterhood and the army, it might lurch to its feet once again, but I saw no sign of that happening on my travels. The remains of the Empire will not fall overnight, but it will fracture into a thousand little clans, I think, each with a leader who possesses a spell-chain."

"Do you think the Alashi are safe?"

"Yes. The Greeks are in no position to threaten us. Someday, perhaps, but not in our lifetime." Janiya sighed. "Though the influx of newcomers may be almost as dangerous to us as an army. We don't have enough food. Our flocks aren't big enough . . ."

"Send people south," I said. "Have them organize clans to farm the lands down there."

"That's a good idea," Janiya said. "I'll suggest it to the elders and eldresses."

I shrugged. "Do we need their approval? Maybe you should suggest it to Ruan. Or others from the sisterhoods and brotherhoods who might enjoy a new challenge."

Janiya shrugged, a little uncomfortable with the thought. "We aren't bound together by magic, but we're bound together by our customs. This isn't the time to challenge them, or we might crumble as thoroughly as the Penelopeian Empire."

The big initiation ceremony for new Alashi took place near the end of the fall gathering. Tamar had initiated me in absentia when she'd been here last spring, so I didn't have to go through it. Zivar was not yet ready to be initiated, so she sat with us as well, looking a little wistful. She still wore her spellchain, but kept it hidden.

Prax walked under an arch of torches, and the men from his brotherhood clustered around him to clasp his hands in welcome. Tamar and I hung back, but Prax sought us out. Tamar stood on tiptoe to press her lips to his forehead. Prax clasped my hand and met my eyes, then bent his head to let me kiss him, too. "Welcome back," he whispered. Another former mine slave was already swearing his loyalty, and many others were still waiting their turn. What was next spring going to be like, with hundreds of new-comers already swarming the steppe?

Prax came over again to sit with us during the celebration. "You remember what we said about starting our own clan?" Prax asked. "I'm thinking that now is a good time. Not *right* now, but next spring."

"Are you thinking we'll go to the site of the reservoir?"

"Yes, with herds—and something we can trade for seeds. The stories all say that it was the most fertile lands that were flooded."

"Do you really think it will be inhabitable yet?" I asked.

"I do. But you're probably right that we should make sure of that. Maybe we can ride there together as soon as the snow melts, before the spring gathering." He glanced around the little circle, at me, Tamar, Alibek, and Zivar. "Maybe just the five of us. What do you think?"

I glanced around; everyone was nodding. "Let's do it," I said. "As soon as the snow melts."

*I*t was a long, difficult winter. Janiya invited Tamar, Alibek, and me to stay with her clan for the winter. Since Xanthe and Zivar were still blossoms, they were sent out with another clan. I was just as glad not to have to spend the winter in close quarters with Xanthe, but I missed Zivar.

There were several young girls in the clan who were back from their first summer with the sisterhood. I saw their mothers fussing over them, including one who got all weepy over her daughter's shorn hair, and my throat went unexpectedly tight.

Uljas had been able to bring Burkut's body up to the Alashi for burial. I hadn't been able to bury my mother at all . . . I had no idea what had happened to her body. Then again, I was certain she wouldn't have wanted to be buried on the steppe. This wasn't her home. If anything, she might have liked being buried with Kyros—which would have been even more impossible, since he hadn't left behind a body at all.

Still, not being able to bury my mother was one of the things that gnawed at me in the early months of winter. If I spoke with the eldress, I thought she would probably let me initiate my mother in absentia, but my mother wouldn't want that, either. What *would* she want? *A proper daughter. A respectable son-in-law. Grandchildren. All the things I was never going to give her.*

I decided that I would grow out my hair, as a memorial to my mother. Brushing my hair always made me think of her.

I had dreams some nights where I stood in darkness and heard the roar of water approaching. I always wrenched myself awake with a gasp and found myself drenched in sweat. Awake, I couldn't bear to think about the horrors I had unleashed; my thoughts recoiled. Tamar didn't seem to feel the guilt I felt. I broached the issue with her once, and she gave me one of the steady, slightly patronizing looks she'd used when I was in the grip of the cold fever. "You said yourself the djinni would succeed in making a gate, sooner or later. And as long as our gate stood, the djinni would keep being bound. And we saved the Alashi from the Greek army. If you could do it over, would you leave the river bound?"

"No."

"So?"

I tried again to put it out of my mind.

$\mathcal{F}$ood was short through the winter. The Alashi were not prepared for so many new members, and the supplies left behind by the retreating Greeks did not fill the shortage. The days were cold, and the nights colder. I dreamed one night that I was back at Zivar's house in Casseia, in a soft bed within a warm room; I could even smell the meal that waited for me. I was almost disappointed when I woke up, though when I thought about the food I'd smelled, I realized that it wasn't the comfort I missed—it was Zivar.

It also occurred to me that it had been a long time since I'd had one of those dizzying surges of energy that came with the cold fever. Nor had I felt despondent and unable to rise from bed. I wondered if Zivar and the other sorceresses were similarly even-tempered now.

$\mathcal{Z}$ivar, I found out, was only an hour's ride away. On a day of cold, bright sunshine, I rode out to where Zivar was staying. She had been having a rough winter. They were making her take tests; of course, she was mostly failing them, just as Tamar and I had. I wanted to tell her that the tests didn't really mean anything, but I feared that if I did, I'd just make it more likely that she'd never be allowed to join the Alashi.

I took her out for a walk. The sky was blue, and the snow reflected the winter sun like shards of broken mirror. There was no wind, which was the only thing that made it bearable to be out in the cold. We kept walking, trying to stay warm.

"Do you feel different these days?" I asked Zivar.

"I feel like strangling the eldress. Is that what you mean?"

"No. I mean the cold fever. Is it still with you?"

Zivar stopped in her tracks. "No," she said, after a moment. "Or if it is, it is quieter than it's been in years."

"I wonder if that's true for all the sorceresses?"

Zivar shrugged. "I could send my aeriko and ask, I suppose, if you really want to know. Does it matter?" Her hand traced the chain under her coat.

"I suppose it doesn't, really."

We kept walking.

"I think the eldress wants me to give up the spell-chain," she said. "Those stupid blue beads! I have a dozen of them now but she still acts like I don't have enough. I think she wants me to free my aeriko. That will prove something, that I've 'changed' or whatever."

I made a noncommittal noise. She was probably right.

"I don't even *want* it anymore," Zivar said. "I haven't used the aeriko for anything in ages, and I don't like looking at it. But what if they don't let me stay? How am I supposed to survive?"

"You're strong, Zivar," I said. "You don't need it."

"I can't survive on my own, Lauria!"

"You won't be alone. Prax wants to start a new clan—you heard him talk about that at fall gathering. He told me I would always be welcome, even when I was in exile. That's where I'm going in the spring, and *that* clan will take you in."

"What would you have me do?" Zivar asked. "With the spell-chain, I mean."

I sighed. "The djinni are people. When they are bound, they are taken away from everything and everyone they know. And not even death can free them. They're stuck. I know the temptation of holding a spell-chain, but I would never keep one for long. Not now."

Zivar fell silent. Then she loosened her wrappings and slowly drew the spell-chain from under her coat. "Take it," she said, holding it out to me.

"I don't want it," I said.

"I don't want it either, so take it!"

I swallowed hard, squinting at her in the sun. "If you don't want it anymore, then break it, Zivar."

Zivar took a deep breath, and let it out. "I don't have a stone," she said.

"I have a hammer," I said. I had brought it along just for this. Zivar gave me a slightly suspicious look—who brings a hammer along on a midwinter ride?—then laid the necklace out on a patch of ice. She summoned the djinn; I could see it, barely, in the dazzling sun. Then she raised the hammer and smashed the binding stone.

The djinn shimmered for a moment; then it was gone. If it spoke, it was only for Zivar's ears.

"Well," Zivar said. She picked up the chain. "I guess we should go back to camp before we freeze solid."

When we stepped into the big yurt, the clan eldress saw the broken spell-chain and took out a blue bead for Zivar.

Zivar flung it back at her. "I didn't destroy my spell chain for *you*," she said. "Keep your damn bead. In fact"—she wrenched off the necklace with its fifteen blue beads and threw it to the ground—"take them *all*. I don't even care anymore."

"Well," the eldress said, and stepped back with a slightly nervous smile. "Well. I think you're—I think you're ready. If you *want* to be a full member of the Alashi, at spring gathering—you're ready."

"I don't care about spring gathering," Zivar said. "If I'm ready, then I'm going to go stay with Janiya's clan. *Today.*"

"I don't see why not," the eldress said, looking as if she'd be very happy to have Zivar off her hands. "I'll send for a horse. You can ride back with Lauria."

*P*rax arrived with the first of the warm spring winds. We took enough horses to travel quickly, and Tamar, Alibek, Prax, Zivar, and I rode out together toward the valley where the reservoir had been. My hair was long enough to braid again. It bounced against my shoulders as I rode.

"This was a lot faster in a palanquin," Zivar muttered the first night, but didn't complain beyond that.

We reached the river and traveled near it. It flowed within its banks now, as if it had never been gone, deceptively calm. Tamar looked at it in awe for several moments, then said, "It would be hard to cross this, if you were a slave coming to join the Alashi—most can't swim."

"Maybe we can persuade people to help us build a bridge," Prax suggested. Alibek laughed skeptically at that. "Or we could expand Alashi territory beyond it. If you don't have to cross the river to reach the Alashi, it's less of a problem."

"What's left of the Greek settlements?" I asked. "Do you know?"

"Not much. Some were wiped out by the flood. There were slave uprisings in the cities that were left."

I shuddered a little, trying not to picture Elpisia.

I had slept very heavily through most of the winter, but that night I dreamed that Kyros was calling my name. I woke early, feeling uneasy. I still felt uneasy when I went to sleep that night, but I didn't dream of Kyros again until we reached the valley.

The valley had been dead and black when I saw it last, and despite Prax's optimism, I'd expected it to still look like that. Instead, it was a lush paradise, covered in thick grass with a scattering of vivid flowers. "This could be farmed," I said to Prax. "You were right."

Prax nodded. "Let's spend the night here tonight, then head back at dawn. It's tempting to explore it, but I want to get the rest of the Gulzhan clan up here as quickly as we can, along with the men from the brotherhood who I think would be interested. If we don't move in, someone else will."

"There's plenty of space . . ."

"We should lay claim to some of it as soon as we can."

We did at least spend the afternoon exploring. We were a long way from the remains of the gate, but we found the ruins of houses, a piece of a jug, and a tarnished silver spoon. Prax, who had found the spoon, put it in his pack.

I dreamed of Kyros that night. First I heard him

calling my name. It was a distant, muddled sound, as if I were swimming underwater. Then his face came out of the darkness. He looked haggard and afraid. "Lauria," he whispered again. I expected him to say more—to ask for my help, to curse me, anything. But all he said was my name.

"Go away," I tried to say; the words caught in the darkness, smothered into silence. I jerked awake. It wasn't yet dawn, but I didn't want to go back to sleep, so I rose quietly and slipped out of the yurt, taking my blanket with me for warmth.

I'd thought I'd left quietly, but Tamar joined me a short time later. "Nightmare?" she asked.

"I dreamed of Kyros," I said.

"In the borderland?" she asked.

I nodded.

"Was he searching for a way out?"

"He might have been," I said. "He called my name."

"You returned," Tamar said.

"With your help, and Alibek's."

"Do you think it was real, what you saw?"

"I don't know," I said. That was a lie. I knew it was real. I shivered.

"What's it like there?" Tamar asked.

"In some ways, it's not a bad place. There's no pain, no hunger, no cold. If he believes that Zeus is hidden there, he even has something to do. He can look for Zeus."

"We don't know when that doorway was built," Tamar said. "Maybe its purpose was to push Zeus through."

My hands were cold. I pressed them between my

knees to try to warm them. "How *did* you bring me back?"

"Alibek forgave you. And you and I, we had vows that bound us together."

I thought about the ritual I'd gone through with Janiya, repudiating my vows to Kyros.

"I think he's stuck there," I said.

$W$e had agreed to leave the valley at first light, but we lingered a bit. As I rounded up the horses, a sparkle caught my eye. I looked down. It was a gold pin, shaped like a rose, set with sapphires and—I suppressed a laugh—a piece of karenite. It was a lovely thing, and I picked it up, thinking about how my mother would have liked it.

We rode out along the river. My mother, and my grief for her, rose up again, and for once I didn't try to push the thoughts away. When we stopped to rest, I took my knife and cut loose my braid. I looped it once, pinned the loop closed with the gold pin, and threw it into the river.

"An offering," I said. "In honor of my mother. She worshipped Athena, but not because she believed in her. My mother was Danibeki. She believed in the river."

Tamar had been sitting in the grass; she rose, then bent to look through her own pack. "Your mother was a brave woman," she said. "She had your voice, but she was unlike you in almost every other way. Except for her courage. I would like to make her an offering as well." Tamar found what she was looking for—a small shovel. She held it up, as if making a presentation at an altar, and then threw it into the river.

Alibek had been watching with half-lidded eyes; now he stood up. "I heard many stories about your mother when I was Kyros's concubine," he said. "Your mother won her freedom through flattery and trickery. I thought of her with a mix of envy and contempt. When I met her, she was not what I had imagined. But I could well believe that she had once won her freedom with her ability to persuade." Alibek took out a wineskin. "Andromeda, I drink to you," he said. He took a swallow of wine, then poured out the rest into the river.

Prax stood up next, a little hesitantly. "Like Alibek, I heard stories of your mother when I was Kyros's slave. I once heard a story you might not know. Some years before I tried to escape, a sickness swept through Elpisia. It struck slaves harder than masters, and many became very ill. Kyros thought that the slaves who claimed severe illness were lying, to evade work; it was Andromeda who persuaded him that this wasn't the case. Your mother's silver tongue may have saved many lives." He took out the silver spoon he'd picked up yesterday. "I honor her." He threw it into the water.

Zivar was the last to speak. "I never met your mother," she said. "I only met you." She took out the broken spell-chain. "I honor the honor and courage that she passed on to you." She looped the chain around her hand, whirled it a few times to let it build up speed, and loosed it into the river.

"Thank you," I whispered, scarcely able to speak. We rode on a short while later.

Near the end of the day, Alibek shouted and

pointed at figures across the river. I squinted. Soldiers, or escaped slaves, or something else? Slaves, I decided as they grew nearer. They were all on foot, and some were limping, obviously footsore.

The group was within shouting distance now, and Tamar waved. Then she pointed. "Do you know her?" she asked.

"Who?"

"The woman on the left. The short one."

I squinted. I couldn't make out faces. "I think your eyes are better than mine. Who is it?"

Tamar shaded her eyes against the glare of the sun and waited a few more minutes. "It's Zarina," she said, finally. "The bath slave from the inn. Zarina, who didn't want us to free her."

I fell back a step. "Well," I said. "How about that?" I started to shrug, then shook my head. "The river returned," I said finally, and we rode south to meet Zarina.

# EPILOGUE

# TAMAR

*Three Years Later.*

Everyone warned me that childbirth would hurt. They also told me that it was worth it. They were right about both. At least it stopped hurting as soon as the baby was out. "It's a fine, healthy girl," Maydan said. "Shall I send in the anxious people waiting outside?"

I settled back against the pillows and rested the baby against my thighs, looking at her. Her dark hair was sparse and wispy, and softer than fur against my fingertips. I touched her hands and feet. She curled her little fingers around my big one. I'd seen plenty of newborns, but most of them were red and puckered and funny looking. I'd been prepared to have an ugly newborn—most babies did seem to get better looking as they grew—but to my pleasure and surprise, mine was beautiful. Stunningly beautiful. She had dark, clear eyes and stared at me like she was trying to learn my face by heart.

Maydan cleared her throat to let me know Alibek had come in, Lauria and Zivar at his heels. I let Alibek take her for a moment. "Touch her hand, she'll hold your finger," I said to Lauria. "Maybe we'll let you hold her tomorrow."

"Hello, beautiful," Lauria said to her. "You look just like your mother. Come look at her, Zivar."

"I make babies cry," Zivar said.

"She won't cry. Just come look at her."

The baby was starting to squirm and look around, opening and shutting her mouth like she was trying to find something with it. "She wants her mother," Maydan said, and helped me settle her at my breast.

Nearly everyone in the clan came in to admire her the following day, from Prax to Zhanna to Zarina, her own toddler resting on her hip. Jaran kissed her soft head and predicted that she'd be a shaman, though the Fair One had returned home and he admitted that this was a wish, not a prophecy. Xanthe visited a few days later and presented us with a gift of apples her clan had gotten from a passing trader. It was a generous gift. The valley was so fertile we had yet to find anything that wouldn't grow, but there weren't very many trees yet.

We named the baby on the tenth day after she was born. I dressed her in her prettiest clothes, and we stood up before the fire, in front of the clan. Alibek formally claimed her as his child, not that there was any doubt. Zhanna invoked Prometheus's and Arachne's blessings, and someone swore they saw a spider scurrying past in the dark, a sign of good luck. When it was time to announce the name of the baby, I took a deep breath. The people in our clan were mostly former slaves, and many of us had Greek names. Still, to give an Alashi baby a Greek name was unusual. But I'd known for a long time the name I wanted to give my daughter, if I ever had one.

"Andromeda," I said, when Zhanna asked me the name of the baby.

"Andromeda," Alibek agreed.

I glanced at Lauria. She was flushed red, and wiped her eyes with the heel of her hand, trying to hide her tears.

We each kissed the baby and sat down for the feast. "Andromeda?" Zarina asked. She'd never known Lauria's mother. "Is that an Alashi name?"

I glanced at Lauria, who was smiling into the fire. "Yes," I said. I kissed my daughter again and took Alibek's hand. "It is now."

# ACKNOWLEDGMENTS

Many thanks, as always, to my editor, Anne Groell, and my agent, Jack Byrne. I get asked sometimes about what it's like to go through the editorial process. I don't think Anne has ever asked me to make a change that didn't result in a stronger book when I was done.

Thanks to my on-call science geeks, Jason Goodman, Karen Swanberg, and John "Rowan" Littell, for answering random questions. Thanks also to my friend Marc Moskowitz, who gave me some Greek language help, to Dr. Lisa Frietag for answering medical questions, and to my father for his willingness to do my offsite backups. Many thanks again to Elise Matthesen, the gifted artist whose necklaces inspired the idea of spell-chains.

Many thanks and a round of coffee to the members of the Wyrdsmiths, without whom this would not be nearly as good a book: Eleanor Arnason, Bill Henry, Doug Hulick, Harry LeBlanc, Kelly McCullough, Lyda Morehouse (a.k.a. Tate Halloway), Sean Murphy, and Rosalind Nelson.

Thank you to all of my beta readers: Dushenka Ani, Blake Bramhall, Ed Burke, Stella Evans, Michelle Herder, Sylvia Izzo Hunter, John "Rowan" Littell, Janelle Lohr, Curtis Mitchell, Lyda Morehouse, Fillard Rhyne, Bill Scherer, Corinne Staggs, and Karen Swanberg. An extra thank-you to Curtis: many things in this world were inspired by ideas that originally came from his fertile imagination.

A huge, huge thank-you, as always, to my husband, Ed Burke. As of this writing, my two daughters are almost five years old and almost two years old. People ask me sometimes how on earth I write with a preschooler and a toddler, and I have to say that a supportive spouse who is an active and involved parent is critical. Ed is a wonderful father and a wonderful husband, and he values my writing and helps me to make space for it in my life. Another thank-you (and a hug and a kiss) to each of my daughters, Molly and Kiera.

# ABOUT THE AUTHOR

NAOMI KRITZER grew up in Madison, Wisconsin, a small lunar colony populated mostly by Ph.Ds. She moved to Minnesota to attend college. After graduating with a B.A. in religion, she became a technical writer. She now lives in Minneapolis with her family. *Fires of the Faithful* was her first novel, followed shortly thereafter by *Turning the Storm, Freedom's Gate,* and *Freedom's Apprentice.*